Storm and Tempest

Brand of Justice
Book 13

Lisa Phillips

TWO DOGS PUBLISHING, LLC.

eBook ISBN: 979-8-88552-286-1

Paperback ISBN: 979-8-88552-287-8

Published by: Two Dogs Publishing, LLC. Idaho, USA

Cover Design by: Sasha Almazan and Gene Mollica, GS Cover Design Studio, LLC

Edited by: Christy Callahan, Professional Publishing Services

Storm and Tempest

Chapter One

"My name is Oliver Jaxton, and I'm an addict."

Jax gripped the sides of the podium, staring at the noticeboard and clock on the back wall rather than the men in the rows of folding chairs. "I used to think cops were heroes. When I became one, I realized we're just as broken as everyone else."

He took a breath. "It all started when I blew out my knee playing high school football. Then I blew it more when I got hooked on the pain meds they gave me. I should've cared, but I didn't. Things got so much easier. I didn't have to care how my shot at playing football had been flushed down the toilet. How my dad didn't have a winner anymore, and my mom didn't have a son she could brag about.

"So I checked out. I..." He cleared his throat. "I didn't want to face anything, but eventually my sister called me out. She knew what was happening. She made me flush the pills down the toilet. My dad offered to get me more, but I knew it wouldn't work to live in that oblivion. I had to face the real world.

"But that place is still in me. That nothingness, where I don't have to care about anything.

"I stayed clean for fifteen years, four months, and three days. Until I woke up in the hospital with an IV drip of that same feeling and a busted shoulder. For a few seconds I was seventeen again, lying in my bed staring at the ceiling. Not caring about anything. I wasn't an FBI agent who'd been held hostage.

"I woke up at rock bottom with a friend there to tell me that my wife is missing." He looked at the clock, fighting against the gathering lump in his throat. Determined to get it all out. "I'd been captured by these mafia guys out of Vegas because of a case I was working on." He had to stop and swallow. "Because of my wife.

"She's been gone for ten weeks now, and my shoulder is healed thanks to the surgery. I've been doing PT, trying to ignore how much I'd like to take a pill and forget about all of this." He rubbed the left side of his ribs where they'd poked him with a cattle prod just for fun. "It's not the first time I've been held captive, or beaten, and I'm not telling you all this so you'll feel sorry for me. My shoulder was dislocated and torn pretty badly. I was prescribed more narcotics, and I didn't say anything because I didn't want to care. I didn't want to feel how much it hurts that I have no idea where she is." He sniffed. "But that wasn't going to help me get her back. I had to fight what I know, and what I want to do, so I can save her. The way she saves everyone.

"So I've been clean for forty-two days now. But I still can't find her. I have no idea where she is, or what's happening to her. This isn't even close to being over. And getting that oblivion back won't make it go away. I can't escape into the nothing this time. Not if I want a shot at finding her." He squeezed his eyes shut for a second. "The pain doesn't make me feel alive. What makes me feel alive is her."

The Bible study leader, Ron Ward, got up from the front row and came to the podium. "Thank you for sharing. Let's all be praying for Oliver and his wife, and the situation. In fact—"

Jax's phone rang in his pocket. He drew it out, left-handed because his right arm still ached all these weeks after surgery, and looked at the screen. "It's my office."

Ron nodded. "You take that. We'll pray for you."

"Thank you." Jax looked at the men who attended the study, a Bible class for those in recovery that his sponsor had hooked him up with. "Thanks, all of you." He skirted the edge of the chairs, and his shoes clipped the varnished wood floor as he retrieved his suit jacket.

He'd come here right from work, but that was no surprise. He spent most nights at the office now so he could be around if they got a lead. Maizie was staying at the townhouse with his cat, Jolene. The young woman he and Kenna had adopted was helping him at work and at home. He just wanted to find his wife—before his whole existence imploded.

Living on a knife edge wasn't going to last long.

Jax drove to the office, the world awash in dark sky and bright lights from the other cars on the road. He'd probably been living in autopilot since he realized she really was gone, and that he had no idea how to find her. For a few days he'd been certain they'd find her within the week. That they would get intel, and her team would go with him and the Phoenix FBI's tactical team, and they'd get her back. Jax had been in no shape to think about joining them, as he'd had surgery within days of Bruce and those lawyers finding him.

The car behind him honked.

The light was green. Jax hit the gas and set off.

This whole thing was a mess. They hadn't found her, and he hadn't been in any shape to get out and do it himself for two weeks after. Swallowed by the thing that made this feeling in his chest go away.

Am I ever going to get her back?

But the man he was—FBI Special Agent in Charge and husband, believer in Jesus—didn't ever go back to who he used to be. Out of necessity he gathered the rules and procedure around him like a blanket. He lived his life by tenets he'd clung to because they meant being the person he wanted to be, and not an addict. He couldn't afford to let go of the life he'd built. Not right now, when being an FBI agent was the thing that would enable him to find her. The Bureau had the means to hunt the people who had taken Kenna, and the resources to get her back.

The alternative was to cut and run and do this himself, solving the case the way Kenna would—solo. But Jax needed the FBI. He needed the rules, the resources and procedures.

If he lost control of himself, he would never get her back.

He pulled into the parking garage and went through security, going up to the floor where his team were situated. He dumped his backpack under the desk in his corner office and headed for the lab.

Special Agent Andrette Herron turned the corner at the end of the hall toward him, wearing tan cargos and a polo shirt. "Boss, you heard the judge signed off on the search warrant for the bar, right?" She jingled a set of keys. "We're gearing up. Rolling out in ten."

"That's great." Jax nodded. "I'll meet you there."

He wasn't going to bother changing out of his suit. He wanted to talk to Maizie about what she had, then go to the bar. It was the best way to not interfere in the work his team needed to do, and when he got there, he'd see if they found Kenna.

If he were honest, he was losing hope.

Before he even reached the door, he could hear the thumping beat of an '80s workout playlist. The one that meant Maizie was trying to figure something out. He pushed open the Plexiglas door, and the volume increased significantly. The room accommodated several technicians, but when Maizie had moved in—hired on as his newest consultant—they'd rearranged.

She worked at a long table that allowed her to stand and face the door, so he could see her head. She looked over the monitors she had stacked one on top of the other, beside them a vertically aligned display, all of which ensured no one walked up behind her and surprised her. It looked like the setup of an emergency dispatcher.

Jax didn't think she'd explained to the other agents why she needed things set up a certain way, same as he hadn't told them that technically she was his adopted daughter. All he'd said was that she was excellent at what she did. Good enough it warranted them hiring her on as a consultant.

If anyone thought that was because he planned to use Bureau resources to find his wife...okay, so they'd be right. But Maizie had helped with several other cases the past few weeks, and she loved his cat.

Her eyes flared seeing him, and she lowered the volume of the music. "You heard about the warrant?"

He nodded, going around her table to see what she had on her screens. At the last second the left side flashed, and the home page for an internet search engine popped up. "I'm heading out in a minute."

Maizie hopped onto the stool beside her, angled toward him. She wore the same kind of cargos that Special Agent Herron had on, but her polo shirt was a gray color and had a different emblem sewn on it. She'd also chosen one that was a size too big so it hung loose on her, and she'd pulled her thick blond hair into a ponytail. Some makeup, but not much. All of it designed to draw as little attention to her as possible.

She was barely eighteen, and for all intents his daughter, so he was fine by that. Later, when she found some confidence in who she was as a woman and started to come out of her shell a little, she was going to be a knockout. He wasn't ready for her to knock some poor young guy on his behind, but if she got into a relationship with someone who treated her like precious china, then Jax figured they could probably come to some kind of consensus.

The kind that would have Jax burying evidence along with the guy's body if he hurt her.

The others in the office had noticed her unique mannerisms. She wasn't exactly skittish. She simply turned to face the person every time she talked to them. She didn't go alone to her car—Jax always walked her downstairs and would often see one of Kenna's team in the parking lot watching out for her as well. And she kept things professional with the agents and other civilian employees.

If anyone looked her up, they wouldn't find a file on the reason she was the way she was. Far as Jax was concerned, Maizie's past was no one's business.

Kenna was gone, so it was up to him to look out for Maizie.

Both of them wanted to find her, and coming here,

Maizie had acted like he gave her the keys to the kingdom. Their tech was pretty cool. She just had to stay within the bounds of the law—something she hadn't technically always done with Kenna.

"Do you think Kenna might be at the bar when they search it?" She bit her lip, which made her look younger. But it was her eyes that told a different story.

One of the women in the office had asked him a few questions that got pretty close to the truth of what had happened to Maizie. No one would guess she'd been a captive her entire life, raised by the man who called her his wife. She'd escaped and he was dead, and now Maizie got to start over and live the life she wanted.

Jax leaned back against the counter and folded his arms. "I don't want to get my hopes up, but I can't help it. And then at the same time, it's so unlikely she's there."

"I know." Her face flushed. "I want her to be there so you can have her back."

"Me, too," he replied, wanting to reassure her.

Maizie had still been in Colorado when he got out of the hospital, and during those rough few days when he was getting clean. She hadn't seen his worst, and he planned to keep it that way.

"You good here, Maze?"

"Yes, Jax." She almost rolled her eyes but didn't. "I found a connection between the bar and...*Dominatus*." She said that last word more quietly than the rest, as they'd both learned to keep to themselves what would sound like a worldwide conspiracy to the other agents. "I need to solidify the connection, but it's there."

"Good." That meant there was a greater chance Kenna was at the bar.

"But it's a front for—"

"Sex crimes?" They had to keep it plain, keep the emotions out of it.

"If she is there—"

"Maze." He had to tread cautiously. "I know what you're saying. But the fact is, she could be anywhere, and we have no way to know what's happening to her. You can't let the unknown drive you crazy. We deal in facts, and things we can prove. Like a connection between this place and our enemy. Tell me what you found."

She scrunched up her nose, her gaze scanning the screens. "It's just a feeling, but I'm going to prove it. There's a connection to shell corporations we've come across before, but it's thin. They're good at hiding their tracks, burying what they own."

A few months back they'd taken down a rogue doctor, formerly with *Dominatus* but operating on his own in a silo buried out in the desert. They'd stopped that, and it had cost them Kenna. Right now, they didn't know what the organization behind all this was up to. But it was definitely something, considering for decades—or more—they'd been directing international events, infiltrating governments, creating genetically superior children, and pretty much trying to rule the world.

And now they had Kenna.

He rubbed his chest. "I need to go."

Maizie reached over and touched his shoulder.

Jax tried not to freeze, considering this was the first time she'd initiated physical contact. He'd had to stop himself from hugging her a number of times, not sure if she would be okay with it. He lifted his gaze to her so she could see the honest fear in his eyes. She wanted to be here to help him, and she had to know she was making a difference. She also had to know how much he needed her presence in his life.

"I've gotta go, Maze." He cleared his throat. "Find me proof."

She let go of his shoulder. "I won't let you down."

There it was. The delicate balance between needing her, and the young woman feeling like she had to prove herself. Not wanting to let him down was one thing—he felt the same way—but she didn't need to tie herself up in knots trying to do it.

"Whatever happens, we stick together." He went out on a limb and held his hand up in front of him with his palm toward his chest.

She clasped it, locking hands with him almost like they were going to arm wrestle.

"Deal?"

Maizie nodded. "Okay, deal."

He squeezed her hand and headed out. Hopefully tonight would be the night he got his wife back. He didn't want to know how bad the alternative was, for any of them.

He just wanted to find Kenna.

Chapter Two

Jax parked at the bank and crossed the street to Twisted Sugar, the late-night spot with bars on the windows and potholes in the parking lot. The team hunkered behind SUVs for a second, and before he'd even reached the sidewalk on that side, someone had given the "go" order and they moved in.

A team of tactical agents with rifles breached the doors and entered. Special agents with a vest over their suit shirt like he'd done, and pistols in hand, followed them in. As yelling erupted inside, Jax went to stand with a couple of agents assigned to catch whoever might make a break for it and run to the door.

"SAC Jaxton, are you taking over command?" Special Agent Farlan was African American, and a recent transfer from Florida.

Jax shook his head. "I'm not here to take over."

Now that he was in charge of the FBI office in Phoenix, he'd had to learn not to act like the other special agents. He was the boss, and it was more of a manager role. He liked being out of the sometimes frustrating work of solving cases, but tonight he needed to be here so he could see for himself who was inside.

Special Agent Herron came out, spotted him, and motioned with a wave.

Guess she already figured it out.

They all knew his wife was missing, and that a lot of what they were working on currently involved that situation. He'd tried to explain about *Dominatus* a couple of times, but the people he worked with shut down when it started to sound less like local federal crimes and more like a grand conspiracy. Those weren't so popular these days, even if most of them turned out to be true.

He'd learned quickly to keep the bigger picture to himself, along with the fact he regularly looped in the president about what was going on. The taskforce he'd been brought into that was trying to take down *Dominatus* seemed to have stalled out, though.

Jax jogged over to Herron, his gun holstered on his hip. "All clear?"

She nodded. "We have everyone secured. I figured you'd want to be here to ask questions."

"Give me the highlights."

She stepped into the dimly lit alcove entryway, toward a skinny Caucasian woman wearing six-inch heels, a tiny skirt, and even more tiny top. An agent standing guard. But that wasn't why Herron had brought him in here.

She was just the first employee he spotted.

"Fourteen *employees*," Agent Herron said. "I use that term loosely. Six are men—the boss and five guys who are muscle. Eight women—the youngest looks like she's fifteen, but we'll run IDs. They have rooms in the back for paying customers, and the menu is whatever you've got the money for."

Jax had been aware of what they would find. But when theory became reality, things were different. These women were someone's daughter, maybe someone's sister. Had they chosen this, either out of desperation or for some other reason, or had they been coerced?

"We have twenty-three customers all over in the lounge," Herron added. "We're running them, too."

What she hadn't done was tell him that his wife was here. Which meant she wasn't.

Jax nodded. "I want Kenna's picture shown to everyone here."

"Already in the works."

"And I want a word with the boss."

She glanced at him, but said nothing, then led him through a set of swinging doors into the main room of the club. A stage wrapped around from two bars—one to the right and another to the left—in a roped off area. Slim catwalks cut through the tables, providing the customers with a nearly 360-degree view of what was on offer. "He's in his office. Guy was deleting files off his computer, but maybe they can be restored. The whiz kid can do that, right?"

"This doesn't go to Maizie," Jax cut in. "You keep her out of it." He needed a good reason, though. "She has enough to work on."

Agent Herron didn't argue, but she clearly also didn't buy his slapshot reasoning.

Didn't matter, though. Just as long as Maizie was kept out of this. No need for her to be reminded that what she'd gone through for years happened every day. That the world was a sick place with so many evil people, which sometimes felt overwhelming. They all had to remember that good overcame evil every day. That God was sovereign and ultimately justice would be done.

He could still stand on the truth even if his prayers didn't feel like they were being answered.

The jobs they had both chosen meant they were a force for good in the world. They had the means to save people, and that was always what they tried to do. It was who his wife was, looking for victims who had been lost. Saving the innocent and bringing the perpetrators to justice.

Even after they had married a few months ago, that hadn't changed.

Until their enemy had targeted Kenna and he hadn't been around to save her.

"You good, Boss?"

He glanced at her and nodded. "I'm good."

"This way." She led him to a back hall, past agents putting zip ties on a couple of guys in black slacks and muscle shirts, and a woman yelling profanity at them wearing an FBI windbreaker to cover her bare skin.

One agent stood at the open door, another inside the small office. The manager was the only one wearing sunglasses. The agent had cuffed him, and the man now sat in a wooden chair in the center of the room.

Jax stopped. "We need to get Forensics in here."

Herron turned to him, and the other agents looked over. "Why's that?"

He backed up and turned up the dial on the overhead light so he could get a better look at the faux wood panels under the chair. "Someone cleaned up this floor. Might've been blood." He drew out his phone and thumbed through to a photo of Kenna. He turned it to the bar owner. "Have you seen this woman?"

"What's this—a missing person case?" The guy snorted, and Jax spotted a couple of broken teeth.

"Just answer the question. Maybe you'll help yourself."

The guy sneered. "Whatever."

Jax waited. Criminals weren't usually reasonable, let alone logical and cooperative. But he needed a second of this guy's attention so he could find out if Kenna had ever been here.

The guy's gaze flicked to the phone screen again.

"Take a good look."

"*Her.*"

Jax's stomach clenched. "You've seen this woman?"

The guy shrugged. "Not for a few weeks. She was in here. Picked up one of the..." He cleared his throat.

Jax shifted closer. "She did what now?"

The guy shifted on the seat.

Herron touched his arm. "We can finish this conversation. You don't need to be here."

"I'm not going anywhere until I have the whole story."

"I want immunity." The guy lifted his chin. "A guarantee I go free. Then I'll tell ya."

Jax twisted his upper body and punched the guy in the face. The chair tipped over backward, and he crashed to the floor along with it.

Other agents grabbed his arms and pulled him back, dragging him out into the hall.

He gritted his teeth. He shouldn't struggle, but what else could he do? It was instinct. "He's seen her."

Agent Herron shoved him against the wall, her forearm across his chest. "You're right. Now we know he's seen her. But if he uses this information to barter with us, then there's nothing you can do to get it out of him without getting fired." Thankfully, she kept her voice low.

"You think I care about that?"

"In the heat of the moment, no. But you'd regret it later. In the cold light of day."

Jax wasn't so sure. Beating the information out of the guy sounded like it would be satisfying. But he got her warning, and she wasn't wrong. "I'm good."

She didn't back off.

"I've got a handle on it."

"I'll find out what he knows." She let go of him and went into the room.

Andrette Herron had three grown kids and a grandbaby on the way, and as far as he could see, she'd been an excellent agent since day one. Her father had been in the Bureau, making her as much of a legacy agent as Kenna. The kind of fed who had the job, and this life, in their blood.

Which made agents like Jax, for whom being a Special Agent had been a kind of Hail Mary play in his life, feel like the odd guy out. They didn't mean it, given it was nothing more than who they were. But for Jax? This job was a whole lot about proving who he was.

Who he could be.

Which meant getting a handle on his tendency to fly off the handle. He needed to keep himself tight. Buttoned up. Straightlaced. Following rules, adhering to procedure, doing things by the book—that was the way to get Kenna back.

Please, Lord.

Jax felt like a bit of a hypocrite talking to God just because they now had an actual lead. He hadn't intended to, but during the past few weeks of silence, he'd sort of given up. He'd ignored the Lord, hadn't prayed much, barely cracked open the pages of his Bible, and just focused on moving forward instead. Searching for leads. Running down avenues of investigation. Anything and everything that would give him the chance to get her back.

He ducked his head and squeezed his eyes shut, but no words came. God knew what he needed without him asking for anything, but that would start with repentance and getting back on the right footing.

But if he did that, would there be answers when he asked?

Or more silence?

He was just about done gathering his thoughts when his phone rang in his pocket. He silenced it, not wanting to talk to his sister right now. She insisted on checking in regularly, but he'd have to call her back tomorrow.

"You good?" The question came from down the hall.

He lifted his chin and looked at the agent on approach. One of the people who worked for him. Jax didn't know them all super well. He'd never been friends with the people he worked for or who worked for him. At least not until Stairns, and that was only after the guy quit the FBI to go work for Kenna. "Did we get what we came for?"

"We'll take all the computers and any paperwork back to the office with us, run everyone's ID, and the women who were here under duress will get a shot at a fresh start. I'd say we won."

Jax didn't begrudge the guy needing it to feel like a contest between them and the bad guys. Each operation was the chance to score a point—and push their defensive line back. All in an effort to gain ground in a never-ending fight.

He'd been tired of the struggle when Kenna was in another state and he had to do his job when he'd rather be with her. After they got married, she'd moved to Phoenix with him, and to her credit she'd made a go of living in a real house rather than on the road in her RV. They probably would've made it work.

Now they wouldn't know.

Special Agent Herron stepped into the hall and nodded. "She was here."

"Tell me what I don't know." He tried not to sound irritated with her, but it probably didn't work. He'd apologize later. "What else did he say?"

"She showed up, picked up a girl they had prearranged purchase of, and took her away. He hasn't seen her again."

"When?" Jax said.

"Three weeks ago."

"You said it was a prearranged purchase." He didn't believe Kenna had gotten herself involved in sex trafficking —if that's what this was. "Who bought her?"

"A client he has who remains anonymous. Anytime they have a specific product, he makes a call and someone comes to collect."

Jax's stomach flipped over. "I want a full report on my desk by morning. And a plan to find out who these people are, buying certain girls."

It definitely sounded like something *Dominatus* would do.

The guy to his left said, "Boss—"

"I don't want to hear it," Jax snapped.

Herron lifted her chin. "We know that. Believe me we *all* know what you don't want to hear. But we still have to say it."

The other agent said, "Seems personal to you."

"Tell me you'd do anything different than what I'm doing if you were in the same situation." Jax glanced between them, daring either one to say it. "I've got it handled."

"No one expects you to be fine," Herron said, her tone softened. "No one expects you to have things tight twenty-four seven until she's found. But if she's part of—"

"She isn't part of it. Kenna had to have been under duress when she came here." He folded his arms across his chest. "I want to see security footage."

"I asked about that. Their system has been broken for a few weeks." Herron hesitated. "He said when she came here, she wasn't scared, or nervous. She didn't say anything that wasn't part of the transaction. He remembers because he offered to buy her a drink and she told him where he could shove that idea."

Jax frowned. That wasn't something Kenna would ever have said. If she was a captive, she'd have surely tried to get a message out somehow.

"I know that look, and I'm sorry," Herron said. "Sometimes we learn things about people we love and they're hard to hear. We think we know the ones closest to us, but we don't always see the truth, even if it's in front of us. We want to trust the person, and it's hard to find out they aren't who we thought they were."

Jax shook his head. "That's not what's happening here."

He'd have to get into conversations about genetic experiments and secret organizations impregnating women in order to explain why he didn't believe that Kenna had gone to work for their enemy. That would only lead the people he worked with to thinking things were far worse than they'd feared—that he'd completely lost his grip on reality.

He added, "Report what you have, and let me figure out what it means."

She started to question him, but he didn't call her on it. He just walked away down the hall. Past the group of girls—women and teens—now being assessed by medics. Past the suspects being loaded into vans to be taken into custody and booked. Back across the street to his car.

He stopped at his door, braced his palms on the roof, and tucked his chin. Then took a few deep breaths. Pretending no one could see him, and that he had himself under control.

"Looking for someone to punch?"

The low voice had a slight Hispanic lilt to it, but not much. He only recognized it because he knew the man approaching to his left. On his offside, so that Jax would have to fully turn around to face the man, and he'd need more time to get the right aim if he had to draw his weapon.

In the meantime, Ramon would have already stabbed him in the back.

"If I was going to punch anyone"—Jax turned—"it would be you. After all, you're the reason she's gone."

"And if I have information?" Ramon asked. The guy didn't even have the decency to look guilty. The day Kenna had been taken by men working for their enemy, Ramon had been stun gunned and left behind. He hadn't done anything to stop it.

"Is the intel you have that Kenna is trafficking young women for *Dominatus?*"

Ramon flinched. "What? No. Who said that? It's dumb."

Jax didn't want to like the guy. He wanted to hate him, blame him, and never see him again. If it wasn't for Maizie and the high regard she had for this man, Jax would have told Ramon to get lost weeks ago. "Then what is it? I need to get back to the office."

Ramon headed for the passenger side. "Team meeting."

"I'm not part of your team."

"Bro, that hurts." Ramon went to the passenger door. "Get in and drive."

Chapter Three

Jax slammed the driver's door shut, completely unapologetic of his bad mood. The sound echoed against the concrete under the overpass like a gunshot. He needed a flashlight so he didn't trip over something, but Ramon didn't offer him one. Before he could ask where the others were and why this meeting was happening under a bridge, a car turned the corner across the asphalt expanse and headed for them. Maizie. Another car pulled in behind it.

He leaned against the car and probably came across as relaxed. Or at least ready.

Instead, on the inside, he was roiling. Everything in him had burned hotter and hotter as he drove here, not listening to whatever Ramon had been saying. Not when all he could think about was Kenna showing up at a bar to *purchase* a person. As if life could be bought or sold.

It was though, far too much in this world, but that didn't mean it *should* be.

His fingers curled into fists by his sides. No way would Kenna ever get involved with something like that. At least not voluntarily. It was entirely possible she'd been brain-washed. They'd seen it before with people captured by *Dominatus*, and he'd read about it from the reports his agents had written after the silo operation. There had been people down there—in that decommissioned missile silo turned into a research center—who had been under the influence of a drug that made them compliant. By all accounts, they'd been little more than zombies who had to be woken up as it were, and then they'd snapped out of it.

Could that be what had happened?

His mind spun with the implication. With questions he had no answers to, followed by even more questions. Like how on earth he was going to get her back.

Moisture gathered in his eyes, and he turned his head. They'd probably believe he was scanning to make sure this clandestine meeting at an out-of-the-way place wasn't under surveillance, and not that he had to blink away the tears in his eyes.

Multiple car doors slammed, and he turned to watch Maizie and Bruce wander over.

Maizie said, "Jax?"

He knew that tone, even if the dim light obscured the expression on her face. The young woman sounded nervous, but that didn't mean there was a problem. He'd become pretty good at reading her over the past few weeks, but it was too soon to find the good in this situation.

Gratitude could come after they found Kenna.

"I'm good." He pushed off the side of the car and went to sit on the front quarter panel, his entire body heavy with exhaustion, wanting to avoid the heat under the hood. "What's going on?"

Ramon stood to his left.

Bruce approached, causing Maizie to turn slightly so he

wasn't in her blind spot. He said, "Amara and Zeyla got tied up doing something."

Jax didn't even want to talk about Kenna's mom and sister—or her aunt and cousin. Whatever those two women were to Kenna, they were the closest thing she had to extended family.

Kenna and Zeyla had never even had a conversation, since they'd only met when Zeyla had been unconscious. The young woman was recovered now, and rebuilding a life. The mom, Amara, was more of a wildcard than anyone Jax had ever met. The woman made Bruce look normal.

Jax didn't want to need their help finding Kenna, but what other options did he have? "Why are we here?"

He'd just been given some of the worst news of his life, and he was expected to make nice with Kenna's team? He needed to hit the gym, lift something heavy, and push all the thoughts and questions out of his mind. Then he would eat something and fall into bed.

Tomorrow he would do it all over again. Every day looking for a break in this case.

How did Kenna do it?

Maizie said, "Ramon has this friend. She's a reporter."

Jax glanced at Ramon. "A *friend?*"

"From my short stint at the FBI." He shifted his stance, shoving his hands in his pockets. Drew out his phone and checked the screen. "She received an anonymous email, untraceable."

Jax looked at Maizie.

"I tried from my laptop at home. I didn't want to use the Bureau's network in case someone discovered it, or there was a virus embedded in the video."

"Let me guess, Kenna is on it. Trafficking young girls for *Dominatus.*"

Maizie stared at him. "She would never do that. And she would never do this. I'm going to prove the video is fake." Her voice thickened, and she cleared her throat. "It's a deep fake."

Ramon shifted closer to Maizie but didn't touch her.

"Maybe it isn't," Jax countered. What the bar owner had seen was real. "What was on the video?"

He didn't want to ask, but he had to.

Maizie looked at Ramon.

"A dead man," he said. "That's how we know it's fake."

Jax waited a couple of seconds. "Whatever it is, just tell me."

"We don't know where they were," Maizie replied. "I'm running the buildings around them through a program that looks at those street view maps online, and it's comparing the image to see if it can find them." She took a breath. "It was Kenna and Doctor Buzard."

"He's dead," Jax pointed out. "Definitely fake. Or old."

Ramon said, "Kenna is the one who killed him."

"The video is date and time stamped in the metadata, and it's from a month ago." Maizie sucked in a sharp breath.

Ramon turned to Jax. "They were making out. Whoever set it up did a great job of making it look like she's in a romance with him. Definitely not under duress this time at least, so don't bother asking about that." He waved a hand. "Doctor Buzard and Kenna. Looks like they ran off together and now they're in cahoots."

"His body is in the ground."

Bruce snorted. "As if no one ever faked their death."

"That doesn't explain why she'd do that."

The two men shifted. Jax didn't want to think what that meant—aside from that they pitied him because his wife had evidently run off with a dead man and was living the high life with her new romance and a thriving business.

He crossed his arms. "We all know Kenna would never switch sides and suddenly start working for *Dominatus*."

He hated that he even had to say it. But the truth had to be spoken aloud so others could hear it. Even if no one ever uttered it, the truth was still truth. And yet, declaring it out loud strengthened the person doing the declaring. It enabled them to believe in it even more. "She would never do that. Not even if they forced her."

"She wouldn't," Maizie said, her voice a little shaky, but she nodded.

"Not even before she got to know you would she *ever* have done something like that." Jax said it for his benefit, and hers. "Those guys from the retirement home pretended to be FBI, they took her and gave her to our enemy, and then they disappeared."

Jax had been trying to find them for weeks.

Dominatus had gone unchecked for decades. Was it any surprise he hadn't found a trace of those men? Their cover stories, impersonating FBI higher-ups, had been impeccable.

"Now they want to destroy her reputation," Jax said. "They want the FBI to shut down my investigation, so I have no way to find her."

His credibility would take a hit. Jax might even lose his job if he pushed it.

He needed the job to keep himself together, because without the boundaries of a day job and the strictures that came with being a Special Agent in Charge, he would have nothing to keep him in check. He might even turn out like Ramon, a guy who skirted the edge and had a limited skillset. Thankfully, Kenna had kept Ramon in the fold, working together so that she could keep an eye on him and help him get out of trouble if it turned out he needed that.

It was the kind of person his wife was that she seemed to collect strays. Ramon. Maizie. Bruce even. People with no family who had a reason to destroy their life trying to right a wrong. She helped them pull themselves together and live on the right side of the law—with enough leeway they could still be who they were. He wasn't sure what that said about him and didn't much care.

He just wanted his wife back.

"My people are working the intel we got from the bar. Maybe we'll find something in their network that can lead us back to *Dominatus.*"

"*Maybe?*" Ramon shifted, aggression in his stance even if he didn't necessarily mean to display that. "You're banking Kenna's survival on a maybe?"

"It's all I've got." Jax thumped his chest. "I'm FBI. That means I run this like the FBI does. It's how we get results."

Ramon huffed. "Your way is taking too long. She's still out there. We have no idea what's happening to her!"

"That sentiment has been shared." Jax wasn't going to take the bait, even if Ramon didn't need to get mad at him. They were all doing the best they could to find her. If this guy wasn't happy with how long it was taking, then he could join the queue to register a complaint.

"You're still thinking like a fed," Ramon said. "Now you've got Maizie tied up working there, doing other cases for you. She needs to be helping us find Kenna." He motioned at Bruce. "We're the ones out there gathering information."

"Yeah? What information have you found?" Jax shot back. The video they'd just told him about had been sent to a reporter. "Friend of yours at a news outlet—is she gonna leak the video? Tell the world that Kenna Banbury has gone dark side?"

"She wouldn't be able to run with it if I had Maizie working with me! We'd have deployed a virus in their computer network by now, and the whole thing would be squashed." Ramon sucked in a breath. "But *no*. You've got her wanting to follow the law so she can live up to your perfect Bureau standards."

Jax pushed off the car. "You're mad that Maizie shouldn't want to break the law? Do you want her to go to jail?"

"No one is going to jail," Ramon argued.

"Right. Because you're going to find a legal way to squash this news story, right? *Dominatus* wants to undermine us. They want to wreck our chances of finding her, which means they believe we might actually do it. Otherwise, they wouldn't be trying to stop us like we're a threat."

"We aren't a threat. We have no idea where she is, no idea how to find her, and...that's it—we have nothing!" Ramon yelled. "But you want to go to your office every day and pretend it's fine that we're nowhere."

"I'm not pretending."

Ramon shifted closer to him. "No? Going to that Bible study. Telling them you're trying to find her. That won't happen while you're waiting for warrants. Or processing evidence. Or telling everyone your sob story."

"You know how the Bureau works."

"I know I won't go back. Kenna will be dead before you find her."

Jax faced off with Kenna's colleague. "Because you're making so much progress working outside the law? You haven't found anything either."

"At least I'm looking. I'm not sitting behind a desk."

Ramon's body shifted again toward Jax, aggression in the movement. "I'm finding her."

"Then find her."

"It's gonna happen faster than what you're doing." Ramon scoffed. "Wasting your time with reports and evidence."

They were nearly chest to chest now. Jax heard Maizie sniffle, but everything sounded like a buzz in his ears. "You think *I'm* not doing my job?" He pointed at Ramon. "You wish you were the one married to her."

"If I was, she wouldn't be missing."

"You're the one who let them take her. If you cared about her, you wouldn't have let that happen." Jax shoved Ramon with both hands because he hadn't denied what Jax said. "You'd have kept her safe, right? No matter what. So tell me, *Ramon*, is it you that's working for *Dominatus*? Is that why I can't find my wife?"

Maizie gasped, and it sounded like a sob.

"You're looking for anyone to blame." Ramon shoved him back. "Because you can't face yourself when you're not in control of everything. You don't even realize you're already spinning out."

Bruce shoved them apart.

Jax stumbled back and sat on the hood of his car. Ramon turned and paced away, running his hands through his hair.

Maizie wiped her face. "You guys shouldn't fight. We need to work together."

Jax pushed off the car to go to her.

She held up a hand. "Don't."

"I'm sorry."

"No, you aren't. You want to fight Ramon because you think it will make you feel better." Maizie sniffed. "Elizabeth said he's an easy target because you know he won't quit looking for Kenna. But that means you shouldn't fight because you're both on the same side."

"We're not fighting, *Hermana*." Ramon rolled his shoulders.

She shot him a look. "Bruce?"

"I got you, Trouble." The former CIA agent folded his arms across the front of his Hawaiian shirt. "Kenna wasn't at the bar. That means everyone goes home and gets some sleep. We won't find her if we're all burned out. We'll miss something important. Like the fact that Buzard is dead, and yet he's on video walking around..."

"No one missed that," Jax said. "It's a lead."

"Exactly." Bruce nodded.

Jax shook his head. "Is this pep talk going to have a point?"

If he was going to be honest, he still wanted to go a few rounds with Ramon. Not for the reason Elizabeth had told Maizie, though. Jax had his own reasons. But he was still going to rely on the guy to help find Kenna.

As long as they all knew it was Jax who was going to be the one to find her.

"We have work to do. Leads to follow. If we work together, we'll get her back," Bruce sounded sure, but all of their hope had waned in the last month.

Right now, it was hard not to hear it as empty sentiment.

"We need to find her," Bruce added. "For all our sakes."

Chapter Four

Jax left his phone in the car. He didn't want to see any more missed calls from Ramon. Until Kenna was found, he wasn't sure he had anything else to say to the guy. After all, they'd made themselves clear to each other last night.

He'd gone home and slept in his room because he wanted to be closer to Maizie in case she needed to talk about what happened. She'd been upset, but that upset led to her sleeping in Kenna's RV in the garage. And when he'd gone over to try and talk to her, he'd overheard her talking— probably to Elizabeth. He'd given her space and left the house before she was up this morning.

Heat shimmered up from the asphalt even though it was still early. He walked the path flanked by rows of neatly planted cypress trees that were all fifteen feet and immaculately manicured. The lawn looked like a golf course, dotted with headstones. One of them would read *Doctor Marcus Buzard.*

Jax tugged the folded paper from his inside breast pocket and knocked on the door of a white square single-story building with peeling paint on the stone exterior. He let himself in and found an older man shuffling papers on a desk. "Sir?"

On the street behind him, several cars screeched to a stop, parking behind his car, going fast but not running lights and sirens. He shut the door just as FBI agents hopped out. At least half a dozen who apparently didn't have anything better to do than come here and find out what he was up to.

Jax cleared his throat. "Sir?"

The guy grabbed a stack of files and a radio, then straightened. He flinched seeing Jax standing there. "I didn't..." He reached for the back of his ear. "Didn't turn on my hearing aids this morning. Didn't even hear you come in."

"Sorry if I startled you. Are you the manager here?"

"Manager, groundskeeper...pest control—you name it."

He shifted his jacket so the man would be able to see the badge on his belt. "I'm Special Agent Oliver Jaxton. This is a warrant for the exhumation of a body." He handed over the paper.

The older man frowned at his document, then looked at the window. "People usually bring equipment. You gonna dig this person up by yourself?"

The door opened behind him, and several agents came in, Farlan at the lead.

"Did you bring a shovel?" Jax asked.

"Sir..." Farlan began. Maybe he had no idea what to say. "Can we step outside, Jax?"

Rather than get into a disagreement with his subordinate, Jax turned to the groundskeeper. "Can you show me where to find plot AC28?"

The older guy wandered to a map on the wall. "AC."

He ran his finger up the map of the grounds, then across a horizontal line. "Twenty-eight is by the fountain, couple rows back to the north."

"Thank you," Jax said. "You can keep that copy of the paperwork." He headed for the door and stepped outside.

Special Agent Herron broke off her conversation with one of the other agents and came over.

He told her, "We're going to need something to dig with."

Right then, Farlan come out of the small building behind him, but Jax wasn't about to be waylaid by him any more than by her.

Herron lifted her chin. "We're going to talk about this before we do something rash."

"That tone might work with your kids, or maybe even your husband," Jax said, "but I'm your boss."

"Assistant Director in Charge Hadley arrived at the office this morning. He wants to speak to you as soon as you can get there." Herron folded her arms. "And he's not happy you're making him wait."

"There's a dangerous man walking around who is supposed to be dead." Jax wasn't going to back down. "I'm looking at that grave."

He strode in the right direction, and the team followed him.

"Don't you need a shovel or something?" Farlan asked.

"I'm here to look," Jax said. "We are getting this thing exhumed, but that can happen this afternoon. We need to secure the scene first."

Farlan snorted. "You think someone's gonna mess with it?"

"If they were going to, it's probably already done," Jax replied. "But there could be clues." Maybe he sounded like a lunatic. But if that's what got him Kenna back, then what did he care? "I want to examine the grave for indications anyone has been visiting. Or something that was left behind. Nothing is out of the realm of possibility right now."

He wouldn't rule out *Dominatus* leaving a surprise for him—likely a nasty one.

They were trying to undermine his search for Kenna.

Jax couldn't explain how she had been at that bar, or why she would be involved in a trafficking ring. At least not any more than he could understand the video of Kenna with Buzard, looking like they were involved in a romantic relationship.

Their enemy wanted the world to believe Kenna had run off with another man. There would certainly be nothing to investigate if that was the case. Jax would look like the guy who had lost his wife and couldn't let her go.

He would be discredited—pitied. The guy who refused to see the truth.

Their enemy didn't need to try and kill them. They certainly had the means to end his life and all of Maizie's friends' lives without firing a single shot. *Dominatus* could destroy them all so easily.

That was why Jax had to figure out what they were up to. Get ahead of them for once, instead of feeling constantly as if his enemy was one step ahead of him. That would be the only way they could deal a blow, let alone take down *Dominatus*. Jax would settle for being a legitimate threat to them—and finding Kenna in the process.

He counted rows to figure out where he should go. But as he neared the stretch of grass, it became apparent he was getting nowhere.

From ten feet away, he pointed. "Looks like someone beat us to it."

The dirt had been piled to one side, and a gaping hole with no casket in it had been dug in front of the headstone that read *Marcus Buzard*.

"So...was he ever here or not?" Farlan squeezed the back of his neck.

"I don't imagine they buried nothing, but I guess it's possible there was just an empty casket. Or it was full of rocks. If there was something here, then someone dug it up."

"I mean, I see that." Farlan shook his head. "Grave robbers?"

Special Agent Herron sighed, her hands on her hips. "Someone didn't want us to find Doctor Buzard."

The man had been dead. So someone had stolen his body, then?

"I'm surprised they allowed him to be buried in the first place." Jax shrugged. "Given who he was, I figured they'd have stolen the body before now or had him cremated to get rid of any evidence."

"Who are these people?" Farlan shook his head. "I mean, I came in late to this game, but this Buzard guy had a facility full of test subjects, and people he coerced to working with him on his grand plan or whatever. But I feel like I need to get up to speed."

"Buzard went rogue from a bigger organization," Jax said. "I figured they would have buried him and everything connected to him." Including people, but everyone that worked for Buzard had taken some kind of vow of silence, going to prison without uttering one word. All of them—and there were at least thirty. Jax had tried talking to a few of them, but still none of them would say anything. "Seemed more like the bigger organization washed their hands of the whole incident."

The only connection he could see were those men from the retirement home, known only by numbers. They'd been registered at the home with clearly fake names, and Maizie had been scouring military service records, trying to find out who they were. It seemed more like they'd been erased from existence.

Something that was *not* going to happen to Kenna.

"Boss."

He turned to Special Agent Herron, and she motioned across the grass.

The groundskeeper came over with a couple of agents, not looking so happy about finding a hole in the ground where there should be a grave. "Well, now," he said, scratching his chin. "That's not good, is it?"

Jax said, "Do you have any kind of surveillance system in the grounds of the cemetery?"

He scratched his jaw. "Usually, sure. But these folks came over last night and told me we were having a whole system upgrade. Knocked the whole thing out for a while and couldn't get it back up. So it's currently down."

"What folks?"

"Older guy, Hispanic guy, and a blonde. Thick ponytail sticking out the back of her ball cap. She was good at what she did. All those ones and zeros racing across the screen."

Jax's stomach clenched. The agents here would realize that was Maizie. "If some of our techs could take a look at your system, we would appreciate it if you give us access. Just in case the footage is recoverable." He wandered off, heading for his car.

If there had been something to find, Kenna's team would have found it. After all, they were the ones who had beaten him here to do exactly what Jax had intended this morning. Bruce, Ramon, and Maizie. None of them had told him what they were doing, or what they'd discovered if they had found something.

Jax stopped by his car and fired off a text, asking them what they did with Buzard's body. Then he climbed in, ignoring the stares of his agents. If his boss wanted a meeting, then Jax wasn't going to make him wait any longer.

He drove to the office, thinking how Kenna would always want to stop for coffee. He'd stopped making a pot in the morning when it was only him who drank it. Then Maizie had shown up at the house because Stairns was in to California so he could be a bodyguard for Jax's sister and her family. Just in case they were targets.

He didn't know whose idea it was that he have her company, but it was better than her being in Colorado by herself.

Jax wanted to know why Maizie let the others talk her into bringing down the surveillance system so they could steal Buzard's body.

His phone chimed in his pocket as he walked past Maizie's lab, but it was the verse of the day from his Bible app. Something about giving the Lord the first fruits.

He didn't see Maizie at her desk, so he sent her a text.

Are you at work?

The bubbles that indicated she was typing popped up, then disappeared.

He got irritated waiting for her to reply and went to find his boss. The Assistant Director in Charge was directly above Jax and reported to the Director of the FBI. If he was here, then there was a serious problem.

Jax knocked. "Sir?"

"Come in."

Jax could tell the guy seldom used this office. There were no personal items on the desk, except for a steaming cup of coffee and a half-eaten donut on a paper towel. The top of the sideboard was empty, with one drawer slightly open. And a painting that was fit for a low-budget hotel room hung on the wall. He'd had seen better artwork at the big box store.

At least Jax's office looked the part.

Assistant Director in Charge Hadley slid his suit jacket on the back of his chair so the lapels were on either side of his head. "Take a seat, Oliver."

"Everything okay, sir?"

"The director and I met with the president recently, and he filled me in on some things. Experiences you had in the United Kingdom that might have had a more lasting effect on you than anyone realized." Before Jax could ask what that was supposed to mean, his boss said, "Have you met with the department psychologist since your wife left you?"

"She went missing. Sir, she was kidnapped by a dangerous group." He explained how Ramon had been stunned and the men who took Kenna from the area outside the silo, right after her debrief by Special Agent Herron, had been agents of a dark organization. "I've only started to scratch the surface of what happened. I need a lot more resources if I'm going to get to the bottom of what's going on."

Kenna's team were hot on the trail, working the case.

Jax was here, relegated to being reprimanded by his boss while they did the job he wanted to be doing right now.

But no, being a fed had saved his life so many times.

Doing his job was what would get her back, not running off chasing random leads with no backup.

"Right." ADIC Hadley linked his fingers together on the top of the desk. "Everything the president told me was quite sensational, but really only speaks to the delusion he's under about shaking things up. Clearing the swamp, or whatever he ran on. I mean, does he really think there's some kind of grand conspiracy going on in the whole world? The man should just worry about this country. The one he's supposed to be the president of. Everyone on the planet isn't under his jurisdiction, no matter what people might think. Other countries will take care of their own business."

"Sir—"

"I'm not finished. What I'm saying is, just worry about what's in your jurisdiction. You were put in charge of this office. Now's the time to act in accordance with your position. That means not using more Bureau resources than necessary to look for your wife. An investigation is one thing, and I'd be right where you are if it was me. But you can't have most of the agents in this office and half the technicians and analysts in the place working on finding your wife. There are other cases to solve. Got me?"

"Yes, sir." This guy disagreed with the president, and he was making this visit about politics instead of it being about the case Jax was working. But Hadley was right that Jax's people had other cases to work. He couldn't pull everyone off what they were supposed to be working on just to find Kenna.

As much as he might want to do exactly that.

Jax continued, "I should give the team updated assignments. That way they know what they're supposed to be working on."

"Right. That brings me to that consultant of yours. The one you gave access to our entire system."

"Maizie is excellent at her job."

"That's part of the problem, I'm afraid. A couple of the agents are questioning her now, trying to find out who has been worming their way through our computer system. She's the most recent hire, so she's first."

"She's being interviewed?" He was technically her guardian, but she was also an adult. And no one here knew she was his adopted daughter. "Does she have representation?"

"Why would she need that?"

Jax had to act like the dutiful agent. Not just because it kept him from descending back into the darkness of addiction, but also because that was what everyone around him expected. "Sir, if you'll excuse me—"

"You're going to jeopardize your career on a wife who may not be who you think she is, and a consultant?"

Jax nearly said yes. But the last thing he could do was burn it all down and walk away. No matter how much he might want to.

"Take a few days," the ADIC said. "I'll cover for you here at the office and keep things running while you get your head straight. That work for you?"

As if Jax could say no.

Chapter Five

Jax strode down the hall and headed for the elevator so he could go to the fourth floor, where they had interview rooms and the holding cells. On the way, he grabbed his phone and called Stairns.

"Morning, Jaxton."

There was a reassurance to hearing it. Possibly because Jax respected Stairns far more than he respected a lot of the people he'd worked with.

He held the phone to his ear and pushed the UP button. "How's everything there?"

"Kids are off to school. Laney is having lunch with Elizabeth, and then they're going to play tennis at the country club."

Jax looked at his shoes, a smile pulling at his lips. "Thank you."

"And our Maizie girl?"

Jax's nose started to itch. He wanted to open up to Stairns, but they'd never been like that. "She's being interviewed by a couple of agents about a worm in the network. I'm headed there now to find out what's going on."

He wanted to tell Stairns how it felt not knowing where Kenna was, or how he didn't know how he was even going to begin to find her. The lack of leads told him enough about the enemy they faced. But how was it supposed to get Kenna back?

This building, this job, was supposed to be his support network—the way he understood how the world worked and how he could navigate it, knowing that he could keep everything contained. All those self-destructive tendencies were in check if he had to pass regular drug tests, act within the bounds of procedure, and operate with integrity. Sure, some agents didn't. That was why they had an Office of Professional Responsibility. But it wasn't the way he operated.

"Fix it."

"Yes, sir." Jax didn't work for the guy, but he had immense respect for what Stairns had done with Maizie. Craig and Elizabeth Stairns had three grown daughters and grandchildren, and they'd opted in their retirement to take on the challenge of helping Maizie navigate recovery from trauma and rebuild her life. Likely out of respect for Kenna.

"Any new leads?"

Jax told him about Buzard's body and talked enough around the hole in the ground and what the groundskeeper said that Stairns would know what happened—that Kenna's team had dug him up and taken him. "I need the funeral director's name, I think. To find out if there was anything odd about the body or how it all transacted."

"Good idea."

"Have you ever come across Assistant Director in Charge Hadley?" Jax asked. "He's here, shaking the trees and asking me if I'm seeing the psychologist."

"I'd say, 'Don't act unhinged and they won't think you're unhinged,' but it doesn't always work like that."

Stairns could say that, because when Kenna was retired with no room for debate, it was Stairns who'd signed the papers, thinking he was doing her a favor. Someone needed to do Jax a favor and just let him look for his wife. The other agents in the office could take care of their cases. He needed to be a man on a mission.

Finding Kenna.

"There has to be a way to get to her." The elevator doors opened, and Jax sniffed, stepping out so no one would think he was having a breakdown. "I need to find her."

"Talk to Bruce. Both him and Ramon called me this morning. You need to get with them and work this." Stairns paused. "As far as Hadley goes, watch yourself. He hasn't risen to the top without stepping on a few heads on the way up."

"Copy that."

"I'll let you go," Stairns said. He must've heard the shift in Jax's tone.

"Thanks." Jax hung up.

He ducked in the surveillance office, logged into the closest computer, and pulled up the feed for the room where Maizie was being questioned. Anyone who checked the records would know he had observed the conversation.

He slid the headphones on.

"...explaining how it is that your station interacted with this worm more than once," the agent stated. She was older and didn't go out in the field much, but she was whip smart and hopefully astute enough to treat Maizie with compassion.

His girl sat across the table, straight with her shoulders back. Chin high but not high enough to be defiant. To her credit, she didn't look as tired as she should be after being up half the night, digging up a dead body and stealing surveillance video. "Everyone in this office likely interacted with that worm," she replied. "The fact I did it only a couple of times means I likely brushed past it in the course of my normal duties."

"Let's talk about those 'normal duties.'" The agent made air quotes. "The Special Agent in Charge personally invited you to work here, even vouched for you."

Maizie stayed quiet longer than someone just thinking what to say. As though taking a more measured approach, keeping herself from saying something she didn't mean to and landing in hot water for it. "If I brushed past the worm, that's likely the same as anyone on the network has done. There's nothing special about my activity." She spoke calmly, as if she'd been advised how to treat this interview, and was reserving judgment on how much trouble she was in.

"You're eighteen years old, and you work as an FBI consultant technician. You think there's nothing special about your situation?" The agent relaxed in her seat. "When did you first realize you were so good with computers?"

Trying to make friends with Maizie so she would let down her guard.

The agent had no idea what kind of person she was dealing with. A fact that could help Maizie keep her own confidence and come across as unflappable, and equally meant she might break more than anyone this woman had ever met. Jax knew it had happened. Her trauma whipped up and slapped her across the face when she least expected it, as it often did to former victims.

The question was, how far would this agent push—and how would Maizie react?

Maizie cleared her throat. "The worm you showed me on that device is pervasive. Everyone has likely interacted with it, unknowingly." She motioned to a tablet on the table. "That's what we're talking about right now, because that worm is a threat to this office, and you need to deal with it." She leaned forward. "You need *me* if you want to get rid of it."

Jax absorbed those words, wondering when she'd decided to make a power play. To shift the balance from the agent to her. She was the one in a position to help the Bureau rather than the agent having all the power. Maizie didn't need to simper and bargain for concessions.

Effective, but not the tactic that Jax would have told her to use.

Maizie's lips curled up, just a fraction. Not enough that anyone who didn't know her would recognize.

Jax shook his head and muttered to himself, "Who is talking in your ear, Maze?"

He would put money on her being coached in the moment. Maybe by Ramon, but more likely it was Bruce the former CIA agent. Or both. Men he wanted to blame, rage against, and pummel until they got him Kenna back. But right now, he couldn't muster up the anger that seemed to have been burning in his chest since he found out she was gone.

In fact, he was angrier at the FBI than at Kenna's team right now.

"What was that, sir?"

Jax hadn't realized the agent on the far side of the room could hear him. He shook his head, holding the earphones in place. "Nothing."

The agent across the table from Maizie in the interview room tapped the tablet screen. "You might be able to help us, but that means answering my questions." She lifted it to Maizie, which meant he couldn't see what was on the screen. "Like explain to me why you've been looking at this page of the silo after action report more than any other." She paused a second. "Is there some kind of code embedded in this data?"

Maizie didn't answer right away. "His name is Sean Reed. He's one of the victims that Kenna Banbury rescued from that silo. He's twenty-one, and he was taken captive when he was fifteen. Experimented on."

"And the code embedded in the page? Is this the back door into the whole network?" The agent stared her down. "Who did you sell access to the FBI system to?"

"When the victim has a face and a name, then they have a story. And when they have a story, you know it hasn't ended yet. And if you have the power to help someone have a happy ending, then that's the best kind of life to live. One where you can change someone's future." Maizie sat back in her chair. "That's what Kenna Banbury taught me."

Jax blinked at the sheen of moisture in his eyes. He set the headphones down and wandered to the door of the interview room. He didn't bother knocking, but opened the door and strode in. "Maizie, who is Sean Reed?"

Maizie looked at him, her eyes wide.

"I want an answer, young lady. Have you been talking to boys online again?"

The agent glanced at him, but he didn't take his attention from Maizie.

"It wasn't about the case, or any sensitive FBI information," Maizie said. "I promise."

He was surprised she didn't add *Dad* to the end of that.

The agent said, "Uh, Boss?"

"We'll talk about this at home. I'm very disappointed in you." Jax turned to the agent. "This conversation is done. If you have more questions, those can be asked at a later time."

"Ms. Morrow is free to go...for now, sir." The agent frowned. "But I may have more questions for her, and her duties here will be limited until we can clear this up."

Jax nodded. "Understood."

Maizie had already stood.

He held out his hand as she approached him, and she took it. If she hadn't, he'd have held it up as if leading her by the small of her back—just without touching her. She squeezed the life out of his hand, and they stepped into the hall.

He kept his grip loose so she could let go as soon as she wanted to, which was at the elevator. "Okay?"

She glanced at him, her attention elsewhere. "Got it." Then she focused on him. "We have lunch plans."

"Ramon?"

"Bruce. Ramon said don't bother calling him back, because of course you were definitely going to do that. He said he'll tell you everything at lunch."

The elevator doors slid open, and they stepped in.

Jax told her, "I need my backpack if we're going out."

She nodded. "There's a lot to tell you."

Yeah, he'd bet that was true. He wanted to ask her outright now, but someone could be listening even in the elevator.

Half an hour later, he parked not far from her in the restaurant parking lot and jogged to catch up. "Sean Reed?"

She ducked her head. "Can't we talk about something else?"

"You've taken to driving. Some of those corners were a little fast, though."

"You totally sound like a dad."

He smiled and held the door for her. "At least you think that's a good thing."

She went right to the back corner of this Mexican joint that smelled amazing and looked a little rundown. He'd never even noticed this place, which could bode well for the food. Not that he was here to enjoy it.

When Kenna was home, they could come here.

Maizie took a seat beside Ramon, which left Jax on the side with Bruce.

Before he even touched the seat, Jax said, "Someone tell me where the body is."

"That would be difficult, bro." Ramon took a sip of his soda.

Bruce shrugged. "There was no body. No casket. Just dirt."

Jax glanced around, not sure if he should even believe that. "So y'all took it upon yourselves to jump the gun and dig up a body?"

"Can't dig up a body if there's no body." Ramon was completely unrepentant. "We were uh...landscaping."

Jax eyed him. "So Marcus Buzard isn't actually dead?"

"He *was* dead," Ramon said. "Kenna shot him. That guy wasn't coming back."

Jax clenched down on his molars.

Bruce said, "I'm thinking...cloning."

"Identical twins would be a lot less fantastical," Jax said. "And more plausible."

"We're talking *Dominatus*. Plausible went out the window a long time ago."

Jax glanced at Maizie, who had kept quiet so far. "You went into an FBI interview wearing an earpiece so they could feed you answers?" He motioned to Ramon and Bruce.

"We weren't going to let her go in alone," Bruce said.

Jax glanced at them. "I was there."

Ramon shrugged, taking up the baton. "We did our job. Kenna wants Maizie safe, so that's what we do."

"Any leads on finding her?" Jax turned to Bruce.

The former CIA agent said, "The doctor's body was our best bet. Maizie needs to go through the footage to see if she can find out who took him. Someone was covering tracks for *Dominatus*."

Jax needed more of a universal update than that, so he said, "And the lawyers, and Amara and Zeyla..." Plus avenues to get more evidence. "The funeral director. Those old guys from the retirement home. Financial companies we know are connected." He looked at each of them. "Am I forgetting anything? Like maybe young men you're chatting with online."

"We haven't talked." Maizie actually looked nervous.

Jax left that one alone. For now. "We need leads."

"That's why I'm here." A woman approached the table, giving them all plenty of warning before she slapped a file on the table.

"Amara."

Behind her was a younger woman. Both looked so much like Kenna it hurt, but he didn't rub his chest. They were even wearing tactical pants and T-shirts like Kenna often did. They looked like a mother-daughter crime fighting, investigating duo.

Jax cleared his throat. "How are you both?"

Zeyla only nodded. She'd had several organs removed while in captivity with another branch of *Dominatus*. The fact she was on her feet and functional was a miracle by itself.

"How we are is irrelevant," Amara said. "We have a lead. Maybe."

"I'll take a maybe."

Amara nodded. "I thought you might."

Ramon reached over and took the file before Jax could open it. Jax shot him a look because *he* was the one who would be investigating any possible leads. Ramon totally ignored his issue.

Amara continued, "An agent of the FBI was dispatched to find the transport that took Kenna from the silo. The men who pretended to be agents had airtight covers, but an agent was sent to investigate where they went after she never arrived at the federal prison they were supposed to take her to."

Jax had a lot of questions but held his tongue. He hadn't known anything about this. At the time, he'd been in the hospital. When he finally got back to the office, no one mentioned it.

Maybe it was in a report somewhere, but he'd read everything. Hadn't he?

"The agent was never seen again," Amara added. "And no one is looking for him. The whole thing was brushed under the rug."

Chapter Six

J ax left Ramon to his file and went after Amara and Zeyla, catching up to Kenna's mom and sister—or aunt and cousin—just outside the door.

"We didn't want to disturb your meal," Amara said.

As she had inside, Zeyla stood by her like a bodyguard.

"I didn't come here to eat," Jax said. "Is there anything else you can tell me?"

Amara was almost five ten, just an inch or so shorter than him. Zeyla had a similar build to Kenna, but curvier, and was maybe only five six. Her short haircut and thick bangs framed her face, whereas Kenna's hair was long down to the middle of her back.

The matriarch said, "As you know, the men who took her have completely disappeared. Totally off the grid. We did manage to track them down to a municipal airport to the northwest of Phoenix, but that's where the trail goes cold."

"That's farther than I've managed to get," Jax said.

Amara nodded. "If they left on a plane, we can't find it. Which in this age is next to impossible."

"Unless you have someone in the FAA and the NTSB.

Agents embedded in the government and air traffic control, and cops on your payroll."

"And more money than God," Zeyla added.

Jax didn't like the sound of any of it. This whole thing seemed almost impossible. He needed to lean on the God who did impossible things and worked in the lives of people who trusted in Him. The believers who yielded to His way and followed it.

But Jax didn't want to be all-in only for what he could get out of it—namely, having Kenna back. That would mean his heart was all wrong. He didn't want to acknowledge that God might be testing him. Asking him to trust, even if he didn't get what he wanted.

Which made him want to rage all over again. Get in another shoving match—and more—with Ramon. He needed to take his frustration out on someone. Or a heavy bag at the gym.

Otherwise, he was going to ruin his sobriety with the wrong choice.

Right now, he didn't want to be a better person, or a better Christian. He just wanted Kenna back.

Zeyla shifted. "The only shot you have of finding her is if she can escape and contact you. The chance of that is slim to none."

"We would have a better chance of rescuing her if we knew an area where she's likely being held. Or a facility."

That was a gross assumption—first that she was still alive. Something he refused to give up hope on. He wasn't going to say he'd be able to "feel" it if she died. That was just hokey. But he wasn't even considering she was really gone until he knew for sure.

The other assumption he was making was that she had been taken somewhere, rather than kept on the move. Or that it was somewhere that was even accessible.

The odds were more than stacked against him.

Didn't mean he planned to give up.

Amara's expression shifted while she thought about that, and after a few seconds she said, "There are facilities all over the world. We don't even know if she's still in the continental US. She could be anywhere."

"Can we get a list of facilities, places we can start looking?" Jax asked.

Zeyla shook her head. "By the time you have data, it's obsolete. No one knows the full extent of *Dominatus* except the Imperatoris."

He tried to remember that word from Latin class. "Isn't that like an emperor?"

"He's over the whole thing, commanding the grand masters like he's the Pope and they're Cardinals."

And Jax had thought the grand masters were the ones in charge. "Who is it? Who is the current Imperatoris?"

Zeyla said, "I doubt you'll find someone alive who can tell you."

"Like a grand master?" He could find one, surely. Question them.

The man with the senator in Colorado who'd captured Kenna had been one. He'd died around the same time, so Jax would have to look up him and all his known associates. "What about when one is replaced because they die? Does a son take over, or is there a vote?"

Zeyla shook her head again, looking upset.

Amara said, "Another would be installed, but there's no way to know who it is. Each part of *Dominatus* operates independently like a splinter terror cell. Instead of taking their orders and going out there to cause as much destruction as possible, it's a piece of a larger puzzle. The grand plan."

"But if we identify him, we can take them down from the top." He glanced between the two women. "Right?"

"Or at least severely cripple the organization," Zeyla said. "But if I knew how to find the Imperatoris, I'd have put a bullet in his head already."

"We need to guarantee we can find Kenna, and we need to cripple the *Dominatus* as much as we can. This is about more than killing one person." He folded his arms across his chest, ignoring the burn in his shoulder.

Amara said, "That's an impossible task. Which is why I brought you a case file much closer to home." She lifted her chin. "Find that agent. Rooting out corruption in the FBI will go a long way to you getting your standing back within the Bureau."

"I wasn't aware I'd lost it."

"Then you should open your eyes." Amara turned and walked away, Zeyla beside her. They went to a black Nissan with some damage on the front right quarter panel. Like they'd been in a scrape of some sort with a red car that had transferred paint onto their vehicle.

Jax went back inside, returned to the table, and sat. "Anything in the file?"

"Anything we should know that they couldn't tell all of us?" Ramon echoed.

Jax wasn't going to get mad that the guy had an irritated tone. He just had to remind himself they had the same goal. Jax told them about the Imperatoris and the rest of it, hitting the highlights. "What do we know about this case, other than that someone in the FBI is working for Dominatus?"

Bruce shifted in his chair, wiping his scruffy face on a

napkin that caught in the stubble on his chin. "The agent's identity was scrubbed from the system."

"I'll pull the official report for the silo operation again," Jax said. "See if anything sticks out."

"This file is pretty thin." Ramon waved it. "Doesn't say who assigned the task to this agent and doesn't say he disappeared. It's just a personnel file for an agent who we can't even prove exists."

Jax didn't like that. He looked at Maizie. "And someone thinks you put a worm in the computer network at my office."

Maizie winced.

He couldn't help wondering about what Amara had just said. That he was on thin ice with the federal agency he worked for. He'd thought he was doing all right, balancing it all. But giving up the fight to find Kenna just to get his career back on more solid footing didn't sound like a great idea. In fact, it sounded like the last thing he wanted to do.

Maizie said, "I wasn't the first to put a worm in the network. I can't trace who did the existing one I found, but mine mirrors it, and everything they copy from the network is also sent to me. I also programmed it to tell me if they change or delete anything."

"And?"

"It's only been running since yesterday."

Bruce said, "Means *Dominatus* found it, and this is their way of shutting you down."

Maizie frowned. "But their worm will be disabled at the same time."

"Scorched earth."

Even if that was true, Jax didn't like the sound of it. "You're walking a fine line between freedom and winding up in jail, Maze."

Ramon said, "Can't put her in jail if you can't find her."

Maizie gasped.

Jax glanced at him, disapproval probably plain on his face. "Maybe don't say stuff like that."

"I agree with Jax," Maizie said, her voice shaky.

"Sorry." Ramon mostly looked at Maizie.

Jax turned to Bruce. "Can you find out who the coroner and funeral director were who interacted with Marcus Buzard's body?"

The older man snapped a salute. "Yes, Boss."

Jax figured he likely did that with Kenna, too. "Ramon and I will go find this agent. Maizie, get on the computer and look for anything left behind when those files and the existence of an agent were scrubbed from the system."

"What are Amara and Zeyla going to do?" Ramon asked, one brow raised. "Just disappear again and come back later with some vaguely helpful information?"

"They didn't tell me, so I guess we don't get to know."

"Sounds about right," Ramon grumbled.

Bruce straightened in his chair. "I'll touch base with Amara. See if I can find out."

"Good. So we all have work to do." Jax whipped around to Maizie, who had her head ducked and was trying to make a clean getaway. "Not so fast, young lady. We still need to talk about Sean."

She didn't look at him but busied herself pushing her chair in and slipping her little crossbody bag over her head.

"Maizie."

She lifted her gaze, her eyes full of unshed tears. "I don't want to talk about Sean."

"Have you contacted him? Are you guys talking?"

She scrunched up her nose. "I don't want to talk about it."

"Maizie," Jax repeated, leaning forward. He wasn't going to stand and tower over her. He wanted her to feel like she had the high ground, and not like he was trying to use masculinity to overpower her. She didn't need that in her life. She needed people who treated her with empathy and respect for the things she had to carry from her past. "I need to know if you've contacted him."

"I haven't! Okay?" She swiped at her cheeks, the tears running freely now. Her yell drew some attention, but there was nothing he could do about it. She had to feel free to express her emotions. "You think I don't want to talk about it with someone?"

"So tell us. You know you're safe with us."

"I can't talk about it with..." She waved her hand.

"Men," Ramon said quietly. "You have girl stuff you need to work through, *Hermana?*"

She squeezed her eyes shut, her breaths coming sharply. On the verge of having an anxiety attack. "She's not here. She's just...she's not here!"

"Elizabeth will make time for you if you call her, right?" Jax hadn't taken girl stuff into account when Stairns and his wife had dropped Maizie off with him and gone to California to watch out for Laney and her family. "I'm sorry she's not nearby."

"I'm talking about Kenna!" Maizie blurted, mascara now smeared on her cheeks. She looked...broken. "I need to talk to her. I need her *here*, but she's...*gone*."

The server entered the periphery. "Is everything okay?" She glanced at them, then back at Maizie. "Are these men bothering you?"

Maizie stiffened, each inhale still sharp as if she was on the verge of breaking down and sobbing. "They aren't bothering me." She looked at Jax then, and he stood. She slammed into him, wrapping her arms around him.

Jax gave her a second to get used to it just in case she changed her mind. Then he hugged her back. "We're going to find her."

She shifted her head. "What if we don't?"

"We will." He angled his head and kissed her forehead. "We're going to find her. We have to."

Tears gathered in his eyes as she cried in his arms. Jax dipped his head and rubbed her back, hearing Ramon and Bruce talking to the server. In a way, he'd been waiting for this to happen. He was a wreck, but focusing on work helped.

Now he had a few days to "get his head together"— whatever that meant. He wasn't going to stop looking for his wife. More than likely, the ADIC was making a play to take over the office and get rid of Jax. Maybe he didn't like his current role and wanted to go back to bossing around everyone that worked under him rather than being the middleman between Jax and the director of the FBI.

Part of him barely cared about his job, but he did need it. The Bureau had kept him in check for years, and if he was going to survive this, he needed to lean in on that. Procedure. Rules. No matter how long it took, he wasn't going to give up the search.

"We have to," she whispered. "Before it's too late."

He gave her a squeeze and stepped back.

Even Ramon looked like he had unshed tears in his eyes. Bruce cleared his throat, wiping his nose on a napkin he dumped on his empty plate.

"We all have work to do," Jax said. "And we should get to it."

Ramon eyed him but nodded and got up. He said something to Maizie in Spanish, and she nodded.

"Welp," Bruce said, tucking his chair in. "Not the way I thought lunch would go, but I'll take it."

Jax found a smile, but it took effort.

He turned to follow Maizie and the two men out of the restaurant. Strategically ignoring the fact they'd drawn attention to themselves just now. He didn't know what people thought of their group of four misfits, and he didn't care. People could think what they wanted. He was going to find Kenna, and her friends would help.

Outside, car tires squealed. A second later, the glass all down one side shattered as automatic weapon fire from more than one source cracked across the open space.

A split second later, Maizie yelped.

Ramon hit Jax at a full tackle and slammed him against the floor. Bruce covered Maizie with his body, using himself as a human shield.

Jax looked over and saw Ramon hunkered down beside him on the tile.

Again and again, shots cracked off like fireworks, exploding across the room. Wood splintered into the air. Dust rained down on everything. Someone screamed. Car tires squealed again, and the automatic weapons fire continued.

Jax slid out his phone and dialed 911.

Ramon grabbed the phone and ended the call. "We need to run."

"I need to call this in!"

People could be hurt. They needed police, FBI, and ambulances. Minimum. He prayed they wouldn't need the coroner as well.

Ramon grabbed his shoulder. "No, we need to get out of here before we get someone killed." He looked at Bruce. "Let's go!"

Chapter Seven

"I shouldn't leave the scene of a crime," Jax said. He'd checked that no one in the restaurant had been shot at least. One older man had bumped his head, diving for cover, but that was the extent of the injuries in the room.

Ramon shoved him toward the passenger side of his own car. He'd already swiped the keys as soon as Jax had pulled them from his pocket.

"Is this how you deal with Kenna?" Jax wasn't sure he liked that.

"Goes both ways." Ramon unlocked the door. "You aren't thinking straight."

"I'm not thinking like a mercenary, that's all."

"All of us need to think like a mercenary from time to time. And what's that saying? 'Rescuer safety first,' isn't it? You want Kenna back, get in the car."

"I'm trusting you." Jax slid in.

Ramon jogged around to the driver's side. Jax thought about making a run for it, but what would that prove? He'd be without wheels and without backup if he left on his own.

"Shut your door." Ramon fired up the engine and

pulled out fast enough Jax had to grab the handle at the top of the door.

"I thought *Dominatus* was being subtle. Undermining me." Jax shook his head.

"They want you dead, apparently. Nothing subtle about what just happened. We're lucky no one got killed."

Jax didn't count that as luck. *Thank You.* "That's exactly what will happen if I leave. They'll find more ways to discredit me and put my job on shaky ground."

"We have a case to solve." Ramon steered with both hands, turning corners like this was a tactical driving course. "You get a slap on the wrist, and everything that would've happened if you'd hung around back there still happens. It's just that you gave yourself time to work this case for real without getting delayed by the people we're hunting."

"You're looking to take down *Dominatus*?"

"That's the case, isn't it?"

"So you follow where Kenna leads?"

"You need to focus up." Ramon squeezed the steering wheel. "This should have been over already."

"You think I've been slacking on finding her?"

"Everything the Bureau does takes too long. Why do you think Kenna and I quit?"

"I know why you quit, and I know why she did. Neither was about procedure or how much time things take, so don't try to fool me with that argument."

"Are you done? Because we have a case to work."

Jax glanced over, staring at Ramon's profile. "When Kenna does it, I usually end up laughing."

"But both of us are a poor substitute for her."

"That's the truth." Not just because Kenna could shake anyone out of their funk and get them to laugh. She did it with each of them when things were serious and they all needed a moment to breathe. Some way to bleed off some of the stress, like a pressure cooker release valve.

Ramon said, "Let's figure out how to make do—and get her back."

"Agreed." Jax needed an answer to one more question, though. "Why do you have such an issue with me being a fed?"

"The issue isn't with you being a fed. It's with you *still* being one." Ramon shook his head. "You should've already quit."

"I need their reach, and their resources."

"Has it helped? Is there any sign it's helping?"

Jax needed them. "You wouldn't understand."

"I understand the Bureau never did me any favors. Kenna Banbury is the only person who ever stuck up for me. So I'm not going to quit until I find her."

"Good." Jax swallowed. "I didn't want to say it in front of Maizie, but I'm getting really worried that finding Kenna will take everything we've got and then some. That it might destroy all of us, and we may never find her."

"So? They want it, let's give it. But we don't stop until we get her back."

Jax could respect that. "Okay."

Chances were, he and Ramon would always be at odds. For a lot of reasons, they would butt heads, and most of it had nothing to do with how Jax had thought for a while that Ramon had been in love with Kenna. Maybe he wasn't now. It didn't really matter. If this was about repaying a debt to Kenna and the guy was all-in with finding her, then Jax would deal with it. He wasn't going to get jealous when he had help to find her, and that help happened to be almost as motivated as he was.

Ramon turned another fast corner. "Reason number

twelve why you shouldn't trust the FBI, let alone work for them." He reached over and tapped the file on the dash, up by the window. "Someone in your agency is working for *Dominatus*, and they're covering up what happened to Kenna."

"At the least," Jax said. "At most they're also responsible for the murder of an agent who worked for me. And that might not be the first time."

"Doesn't mean it's your fault. Guilt isn't a good look."

"I'm not going to go off the rails just because I feel like crap that someone disappeared and I didn't even notice the cover-up because I was in the hospital."

"Just checking."

"You're telling me you have no vices?" Jax shifted in his seat, wondering how Ramon knew where to go. Or was he just driving around in circles? "What do you do to blow off steam, or relieve the stress?"

"It isn't stress. It's night terrors, waking up in a cold sweat with the taste of blood in my mouth."

"How do you deal?"

"I find a bar, and I pick a fight with someone."

Jax paused. "Does Kenna know about this?"

"I've got it under control."

Whether he did or not, Jax felt a little like he was on more even footing now with Ramon than he'd been before. They knew each other's weaknesses, so they could work together to avoid them, but it was also about being vulnerable enough to admit you couldn't do it all on your own. Which only made him wonder why he was currently thinking of working with Ramon at all.

Yet here they were, together.

For Kenna.

"I'm still gonna get fired," Jax said. He didn't like how

this was playing out. "My boss showed up at the office. He's going to use what happened at the restaurant to undermine me and put me on leave."

"Good." Ramon shrugged. "You'll be able to work this case for real."

Jax wouldn't see eye to eye with him on everything.

"Better that you're free than they get you committed, or put you in jail. Or kill you. You need to leave on your terms so they don't have the upper hand."

"They already have it," Jax said. "They're waiting for me to make a misstep so they can hang me."

"Bruce has Maizie covered so you and I can work this case. Someone is going to talk, and we're going to find out what happened to this missing agent."

"Which means I couldn't hang back and oversee that scene because..." Jax began. They could've at least asked witnesses outside for descriptions of the shooters, and license plate numbers.

"Because I'll bet you a hundred bucks the investigation will turn up someone who says you paid them to do that and make it look good," Ramon finished. "Or they'll 'discover' evidence that money changed hands. We need Maizie away from these people as much as we need you out of the Bureau. Before *she* ends up in cuffs."

Ramon clearly didn't like that Jax had brought Maizie on as a consultant, but hopefully that was all they were going to say about that. He hadn't liked seeing her in an interrogation room even if it was only about her being questioned.

Ramon pulled into a condo complex and headed for the farthest building.

Jax looked around at the manicured bushes and white-washed siding. "Who lives here?"

"The missing agent. Where did you think I was going?" Ramon navigated to a space, avoiding the rented moving truck blocking several spaces at the end. He frowned at the open door to the condo at the end, first floor. "Let's go find out what's going on."

Jax opened the file, reading it while he got out and shut the car door. Special Agent Elliot Adams, twenty-eight. He'd only been an agent for just over a year. Originally from Chicago, he had a sister, but the parents were deceased. Nothing much in savings and only the basic government retirement fund account, which he'd been putting hardly anything into since he started with the Bureau.

His superiors found him to be competent and said he had promise.

"Seems like a solid guy." Jax stepped up onto the sidewalk.

Up ahead, Ramon jogged up the stairs, meeting a woman at the top carrying a heavy box. As Jax approached, Ramon said, "...just a minute of your time. It's about your brother."

Jax didn't like feeling as if everyone around him was a step ahead, but in this case, it was efficient. "I'm Special Agent in Charge Oliver Jaxton," he told her. "We'd like to speak with you about Elliot."

The woman had blond highlights in her light-brown hair, and a round figure. She wore denim shorts, canvas shoes, and a gray T-shirt with flowers on it. "Not sure I wanna speak with the FBI since they're the ones who killed him."

"You know for sure that Elliot is dead?" Jax confirmed.

"If he was alive, he'd have come home already." She set the box by her feet and brushed hair back from her face.

"But he hasn't, so he's got to be dead. He would never stop calling me or let me wonder if he was all right. Never."

"I'm sorry." Jax knew exactly how that felt. "My wife is missing. She's the one Elliot was trying to find, so he could follow up on the transfer. What's your name?"

"Sandra." She shook her head. "Is that normal? I mean sending one agent to find another, when she was being transported by officials with the Bureau."

"There's nothing normal about what is going on," Jax replied. Then he needed to ask, "How did you know that's what Elliot was working on?"

"He told me everything." Sandra shrugged. "He called me the day he went missing, told me what he was working on. Said he might be late for dinner."

And he'd never shown up.

Jax's chest ached. "If you can help us figure out what happened to him, we may be able to find him and my wife. I'm going to keep hoping they're both alive until I know otherwise."

She didn't seem convinced. "How am I supposed to help you?"

Ramon hung back, leaning against the railing and keeping an eye on their surroundings. Watching for more gunmen? They'd both shaken off the adrenaline of being shot at quickly. There were many ways they were similar, and Jax could see why Kenna liked the guy. Not just because he hung back and let Jax be the one to take the lead questioning Sandra Adams.

Jax waited a beat. "Did Elliot seem different, like he was worried about anything?"

"He was confused." She glanced aside, thinking. "Didn't know why he'd been ordered to follow up on a custody transfer. Considering the men who took her worked for an Assistant Director in Charge."

The ADIC on scene after the silo operation had been one of the men from the retirement home pretending to be a bureau employee. Fake name, excellent cover story. Impeccable credentials.

Which made Jax wonder if his real ADIC, Hadley, had something to do with it. Not many people could fake that. Enough people kept up on who the FBI had as current ADIC's that someone should've called them on it. But in the heat of the moment, who would question a superior?

Special Agent Herron hadn't, which meant she had to be on the list of people who could be the *Dominatus* mole, assuming there was one. Even if he didn't think she was dirty, it was something he'd need to consider.

"What about the agent who assigned him the task?" Jax asked. "Did Elliot say who it was that told him to follow up on the transfer?"

She shook her head. "He seemed shaken, and he told me a little of what you all found in that silo. The research that crazy doctor had been doing. That he had people in there who were captives. Even children. He said the private investigator shouldn't have been arrested. But he did his job. He wanted to be part of the Bureau forever, not just for a few years. He believed in it."

Ramon glanced at Jax, the implication clear.

Elliot had believed in the FBI, and it probably got him killed.

Sandra sniffed. "I called and called, but no one at the office ever called me back. No one would tell me what happened to Elliot, and after a few weeks, they told me to stop calling. That they didn't know who Elliot Adams even was—and they didn't think he'd ever worked there."

Jax nodded. "Do you have the information for anyone he worked with directly, like a partner?"

The man couldn't have interacted with no one. Agents often teamed up to work on cases, and Elliot had been at the silo. It was impossible to completely erase someone in this day and age.

She shook her head. "He didn't mention anyone, and he only hung out with me. He had a few friends from college he kept up with on socials but hadn't found friends locally. We both moved here when he was assigned to the Phoenix office. He rented this place, and my apartment is a couple of miles away." She sniffed. "Now the owner wants to sell the condo, and I have to clear his stuff out."

"I'm going to find out what happened." Jax couldn't promise that he would find Elliot, but a man's professional life had been erased because of a case Kenna and all of them had taken. "I promise I won't quit until I get to the bottom of this."

Sandra nodded, biting her lip. "Thank you."

Ramon pushed off the railing. "Does Elliot have a personal computer, or a personal phone that was left behind?"

"He has a laptop." She thumbed over her shoulder. "I don't know his password."

"Could we have it?" Jax asked.

"It's of no use to me." Sandra wandered into the condo.

Jax spoke in a low voice. "I don't get how a man is erased from FBI records."

Ramon's expression darkened. "They don't get to just delete a person's life." He might've been talking about Kenna as much as about Elliot, but the sentiment was the same either way.

"We need to find those guys," Jax said. "Two, Four, and Five."

"Those are stupid names."

"So find out who they really are. And then *find them*."

"Don't tell me what to do just because you're frustrated you have no answers."

Jax folded his arms right as the sister walked out of the condo. She held out the laptop to Jax, but Ramon took it.

"Thank you for talking to us." Jax took a business card from his wallet. "I'll be in touch, so save my number. And call if you remember anything, or if Elliot contacts you."

She took the card. "Do you really think he could still be alive?"

"Don't ever give up hope. Not until you know for sure."

Ramon shifted, holding the laptop. "We'll call if we find anything."

She glanced between them. "Thank you for trying."

Maybe she'd already given up hope. It kind of sounded like it. But that didn't mean Jax was going to. Because if Kenna had taught him anything, it was that when you gave up hope was when the bad guys won.

Chapter Eight

Jax's phone rang just as they climbed back in the car, this time with him in the driver's seat. He was tempted to go back to the scene at the restaurant, talk to whoever was working it. The car connected to his phone, and the dash screen read *M calling*.

"Hey, Maze. Everything good?"

"I have something already."

"That was fast." Ramon opened the laptop on his knees. "So do we, but we'll have to drop it off. Where are you?"

"At the RV with Jolene, locked up tight."

Jax had surveillance on his house, new since the last system had been breached before Kenna was taken. In fact, his place had been broken into multiple times, and he hadn't really believed it until he saw how his system had been manipulated with his own eyes. Now the house had cameras outside, cameras inside, and the RV in the garage bay that had been built to accommodate the tall vehicle had its own system. All of it couldn't be hacked without physical access.

"We're dropping off a laptop," Jax said. "What do you have?"

He drove toward his house, realizing he was hitting after-school traffic. How had he lost most of a day to all this? Seemed like a lot had happened in a short space of time. Maizie and Bruce probably both needed a nap after being up last night unearthing a grave with no body, while Ramon looked like he usually did—not exactly well rested, though.

Jax didn't need to start worrying about the guy's sleep habits. They were barely friends at best. It was closer to a stalemate and purely because they had the same goal.

Maizie said, "I found the coroner who signed off on Marcus Buzard's death. I have a copy of the certificate, and everything lines up with what was reported by Ramon and Kenna as to how he died. So the doctor definitely saw Buzard's body at some point."

"Or someone gave an extremely accurate description," Ramon said.

Jax nodded.

"After that, it must have been taken," Maizie said. "Or misplaced. Is that a thing? Misplacing a body?"

Jax shook his head, pulling up to a stoplight. "Not as far as I know."

Ramon shook his head. "Doesn't explain how he ended up alive and running around with Kenna."

"You can't believe that's her." Maizie's voice had a higher pitch than usual. "It has to be faked."

Jax winced. "The bar owner saw her, talked to her. I don't want to believe it either, but we need an explanation."

"Brainwashing." Ramon sounded so matter-of-fact. Not that it was so farfetched with these people.

Jax didn't like it. "Not something I try to think about."

"Me either," Maizie said. "I much prefer suspicious car accidents."

Jax's foot switched to the brake, but he caught himself. "What's that?"

"The coroner died in a car accident, along with his wife, a week after he signed Buzard's death certificate. They were on a highway headed north, toward the Grand Canyon. Went off a cliff. The car caught fire, and they both died pretty much instantly. So I have two more death certificates open on my computer, a news obituary, and a social media post. The wife's friends can't believe such a tragedy occurred. Apparently, it was a brand-new car."

"Cars fail." Jax didn't like saying it while he was driving, but it could've been a freak accident. If the timing wasn't incredibly coincidental.

"And people are murdered," Ramon said. "Especially people who get in the way of what *Dominatus* wants."

Maizie was silent.

"If they wanted Kenna dead," Jax began, "they wouldn't have gone to the trouble of taking her. And the fact they took her from the scene outside that silo means they couldn't wait. So she knows something, or they needed something from her. Either way, she's of value to them. That means she's alive somewhere."

Ramon said, "Amara better come up with some intel. I need to kick a door in and shoot somebody."

Jax couldn't disagree but needed to know why Maizie had gone quiet. "Maze?"

"I'm okay. I just... We all miss her. Not just me."

"It sucks. And it hurts."

"Are you okay?" Maizie said.

Jax had to tell her the truth. "I'm holding on. But it's hard."

She sighed across the phone line. "Sorry the coroner is a dead end. Bruce is looking for Elliot Adams's car, or someone who saw him after he left the silo going after the transport. Maybe he'll find something."

"I'll pray for that." Jax heard the hollowness of his own words. He shouldn't say that if it wasn't going to be true. There was no power in an empty sentiment. "I will."

He made the promise to himself as much as to her.

This wasn't going to be solved by working in his own strength, trying to succeed in his flesh. He knew probably better than a lot of people that his flesh was so weak. He needed God to supply him supernaturally with the ability to keep the faith until Kenna was found.

To not give into despair the way her previous partner had.

He hung up with Maizie when they pulled into the drive, and Ramon dropped the laptop off to her in the RV next to where he parked his car. Soon as Ramon was back in the car, Jax pulled out again.

"Where to, Boss?" Ramon asked.

Jax ignored that comment. "I've been trying to work out who ordered Special Agent Adams to go after Kenna's transport, and if that person is also responsible for his disappearance."

"Why send the guy after the transport if you want the people who took her to be able to get away?"

"Exactly." Jax headed for a coffee shop they'd tried but which Kenna hadn't liked. Going to her favorite place would hurt too much. "If someone sent Elliot after them, maybe it was because instinct said the whole thing might be suspicious. Whoever is dirty found out, intervened and stopped Elliot."

"Okay, so who in your office would do that?"

The new guy, Special Agent Farlan, must have been transferred in to take the place of Agent Adams. "I still don't understand how an agent goes missing and no one raises an eyebrow," Jax commented. He called a guy that worked in Farlan's group, listening to it ring before the guy picked up.

"Browne."

"It's SAC Jax. Got a minute?"

"Uh, yeah. Sir. Heard you were out for a day or two. Sick or something."

At least he didn't mention the shoot-up at the restaurant. The Bureau either hadn't figured out he was there yet, or this guy simply hadn't heard.

"Or something," Jax said. "Listen, I just have a quick question. It's been niggling at me. Special Agent Farlan came in to fill an open spot, right?"

"That's right," Browne said. "You were laid up in the hospital, so Hadley took care of the whole thing."

Of course he had. "Who did Farlan replace?"

Ramon whispered, "And when did Hadley show up in town?"

"This young guy, Special Agent Elliot Adams," Browne answered. "That's who Farlan replaced."

"First I've heard of him," Jax said. "Did you work with him long?"

"Maybe a year. Something like that. He didn't talk much, but he was a decent agent. Never hung out after work, or on the weekend. Didn't come to any team stuff like barbecues. Kept to himself."

"When's the last time you saw him?"

"He was on the silo operation. Not sure if I saw him after that. Hadley said he had some kind of breakdown. Like he couldn't hack what he saw, or something. I never saw him, so I dunno. Hadley said he transferred out and went to a different office."

"So why has he been erased from the computer system?"

"Has he? Probably someone deleted him by accident or something. It happens." Browne paused. "That all you need, Boss?"

"Who was in charge of the silo operation?"

"Special Agent Herron."

"Thanks, Browne. I appreciate your help."

The line went dead, and music came back on through the car speakers. A local Christian radio station playing worship music. Jax wanted to shut it off, to cut off what God might want to say through the music. So he left it on just to prove he could deal with all of it.

Whatever it took to get her back. Even if that meant God wanted to grow him in ways he didn't want to grow.

Things were already uncomfortable enough.

"Herron?"

He glanced at Ramon. "I'd have told you she's solid. I'd have banked on it."

"Maybe not as much as you thought."

Jax sighed. "Have Maizie look into her financials. See if there's any evidence things aren't as they seem."

Ramon slid out his phone and started texting.

Jax drank his coffee, heading for the after-work spot most of the agents went to. At this time on a Friday, it wasn't going to be busy yet. Just because he didn't want it to be Special Agent Herron who was dirty didn't mean he'd get his wish. After all, that's all it was—a wish.

They checked out Herron's house, but with her at work and no cars in the drive, there wasn't much to see. Jax stopped at the drive-through of a chain restaurant he liked because they did protein grain bowls. Ramon didn't seem impressed, but he ate what he ordered like he enjoyed it.

Jax parked across the street where he could see the back of the bar, and the parking area where the agents left their cars while they blew off some steam playing pool or darts after work. He shut off the engine and rolled the windows down enough they'd get some airflow, but even under a tree in the shade, it was going to get hot fast.

He took off his tie and unbuttoned the collar of his shirt, rolling up his sleeves to settle in for the long haul.

"I could go around front, see what I can see," Ramon offered. "Or go inside."

Jax shook his head. "We need to stick together with Bruce off doing whatever he's doing. We need intel in a way that doesn't let them know we're onto them."

"Pipe dream. Considering they're constantly one step ahead of us."

"Still."

Ramon probably expected Jax to say more than that, but he didn't. He was too busy trying to figure out who in his office was dirty and working for *Dominatus*. Ordering people to their deaths and squashing all kinds of investigations.

He liked Special Agent Herron, and under different circumstances would call the wife and mother a friend.

Jax tapped his fingers on his lap and watched the back door of the bar.

"How long is this going to take?" Ramon grumbled.

"Could be hours."

"That's why you should let me go in. Shake some trees."

"When you told me you take out your issues on innocent people in bars?" Jax almost smiled.

"They might not be innocent."

"How do you know?" Jax eyed him. "Some kind of instinct?"

Ramon shifted in his seat. "Maizie looks people up. If someone has an outstanding warrant and I happen to leave the guy somewhere he'll be found and receive medical attention, I figure I'm doing the law a favor. Soon as they run his ID, they'll take him into custody."

"A public service." Jax shook his head. "Sounds like a 'Kenna' way to do it."

"Actually, it was Bruce who suggested it, but I guess it might be something she would say. Since you guys got married, she's had a lot on her mind, with not feeling good and everything that was going on. I'm just glad I got to help at the silo."

"So am I." Jax figured that was as close as he was going to get to the apology that Ramon likely didn't think he needed to offer.

"Wish I could find those old guys. I wanna do a public service on their—"

"I know what you mean," Jax cut in. Then he bit the bullet. "Thanks for coming out with me today."

"You think she'd forgive me if I let anything happen to you?"

Jax nearly chuckled. "No, I don't suppose she would."

His phone buzzed, and he checked the screen. It was the number for the taskforce that the president had set up to take care of *Dominatus* in the US. Jax had connected with them after being imprisoned in the UK earlier this year. He'd been roped into an operation in Europe that meant leaving Kenna behind, but when the president asked, it wasn't advisable to say no.

Right now, Jax didn't have privacy to make an update, and with what he'd learned today, he needed to find out what else he could uncover so the report would be fuller. And he needed to do it when Ramon wasn't in the car.

Jax didn't like that he had been keeping the updates from Kenna and her team, but given the situation and the fact that even his office had been compromised, he had to keep things tight. The president had promised to turn over anything that related to Kenna, but Jax wasn't going to hold his breath waiting for intel from up top. Every call was about what Jax had found, and even those were few and far between. Today there might actually be something to report.

Maybe the president knew who the Imperatoris might be.

"Movement," Ramon commented.

Which jogged Jax out of his thoughts as the back door opened and Special Agent Farlan came out. They watched him gesture widely as he talked on his phone.

"This is a waste of time." Ramon shifted in his seat. "He's probably lying to his girlfriend about why he didn't come home yet."

"This is police work," Jax said.

While Farlan talked, Special Agent Herron stepped out. She had tied back her short dark-brown hair, her sunglasses pushed up to the top of her head. When Farlan saw her, he ended his phone call and spoke to her.

Herron's body language immediately went on the defensive.

"Lover's tiff," Ramon said.

Jax watched the interplay. Herron said something and Farlan moved in, his body language aggressive. She pointed her finger in his face and said something.

Farlan stomped away, chastised and unhappy, back into the bar.

"Guess we know who is in charge in that relationship," Ramon added.

"Go make a friend," Jax told him. "Find out what he knows."

"Finally." Ramon shoved out of the car and strode toward the front door of the bar.

Jax got out as well, walking to where Special Agent Herron stood alone. Hands on her hips. Looking at the sky and thinking.

"Everything all right?" he asked.

She spun around to him. "SAC Jax, you scared me."

"Did I really?" He stopped in front of her and waited for the answer.

Chapter Nine

H erron chuckled, and it didn't sound convincing. In fact, she sounded nervous. And apparently, she didn't even know he'd seen that whole interplay with Special Agent Farlan.

"You're probably wondering how I'm doing after I was caught in a drive-by shooting earlier today." He shifted his stance, trying to appear casual. As if he hadn't been surveilling an FBI bar and witnessed her heated conversation with Farlan.

"A drive-by. When?"

Jax frowned. "I went to lunch. Someone shot up the whole place. You didn't hear?"

"Maybe local police took it." She looked confused. "You were there?"

Considering he'd fled the scene, probably that was about all they needed to say about it. When the local police investigating the crime caught up to him first—because it was harder to find the rest of Kenna's friends—he'd have to explain. At which point the funk would *really* hit the fan.

But whichever cops came around asking questions he

wasn't going to want to answer, they probably would have no clue there was more going on here than one drive-by. Or so he presumed. What Jax needed was hard evidence someone had directly targeted him.

Or evidence it was about someone else entirely.

He squeezed the bridge of his nose, then dropped his hand. "Andrette, I need you to answer some questions with straight answers. Not the runaround you've been giving me for weeks. My wife is *gone*. And apart from her associate, you're the last person who saw her. You let them take her."

He'd said the same to Ramon, but as far as Jax was concerned, there was blame enough to go around. And that included him. Piling shame on all of them achieved nothing, he figured. So, what was the point shoveling on more?

It wouldn't help them find her.

She shifted, defensiveness infusing her movements—in the way she rolled her shoulders, and her hands. As if she needed to grab onto something. But there was nothing out here in the semidark of the back step and the parking lot.

"I need you to tell me if those men at the silo said anything about where they were taking her," he pressed. "If they gave you any impression whatsoever that they had evil intentions. Even just the tiniest thing. You saw them. You spoke to them." He took a breath, knowing he needed to stop, but also had to understand how big this was for him. "She's my whole life. I need her back."

She swiped a tear from the corner of her eye. "I'm sorry I couldn't help more. I put everything I could remember in my report as soon as I realized she was gone. Hadley and I talked about it, and he agreed we should send an agent to look for her."

"One guy?" Far as Jax was concerned, she should've

gone herself if she thought there was a chance someone had posed as a team of agents and taken Kenna.

"Hadley said we couldn't spare anyone else. Special Agent Adams was supposed to check in with me, but he never did."

"So you raised a stink that he was missing as well? Two people kidnapped, maybe murdered, and you say nothing?"

"Hadley—"

He took a step toward her. "Eventually you're going to have to take responsibility for this yourself."

She flinched and backed up. "I filed reports. I went to Hadley. He was covering your position while you were in the hospital. I went to him so many times. He told me that Adams requested a transfer and he was gone."

"And you bought that?"

"You don't..." Her voice thickened. "You don't understand, Oliver." It was so rare for someone to call him by his first name that it sounded jarring. Maybe even insincere.

"Andrette, she's gone," he said, "and an agent is missing as well. Elliot Adams would never have left his sister. Not without calling. Something happened to him."

"Because I sent him after her." She drew in a choppy breath.

"And you didn't push hard enough to find out what happened."

"I couldn't."

"You could have," Jax corrected. "You didn't."

"I *couldn't.*"

There it was. "Why not? Why couldn't you push and push until you got to the truth."

"Don't ask. I can't tell you." She moved to step away.

Jax caught her elbow but held it gently. "This is my wife."

"And my children."

He sucked in a breath. "They were taken?"

She shook her head.

"Then you should've shouted to anyone who would listen. Something is wrong in the office. Someone is covering up crimes."

"I can't help that. There's nothing I can do."

"Why not?" He let go of her arm. Neither moved. "What's going on with your kids?"

"I got a text. A threat." She gasped. "If I made a fuss about Kenna, or about Special Agent Adams, my children would die."

"Did you trace the number?"

"It came through unregistered. I ran a trace on it at work, and it came up as a payphone in New York City, probably what the number used to go to." She blew out a quick breath. "The next day my kids said a man came up to them while they were waiting for the school bus. He gave them a note to give to me."

"Did you keep it?" Testing it for trace evidence was a longshot, but they had to try.

She shook her head. "Burned it."

Jax sighed, shaking his head. "They got to you."

"They knew I wasn't going to work for them. So they threatened to hurt my children, which means they're the most horrible kind of people you can imagine. But they know I would *never* betray my oath."

Until it became personal, and she risked the life of her family. "I understand."

"But you still think I should've said something."

"I understand," he repeated. After all, she'd taken the risk of telling him now. "Take some time off, take your kids, and go out of town. Somewhere safe."

"Henry already took them to his brother's house. They're as safe as I can make them." She touched her forehead and winced. "I want to help you find your wife. I really do. But I can't do anything that'll jeopardize my family."

Jax relaxed a fraction. He would've done the same.

"Andrette, you said yourself they're as safe as you can make them. There's a sister out there who needs to know what happened to her brother. I want my wife back. But this is bigger than just me." Meanwhile, his heart was about to burst out of his chest. "And it's bigger than you."

He wanted to scream or start a fight. Run hard and fast, sprinting toward Kenna. But he would just be running. A bullet fired with no aim. A rocket with no course plotted.

How can I find her?

Herron studied him. "It's not Hadley, if that's what you're thinking. The ADIC is a selfish turd. But he isn't dirty, he believes in the FBI. He just believes more in what the FBI can do for him long term, especially when he runs for governor."

Jax didn't disagree. In fact, it pretty much lined up with his thoughts about Hadley. "Is there any chance someone leaned on him to squash it?"

The boss could be under someone's thumb the same way Andrette was. Or he was the one calling the shots.

But would a shot caller keep Jax around?

"Makes sense that Hadley might have been given orders from someone else, a person we'd never suspect." She shook her head. "But he never gave me the impression he was under duress."

Given the man's skills as a politician, Jax wasn't entirely surprised that Hadley might be a skilled actor. Someone who played his cards close to the vest. "He might be, and you'd never know."

"And yet I cracked."

"Because it's me."

She didn't argue with him. They had become friends as well as colleagues, or as close as two FBI agents became without hanging outside of work. He'd never met her family, but she'd met Kenna. Andrette knew how much he cared for his wife.

She lifted her chin. "You were really shot at earlier?"

"I have no idea why, or whether it's even connected."

"Or you're closer to answers than you realize."

He shrugged.

"Elliot Adams didn't transfer?"

"No one has seen him since you sent him to follow up."

She sniffed. "I knew there was something not right about it."

Jax squeezed her shoulder. "What was that about with Farlan earlier? You two were having a pretty heated conversation."

"We knew each other at a previous posting. He isn't a bad guy, but he takes risks. He knows something is off at this office. I told him to leave it alone."

That meant Jax might actually be able to trust the guy. "I need to know if Elliot found anything, as well as what happened to him. Did you hear from him at all after he left?"

Amara had told him the retired guys had been at an airfield. They could've flown Kenna anywhere after that. She could be in Mongolia for all he knew.

But he couldn't lose his cool, freaking out that he'd lost her for good.

He *couldn't.*

The second Jax lost it, anything was liable to happen. He knew what self-destructing felt like all too well. He was banking on the prayers of the other men at his Bible study and a lot of other things to help him hold it together.

"He called me later that night. Said he'd caught up to them on the highway, but he'd been having car trouble and stopped at a gas station."

"And you couldn't follow up?"

She nodded. "I probably owe it to him now to find out what happened."

"There are people, Kenna's people, who can find Elliot. You don't have to risk your children."

"They'll realize you're interfering. That you're uncovering things that they don't want uncovered. Someone in the office works for whoever took Kenna."

Jax had explained that there was an international criminal organization so many times that people had started to roll their eyes. He didn't know how else to make his point but to say, "They have reach. They're a powerful group. You know that now."

"They have the office in a chokehold, and it isn't only me they've targeted." She sniffed and looked down at the ground. "I don't want anything to happen to you."

His phone vibrated in his pocket, but he ignored it. Ramon was inside the building, and the guy could take care of himself. A glance at his watch told him he had a message from Bruce. Jax focused back on the conversation.

"I'll help you find her," Andrette said.

Jax shook his head. "Don't put your family at risk. I need someone in the FBI who can pass me information."

"The person in the FBI is *you*, Jax."

"Maybe not for much longer." He needed the job to

hold him together, but he could also see the writing on the wall.

The back door of the bar flung open and slammed against the siding before bouncing back. Two agents tossed Ramon out onto the ground, laughing their drunk butts off as he thumped onto the gravel. One of them muttered a curse about the guy, and the door shut again.

Andrette's phone rang, and she answered, "Special Agent Herron."

Jax rolled his friend to his back. "How did it go?"

Ramon groaned. "Better than you'd think. One of your agents is dealing. There are several alcoholics in the group. The alpha is some guy named Peterborough."

"Interesting." He had written the guy up a couple of times.

Jax held out his hand and helped Ramon to his feet.

Andrette had her gun pointed at them. "I'm sorry. I don't want to do this."

"What are you doing?" Jax held his hands up, not wanting to surprise her and wind up with her squeezing that trigger finger too hard.

"I have to do this. For my children."

Ramon swung out, moving toward her at the same time he slammed his hand down. The gun went off, and the shot pinged off the ground. A piece of concrete slammed into Jax's shin. He barely had time to yelp before Ramon shoved Andrette into him.

Jax held on to her.

Ramon had the gun.

"This never happened," Jax said to Andrette.

Ramon didn't like that idea. "I'm taking her gun."

"No, you aren't." Jax didn't let go of the agent in his arms. "This never happened, Special Agent Herron. My associate and I are leaving. You aren't going to shoot us in the back."

"She leaves first." Ramon didn't hold out her gun.

Andrette sobbed.

"I'm sorry your children are in danger, but nothing is going to stop me from finding Kenna." He let go of her, Ramon handed over the weapon, and she raced away.

"Coercion?"

Jax nodded. "Let's get out of here."

As they walked to the car, periodically both glancing over their shoulders, Ramon said, "Are you going to accept that the FBI isn't how you're going to find her now?"

"I think I'm closer than ever to the truth. That's why we got shot at earlier."

"You stick around the Bureau and you'll only get tangled up in a mess that's designed to distract you."

Jax wasn't sure that was true.

"You want to find Kenna?" Ramon paused. "Maybe you should do this her way. Seemed to work just fine."

"I don't need to justify to you why I'm an agent, and I always will be." But saying that sounded hollow. Part of him had kind of assumed he would quit and go to work with Kenna if she wanted him to be by her side 24/7. Some people lived and worked together, and others worked separate jobs in different fields.

He didn't want to quit the Bureau if she wasn't even here.

"Maybe not." Ramon looked at him over the roof of the car. "But no one there is going to help you. You're on your own. While out here in the PI world, you've got a whole team, and all they're trying to do right now is find her. No other cases. No other priorities. Just finding Kenna."

"You think I should jump on board with you guys when I'm just starting to get real leads."

"I think *Dominatus* believes they can control you while you're an agent. Once you walk out that door for good, they have no idea what you'll be doing. So stick it to them and come work with us."

It was probably the closest thing to an offer of friendship that he was going to get from Ramon. The man's loyalty would always be to Kenna first and then Maizie. Considering Jax felt the same about the two women, this might actually work.

But did he really want to accept the offer when he could be throwing away the only chance he might have to figure out what happened to her?

"You have gravel in your hair." Jax pulled the driver's door open.

Ramon didn't respond to that. He was looking at his phone. "Bruce found Elliot Adams."

Chapter Ten

The sun had barely peeked over the horizon when Jax pulled the car into the entrance of the Altern Brothers junkyard in Wickenburg, a small town northwest of Phoenix.

Ramon shoved his door open. "This town has a municipal airport. Same one that they took off from?"

"I doubt it's a coincidence." Jax wasn't going to correct Ramon that they didn't know the men who kidnapped Kenna ever took off in a plane from the airport. After all, that might have been misdirection. But according to Amara, they had been there.

Ramon slammed his car door. "We're going there when we're done here, right?"

A police unit pulled in behind them, running lights and sirens for a second as the black-and-white passed Jax and Ramon and went through the gate into the junkyard. The exterior walls were corrugated metal, and the sign out front needed painting. Bruce's car was parked next to theirs.

Jax went through the open gate, Ramon right beside him.

Two skinny Rottweilers prowled around just inside the entrance.

Jax stopped. Ramon took a couple of steps, and one of the dogs growled at him. Jax chuckled. "I don't think he likes you."

"He can smell an alpha."

Jax laughed outright. "Sure, that's what it is."

A man in overalls ambled over to them, more hair on his chin than on the top of his head. He had a rag tucked into one pocket and his sleeves rolled back to reveal tattoos up both arms. "Help you guys?"

"They're with me, Charlie." Bruce came over wearing a white button-down shirt.

Charlie whistled, and the dogs laid down on the dusty earth. Ears up but following orders.

Bruce waved them to him. "This way."

"Want to tell us what you found?" Jax strode over to him.

"And why the cops are here." Ramon didn't look so happy about that.

"Charlie's brother insisted, and I didn't have a good reason to say no." Bruce shrugged. "They hid it pretty well."

"Charlie and his brother?" Jax glanced at the rows of junk cars piled on each other on either side, four high in some cases. Compacted vehicles and farm equipment, odd scraps of metal. He even spotted a few washing machines dotted about—and the body of an old plane.

"Nah, Charlie and his brother are good people. Charlie was in 'Nam. His brother Petey was a cop for years. That's why he called his buddies at the state police about the blood."

They rounded the corner at the end of the row and spotted who he assumed was Petey, chatting with an older uniformed cop with a potbelly, while a younger officer climbed up a stack of cars. He stood on the frame of an open window belonging to a blue Taurus and looked in the window of a small red SUV.

Bruce said, "They never even knew it was here till I did a walkaround. Someone must've smuggled it in, because the boys didn't remember it and there was no record of this car in their ledgers."

"Paper ledgers?" Ramon asked.

"Can't hack a piece of paper. And it ain't like they get good cell signal out here."

Jax did a circuit around the car, including the police car. He hadn't brought his credentials to prove he was an FBI agent, so he couldn't be here in an official capacity. But he did want to take a look.

The cop scanned the interior.

"You see a body?" Jax found the license plate—or the spot where it should be. Nothing. He went to check the front. They could run the VIN numbers and see who it was registered to.

"Nothing but blood." The cop looked at him. "Who are you?" He shifted back and jumped down, brushing his hands together.

"Someone who'd like to know what happened to Elliot Adams." Jax went to the front. No license plate number there either. "Is there a VIN number, or did that get removed like the plates?"

The officer lifted one brow. "Sergeant?" He glanced at the older officer.

"Let's pop the trunk, Son. See if there's anything got left behind." The sergeant had a moustache, and flat brown eyes. His skin had a yellow tone to it.

"Yes, Sergeant." The officer looked around.

"Fetch a crowbar, Son."

The officer jogged away toward Charlie, who'd wandered off.

A breeze kicked up down the aisle between rows of junk. Through the dust, Jax spotted a small plane taking off from the airport that had to be several miles away, maybe even all the way across town. Elliot Adams had made it as far as where those men took Kenna. Then something had happened before he could prevent them from leaving with her.

Jax owed it to the special agent to find out what happened to him.

He went to the end of the row, walked up the next aisle so he could see the other side of the small SUV, then turned to Bruce. "How did you find it?"

"Don't ask questions you don't want the answer to."

"At least you didn't call me *Son*."

Bruce laughed. "We've all been there." Then slid on the pair of old Ray-Ban sunglasses he'd retrieved from his shirt pocket.

"Have you been over to the airport?"

Ramon came over. "What are we talking about?"

"This case." Jax surveyed the car, spotting what looked like evidence of a collision on the side.

Bruce peeked over the top of his Ray-Bans. "The airport is my next stop."

"Maybe you'll find someone we can interrogate." Ramon stuck his thumbs in the pockets of his jeans.

Jax glanced at him, wondering how come Kenna had never mentioned Ramon's need to blow off steam by punching people. "I'd rather deliver good news to a young woman missing her brother."

Ramon made a face like he was skeptical. "You really think he's still alive?"

"Isn't that why we're searching for Kenna? Because we're not giving up hope that she's alive?"

"Good point." Ramon shrugged, moved past Jax, and climbed up to the passenger window. "Did that cop know the keys are still in the ignition? This thing's a bit mangled, but it's still mostly intact."

"It's a wonder the junkyard guys didn't realize it was out here."

Bruce said, "Charlie told me they don't come down this aisle until spring, but it's all depending on inventory. New drop-offs get loaded on the far side."

"Not much call for random parts?"

"They do all right selling scrap metal."

The car engine turned over, coughed, and then died. On the far side of the car someone said, "Hey!"

Ramon shifted back out of the window, and the trunk door popped open an inch or so. "Guess we didn't need that crowbar."

Jax climbed up to the rear. When he spotted the sergeant, he said, "Just looking. I know not to touch anything."

"Your friend there is gonna answer some questions." The sergeant glared at him, instead of Ramon. Which wasn't really fair.

Jax didn't want to wonder if Kenna was dead in the back of this vehicle. But the thought went through his mind anyway. For all his talk about keeping hope that she was alive, it was getting hard. It had been weeks since she was taken, and she seemed so far out of reach now that he had no idea how to get her back.

Surely someone out there knew where she was.

He peered into the back of the vehicle, but from what he saw, it was empty.

"Wanna back up?" The officer tugged on the door with a pair of gloves.

"I'm looking for a friend," Jax replied. "A federal agent. I believe this is his car."

"The VIN has been scratched off. No plates. So how do you know it's his car?" The officer shot the question at him like an accusation that didn't require an answer.

Jax reached for something. "The sticker on the window. It's his." He didn't have anything better to offer than a sticker that indicated Elliot had run a marathon in his life— or the car's previous owner had.

"He isn't in the car. No one is." The officer sighed. "Anything else?"

"Do you have any reports of a local hit-and-run? It would've happened about two months ago."

"Are you a journalist?"

Jax shook his head. "Just asking questions."

"No, we didn't have any hit-and-run reports. I would know if we had because it'd mean something exciting actually happened in this backwater strip of desert."

"Right." Jax climbed down off the stack of vehicles.

"Don't leave without showing me some ID."

Jax glanced back. "You have good instincts. Transfer to a bigger department."

"Can't. Mom is sick and she's local, so here I am."

Jax nodded. He wandered back to Bruce and Ramon. "Elliot isn't here."

And neither is Kenna.

Bruce scratched his chin, then motioned to the car. "Someone slammed into him."

"I saw that." Jax went to get a closer look at the scrape.

Ramon said, "Someone with a black car collided with this one and probably forced him off the road. So, does that mean they took the FBI agent with them? Maybe we're looking at a string of kidnappings, not just Kenna."

"More likely he was in the wrong place at the wrong time." Jax thought about it. "I hate to say this, but he's probably in the desert in a shallow grave and we'll never find him."

Bruce said, "Your bureau can't do some magic with forensic analysis and find the black car that hit him? They do that stuff on TV all the time."

Jax shot him a look, then remembered where he'd seen a black car recently. With a scraped-up front corner, and red paint transfer. He whipped out his phone and called the number he had for Amara. She didn't answer, so he left a message that amounted to, *Call me back immediately.* When he hung up, he said, "Let's go." And over his shoulder said to the deputy, "We'll get out of your hair."

"Hey!" the officer called after them.

Jax ignored him and walked away with Bruce and Ramon, moving fast and not wanting to get waylaid. They made their way to the office where Charlie met them. The cops would catch up in a second, no doubt. Intending to make life difficult for him and Kenna's friends under the guise of finding out what they knew.

Jax said, "Any idea who brought the car in and when?"

Charlie leaned against the doorframe. "No cameras. Don't need Big Brother watching me. And we were in Vegas at a car show two months ago. Probably showed up then." He shrugged, apparently not all that bothered by the appearance of a mystery car.

The officer approached, thunder in his expression.

"And you didn't notice a car with blood on the steering wheel in your lot?"

Elliot had been hurt.

Jax glanced at Ramon and mouthed, *Hospitals.*

Ramon nodded and slid out his phone, texting furiously. Probably contacting Maizie so she could call around local places where Elliot might have been taken if he was found.

Charlie shrugged. "I don't do inventory until September. Right now, we're filling rows A through C. What can I say?"

"I have the sister's information," Jax told the officer. "In case you want to contact her with the news you found her brother's car."

Bruce and Ramon spoke quietly with each other off to the side.

"You still haven't explained who you are. You don't act like a civilian."

"He's a fed, Son." The sergeant came over. "I've seen him on the news. FBI out of Phoenix, is that right? One of them big-city bigshots who like to tell us small-town folks how to do our jobs." A big man, he rocked back and forth on his boots. "Only it turns out this is a major corridor for trafficking guns, drugs—you name it. So we don't just work petty crimes. We do the big stuff, too."

Jax wanted to ask if the airport was on their radar, but didn't figure the question would go down well. He could request files from the state police. Going through them would take time he didn't have.

"This isn't just a case," he finally said. "It's also a personal matter."

"When the missing driver of that vehicle was one of your agents, right? I don't think so." The sergeant shook his head. "Has to be a fed thing. Or a cover-up. Did you run him off the road? Now you're here to run interference. Is that right?"

Jax ignored the fact this guy mistook what he'd said. "Call my office. I'm sure they'll fill you in about Elliot Adams. Pretty sure he transferred out of the Phoenix office, but I wouldn't know. I was in the hospital at the time recovering from surgery."

"I see." The sergeant rocked back and forth on his heels, eyeing Jax.

Probably thought he was unhinged. Or lying.

Jax's phone rang in his pocket.

Thank You, God. Otherwise, he didn't know how to get out of this conversation without handing over ID and spending hours answering questions.

"I need to take this." He waved the phone at them. But when he walked away to see who was calling, it was Special Agent Herron.

"Jaxton."

He stared at the sky in the direction of the airport but saw nothing as he headed slowly in the direction of the open gate. Not like he was leaving, just wandering and talking on the phone.

"I thought you might want to know," she began, "Assistant Director in Charge Hadley was on the warpath this morning. He's acting like he's sticking around for a while, bringing his things into your office."

"Great."

"He's talking like you aren't coming back."

Jax winced. "We found Special Agent Adams' car. Looks like he was in an accident and someone tried to cover it up, but that's just supposition from the remains of the car. I'm going to have Kenna's people call around hospitals and find out if he's in one as a John Doe."

Or the man was under that name, unclaimed in the morgue. Hopefully, they'd be able to find him and give his sister good news. Not the worst news, the kind Jax dreaded.

"If we find his body," Jax continued, "or find him alive, I'll let you know. We can go talk to his sister together."

Andrette sniffed. "Thank you."

"Anything else?" She'd called him, after all.

"I looked at Hadley's calendar. He has a meeting on his schedule for lunch. It's part of why he's so antsy. He wants reports from everyone on what cases they're working and the progress they've made before he goes out."

"Who is the meeting with?"

"I don't know, but the calendar appointment says *D*. That's all. Just *D*."

D, as in *Dominatus*? A long shot, but it could be the break they'd been looking for.

Jax said, "Thanks."

"I hope you find her."

The line went dead.

Ramon met him at the car. "What now?"

"We need to track down Amara." Jax opened the driver's side door. "She's the one who ran Elliot off the road."

Chapter Eleven

Ramon pocketed his phone and turned to Jax. "There are no John Does at any hospitals within a hundred-mile radius who match Elliot's description. Same with the local morgue."

"So he's not dead, or in a coma and unidentified." Although, with Amara's skills, she could have hidden him in such a way that all Ramon's work just now would be moot and the guy was in a hospital under a fake name. "She has a lot to answer for."

Jax made a call from his cell in the phone holder on the dash. When it connected, he put it on speaker. "Bruce, where's Amara?" He gripped the wheel, doing eighty on the highway back to Phoenix.

His phone lit up. "How should I know?"

"Why not use your contacts to find her?" Jax replied. "Because she knows more than she's saying."

Ramon huffed. "You think?"

Focused on the road, Jax didn't see the expression on Ramon's face. Why did Ramon need to cut into his conversation with Bruce? Jax shook his head. "What?"

"Of course she's hiding stuff," Ramon said. "She's connected. Out, but in. Fighting them. Getting targeted. Captured by that senator. Escaping. She and Zeyla could've made a deal at any time, and it's why they're both still alive."

Jax didn't like the sound of that. "It's sloppy that she let me see the damage on her car. She parked so it faced anyone who looked in that direction. That wasn't a mistake. I don't think she makes mistakes."

"Amara wanted you to make the connection," Bruce said. "She brought you the file."

Jax looked in his rearview at Bruce's car behind them. The search of the airport had been a bust. Every building had been empty, and only a couple of guys with a hobby plane in one hangar were there to let them in a gate and answer questions. Of course, they knew nothing, since they hadn't even been at the airport on the night Jax and his friends were asking about.

Jax said, "We're being played."

"Again, *of course*," Ramon insisted on saying. "We're all pawns. All of us. That's all Kenna has ever been to them. We try to fight, but how are we supposed to go up against people like this?"

"So you're not onboard with taking them down?" Jax glanced over for a second.

"Once Kenna is back...it's up to you guys." Ramon shifted in his seat. "But my vote will be to disappear. At least as far as they're concerned. We never bother them, and they never bother us."

Jax gaped. "You want to make a deal with them."

Bruce said, "I tried. Look where it got me."

"You want a life, don't you?" Ramon asked them both.

"I say live and let live. It's the only way we're gonna survive."

Everything in Jax wanted to find Kenna and just disappear. Build a life with her that included fulfilling careers for both of them, kids, and a peaceful life. Whatever that might look like. "She would never be happy until there's justice. You think she would rest if she knew *Dominatus* was out there hurting people?"

Ramon just sighed.

Jax continued, "Until we find Amara and Zeyla, we should go back to Phoenix and double back on exposing the mole in the Bureau. Whoever is their handler, or feeds them information, we need to talk to that person. They have to know how to find her."

"For the sake of your precious justice?" Ramon's tone cut across the interior of the car like a knife.

Jax wanted to give the guy a long speech about Kenna and the way she got things done. Instead, he asked rhetorically, "You think she'd let corruption in the FBI go unchecked?"

"She'd be first in line to bring that stuff into the light," Ramon admitted. "Expose it."

"Let's do it, because it's what she would do."

"Agreed."

"Pull into that gas station." Ramon turned. "Bruce?"

"What are you going to do?" Bruce asked him.

It was like listening to shorthand, but Jax figured the quickest way to an answer was to do as Ramon had asked.

Bruce pulled off the highway and into the parking lot behind him.

"Find Amara," Ramon said. "While you guys clean house at the FBI."

Sounded like he didn't want anything to do with the

Bureau. And considering he'd been an agent burned and discredited by his handler, Jax didn't really blame him. "How are you going to find Amara?"

Ramon shoved the door open. "Don't worry about it. I'll call if I get anywhere."

Bruce got out of his car, and the two men shook hands. Ramon got into Bruce's car, and Bruce got into the passenger side of Jax's.

Ramon peeled out of the lot faster than necessary.

Jax followed, heading toward Phoenix. "Maybe he's the one who needs a bodyguard."

"Do you think Kenna would—"

"Fine. Use my logic against me." He'd won a debate with Ramon with the same tactic, and Bruce had been listening. No, Kenna would not let corruption in the Bureau gone unchecked.

Bruce chuckled.

Jax wasn't quite as amused. "He's a big boy. Or expendable. I'm the one who needs a bodyguard. Got it." He nodded, hitting the gas like Ramon had because he could—not because he had anything to prove.

Bruce shook his head. "He's going to check on Maizie first. Make sure she's good. That's the deal."

Jax hadn't known about that deal. "How will he find Amara?"

"Not sure it's her he's gonna find."

Jax frowned. "Zeyla?"

Bruce shrugged.

"I thought he was friends with some reporter who got an anonymous video." Just thinking about that made his stomach turn, but this was a conversation about Ramon and the revolving door of women who seemed to come and go from his life. "And before that it was Forrest Crosby."

"We're all looking for something."

"Even you?"

"Life never works out the way we think."

"Kenna told me a while back that you had a moment with her mother." Jax glanced over. "Things didn't work out?"

"She's not the kind of woman you pin down. But I guess that's what makes it exciting."

"And the lawyers at that firm?"

Bruce sighed. "Figured you'd get around to interrogating me. You know you could've called anytime the past two months. Just asked."

"Sorry." He navigated through downtown to the restaurant Andrette had sent him from Hadley's calendar. "I should've worked closer with you guys."

"Hasn't been easy for any of us. You don't wanna believe one person is the glue that holds all the others together, but some people are just like that."

"You all became a family." Because of Kenna.

"We needed it."

Jax nodded. "So did I." He found a break in the line of cars at the curb and pulled into a space.

"And it was the Bureau you found," Bruce said. "But sometimes life surprises you, and you realize it's time to make a different choice."

"The reason I'm an agent is more complicated than that. It wasn't just the first thing that came along. Being an agent has meant everything to me." Because Special Agent Oliver Jaxton was the man he'd always thought he should be—the man his father could be proud of.

"Long as it's not the only thing you are. Otherwise, when it gets taken away you have nothing left. You wind up rebuilding your life, like Kenna did." Bruce glanced over. "She told me her story. Is that what you're gonna be?"

"You think we won't find her." Jax gripped the wheel, squeezing it to get some of the tension out, not liking where this conversation was going.

"I want you to survive either way. To not lose yourself. She wouldn't want that." Bruce ran his fists down the knees of his tan jeans.

"No, I don't suppose she would want that."

Bruce let him think on that, and Jax drove in silence—his thoughts full of what Bruce had said, his heart aching for his wife.

Everything they were doing...all of it felt so much like wasting time. Spinning their wheels and never getting anywhere. Constantly believing this next thing they did would be the step that unlocked everything. That eventually they'd happen upon the answer.

Jax was more worried about who they would all become while wrestling with the question of whether Kenna was alive or dead. Wondering if they would find her or spend the rest of their lives looking. Each of them could so easily fall back into who they used to be.

He'd been made new by Jesus a long time ago. But right now, even that felt tenuous. As if he only had a weak grip on who he was in Christ.

The rest of them weren't believers as far as he knew. Jax should take some time to tell them the story of why he'd chosen to believe. They could decide for themselves what they wanted to do with the information.

"Where's our guy?" Bruce motioned out the windshield at the restaurant on the other side of the street.

"On the patio, the second umbrella from the right."

They even had cooling units out there, under the umbrellas, so people could enjoy their lunch alfresco.

Jax left the engine running for the sake of the air-conditioning, since it was over a hundred degrees outside right now. Kenna would've hated it even if she hadn't complained all that much. She'd moved here so they could make a life together. Happily ever after wasn't the time to get vocal about complaints, but it was a time to make the best of things and work through problems together.

He'd been planning to take her somewhere with snow over the winter, and they both knew they weren't going to live in Arizona forever. With a powerful enemy in the world, they hadn't made many plans for the future.

Now he wanted to have those conversations, but she wasn't here. Talk about having kids. Move somewhere they could raise children in peace. He could even see them being the home base for a team of investigators who worked for Kenna. People like Bruce and Ramon, even Maizie.

It sounded like a good life.

"Waiting for someone." Bruce shifted in his seat, getting antsy. "I could get closer."

Jax nearly laughed that the two men were so different yet similar in a lot of ways. "Ramon wanted to do the same thing. He wound up getting thrown out the back door of a cop bar."

Bruce chuckled. "He has all the fun."

Jax saw a woman approach Hadley's table. A blonde, so maybe one of the lawyers they'd met—resistance fighters who worked to undermine *Dominatus*. Or it was an agent of the company who had been trained her whole life to be one of their operatives.

The woman walked by.

Jax relaxed in his seat. "You never did tell me about the lawyers."

Bruce shrugged. "Haven't spoken to them in weeks. They shut the office in Phoenix after the doctor was killed at the silo, and I couldn't trace them."

"They wanted him dead," Jax said. "Someone should tell them he's running around making waves."

Bruce muttered, "Clone," under his breath, but Jax ignored it.

A guy in a suit walked out of the restaurant, looked around, and made a beeline for the Assistant Director in Charge.

"Binoculars?" Bruce asked, a tightness to his voice.

Jax dug in the duffel on the back seat and handed over a pair. "You see him?"

Bruce put the viewfinders to his face and swore.

"Excuse me?"

"Sorry. Kenna doesn't like when I do that either, but this time it was justified." Bruce's jaw flexed. "I know that guy. The one who just sat down with your boss."

"Who is it?"

"Samuel Chistane." Bruce lowered the binoculars. The two men at the table talked, settling in for lunch. "I want to take my pistol, cross the street, and put a bullet in his head in broad daylight in front of all those witnesses."

"But you aren't going to do that," Jax said. "What you're going to do is tell me who he is." He kept one eye on the two men. "Talk to me, Bruce."

"Doesn't mean I won't kill him later." Bruce blew out a breath. "We were partners. Did a lot of jobs together, because the success rate was higher when we could cover for each other. We went in as partners who ran an investment company. Got a lot of intel that way. Until I realized

Samuel was also selling the intel to competitors of whoever we were trying to take down. The CIA wanted the information, but he'd copy it and get himself an influx of cash. Probably to pay his loan shark."

Jax winced. "Did the CIA know he was gambling?"

"Of course," Bruce said. "Doesn't mean they ever did anything about it. Pretty sure they encouraged it. Paid his debts a couple of times to keep him in house, keep him loyal to them. They probably knew he would switch sides at the first sign someone else might give him a better deal."

"So he played both off against each other, balancing his vices, his creditors, and his country."

"Mm-hmm. Samuel liked the rush, but I didn't want anything to do with it." Bruce paused. "He did his thing. I did my part. All of it was hunky-dory."

"Until?" Jax watched the two men across the street drink wine and eat their lunch. What was Hadley doing with a former CIA agent? And why was Samuel Chistane in his calendar as simply *D*?

"Until an operation in Belgrade where the client didn't want the CIA to get anything. Samuel was going to tell our handler we got nothing, but that would've meant I failed as well. No-go, not part of our deal. In the end, that mission cost us an informant." Bruce continued, his voice rough, "She..." He cleared his throat. "Samuel tried to kill me when I realized he was the one who'd killed the informant. I fought him. He injured me and got back to the CIA first. Told them I was the one who'd turned. They burned me, and the rest is history as they say."

"What do you want to do about him?"

"We know he's connected. The finance company he owns is in deals with companies whose sole customer is *Dominatus*. It would be satisfying to learn he's one of them, because then I could torture him before I kill him. But we both know that's not how life works."

"He might know something," Jax said. "Not that I'm advocating torture."

"I'd say I'll take your guy, you take mine, but I want to see his face when he's asked about *Dominatus* and his role with them."

"This is just lunch between a businessman and an Assistant Director in Charge at the FBI." Jax shrugged. "It could be nothing."

"And he might know where Kenna is."

Jax blew out a long breath. "When he gets up to leave, we follow Samuel and find out where he goes. Maybe we'll get a result."

"No maybes," Bruce said. "Either way, there will be a result."

"Revenge isn't going to satisfy you. It won't get you your life back. And you know that because you're building a life, and it has nothing to do with what he did to you."

"Maybe not, but it'll feel good when I kill him for it."

Jax could argue with that, but not right now. The tone in Bruce's voice made him hold off. The guy didn't sound angry. He sounded resigned. "We could hand him over to the government with evidence he was selling secrets to enemies of the United States. Do you have any evidence?"

"I'd like to see his face when they slap cuffs on him, but I have no proof. It's all hearsay."

"Did he build that company from the ground up?"

"Sure did," Bruce said. "Since he got back."

"Why don't we take it apart. Give all his money to kids' nonprofits."

Bruce chuckled. "That would also be satisfying."

"Revenge doesn't have to involve bloodshed." Jax

watched his boss, who was currently moving into Jax's office and undermining his role at the FBI, laugh at something Samuel Chistane said. "Sometimes it's better with a careful plan that ends up with their life in pieces and you walking away still a whole person."

"Remind me not to underestimate you."

Jax smiled. It was *Dominatus* who needed to watch out, because he was coming for Kenna, and then he was coming for them. Forget what Ramon had said about walking away and living a quiet life.

Right now, he wanted to burn it all down.

Chapter Twelve

"Where is he going now?" Jax shook his head.

They'd followed Samuel from the lunch with Hadley to a local community park where he was now wandering the network of paths between wide stretches of grass where people played ultimate Frisbee or tossed footballs. The whole place had been manicured to within an inch of its life, but kids on the playground and splash pad seemed happy enough with the setup.

Bruce huffed beside him. "Clandestine meeting?"

"Or he knows we're following him and he's stringing us along." Jax hung back. "Going for a stroll to clear his head."

Between his federally ingrained skills and Bruce's former life as a spy, Samuel Chistane shouldn't know they were behind him. Except for the fact he was from the same line of work as Bruce—and maybe he'd never left. After all, he could still be working for whoever wanted to pay off his debts.

Jax palmed his phone and dialed Maizie. As soon as she picked up, he said, "Everything good?"

"Yeah," she said on a sigh, sounding tired—or something else he couldn't figure out. Had she been crying? "Ramon dropped off the laptop, so I've got a program going through the files, indexing everything. Local police are looking for gangbangers who shot up a restaurant yesterday morning. There's nothing in any of the reports about you being a fed, and the footage from inside the place was lost. The police never got their hands on it."

"Any fatalities?" Jax scratched his nose under his sunglasses, keeping an eye on both Bruce and Samuel—and the two dogs playing on the grass to his right.

"A few of the customers in the restaurant had bumps and bruises. A guy with a preexisting heart condition was taken to the hospital, but it was just to check him over. He's already been discharged."

"Thanks, Maze." That matched his hunch. "Did you get much sleep last night?"

"A little. I'm going to talk to Elizabeth later. We have an appointment scheduled."

"Good. Keep yourself safe, yeah?" He meant that in all ways.

"You, too." She hung up.

He'd be surprised if there turned out to be anything on Elliot Adams' computer. Seemed more like he was an innocent bystander in all this, but it never hurt to be careful.

Up ahead, Samuel took a path that disappeared into the trees. A shaded running trail that would likely be popular in the afternoon heat.

Jax glanced at Bruce. "You good?"

The older man wiped sweat from his forehead with a handkerchief. "Been in hotter places than this."

"I'm sure you have. But I'm guessing you were younger then."

Bruce chuckled. "You'd be right about that."

"Let me know if you want me to keep going alone."

"Kenna wouldn't be offering to go it solo. She'd be complaining about the heat along with me."

Jax smiled. "I'd like to hear about what the two of you got up to in England. But maybe later."

"My side of the story."

They stepped into the shady part, and both let out a long sigh.

"Twenty degrees cooler in here at least." Jax wiped his forehead with the back of his hand. "Thank you for bringing her up. A lot of people have hesitated, like hearing about her is going to make me lose it."

"Maybe you *should* lose it."

Jax shook his head. "That's when things get dangerous for me. If I'm going to find her, I need to keep things tight and my head on straight."

"Like not getting a rifle and taking that guy out?"

"Chistane is more valuable to us alive than dead, and you know it."

"He's more valuable to us if we can find him than if we can't." Bruce motioned to the trail up ahead, where the strip of asphalt between tall trees bent to the right. Samuel Chistane was out of sight. "And if we aren't being watched." He glanced around.

"What is it?" Jax asked. The back of his neck prickled with some kind of awareness. He looked around.

"Whoa," Bruce said.

Jax clocked the red dot on his chest, a tiny light. He was in someone's crosshairs.

But he wasn't the only target.

"You, too." Jax motioned to the red dot from a different laser sight on Bruce's shirt buttons. Which meant they were being covered from multiple angles. "Put your hands up. Don't do anything rash."

Uniformed SWAT officers who were definitely FBI—not local police—emerged from all angles. The fact he hadn't realized he and Bruce were surrounded until the team was almost on top of them impressed him. And made him proud to be their boss.

"FBI! No sudden movements!"

Jax stood very still, both hands in the air. He looked for a familiar face among the crowd of cops, but with their helmets, it was hard to recognize the few whose names he would know.

One grabbed the back of his shirt. "Down on the ground!"

"I'm Special Agent in Charge Oliver Jaxton. What's going on?"

Bruce was slammed to the ground, held there by a knee. To his credit, the older man didn't fight back. But he yelled, "We didn't do anything!"

"What's going on?" Jax looked around and spotted an agent he recognized at the back. "Farlan!"

The agent nearest Jax said, "We got a report. Male of your description brandishing a weapon with civilians around, threatening to shoot."

Jax shook his head. "We're just walking. That's it."

The agent lifted his chin, and the man behind Jax let him go.

Special Agent Farlan reached them. "Guys, this is the Phoenix ASAC." To Jax he said, "These are agents from Albuquerque. They're here doing a training, and we were closest when the call went out."

"This is a setup." Jax motioned to Bruce. "Let my friend up, please."

The agents lifted Bruce to his feet. He looked like he wanted to push them away, but Jax shook his head and Bruce contained himself.

"Sorry you wasted your time," Jax said. "Someone is obviously targeting me."

Farlan tipped his head to the side, and they stepped off to the edge of the group. "You need to come to the office. Write up a report. Let us know what's going on."

Jax would've said yes, normally. But right now, that was the last thing he wanted to do. It seemed like, for the first time, being an agent who followed the rules wasn't going to get him what he wanted. "I'm not coming in."

"Hadley is going to want to talk to you. He was asking where you were this morning."

"He told me to take a few days."

"And make an appointment with the department shrink, right?" Farlan stared him down. "But you didn't do that. Now you're out here...what—recreating? Going for a stroll in the afternoon heat. More likely you're chasing a ghost, trying to find a woman who doesn't want you and making up leads so everyone thinks there's some grand conspiracy."

Which is likely why in just two days Kenna's friends had gained more leads than the FBI had in two months. Not counting whatever Amara was up to, handing him that file and sending him after Elliot—a man she had run off the road and probably killed.

Jax took a step back.

"Boss, you need to come back to the office with us." The agent tilted his head. "Your friend, too."

A couple of other agents crowded around.

"Hadley told me to take a couple of personal days," Jax said, loudly enough more than just Farlan could hear it. "So that's what I'm doing. Because he's running the office, so everything goes smoothly." Meaning Jax was expendable.

In a big organization, that was a good thing. The success or failure of the FBI as an agency shouldn't rest on just one person's shoulders. It should continue on, no matter who was in what role.

He could walk away, and they would be fine. But Kenna wouldn't be.

Farlan frowned. "He threatened to suspend you if you didn't show up."

That cleared that right up—and solidified his resolve even more.

Jax slid his gun and its holster from his belt and handed it to Farlan. "My duty weapon. And my badge." He slid the cred pack from his pocket and handed it over. "Take these to Hadley. Maybe ask him why no one in the department is considering the fact that my wife was kidnapped recently. Except Special Agent Herron. She sent an agent to find Kenna after the transport left. That agent went missing, but everyone thinks he transferred out."

The skin around Farlan's eyes creased.

"If he was transferred, then find out where," Jax continued. "Get Special Agent Elliot Adams on the phone and speak to him. Find out if he really transferred out of the office right after the silo operation. Ask questions about what's going on in the office. Because something isn't right." He looked around. "Unless you're all in on it."

"There isn't a conspiracy," Farlan said.

Bruce barked a laugh. "Son, I've seen empires rise and fall. Conspiracies are the air you breathe. Ain't no getting away from them or avoiding them when they're all around you. Question is, what side are you on?"

Farlan looked like he wanted to say something else, but instead a sad expression crossed his face. He turned, and the agents all disbursed. Walking into the woods the way they'd come, leaving Jax and Bruce on the path alone.

"Did you just quit the FBI, Son?"

Jax winced. "I probably shouldn't have done that."

"You already did the hard part. Don't take back what you let go. Release it, move on, and let's find Kenna."

Jax looked around. "Where did Chistane go?"

"Guess we'd better find him first." Bruce shrugged. "Good thing I put a tracker on his car. I just hope he goes back to it now and doesn't dump it for a new one."

"You think he's switching vehicles, covering his tracks?" Jax glanced at him as they headed down the path back to the parking lot.

Bruce took a pair of aviator sunglasses from his shirt pocket and slipped them on. "That's what I would do. But it feels more like this whole thing has been a trap. He's baiting me, stringing us along."

Jax nodded. "I don't like it, but I think you're right."

When they got near enough, Bruce pulled out his phone. "His car is gone."

"When did you put on a tracker?" Jax asked. Somehow, he'd missed that.

"Tricks of the trade." Bruce chuckled. "A magician never reveals his secrets."

"Any tricks to find Elliot, and Kenna?"

"I wish I could." Bruce's tone rang with a grief so strong that Jax could taste it.

She was gone, but she wasn't dead. Jax refused to believe it.

His phone buzzed with a text from Ramon.

Jax read it, then said, "Amara and Zeyla are at Elliot's sister's house."

"Then let's roll." Bruce pulled the passenger door open.

Jax didn't know how Kenna's team ever found all the things they managed to find. It was entirely possible he shouldn't ask about the tricks of Bruce's trade. All of them had skills—Ramon and Bruce. Even Maizie. Since most of their methods might not be within the bounds of the law, he figured he probably didn't want to know.

But he thought about it the whole way, and half an hour later pulled into a neighborhood of older homes with neat lawns and chain-link fences. One had an ocean of flamingos on the artificial grass between the house and the fence. Bruce's car was parked in the cul-de-sac, at an angle at the curb, which meant Ramon was here. Another vehicle sat on the drive. The giant rental truck Sandra had at Elliot's house was parked on the street—and probably needed returning.

Jax, followed by Bruce, entered the front door. "Ramon!"

"Kitchen!"

Jax found the crowd in the kitchen. Amara and Zeyla, Elliot's sister and Ramon—with his gun in his hand by his side. He lowered his weapon. "What's going on?"

"Amara was about to explain," Ramon said.

Elliot's sister, Sandra, looked freaked but lifted her chin. "I'd like to hear it as well, but that's only because I'm not going with you until you tell me what's going on."

Amara shook her head, looking disappointed. "It would've been easier if you just complied, Sandra."

"Do people do that often?" Ramon asked.

Zeyla shot him a look.

"Amara?" Jax needed her to talk, or he was going to tell

Sandra that Amara was responsible for her brother's disappearance.

"I'm here to take you to your brother," Amara said.

Sandra gasped. Jax glanced at Amara. "He's alive?"

Amara nodded.

Jax said, "You're the one who ran him off the road."

She needed to admit it so they could start being honest with each other. Not only because Sandra deserved the truth, but also because Jax wanted to know what she hadn't yet told him.

Sandra yelled, "Where is he?!"

Zeyla turned and walked out the back door. Ramon went after her, and Bruce shifted closer to Amara. Adjusting the huddle. Jax crossed his arms.

Amara said, "He's safe, and staying with people I trust. I can take you there. And I'm sorry, but you won't be able to leave for a while."

Sandra shook her head. "What's going on?"

"I can explain on the way." Amara shifted, motioning to the door. "We should hurry."

"Great," Jax said. "We'll escort you just in case, and you can explain everything once Sandra sees her brother."

Amara looked at him. "I don't know where Kenna is."

"I hope you're being honest about that, at least, even if you haven't been honest about much else. But considering what else you lied about, I'm not sure I'll ever completely believe you." How could he? She'd manipulated them, thrown Kenna to the wolves without the knowledge to protect herself from *Dominatus*, and might be the reason why that group had her now.

She might have been able to stop it. Had she at least tried?

Bruce said, "Have you lied, Amara?"

She whipped around and looked at Bruce. "I never lied."

"But you withheld the truth," Jax said. "So it's time for answers."

"I want to see my brother." Sandra turned and grabbed her purse from the counter. "Take me to him now. Then you guys can talk after, because I don't care about whatever this is. I just want to see Elliot."

Bruce gestured. "You can both ride with Jax and I."

Sandra followed Bruce out.

Amara stared at Jax, lines around her eyes. She seemed fatigued. As if the weight of everything lay heavy on her shoulders. But he didn't know if it was guilt or just the stress of what was going on.

"We could be working together." He stared at her.

"With the FBI?" She barked a hollow laugh.

"I just quit. So I guess you don't have to worry about that now." As if that had been a problem. More like it was a convenient excuse. Could he trust this woman? Maybe not further than what he was able to verify.

Amara shook her head. "Once a fed, always a fed."

"Do you know who has Kenna, or where she is?" He waited, and in the silence studied her. The woman was an enigma he didn't know how to unravel, but he had to. Kenna's well-being and both of their futures counted on it.

"She's alive."

Jax sucked in a sharp breath. "Is she with Elliot?"

Amara shook her head. "I'm doing what I can. I'm doing *everything* I can." A sheen of tears filled her eyes. "You don't understand, but I'm doing all I'm able to do. For her."

"I would understand if you'd bothered to explain it rather than keeping everyone in the dark. Instead, you tell me how hard you have it. How much stress you're under."

Jax slammed a hand on his chest. "As if it's nothing that I don't know whether to grieve or keep searching. I don't know who to trust. I don't know how to find her."

Jax closed the gap between them, unwilling to check his anger.

"WHERE IS SHE?" he yelled.

Chapter Thirteen

Let's go.

That was all she'd said in answer to his question. As if his world wasn't currently tearing itself apart—and he knew he was next. That he wouldn't be able to hang on much longer before it all just...fractured.

"Elliot is down there." Amara led them down a hallway, past several of the lawyers from Hann, Anthony & Associates. Five, if he'd managed to spot them all, standing around in khakis and polo shirts like this was a private security convention.

A lawyer he recognized stood beside a plain door in this plain hallway, the building an office and warehouse in a business district on the west side of Phoenix. Outside in huge letters on the exterior of the building was a fading sign for a plumbing supply business—and yet no one worked here.

"Oliver." The lawyer, Lisa Romeo, nodded.

"Ms. Romeo." He returned her nod.

Sandra said, "Is he in there?"

Sandra raced ahead of Jax. He wanted to stop her so

that he went first, but with guards all around, there likely wasn't any danger.

Depending on Elliot's condition.

The door beside her whipped open, and a man stood there, late twenties. Slender, wearing tan slacks and a white shirt that was untucked. He had two pens in his breast pocket and glasses on his nose. "Sandra!"

Jax realized he did recognize the guy. But instead of remembering when they'd conversed at the office, he didn't think they'd actually spoken directly. Elliot Adams had been present at some meetings Jax had led. He was the forgettable kind, a guy who didn't stick out—which made Jax wonder who else he hadn't noticed because he was too preoccupied. He might not be able to know everyone, but were there others who had slipped through the cracks?

Elliot and Sandra Adams collided in a hug, a mess of words exchanged between them.

Jax glanced at Amara, who had a blank look on her face, then stepped aside with Ms. Romeo.

"You look a lot better than you did the last time I saw you," the lawyer told him.

That had been when they'd rescued him from those mafia guys, injured and barely conscious.

He chuckled. "Not surprising."

The brother and sister stepped into the room, arms around each other and talking low with their heads together. Jax wanted the information they were sharing back and forth, not entirely sure whatever Amara had to say to him would be the truth.

Ramon and Zeyla stepped into the hall at the far end. Ramon lifted his chin, and Jax returned it.

"I need answers." Jax glanced between Ms. Romeo and Amara. "Now. I need to know what's going on."

Bruce hadn't come inside with them. He'd dropped Jax off and then taken the car so he could go do...whatever it was he was going to do. Presumably follow the tracker to his former partner and then hopefully watch, or secure, Samuel Chistane. But if Bruce killed the guy, it really wouldn't be so surprising. Jax wasn't going to babysit the guy, but realized he needed to put a stipulation on things, so he sent Bruce a text.

> Don't kill him. We need information, remember?

It was as much a reminder to himself as it was to Kenna's friend. After all, it was Zeyla who had stopped Jax from yelling at Amara earlier. She and Ramon had come in right after he yelled at her. Now the anger in his gut was roiling. But every time he looked at Elliot and Sandra off to the side in a room—reunited—it wasn't anger he felt. It was jealousy. They had each other back.

What did he have?

He turned to Amara. "You know where she is."

Kenna's mother said, "That's one of the few things I don't know."

Jax shook his head. "You work for *Dominatus*, don't you? That means you all do." He waved a hand, incorporating Ms. Romeo and Zeyla. "Am I wrong?"

"Don't be ridiculous," Amara hissed. "You think this is so black-and-white. We're either good or evil. As if the world is so simple." She shook her head.

"So I'm the naïve one, and I guess you're going to have to explain this all to me. Because it looks like you ran an FBI agent off the road and then kidnapped him in order to allow those retired guys to take Kenna from me." He folded his arms. "So tell me why I shouldn't call a team of agents here to tear this whole place apart. See what else you're hiding."

Ms. Romeo shifted. "Please don't blow this safe house. She shouldn't have brought you here, and we'll clear out as soon as you're gone. This place is burned with just you guys, but that doesn't mean anyone needs to find out about it."

Jax clenched down on his molars.

Amara slid a phone from her jacket pocket. The move, of course, put him on edge, just in case she was drawing a weapon from out of sight. Instead, she showed him the screen of her phone.

Jax grabbed the cell and looked closer. *Kenna.* "Where did you get this?"

Ramon moved to him and looked at the screen over his shoulder. "That looks like a hospital bed. She isn't secured to it."

Kenna was tucked in on the screen, under blankets. Fast asleep—or unconscious. No IVs, and no monitors attached to her taking readings of her vitals.

"Is she alive or—" The question caught in his throat.

"I'm making sure of it." Amara took the phone.

Jax didn't want to give it back. "Send me that image. And any more that you have." He saw her expression pinch a little. "You have more?"

Amara's lips pressed into a thin line. "I have three others."

Ramon started to move by him.

Jax slammed a hand on the guy's chest. "If you kill her, we don't get information."

As much as he wanted to rage at Amara right now, he was also surprised to find himself the voice of reason with Ramon.

He was still processing the fact she'd been receiving images of Kenna. "I can't believe you never told me you have images of her."

His gut burned.

Amara stood there, looking a little guilty at least. But not much.

Ramon's body tensed. "I can't believe you never told *us*. You think we wouldn't want to know about Kenna?" His voice rose in volume. "You're a piece of work."

"Ramon." Jax had to get answers, not just go around and around with accusations.

His friend said, "I don't think you understand what I can do to get information. She might wish she was dead."

"But we aren't going to do that." Jax could guess well enough what the guy meant. Having worked for a cartel in Mexico for years, Ramon was a wildcard at best, and thankfully they were on the same side in this. But if Ramon committed a crime, Jax couldn't exactly ignore it, even if he had turned over his badge. "Maybe don't incriminate yourself in front of an FBI agent."

"I thought you were suspended." Amara eyed him. "Or did you quit?"

Jax didn't back down. "And I thought you wanted Kenna back with her family, but I guess I was wrong."

Amara's expression hardened. "She's alive because of me."

Ramon shifted, standing behind Jax's right shoulder. "Explain."

Jax lifted his brows.

"Fine," Amara said. "I made it obvious enough that it was me who ran Elliot off the road. Foolishly I thought you might like to know that Kenna is alive. That I didn't kill Agent Adams, and I *thought* you'd know I am on your side."

"Where is she?" Jax asked.

"I have no idea."

Jax shook his head. "Not good enough."

"She's alive. Even if you did find her, which is impossible because no one has any idea where she was taken, then she dies. They'll kill her if you even start to get close. You stay away and she lives. Got it?"

"We aren't going to agree on this." It was how Amara had worked her whole life, or at least Kenna's whole life. Staying away in order to protect Kenna. But that hadn't been what she needed, because Jax and Kenna had talked about it at length. Amara did what she wanted. Nothing could change what had already happened.

Kenna had needed this woman in her life so she could have a mother. Not a memory, or a headstone for a dead woman. But did Amara stop long enough to realize that?

No, she hadn't.

"I'm going to get her back whether you help me or not." Jax wasn't backing down. Ever. "Why didn't you at least tell me you were being coerced into working for them in order to keep her alive?"

Ms. Romeo hadn't moved or said anything. He figured she was acting as counsel—but he didn't know who she was representing here. Amara didn't seem to need anyone to tell her what to say or not say so as not to incriminate herself. Zeyla remained quiet as well. Ramon might know more about where she was at with all this, given they'd spoken at the house. Otherwise, she kept to herself. Another enigma it would take time to figure out.

Amara said, "Would you be inclined to admit it if someone had you over a barrel and you had no way out?"

"Except it seems like everyone apart from us knows, because no one else here is surprised to discover you're aware of Kenna's condition." He motioned between himself and Ramon. "First off, how about you explain better what happened with Elliot."

He should be furious with her, but grief was like a wave that dampened the fire of his anger and put it out. He wanted to demand to see more pictures of Kenna. *She's alive.* He needed to tuck that thought close to his heart so he could save the feeling. If Amara sent the images to him, Maizie would see them. She would know that Kenna was alive.

The search for her would be renewed, because Maizie wasn't going to let images get past her without a thorough analysis of the elements in the image—and where they'd come from. Now that the information was out, they might get a real lead.

Amara said, "*Dominatus* knew that Elliot was going after those men to find out what happened to Kenna."

She paused long enough he said, "We already know he was a scapegoat. No one at the FBI knows he's gone. They all think he transferred, and the computer system is conveniently missing any record of him."

"That was intentional." Elliot stepped out of the room. "We decided to have evidence of me scrubbed from the system and planted the story that I transferred. That way no one would come looking and find me. Amara planned to get Sandra and bring her here so we can go into protective custody together."

His sister side hugged him and stayed there, under his arm. Holding on to him. "I thought you were dead, but no one cared. They didn't think they needed to look for you."

"So it wasn't whoever in the office is working for *Dominatus* who came up with the cover story?" Jax turned to

Amara. "Did you use Maizie to plant the files in the FBI computer network?"

She shook her head. "Your girl is clean. Which means she's likely a target like the rest of you."

Jax didn't like the sound of that, but it wasn't a surprise since Maizie had been interviewed about that worm in the FBI system. Had that been Amara's doing?

Jax sighed. "Now go back to the subject of Kenna."

"I don't know where she is, and I can't even look for her, or they'll kill her."

"But you've discovered everything you possibly can from the photos and the accounts they were sent from?" Jax lifted his chin. "Send them to me."

She tapped her phone, and his vibrated. She'd sent them to him over Bluetooth.

Maizie would see them automatically because every-thing from his personal phone connected to her system now. The way Kenna's had always done and how every photo she took was immediately uploaded. He texted her to be careful looking into the source of the images in case *Dominatus* was watching for her.

"I've tried my best to keep you guys from getting caught up in this mess." Amara rubbed the spot between her eyes. "So you can keep the freedom you have to search for her while my hands are tied."

Zeyla said, "Are you getting a migraine?"

Amara shot her a look. Was she really mad because her daughter had said that aloud?

It wouldn't surprise him if she had more secrets she hadn't shared with the rest of them. But they should know it was better to be vulnerable with each other. Opening up made them all stronger.

Amara glanced at Jax. "I've been tangled up with *Domi-*

natus for as long as I can remember. Once you're in, there's no getting out. That's why they know I'm vulnerable. They didn't take Kenna so they could manipulate me into working on their behalf, but it's a nice perk for them. They know I'd never do anything that would lead them to harm her."

"Demand proof of life," Ramon said. "The next time they contact you, tell them you want to speak to her. We can have Maizie trace it."

"What do you think those photos were?" Amara paused. "And even if I can get her on the phone, or a video call, you aren't going to be able to trace it. These people have better tech than the people who are making the cutting-edge stuff."

They also had a computer program that allowed one person to pretend to be someone else on a video call. Even if they talked to Kenna, Jax wasn't sure he would trust it.

Elliot shook his head. "I've been hearing all about these people for weeks. And I still can't believe what all they are capable of, and what they're doing, is true. It's unbelievable."

"Why you?" Jax asked. "Special Agent Herron sent you after the transport. That's as much as I know. But you were targeted. Put in the middle of this."

Elliot's expression darkened. "I was investigating them. I just didn't know it."

"*Dominatus?*"

Elliot nodded. His sister shifted and withdrew from him, and he said, "I'll explain it all." He looked at Jax. "I work mostly white-collar crimes. Financial, usually."

Jax nodded. "That tracks with the meetings I remember you from. Sorry I didn't—"

"Don't be," Elliot said, cutting him off. "We're past that

at this point. Besides, there are more important things going on here than whether or not my manager's boss noticed me in an ocean of agents." After a second of pause, he said, "I was looking into a series of connected financial companies. We'd had reports that they might be involved in some form of insider trading, or possibly even money laundering, so I was running down all the subsidiaries and other connected firms."

"You got too close, and when they needed you to disappear, they had Agent Herron send you after the transport. And Amara here"—Jax glanced at her—"was supposed to—what—kill you?"

"I've taken enough lives," she replied. "So I had Hann, Anthony & Associates aid me in securing Mr. Adams in this safehouse. The goal was to set him up with a new life, but Elliot wasn't about to go without his sister. He's been helping us in the meantime with what he found in his investigation into those companies."

"And?" Jax glanced at Elliot. "Is it enough for probable cause?"

"Not for a warrant any judge is going to sign," Elliot said. "But it's enough we can trace the money back to other companies that could be part of this conspiracy. They're spread all over. I couldn't believe it when every time I turned over another rock, there were more companies connected. It's huge."

"I need a report of everything you've discovered."

Elliot flinched. "We can't turn this over to the FBI when you've already said they have agents in house, doing their dirty work. We'll be giving it right into their hands."

That wasn't a bad way of labeling what Amara had done as well. Certainly felt like "dirty work." But that wasn't who Jax was going to turn it over to. "Let me worry about where the information is going to go. It's time to be done keeping secrets and working separately. We need to work together, or the people we care about continue to be targeted."

After a second, Elliot nodded.

Jax looked at Amara.

It was Ramon who asked, "Are you in, or not?"

And Elliot who answered, "They were going to have me killed, so I'm in for taking them down." He glanced at his sister. "You feel like hiding here with me until we get sent somewhere safe?"

She said, "Get me a secure laptop and I'll help."

Elliot smiled. "Okay."

Jax didn't take his attention from Amara, who seemed to be allowing things to develop without her input. Because she wanted to be able to report back to *Dominatus* that things here had been out of her control?

"A nice speech isn't going to win this." Zeyla's hands curled into fists by her sides.

Jax had never seen her so animated. In fact, he didn't think he'd heard her say more than a few words.

She continued, "You think working this like a case, trying to catch them for tax evasion like they're mobsters, is even going to work? This is psychological warfare." She waved at her mom, then said, "These people carved me up."

"Everyone knows how serious this is." Jax stared at her. "Me most of all."

"You?" Amara looked like she wanted to laugh. "You think you know *anything*? I've been fighting these people since before you were born. I know how to play their game."

"You really think this is a game?" Jax stared at her. "I want my wife back."

"What do you think I'm trying to achieve?"

"We pull Maizie in," Jax said. "We all sit down and go through everything. There has to be something to work with. We need a plan."

They were going to break this case. He had no other options.

His phone started to ring. He answered, "Good timing, Maze."

The teen gasped. "She's still alive."

Tears filled his eyes, and he turned away. "Yeah, she is."

"I was so scared that they did something to her."

"Me, too." He sucked in a breath. "Pack up your stuff. I need you here. We've got a case to solve."

"Okay, but I don't want to leave Bruce hanging. He needed surveillance."

Jax gripped the phone. "He caught up to Samuel Chistaine?"

"He's snapping the trap shut now."

Chapter Fourteen

The roll-up door at the end of the warehouse ascended, and Bruce pulled in. Maizie had been at the RV, so she was across town still but on her way, and Jax was watching her progress on his tracking app.

The slam of the car door echoed in the otherwise quiet expanse of space. A couple of birds took flight up in the ceiling, soaring out an open window.

A couple of the lawyers he'd met a few months ago at their office were at the far end of the room, standing guard. One of the two had been there when they rescued him, he was pretty sure. He'd been badly injured and didn't remember a lot of it, but he thought she looked familiar.

The mafia guys who had captured him, trying to get Kenna to rescue the leader's niece in exchange for Jax's freedom, hadn't been seen since. He never asked anyone where they were. Whether the lawyers killed them, or someone else had, Jax wasn't sure he wanted to know.

But where did that get him? Maybe he should've asked a whole lot more questions, given Amara had been keeping the secrets she had. Then there was Ramon and the thing he seemed to have going with Zeyla—even if it was antag-onistic.

Bruce stopped by the trunk of the car, a sheen of sweat on his forehead. Blood at the corner of his mouth. His former partner had put up a fight.

Jax strode over. "Were you going to tell anyone you caught up to Samuel and were moving in?"

"I told Maizie." He reached for the trunk. Jax grabbed his shoulder and turned the man back around. Bruce twisted to him, already swinging.

Jax blocked the punch. "We're going to establish some ground rules."

"Like no one puts their hands on anyone else?"

Jax wanted to say, *You started it*, but didn't. "Fine." He folded his arms. "But clue us in. You don't want the guy loose, and he needs to explain his involvement while also giving you an answer as to why he betrayed you. Did I get that right?"

Bruce nodded.

"Great. But now is when we quit doing things solo and call each other for backup."

After all, if he'd quit the FBI to help them full-time, then they needed to start acting like a team.

Ramon, staring at his phone, muttered, "Who put you in charge?"

Jax glanced at him.

Bruce flipped the lid of the trunk open, and he and Amara hauled Samuel out. The guy was breathing hard behind the cloth tied around his head. Both his hands and feet had been taped together, and he'd soiled himself.

Jax wrinkled his nose, but couldn't help noticing how it seemed Bruce and Amara were in sync. There was a pattern to their movements, most likely similar to him and

Kenna. As if they'd spent a lot of time in close quarters—living and working together.

All that since Bruce had met her only months ago? The guy certainly kept his secrets, but it wasn't like he was playing both sides in the same way Amara did. At least, not according to Kenna he wasn't. Now that Jax knew Amara had been hiding Kenna's situation from all of them, he'd have to ask them straight-out what was going on.

"I'm just saying." Ramon shrugged. "Kenna lets us do our own thing."

"And look where that has us so far." Jax wasn't going to back down on this. "It's time to change how we've been doing things." Ramon didn't look up, so Jax peered at what was on his screen. A small circle moved across a map. "You're tracking Maizie as well?"

"She's almost here."

Jax nodded. "When she gets here, we're having a team meeting." Someone grumbled, but he didn't wait around to figure out who. Instead, he went to the front doors and watched for Maizie to appear in the direction she was coming from.

Bruce followed him outside, and then Ramon.

Bruce said, "They're getting Samuel settled in a spot that's good for questioning."

Jax didn't look at either of them. "They've done that before here?"

"Probably thought they'd have to do that with Elliot," Bruce said. "But he just told them everything after Amara brought him here."

"Even though she's the one who ran him off the road?" He didn't understand any of these people. They didn't operate the way he'd been trained to at all.

Bruce started to say something but didn't.

Maizie pulled into the parking lot at that moment, turning haphazardly into a space across two white lines and barely shutting off the engine before she ran over. The young woman didn't slow down. She slammed into Jax and wrapped her arms around him. "She's really alive? When did Amara hear from them?"

He hugged her back, careful to keep his arms loose for when she wanted to step back. "She's alive," he repeated back to her. Rather than dwell on the when, he just wanted a second to absorb the fact they hadn't killed Kenna.

She stepped back, swiping her face, and groaned, "Ramon."

"I know. It's good news."

She gave him a hug as well, briefer than the one she'd given Jax. Then she hugged Bruce. The old man said, "Trouble," sounding like he had a lump in his throat. When he stepped back, he sniffed.

"She's alive," Jax said, just to voice it aloud again. "That means we need to double down on finding her while we have this fresh evidence."

"With team meetings?" Bruce eyed him.

"All or nothing," Jax replied. "We do this together."

Ramon shook his head. "Isn't it supposed to be 'all for one and one for all'?"

Maizie said, "What are you guys talking about?"

"There's work to do." Jax motioned to the door. "Because the longer we let them have her, the greater the chance—" His voice caught in his throat. That image flashed in his mind again. Kenna in a hospital bed. "That we never get her back."

Given who these people were, the ones who had her, they could be doing anything. She could be...

He rubbed his chest, his breaths coming hard. "We need to..." He gasped, and the world swam around him.

The others grabbed his arms and walked him inside, making the front door clang. It echoed through the entry-way, and he shrugged off their hands to turn and pace.

Jax tried to catch his breath.

Vulnerable was one thing. But he couldn't completely lose it in front of them or Maizie—get freaked out beyond anything he'd ever felt—over the fact that horrible things were happening to Kenna. Even the best-case scenarios were a kind of torture. And all of it boiled down to the fact that she wasn't here with him, enjoying their life together. Living a peaceful existence like the one she'd craved before they all barreled into her life.

"We're going to find her," Bruce said.

Ramon nodded. "We won't stop. Because you know she would do the exact same for any of us."

Maizie touched Jax's arm. "She wouldn't quit. Ever. That's why we aren't going to either."

He was making them all waste time standing here dealing with his freak-out. He ran his hands down his face and scrubbed against the stubble on his chin. "I need her back."

Maizie nodded. "We all do."

"Can you even imagine if one of us was missing?" Ramon said, a smile tugging at his mouth. "She would be on a rampage. Yelling at all of us. Drinking too much coffee and never sleeping. We'd never hear the end of it until whoever it was got found."

Maizie giggled. "That's true."

Even Bruce smiled.

"Thanks, guys," Jax managed.

Ramon clapped his back. "You want a team? I guess you got one."

"You want a meeting? Make it a quick one." Bruce eyed him. "No wasting time."

"I know you want to question Samuel, but it might be best if someone else does it," Jax pointed out. "Just in case he feels like accusing you of being vindictive."

Ramon said, "I'll do it," following Bruce through the doors.

Which left Jax in the entryway with Maizie. He said, "Are you okay?"

Something shifted in her gaze, but he couldn't pin down what it was. "I'll be okay when we find her."

He nodded. "Me, too."

Jax pushed through the doors, and Maizie went with him to the same hall where they'd spoken to Elliot. The lawyer stood waiting. "Ms. Romeo, will you take Maizie to speak with Elliot and his sister."

The woman nodded. "I can do that."

"And stay with her until I get there." Jax wasn't going to budge on that.

"You believe she might be in danger from Elliot or Sandra?"

"We're all in danger all the time. Prudence dictates we pay attention to security. Especially when we have so much to lose."

She eyed him, a tiny bit of admiration in her eyes. "Very well. I'll stay with Ms. Morrow."

He looked at Maizie, who tipped her head and said, "Go. I'm good."

Not the first time he hadn't wanted to leave Maizie, but he did it. Jax followed the sound of conversation down the hall, around the corner. Ramon stood in the hall with Zeyla, their stances a whole lot like they were in a standoff.

"What now?"

Ramon glanced over his shoulder at Jax. "Nothing."

"Right."

Zeyla said, "I didn't do anything. Ramon is just being *Ramon*."

Her voice was so similar to Kenna's it made his chest squeeze. He'd wonder if he needed to see a doctor if not for the fact this felt exactly like the weeks after his grandpa died. The same steel bands wrapped around his chest.

But he wasn't grieving Kenna, because she wasn't dead. *She's alive.* He was going to find her. Which meant this feeling was fear that he might not.

"See?" Zeyla waved an arm. "He won't even look at me."

Jax shifted his attention to Ramon, who shook his head and said, "So you're all butthurt about that? It's hardly the time to be petty."

Zeyla scoffed. "You think that's what this is?"

Jax said, "You look like her. You sound like her."

He wasn't sure he could explain it more than that. But he figured it could very well be the problem Ramon had with this woman.

"I get it. I make things hard." She started to turn away.

Ramon clasped her elbow. "Zey—"

"Don't bother." She pulled her arm from his grip. "It's not like I'm asking to be part of your team." She walked away.

"We need to get in here and talk to Samuel," Jax said. "But what's going on? You know Kenna would ask. She would want to know."

Ramon shook his head. "I wouldn't tell her either. I'd say I'm dealing with it."

Jax figured he knew. "But you're still going to tell me."

"I don't trust her."

"Okay, not what I expected you to say." He'd figured this was about Ramon having feelings for Zeyla, and her rejecting him, or something like that. Or he was conflicted because she looked so much like Kenna. "You think she's going to betray us, or lie to us like Amara has been?"

"I always think everyone is going to betray us. It's why I'm still alive."

Jax was pretty sure that was from a movie but couldn't remember which one. "Do you have actual evidence or just a gut feeling?"

Ramon scratched his jaw.

Jax winced. "She seemed kind of hurt that I haven't talked to her. Maybe I should've made more of an effort, but she's always with her mom."

"If Zeyla wanted to get to know Kenna and any of us, she could've done that weeks ago. She's going to get mad about it now like that's her prerogative."

"Maybe she thought she had time, and when Kenna was taken, she realized the opportunity she'd lost." Jax shrugged. "I can certainly understand that."

Ramon glanced at him. "Do you have to be reasonable about it?"

"It's called empathy."

"I'm sure it's easier to feel other people's pain than your own. Because then you don't have to deal with your problems. You're just so worried about everyone else's."

Jax clapped a hand on the other man's shoulder. "Now he gets it."

Ramon almost laughed. "I'm gonna go check on Maizie's progress."

Jax had never thought he would come to appreciate Ramon's role in Kenna's life, but if this continued, they might actually wind up friends. The reality was, Ramon probably had feelings for Zeyla, but didn't know if he could trust her with what her mom had done—keeping from them the fact she knew that Kenna was alive.

And yes, Jax was pushing away his own feelings while focusing on others. If he didn't, he would end up spinning out. He'd find himself in over his head more than that extremely mild anxiety attack he'd had in the entryway. Kenna needed him focused, not fractured.

He had to hold it together.

Jax stepped into the drab office where Amara and Bruce stood watching Samuel, who had been secured to a simple wooden chair. Cords came out of the wall where equipment had been plugged in. A stack of boxes had been flattened and laid in a pile. Ceiling tiles lined the space above him, one of which was askew.

Samuel's chin hung on his chest, his breathing steady. He might be faking being unconscious, but Jax wasn't sure. Why fight his way out now when he could wait until there were less people around?

"Out." Jax motioned them to the door, and they stepped into the hall. He said, "Maizie is working with Elliot. You're going to give her access to every communication you have with these people so she can try and find Kenna with it. And no one leaves this building without me knowing." He glanced at Bruce, then looked at his watch. "We're having a team meeting at six."

"I'll call for dinner. Get something delivered."

Amara looked at Bruce. "You're onboard with this?"

"Cards on the table."

Amara didn't like that.

Jax said, "If we're going to find Kenna, it will be because we worked together."

He wanted to call Preston Lightwood for the additional resources, knowing he would come with Miami Security International—the men who had rescued them from Mexico. But those same people had also lied to Kenna, dropped a bomb of information on her about her mother, and somewhat helped her resolve the situation. He should warn the team that if things moved in the direction where he needed a tactical team, he wanted them on standby. After all, he figured they owed Kenna a favor.

How he would pay for their services, he had no idea. The only savings he had was the downpayment for the "forever home" he wanted to buy when he and Kenna had kids.

He didn't want to use it on...never mind. There would be no forever home if he didn't get her back. So he figured he could pull together the money if he needed it.

"If we get her back, it will be because we *talked* to each other and helped each other," Jax said. "Secrets get people killed. It's who these people are, pitting us against one another and undermining what we think we know. Hiding things from each other isn't going to get us a result." He leaned against the doorframe. "Unless you don't want her back. Maybe that's your plan. Keep her in there, so you have an 'in' with them. Is that your game?"

"You keep saying that." Amara started to walk away. "But you don't realize I'm not playing."

Bruce lifted his chin and followed her.

Jax watched them go, then stepped into the room and closed the door.

Samuel sat there staring at him, probably having

listened to that entire exchange. His suit was sweat stained and dirty. One shoe missing. His hair mussed. They hadn't given him clean clothes, and the smell had a tang.

Samuel lifted his chin. "Guess you've got this all figured out."

Of course, a CIA agent no doubt trained in interrogation tactics would try to spin this to catch Jax off guard. Or use a tactic that made Jax question his resolve.

Samuel continued, "I'm the ticket to all this. The way to get your wife back."

But this guy didn't know anything about him, and Jax wasn't going to explain. He stayed silent since Samuel had started talking. How long would he go before he stopped? Jax grabbed a chair and sat facing Samuel.

"You can do whatever you want to me," the guy said. "I'm not telling you anything."

Jax stretched his arms above his head and leaned back in the chair. "Then I guess there's nothing to say."

He wanted to ensure that *Dominatus* had made a mistake when they chose Amara to lean on. Maybe they simply believed they had more power over her, in order to coerce her into murdering on their behalf. She was a known component to them, where Jax simply had more integrity. That might have been why they didn't choose him.

But they misunderstood the resolve he had to clean house.

Jax stared at Samuel. "You're going to tell me everything you know."

Chapter Fifteen

"Bruce!"

Jax tried not to wince, still sitting in the same chair. This guy was loud, and he'd been yelling so long his voice was hoarse. Instead of sitting quietly and saying nothing, Samuel had decided to scream and taunt everyone in the building at the top of his lungs. For an hour so far.

"It worked because you made it easy!"

Jax looked at his phone and saw a new message from Bruce, which read,

> You aren't gonna break him.

Jax replied,

> Then why capture him?

Bruce wanted revenge. He wanted to bring down the man who had betrayed him and caused him to be burned by the CIA. Who wouldn't want to take down the person they'd trusted that stabbed them in the back? Of course, he made sure Samuel didn't get away from them.

"You're the chump who never realized!"

Bruce's reply said,

> He shouldn't get away with what he did.
> But if he's here then they don't have him.

Another message popped in.

> It's not just about me. He's ruining lives,
> aiding and abetting these people. He
> considered me expendable, so now I'm
> returning the favor.

Jax thought about that. Of course, if Samuel was supposed to check in with *Dominatus* or whoever he reported to, then being captured would cause problems for him. If the guy was meant to show up at a certain place at a certain time, they would've noticed he was missing and realized something had happened.

They might even believe he'd turned on them.

Returning the favor.

Jax let out a loud sigh. "You may as well save your breath, Chistane. You aren't going to goad Bruce into coming here."

"Did you know your friend *Bruce* killed three children in Singapore? He shot them in cold blood."

Jax wasn't going to react, because that was exactly what this guy wanted. "I'm sure it's a very interesting story." Samuel knew he was going down. If he could undermine their team on the way, that would be satisfying to him. "But to be honest, what are three children compared with everyone whose lives you've ruined?"

Samuel lifted his chin. "I don't know what you're talking about."

Jax just needed to wait out Maizie and whatever she and Elliot found on Samuel's phone when Bruce grabbed him, or what they discovered in the files Elliot had been working on. Until then, he didn't have specifics to question Samuel.

Jax sighed and said, "Sure you don't." Then tipped his head to the side. "And if I call the head of my taskforce, tell him I have an operative for *Dominatus* in my custody and he should send a team to pick you up...what do you think will happen then?"

Samuel smirked. "Nothing, because we're everywhere."

Jax didn't want to believe that the president's taskforce had been compromised, but it would explain why communication seemed to have shut down. "You realize that just means wherever we point our target, we'll hit one of you. So I guess we can't miss."

The smirk dissipated.

"Here. Overseas. Doesn't matter where we aim, right? Because you're everywhere."

"Walk away."

Jax said, "I might have been convinced to let it go. Live and let live, and all that. But *Dominatus* took my wife. Now there's nothing that will compel me to walk away. Not ever. Not until I find her."

Samuel stared at him, and the skin around his eyes flexed.

"This is where you offer to get her back for me, and in exchange my people and I leave your organization alone." Jax paused. "Unless you don't have the authority to do that, because you're just an underling. Like an errand boy."

Samuel's expression hardened, but he said nothing.

"Is Hadley above you in the hierarchy, or is there someone else I should be talking to?" Jax waited a beat, then stood like he was going to leave. "Seems like this has been a waste of my time." He tried to look disappointed.

"I'm not going to fall for it. Just to save face." Samuel paused. "You think I'll simper and try and convince you I'm someone important? We all play our role. Who I report to makes no difference."

"That and the fact you're all divided up into little sects that have no real authority on their own while one person, or a conclave, holds all the power."

A tendon in Samuel's jaw flexed.

"Kind of sad, isn't it? You're part of this huge organization changing the world, but you're just one of the expendable masses." Jax grasped the back of his chair and stared at Samuel. "At least with the CIA, you were important." He wandered to the door, antsy to stretch his legs and check on Maizie, then turned back. "I guess we'll find out how they feel about you when you don't show up, or check in."

He gave Samuel a second to respond, but the guy just glared at him.

Jax shut the door and glanced both ways down the hall. No one could see him.

He dragged in a breath, then tried to exhale all the fear he felt not knowing if he would ever see Kenna again. Or who she might be when he did get her back. *Dominatus* could have done anything to her.

He refused to believe the fabrication that she was having some kind of illicit relationship with Buzard—or whoever had been in that video Ramon's friend received. Or the implication of that bar owner, that she was trading in the worst kind of vices.

Zeyla had been right that this was psychological warfare. More and more ways to undermine them and cast doubt on what people knew about Kenna.

Two of the lawyers from Hann, Anthony & Associates rounded the corner. One he didn't know, and the other was a woman he'd seen before. The familiar one said, "We'll watch the door. Make sure he doesn't escape."

"Thanks." Jax nodded. "I won't be long. I just need to give him time to think about what's going to happen to him."

The woman he didn't know said, "Sure you don't want us to ask him some questions?"

"Maybe later." He headed for the room where he'd left Maizie and found Sandra handing out coffee, while Elliot and Maizie had their laptops side-by-side.

Four rectangular tables had been arranged in a square, nothing in the middle.

Thankfully, the FBI agent was years older than Maizie, so Jax didn't have to worry about her navigating a crush—or a romance—that might actually go somewhere while Kenna was gone. Jax was technically her dad by adoption, but that didn't mean he was ready for her to be dating.

Maybe he would never be ready.

"Anything new?" He went to the carafe, on a trio of cupboards with a Formica countertop. The smell of caffeine drifted up and filled his nose, which just made him think of Kenna. He turned and sipped the drink, leaning back against the edge of the counter.

"Actually, yes." Maizie looked up from her laptop. "There was this one company among the list of businesses Elliot was investigating. Most of what he had overlapped with the companies I know are connected to *Dominatus*. But he had a few different ones. Including a charter company, like for private flights."

Sandra stared at her quizzically, like she wasn't quite sure what to make of the teen.

Maizie continued, "Ramon and Zeyla went to check it

out in case they used one of their planes to transport Kenna out of the airport."

Jax managed to nod. "Good."

"Bruce and Amara are...I don't know where." She glanced at him, an interesting look on her face. Worried, nervous, and a bunch of other things. "They left a bit ago and didn't tell me what for."

"We have a team meeting later, so we can ask then."

Elliot and Sandra didn't need an earful of Maizie's hang-ups about romantic relationships. She saw healthy examples in the people around her, but Bruce and whatever he had going with Amara might be something else entirely.

At best it was an on-again, off-again or nonstarter thing. The worse might be something unhealthy. Jax would rather Maizie got used to relationships that honored the God he served. Seeing examples of serving others would help her move the needle on her expectations for the future.

Jax wanted Kenna back so they could model a healthy marriage and healthy parenting.

Elliot sat back in his chair, and Jax caught the expression on his face.

"What is it?"

"I can't stay here forever and keep living in this warehouse." Elliot took a sip of his coffee. "I've been in this limbo for weeks. Now that Sandra is here, too, I'm thinking about what's next. Amara said she would set us up with a new life as soon as Sandra came, but then she was asking me to help her. She never actually picked up Sandra."

"She never approached me at all," the sister said.

"We can arrange for protection to continue, assuming *Dominatus* will be looking for you." Jax wasn't sure what the threat level might be, but the lawyers surely had a longer-term solution for a place these two could live. Like a safehouse somewhere.

He could also call Preston, who had provided sanctuary for a young mother Kenna saved. Would he do that again?

Elliot started to shake his head. "What if I went back to the FBI, though? Confronted them with the reality of what happened. I was run off the road, and then I got kidnapped —which is technically true."

"Someone covered that up."

"So I force the issue. Get whoever it is knocked back a step, because I make them face the lie that I was transferred when I'm showing up at the office. I never transferred, and someone outside of the FBI forged the paperwork and changed the internal computer records to show I'm...wherever I'm supposed to be. They can't ignore the fact that I didn't disappear and that it was all fake—not that I'm going to say I know who did it."

Jax reached up and squeezed the back of his neck.

Elliot continued, "This was all a conspiracy to shove me out because of this case I was working. That means I'm onto something." He looked at Jax. "So why don't we go to the US Attorney's office and get them to take the case?"

"We have to assume that *Dominatus* has someone in that office, or a federal judge in their pocket." Jax set his coffee on the table nearest to him and stared across the open middle at the FBI agent. "I know you want your life back, but in my experience, once you get caught up with these people, they don't let it go."

He did have an idea that had been coalescing for a while now about where Elliot could go and keep fighting. After all, the more people who were in on this coordinated fight, the better. "I might have another job you can do," he added. "A way to be part of the group working against *Dominatus.*"

Jax got out his phone and sent a message on a secure app he'd been given access to for the taskforce. Things had been oddly quiet on it lately, but this news might bring a resurgence of efforts. "When I get a call back, I'll see what I can arrange so you can still do your job, but in a way that we're all working together to fight this."

Sandra didn't look happy. "So we're never going to get our lives back?"

Jax shook his head. "Not anytime soon."

Elliot reached over and squeezed his sister's hand. "This is important."

She whipped her head around and looked at him. "I think what you meant to say is, 'Your life wasn't that great anyway,' wasn't it? That's what you wanted to say."

"A fresh start can be a good thing."

She shifted her hand out of his grip and folded her arms. "Starting over *again?* Sure. That's always a great thing."

Elliot opened his mouth to say something but only sighed. "I didn't want to put you at risk. Amara explained to me that they used her daughter as leverage to get her to do things for them."

"She was supposed to kill you, but she didn't," Sandra said. "If you go back to the FBI, everyone will see that you aren't dead. What do you think will happen to the woman they care about who is missing when you do that?" She glared at her brother. "You never think about anyone else but yourself. You wanted me in your life, so you were going to have that Amara woman—who is scary, by the way—drag me from *my* life so you can have what you want. Because what I want is less important."

"Sis—"

"I was grieving you. Packing up your life and moving on with mine." Sandra pushed her chair back and stood. "I didn't ask to be part of this."

Jax said, "None of us did."

She turned to him and glared. "That actually makes it *worse*."

Jax held up his hands but said nothing.

"I'm so glad to see you." She looked at her brother. "*So* glad you're alive, and you're all right. But trying to fight a conspiracy? You could get yourself killed...just like Mom and Dad."

Maizie's fingers zipped across her keyboard. Jax could see the conversation was upsetting her. He needed a way for Sandra and Elliot to figure this out another time, preferably when the teen wasn't around.

Elliot said, "I'm not going to get—"

Maizie gasped. She looked at Jax. "Their parents died in a plane crash."

Jax said, "That's tragic. I'm so sorry for your loss, guys."

"No, you don't understand." Maizie shook her head. "The plane they were in was chartered by Escape, the airline company that changed its name a few years back to Emissary. The one *Dominatus* owns. Where Ramon and Zeyla went."

Jax understood the gasp now. "It was one of their planes."

The brother and sister absorbed this news. Elliot turned to Maizie. "You know for sure it was one of their planes?"

She nodded. "I'm sorry. I was just giving you guys some space to keep talking. I didn't mean to find a connection."

Jax went over and put his hand on her shoulder.

Elliot said, "We don't know that they were part of it, or

innocent bystanders who just happened to charter one of their planes. They could've been simply in the wrong place at the wrong time."

Jax nodded. "They might've chartered a flight, not knowing the company had ugly ties."

"But we're going to look into it, right?" Sandra stepped away from her brother, putting a visible separation between them. "Find out if they were murdered?"

"You might not like what you find if you dig," Jax warned her.

He'd had the same realization with his own parents, and the fact his father seemed to have a distant connection to *Dominatus*. Though, in his dad's case it was more like he'd made some kind of arrangement to stay out of their organization. Jax had tried several times to get his dad to explain the connection. His father hadn't wanted to, but he was definitely linked to the organization in some fashion.

Elliot looked at his sister. "It's up to you whether or not we look into their deaths. If you say leave it alone, I won't dig."

Sandra's face twisted with grief. "It was a long time ago. I don't remember them much more than you do. But I'd like to know who they really were if there's something to find. And what really happened to them."

Maizie said, "I'll send you what I find. I'm still working through the companies Elliot was investigating."

"Thank you, Maizie." Sandra went to the coffee station again and grabbed an apple from the fruit bowl someone had laid out. Several of the muffins had been taken.

"You're welcome." Maizie looked at Jax.

He raised his brows, and she smiled a little. "I need to check back on Samuel, but keep working. If we can get evidence that is undeniable, then we can pass that up the chain, along with the possibility of bringing Elliot on board." He glanced at Elliot. "The group I'm part of is all within the government, and each of the people who are part of it have no idea of the others' identities. So we can't tell anyone who they are because we don't know."

He wasn't sure how much of it was worth sharing. He hadn't heard from his contact in weeks, and it didn't seem that anyone else was submitting reports because he'd have been passed those as well.

Sandra said, "That sounds like what the bad guys are doing. What did you call them—*Dominatus*?" When he nodded, she continued, "Keeping everyone separated so no one person has the knowledge it would take to bring everyone down. How do you know you don't work for them?"

Kenna's people knew he'd made that deal with the president, but Jax wasn't about to say that to these two when he didn't know them all that well.

"I know." Jax lifted his chin. "I have evidence."

Sandra didn't seem impressed by that. Elliot was back on his laptop.

The sister said, "It's a real shame they chose to do it that way, keeping you all separate. Because that means you know nothing. So I don't need you."

Jax turned to her, his brows tugging together. "What do you—"

She swung out toward him with a knife. Jax lifted his arm to defend himself, and the blade glanced off his forearm before he slammed her arm away. He cried out at the sting of pain from the cut, and the surprise. Sandra stumbled back but rallied.

Maizie screamed, and he heard a chair topple back. "Bruce!" She yelled his name so loud it rang in the room.

Jax didn't go to her. He had to neutralize the threat. Hopefully the first and only one. He spun Sandra and locked his arms around her, his fingers squeezing her wrist and confining the bones in her hand until she voluntarily gave up the knife. Or dropped it. He spoke between gritted teeth, aware of the blood dripping down his forearm. "Don't even think about it."

Sandra screamed, pushing against his hold on her. She slammed her head back and caught his bad shoulder, which hurt a whole lot, then tried again to headbutt him.

Jax didn't let go.

The door slammed open.

"Maizie!" Bruce rushed in, and Jax turned Sandra to see the other man had his gun drawn. He pointed it at all corners, then at Elliot.

The agent raised his hands. "I have nothing to do with this. Sandra, what are you doing?" He turned to his sister. "What is going on?"

"I'm doing my job." She wrestled in his arms.

"Drop the knife," Jax barked.

"I figured the target would be Samuel, but maybe he was your next target. *Sandra*." Amara came around the table and stood in front of them. "I'll take care of her."

Jax didn't like the sound of that.

"We need to know what she knows," Amara said. "And who is giving her orders."

Sandra shuddered. "You'll never end this. We will kill everyone you love."

Elliot cried out, "Sandra, why are you *doing* this?"

Jax glanced at Maizie, who stood in the corner with her back to the wall, then looked back at Amara. The older woman had a kitchen towel in her hands. She wrapped it around Sandra's hand and the knife, covering the blade so Sandra couldn't easily stab someone with it.

"Nice-looking blade," Amara said. "Let go of the knife. No sudden movements, okay?"

Sandra shifted against Jax's arms, still determined to get away. He wasn't letting an agent of their enemy go. She'd waited until now to expose her true allegiance, and given the way he was reacting, Elliot had no idea his sister was one of them.

She'd come here to find out what Jax knew, and who was part of the group trying to fight against them.

No matter what, no one could find out what he knew.

Chapter Sixteen

Amara glared at Sandra. "How long have you been working for *Dominatus?*"

Jax needed something he could use to secure Sandra so that he could let go of her, but she still hadn't dropped the knife. Amara held on to the towel, ready to grab the blade as soon as Sandra let go. No one else was going to get cut.

A gunshot exploded down the hall.

Jax twisted Sandra around and slammed her onto the table before she could react. The knife out to one side. To Amara he said, "Watch her."

Amara shoved against Sandra, holding her down. "Go."

Jax raced for the door, reaching out to Maizie with one hand. "Stay behind me."

She grabbed his hand and ran with him. Jax drew his gun from the holster at the small of his back, unwilling to leave Maizie with people he didn't trust. Even if that meant putting her in danger going with him, and yes, even if Bruce had been back there. Amara and Bruce had their hands full with Elliot and Sandra.

They were all already in danger, no matter where Maizie was.

Jax ran toward the room where they'd been holding Samuel Chistane and spotted one of the lawyers who'd been watching the door. On the ground in a pool of blood. Another two gunshots echoed from inside the room, the muffled pop of a suppressor, and he saw muzzle flash through the open door.

He slammed his shoulder into the wall just before the door.

Maizie let go of his hand.

Jax looked in the room.

The second lawyer who'd been standing guard lay on the ground, blood on her chest. Another woman he'd never seen before clutched her shoulder and squared her aim on Samuel. She'd killed two so far, and anyone else who'd come across her before she made it this far.

"FBI!" That part was a reflex, but he couldn't let her kill Samuel. "Put the gun down!"

The bound man stared at her, wide-eyed and breathing hard.

Jax said, "Don't—"

She squeezed the trigger, and Samuel toppled back, along with the chair, a bullet hole in his chest. Jax fired as well, hitting her in the head.

She crumpled to the ground, dead before she hit the floor.

"It's clear," he said to Maizie. He rushed over to Samuel and touched two fingers to his throat.

The young woman said, "That's a lot of blood."

Jax tried to recall where his phone was. "We need EMT—"

Samuel nearly pulled Jax down on top of him by grabbing him by the arm.

Jax's hand landed in the blood-soaked shirt on Samuel's front, and the guy groaned. "Sorry. Hang on. We're gonna get someone to help you."

Samuel shook his head. "Don't bother."

Maizie knelt on the other side, tears in her eyes.

Jax said, "You don't have to die."

Samuel tried to speak again but was forced to cough. Blood appeared at the corners of his mouth.

"Easy." Jax had to ask, "Where is my wife?"

Samuel coughed again, groaning from the pain.

"Where is she? Tell me."

The grip on Jax's arm slacked, and his chest rattled with the next breath. Samuel said, "Offshore," and the life left his eyes. His head tipped to the side and his hand fell away from Jax's arm.

"What on earth?"

Jax looked over at the door and saw Ramon there. Zeyla peered over his shoulder. She ducked away and disappeared down the hall. Ramon said, "We just got back from the charter company. What happened?"

"One of the *Dominatus* operatives came in. Four dead, including her."

Maizie turned to Ramon. "Sandra is one, too. She had a knife."

Jax remembered that Elliot's sister had cut him with that blade and lifted his arm. It stung when he moved his hand toward him and looked down the edge of his forearm. "Ow."

"You just realized it hurts?" Maizie frowned.

"Adrenaline." He rocked on the balls of his feet and stood. "Let's get out of this room. We need to call..." He cut himself off, unsure that informing the police of what had happened was the best idea. At least not until they were safely away from the scene.

Ramon held out his hand for Maizie and helped her stand.

She shook her head. "Two operatives? This one, and Sandra? Why would they need both of them?"

"They'd have had different assignments." Jax holstered his gun and searched the killer's pockets, finding no ID or phone—not even some cash for just in case. Though, maybe it was in her shoe. She wore no jewelry, and her sneakers were nearly brand-new. Neither had anything interesting in them.

He left the gun she held where it had landed on the floor, so that it could be matched to ballistics. The round he had fired into her would come back as registered to his personal weapon. At that point everyone would know it was Jax who had killed her.

"Let's get out of here."

Maizie nodded.

"You good, Maze?" He had no idea if she'd ever seen a dead body up close, but she seemed to be dealing with the scene like a champ.

"I'm good." She blew out a breath through pursed lips.

Ramon slung his arm around her shoulder. "Even if she isn't, she's got us."

Not what he'd thought Ramon was going to say. It was better. "Agreed. Though, don't worry if it hits you later."

Ramon said, "Yeah, if you're crying in the shower...just know you're not the only one, yeah?"

Jax glanced at the guy, not sure what to make of that. He led the way back to the other room. Zeyla stood by

Bruce, who sat in a chair gingerly touching a knot on his head. Bruce said, "Elliot ran off."

As Jax entered the room, Amara straightened to stand. She had the knife in her hand and not one ounce of remorse on her face. "She gave me no choice."

Sandra lay on the floor, blood on her neck.

"Is that when Elliot split?" Jax glanced between Amara and Bruce.

Amara looked at Bruce, and he said, "He got the drop on me and made a run for it."

"Seems like there's a lot of that going on today." Part of it was because of him, and Sandra's reaction to his not knowing who else was in the group the president oversaw. Maybe she didn't even know the president was part of it.

He explained what had happened in the other room, leaving out the last thing Samuel had said. He needed to figure out what "offshore" meant, and if it was at all relevant to the search for Kenna.

Amara shook her head. "Two of them?"

"Different missions." Jax glanced at the dead woman in the room. "We need to clear out."

Not only because Maizie didn't need to be in here with a dead woman. They also needed to figure out what they were going to do next.

Amara stepped away from the dead body. "Great, I'll—"

"Maizie and I are leaving." Jax wasn't sure about the rest of them. In fact, he turned to Bruce. "I don't know you." He looked at Amara. "I trust you even less." He waved at her daughter. "Even Ramon doesn't trust Zeyla, and I barely trust Ramon."

Ramon said, "Fair. But I'm coming with you guys."

Maizie sniffed.

"So you're leaving?" Amara lifted her chin.

"If you want to help, I can let you know when we need backup or more bodies for an op. But you're not part of this." He motioned to himself, and Maizie—and yeah, Ramon as well. "Because you should've told me the minute you heard that Kenna was alive."

Now they had everything from her that had been sent. All the information they'd need to try and track down what they could find.

It was time to get gone.

Maizie swiped up her laptop and Elliot's, wiping her cheeks with her fingers. Apparently, Elliot had neglected to take the laptop with him when he ran off. Though, it looked like that might be what he had used to hit Bruce over the head.

Ramon held the door, and they went out to the car. He and Jax shared a look about Maizie, and when she'd closed the back door of the car, Jax said quietly, "Maybe it just caught up to her."

Ramon nodded, but didn't look convinced. "Seemed like it was more to do with Amara not telling you about Kenna."

Jax's hand shook so badly it was hard to start the vehicle, but he got it running.

From the back seat, Maizie put her hand on his shoulder. "Are you okay?"

He gripped the wheel. *I'll be okay when I get her back.* "We did the right thing, leaving them. Right?"

"I can drive," Ramon offered. His voice was low, maybe even gentle.

Because he knew what Jax was going through. All of them did. It wasn't about who cared for Kenna more than everyone else. They all needed her back.

Jax squeezed his eyes shut. "I'm good."

"First time you killed someone?"

Jax opened his eyes and shook his head.

"I didn't think so."

"It's just...a lot right now."

Ramon said, "We know she's alive."

Deciding that Ramon should drive, Jax looked at Ramon and cocked his head, then got out and switched seats with the guy. In the passenger side, he turned so he could see Maizie. Ramon pulled out fast, and Jax buckled his seatbelt.

She reached for her laptop. "I'm going to use what was sent to Amara to find her. I'm done being too scared to do everything I can to find her."

"I don't want you thinking this is all riding on you, Maze." Jax paused. "You have amazing skills. You can do things the rest of us don't even have the first clue how to do. But finding her isn't solely your responsibility, okay?"

She stared at him, her laptop open on her knees.

"I don't want you to get crushed under the pressure of thinking you're the one responsible for finding Kenna."

"I want to find her. If I can do it, I *will*."

He knew that look in her eyes, because he saw it when he looked in the mirror—grief and the weight of responsibility. "I know."

He twisted back to face the front, closing his eyes and leaning his head back on the seat. First, he'd thought it was the FBI who would help him find her. But given the evidence of Special Agent Herron being blackmailed, and Hadley taking over Jax's job, they only wanted to believe the story that Kenna had run off. As if she *had* turned dark side—and, if that video was to be believed, she was having a relationship with someone else. As if Jax had been somehow holding her back.

Staying at the FBI, trying to keep his job, had felt more like fighting the battle solo, without their backing. He'd been on his own, or working with Maizie. She was the one who'd been his ally this whole time, but with her being *his* responsibility, he couldn't lean on her as an equal. Doing that wouldn't be fair to her.

Now that he'd walked away from the FBI, he almost felt as if he had more support. Add the fact there had been more movement on the case in the past day than in weeks, he didn't know if he should feel reassured or not.

Things seemed to be unraveling rather than progressing toward solving the case.

Ramon glanced over his shoulder. "Any way to track down Elliot?"

Jax met his gaze. "You think he knows more than he was letting on?"

Ramon shrugged.

Maizie looked up. "I have his laptop, so I can set up an alert. And if he logs onto any of his apps or accounts from another device, I'll know about it. Do we need to find him?"

"He could be in danger," Jax said. "But I'm not wasting time looking for him if he's on the run, keeping a low profile." He winced, thinking of how Elliot could implicate Jax in crimes that would get him fired—if not put in jail. But catching the guy and shutting him down just to keep the truth buried wasn't the right course of action.

Ramon said, "Where to, Maze?"

"The RV?"

Jax nodded. "The RV." He tapped the dash screen so it would direct Ramon back to Jax's townhouse, since they were thirty minutes away in a different suburb of Phoenix.

The midday sun beat down on the windshield, and the window beside him radiated with warmth.

He shut his eyes against the glare when what he wanted to do was look at those pictures of Kenna again. It wasn't going to help. In fact, it might make things worse to keep wondering what was happening to her. The implication of a photo of her in a hospital bed.

He wanted to pray, but the words wouldn't come.

What could God possibly be doing through this? Jax thought he'd had the solution all figured out, relying on the Bureau to provide the resources to gain him success. Now he had to do the same with Kenna's team—the people she considered family.

Jax had always thought that him not being an FBI agent wasn't going to be the best version of himself. That would be the version with no boundaries, just his own integrity. He'd proven in high school—by lying to himself and everyone else and hiding the pills he'd been taking—that he lacked the honor it took to be someone people counted on. Fear had held him back from walking away from his job and joining Kenna on hers.

Fear, and the expectations others had always put on him to be a self-sufficient guy who took care of his family. But now that he'd lost what really counted, he wondered why he'd put so much stock in doing what he thought he "should." It had taken losing Kenna to realize what really mattered, and it wasn't being an FBI agent so he could feel good about himself.

Ramon pulled the car into the garage, beside the RV bay. Maizie jumped out and went ahead of him, into the RV. He set up the coffee pot, needing more than anything right now to feel close to her.

Jolene wandered down the linoleum from the bedroom,

where Maizie sat on the edge of the bed, typing on her laptop. The cat wound herself around one of his ankles, between his feet and around the other leg, leaving cat hair on the ends of his pants.

Stuck in the blood on his pants.

Jax looked at his hands and realized they, too, were stained with blood from Samuel, and the operative he'd killed and searched. That, and the cut on the side of his forearm. He strode out of the RV and through the laundry room door into his house, then up the stairs and through the bedroom.

He didn't look at the bed.

Jax stripped off and took a shower, the water extra hot. Trying to cleanse off the grime of everything happening right now so he could get some clarity.

The knife wound on the edge of his arm stung.

Blood dripped onto the tile between his feet and washed away down the drain. But in the end, he emerged from the shower the same man he'd been when he went in. The same guy who considered the FBI to be the height of integrity, even despite the actions of some agents. There were bad seeds in every organization, no matter how pure and upright it was meant to be. He was the same man he'd always been now that he was on suspension, working with mavericks to solve this case.

The addict.

The guy who'd beat the addiction to get clean and stayed that way so long as it was in his power to do so.

All of it was him, no matter what he did or said. Or the ways that he succeeded or failed. Jax would always be the person God had made uniquely to do the things He'd set before him.

To find Kenna—a woman who spent her life on saving others. To always be the one who showed up to save her when she needed it.

For better or worse.

Chapter Seventeen

Jax took his cup of coffee and sat across from Ramon, even though the little dinette in the RV wasn't really big enough for two grown men. "What happened at the charter plane company?"

Ramon and Zeyla had been out getting intel, trying to find details of a flight that might have taken Kenna out of Arizona.

The word *offshore* rolled around in his mind. Samuel's last word.

But what had the guy been trying to tell him? Maybe with all the information about financial companies, the way to find Kenna was through a bank account, following a money trail. Jax didn't know how that could be true, but it was worth a try. He needed to run the idea past Maizie and see what she thought, but they were waiting for her to tell them what she'd come up with once she'd finished compiling everything.

Ramon glanced at Maizie, still on her computer, then said, "They have a hangar—or they had one—at that municipal airport. Someone took the sign down, probably the same person who cleared everything out and packed up."

"They're gone?"

Ramon nodded. "Empty hangar, empty ready room—even the fridge was bare. Cupboards and drawers open. We found a newspaper from a few months ago, just the sports section though, and a flyer for an event happening at the airport." He sipped his coffee. "Nothing we can use."

Jax wanted to believe they'd gained leads in the last day or so, but with this—and the fact they might not get anything from pictures of Kenna sent from an untraceable account—he might have to accept they had nothing else.

Ramon continued, "Spoke with the guys in the neighboring hangar, hobby fliers who hang out there when they're not working and fly for fun. They said they never spoke to the outfit when they saw them—and it wasn't often. Might amount to different schedules, or there might never have been much in that hangar. Except maybe a plane waiting to take Kenna away."

Jax cleared his throat. "What about flight records?"

"You're assuming they filed accurate flight plans, and they were going farther out than just local jaunts. Which is unlikely. But do you really think they're being truthful?"

Jax sighed into his coffee, taking a sip. The coffee Kenna made was better than this. "I guess not. It's just frustrating."

"More frustrating than Amara communicating with the people holding Kenna and not telling us?"

Jax's stomach clenched. "No, probably not." He set his mug down too hard. "They're using Kenna, using Amara. No care for who they hurt in the process. Just destroying lives. And for what?"

Maizie had faced a similar situation. Ramon as well. Now Kenna?

Jax could argue Bruce had also been a pawn of someone with their own selfish ends. "Should we have brought Bruce?"

Ramon shook his head. "He likes to play both sides. See what he can find out."

"How do we know he's on the level?"

"The guy was a spy." Ramon shrugged. "Are they ever on the level?"

"We need to know if we can trust him."

"Kenna trusted him. Maybe not as much as us." Ramon gestured to Maizie and himself. "But she counted on Bruce."

"So I should've told him to come with us?"

"I'd have done what you did," Ramon said. "And this way, Bruce can feed us back intel from Amara and Zeyla. Now he knows Amara has been getting communication from the people holding Kenna, and he's doubling down on that side, finding out what they know. He'll dig, and Amara won't even realize it. And if we need him, he'll drop everything and come to us. He's solid."

Jax nodded. "Okay, then."

Maizie came through the divider between the bedroom and the rest of the RV, holding her laptop. "Okay, I have something you need to hear."

Jax shifted so his back was to the side of the seat and he could face her. She put the laptop on the end of the counter and grabbed a soda from the fridge, popping the top.

"Okay." She sighed and the guarded expression on her face registered.

He said, "We aren't going to like this."

"I'll backtrack and go over it all from the beginning, but it connects to your family, Jax." She waited, likely to see his reaction.

Jax kept his voice gentle when he said, "Kenna is my family."

Maizie nodded, scrunching up her nose a bit. "While looking through the investigation Elliot was working, I found a picture of a hospital ribbon-cutting ceremony that made the papers. Two years ago. The wing was named after the largest donor, which was your father. The Edward Russell Jaxton Wing of the Aspen Valley Medical Center in Flagstaff. It's a private hospital Elliot was looking into because their financials connect to other *Dominatus* investment companies. He didn't know it was them, but he made the connection."

She turned her laptop so he could see the screen, a ribbon-cutting ceremony that seemed to have been broadcast on local news given the lettering around the screen and across the bottom. "As you can see, Doctor Marcus Buzard was present at the event, and standing beside him is your dad."

"We knew he had connections." Ramon kept a measured tone to his voice. "After Colorado we theorized there was some kind of deal, but if he was all-in with *Dominatus*, you would know."

Jax glanced at the guy. "Like Elliot knew his sister worked for them? They were closer than I am to my dad." He looked at Maizie. "Any reason we should go there and look around?"

"Yeah, I need physical access to get into their system and download their files."

"Looks like we're going on a road trip." Ramon sucked down the last of his coffee and set the mug in the sink.

Jax wasn't so quick to get up, so Maizie brought her laptop over and sat in the seat where Ramon had been. "I'm sorry," she said. "If your dad is connected to this…I'm just sorry. About a lot of things, it turns out."

He touched her hand for a second. "Thanks, Maze." On her screen now was a series of open documents. "I think I'm going to call and ask about the agreement he made with them. Maybe for once in my life my father will give me a straight answer."

"You've asked him before?" Ramon rested the side of his hip against the counter with his arms crossed. "About *Dominatus*?"

Jax nodded. "When he showed up in Colorado, I tried to get him to tell me what agreement he had that made my mother and my sister off-limits, but then they were kidnapped anyway. I figured there was something he didn't want to do, and they were taken as leverage."

Maizie frowned. "I thought they were kidnapped because of Kenna's thing?"

"I wondered about that as well. But it seemed like there was far too much he wasn't saying." Jax ran his hands through his hair. "I'll call him, then we can go."

She nodded. "I'll keep working until you're ready."

Part of him needed to rush to that hospital and find out if Kenna had ever been there. She might even be there now. The whole airport lead might have simply been a smokescreen—or a plane had taken her to Flagstaff. Jax needed information, and the closest place he could get it was from his father.

He had to show his father the photo. Marcus Buzard standing beside his father, both cutting a wide red ribbon with a pair of ridiculously oversize scissors.

Jax left the laptop and went into the garage, calling his father's number while he paced the concrete floor. Too much of the house reminded him of Kenna. Enjoying it alone, or even thinking of her there, would seem like too much of a betrayal.

The phone rang, giving him something to focus on. A way to get answers about his family connection to their enemy.

He didn't want to believe his dad had something to do with *Dominatus*, but there was far too much evidence not to ask.

"Oliver?"

"Mom?" He quit pacing. "Why are you answering Dad's phone? Is everything okay?"

His mother's voice had been shaking when she answered the phone. Now a dog barked in the background.

"Mom?"

A shuffle came over the line, and then a woman said, "Jax? It's Elizabeth Stairns."

That meant the dog barking had been Cabot, since Kenna's dog had gone with Craig and Elizabeth when they dropped Maizie in Phoenix and went to California to watch out for his family.

"What's going on, Elizabeth?"

A pause. "Your mother called me a little while ago to come over."

In the background he heard his mom's raised voice. "He's never done this before!" She sounded distressed.

Jax's breath quickened.

Elizabeth said, "Your father left in a hurry. He packed a few things, but didn't take his phone. It was on the sideboard in the front hallway."

"He took his wallet?"

"Yes, I believe so."

"And we're sure he packed his things and left?" Jax put

the phone on speaker. "Is there any way he could've been taken?"

He sent a text on the group thread between him, his sister Laney, and Elizabeth's husband, Craig Stairns, to give them the rundown. He figured Stairns could investigate where Jax's father had gone while Laney supported their mother. Even if Elizabeth was a trained counselor, he wanted his mom to have someone with her.

"I'm still asking those questions," Elizabeth said. "As soon as I know, I'll fill you in."

"Thank you."

Before he could ask, she said, "Adrielle, would you like to speak to your son again?"

Jax heard his mom answer, then she spoke into the phone. "Why would he do this?"

"I don't know, Mom." Jax tried to be reassuring. "What did he say the last time you spoke to him? How did he seem?"

"We had breakfast like always. He was on his iPad, and I was reading a nice devotional Laney gave to me." She took a breathy pause. "Are you going to come here?"

"It will take me a day to get there, but if I need to, I will."

He was hoping his father had simply gone on a work trip and neglected to inform his mom. Was that possible? Or some other meeting. He could have decided to clean out part of his closet and donate the clothes.

"You also may want to think about calling in local police or FBI if something has happened to him," Jax added. "Did he take his car?"

"Yes, of course."

"Does it have any kind of GPS in it? Like the breakdown service where it calls the dispatcher if you get in a crash?"

Adrielle said, "I don't think so."

He couldn't think of another way to figure out where his father had gone. "Did he get a call, a visitor, or some other kind of communication that he might've reacted to by leaving? Maybe something that upset him."

"I was in the garden pruning my rosebushes. I didn't even hear him leave. I tried to call him, and his phone was in the front hall. Elizabeth was already here." She paused. "I think her husband just arrived."

"That's good." Jax noticed Maizie had come out of the RV. "Mom, I need to ask you some questions."

"About your father?"

"Sort of." He squeezed the bridge of his nose. "Do you know anything about a hospital wing in Flagstaff that's named after him? I found a photo of the ribbon-cutting ceremony, and he was there." With the doctor who had altered Kenna's physiology months ago.

"I suppose. We give to a lot of organizations. Hospitals and nonprofits. There might be one in Flagstaff. Why are you asking?"

"It might be connected to Kenna's disappearance."

"Do you think that's what happened to your father?" she asked. "Maybe they took him like they took Kenna, and tried to make it look like he ran off."

"I don't know, Mom, but we'll find out. Okay?"

She sighed. "Okay."

"I have another question." He asked her about the airline that Ramon and Zeyla had checked out and if she knew the name. "Maybe you and Dad fly with them?"

"Of course. We have the platinum membership card, but I'm not sure your father has been happy with the service lately. We're going to Key West in October, and I don't think he's going to book us with them."

"Thanks, Mom. Let me know if you need anything. And have Stairns call me with an update."

"Okay, darling." The call ended.

Jax lowered the phone. Maizie stepped out of the RV with her backpack on her shoulders, Ramon behind her. Something she didn't allow with anyone outside the people in this garage.

He explained to them what was happening in California, at his parents' house. "I'll go if there's any indication me being there will help."

Ramon nodded. "It's no use going there if you'll just end up sitting around having to be supportive."

Jax wouldn't have put it like that, but it was the same thing.

Maizie said, "We need to check out the hospital. The wing is under renovation, so no one's in there."

Ramon stepped down out of the RV and headed for the passenger door before Maizie got there. "Apparently they had a problem with the HVAC, and no one can be in there."

Jax frowned. "So they cleared out a whole wing of the hospital to fix it?"

Ramon slid into the passenger seat, and Jax drove the three of them to the Aspen Valley Medical Center in Flagstaff. The drive took a couple of hours, so he called Stairns after a while for an update.

It looked like his father had packed an overnight bag and left in a hurry, leaving his phone behind. Stairns's next stop was to check with Jax's father's personal assistant to find out if she knew what might be happening.

Jax said, "Thank you."

"You're welcome to come and help, but I've got this if you're working."

A lot went unsaid in that comment, and Jax appreciated the nonchalant way Stairns worded that—without making him feel guilty about staying in Arizona trying to find Kenna.

After they'd gone over all of it, Jax realized it was time to exit the freeway. "We're a couple of minutes from the hospital."

"I'll let you go, then," Stairns said. "Update after."

"Sounds good." Jax tapped the dash screen.

He didn't want to wonder how Stairns had kept him talking for the purpose of distracting him. Allowing Jax something to focus on so that he didn't continue in the thought spiral that had him spinning down into...he didn't want to think about where that ended up.

Not when his arm stung from the knife injury and he could use a little of that oblivion right now.

Jax pulled the car into the parking lot and found a space. Ramon looked up from his phone, and Maizie closed her laptop.

He glanced at both of them, more than grateful he didn't have to do this on his own. "Let's go."

Chapter Eighteen

"I'm good here." Maizie settled at a small round table for two with her laptop, her backpack on the second chair. Good way to keep someone from sitting there in this busy hospital lobby with a wall of glass windows, arched ceilings, and a fancy coffee bar on one side.

"I don't like leaving you." Jax crouched by her chair.

She tipped her head toward him, an expression he wasn't sure about in her eyes. "You need to look for her, and I can wait here and work while you do it."

He wasn't sure if that put her in harm's way or kept her out of it. "I should've called Bruce."

Ramon moved to stand behind the backpack, where he'd have a view of the door. "He's grilling Amara on what she knows about Kenna. Sounds like it's a real knock-down, drag-out fight." He focused on the entrance, and when Jax looked at him, he lifted his chin.

Jax glanced at the front doors of the hospital and saw Zeyla heading toward them.

Ramon said, "She wants to find Kenna as badly as we do."

Maizie glanced over her shoulder, some wariness on her face. But not fear.

"Are you good with her hanging with you?" Jax asked.

Maizie whispered, "She looks like she wants to kill someone, but she's on our side."

"That's who I want protecting you." He touched her shoulder. "But only if that's what you want."

Zeyla strode up to them, her dark hair in two Viking braids hanging over her shoulders. She wore wide-leg black pants and a white cropped T-shirt that revealed a belly button ring. Boots on her feet.

He figured she wore no other jewelry because it could get ripped off in a fight.

"Thanks for coming." Jax straightened.

Zeyla cocked a hip. "Even though you had no idea I would be here? Seems like there's a lot of that going around." She rolled her eyes. "For the record, my mom said she told you about the texts. I can't believe she didn't. I thought you knew. I'm sorry."

"Thank you for letting me know." Jax glanced at Maizie and saw more of that odd look. "What is it, Maze?"

She shook her head. "I want to say, but I can't."

Zeyla dragged over a chair from another table and sat with Maizie. "Being here is better than listening to Mom and Bruce arguing. We can get a latte and get to know each other."

Now that was a scary proposition.

"I have work to do," Maizie said. "We can get to know each other later—like, after Kenna has been found." The confidence in Maizie's voice made him smile. She looked at him. "Can you grab the comms from the side pocket of my backpack?"

Ramon was the one who dug in there and tossed them

to him. Jax handed them out, grudgingly giving one to Zeyla as well.

Maizie clicked the mouse on her laptop. "Check?"

Jax nodded. "I copy you." But he didn't walk away. "You're good?"

"I'm good." She looked like she wanted to say more, but the quicker they got this done, the sooner they could get back to the RV.

As he and Ramon strode to the elevator, Jax said, "I'm leaning more and more toward the way Kenna is with her RV."

"Feel like hitting the road and becoming a freelance investigator?"

"No one gets the deal Kenna got with private investigator licenses."

Ramon hit the button to go up. "I don't have any. She's got a dozen or whatever. Doesn't make any difference to us."

"I think I just want to hide. Or ignore all the bad in the world." With her there, too, of course.

They'd spent their honeymoon in the RV, making their way from Colorado back to Phoenix. Over those couple of weeks, they'd stopped in a few places and burned all his vacation days looking at Zion National Park and the Grand Canyon. Their troubles hadn't been over—fighting *Dominatus* wasn't just a one-time thing, it was an ongoing case. But the trip had been a reprieve from their lives.

Jax sighed. "Or we could just drive with no destination in mind."

"You're looking for peace." The doors opened, and Ramon stepped in. "We all are."

Jax stepped in behind him. "Have you found it?"

"Don't start talking to me about Jesus. I've heard it." Ramon leaned against the wall of the elevator.

"So what's your hangup?"

"A million tiny things I don't have answers for because there are none."

When the doors opened, they stepped out. There was a breezeway between the main building and the wing named after Jax's father. A few pieces of trash and a newspaper had piled on the concrete up against the wall.

Jax looked around. "Different out here than in the hospital."

"I was getting fancy private hospital vibes back in there, but this is more inner city." Ramon grabbed the handle for the Edward Russell Jaxton wing, but the door stuck. "Huh." He drew a lock pick kit from his pocket. "Maybe you should look away."

"Don't worry about it."

"And if I don't want an FBI agent watching me commit a crime?"

Jax turned away. "Fine."

Back on the other end of the breezeway, through the small porthole door, he saw a woman walk by and glance at them. Dark hair. He didn't get a good enough look at her face to know if he'd seen her before.

"We're in." Ramon hauled the door open, and they stepped through.

Jax frowned at the state of disarray. "Wasn't there a ribbon-cutting ceremony two years ago? Looks like this place was never finished."

"They did a tour of the first couple of floors, but not the rest. It was still being worked on so they could expand later."

"So we might be in the unused portion of the hospital?" Jax paused. "We should've gone in downstairs."

"It's boarded up. Locked up tight with guards and everything. This is the only way in."

Ceiling tiles lay discarded on the floor. Wires and metal piping for HVAC hung down below the ceiling. Plastic sheeting had been put up to cover the exposed walls but now hung down from the corners and flapped in some unseen breeze from the air current.

"Split up?" Ramon glanced over.

"Sure. Stay on comms and meet at the elevators."

"Got it." Ramon headed off in the other direction.

Jax set off down the hall. "Maizie, you copy?"

"I copy."

"So do I," Zeyla said. "This latte isn't good. And it cost me seven dollars."

Jax turned a corner and found a hall of what had to be treatment rooms. "Any success getting into their computer system?"

"They have a whole lot of things behind a firewall," Maizie explained. "The hospital itself has all their stuff in a database, but there's a ton more data that I can't see. So it has to be hidden from me. I'll get into it."

"Sounds promising." Also like she was trying to prove herself and going overboard with it.

One hand on his gun, he opened the first door he came to. A hospital bed with no sheets. It could be where the photo of Kenna had been taken, but there was literally no way to tell. Nothing had been left behind but the basics, the bed linens in a pile on the floor with a pillow.

He left that room and tried one across the hall that was empty.

Jax told Maizie, "If you can't access it, that's not a problem."

"We need to find out what they know," she replied. "What information they're hiding."

"Okay, but even if we don't succeed here, it was still worth coming. We're all feeling the pressure on this one, and I don't want you to feel like it's your fault if we don't get a result."

Silence was the only response.

Then Maizie said, "We'll see what I get."

Jax figured there was more to say, but he was searching and she was working. He needed to make sure Maizie didn't feel the weight of Kenna being missing with any sense of guilt for the fact they hadn't found her yet. The only people responsible were those who had taken her. And if—when—Jax got her back, he would see that justice was done.

He spotted Ramon at the end of the hall. The tall Hispanic man shook his head. Jax stepped into another empty room where a machine had been set up, one that had a monitor and a keyboard on a cart, and a wand in a holder beside the keyboard.

Some kind of radiology machine, or an ultrasound maybe?

He looked at the bed. An ultrasound. *Kenna.* Jax sucked in a breath. "Makes sense why they took her now and not before."

"What's that?" Ramon stopped by the door.

Jax didn't want to say it. The idea had barely formed in his mind. "If Kenna is pregnant—or they want to get her pregnant—that might be why they wanted her now."

Ramon kept his voice low. "Is this what you wanna talk about?"

"Of course not." Jax went over to see what he'd noticed on the floor and crouched to pick up the dark scrap of paper.

An image of a tiny person, barely bigger than a peanut.

His eyes burned. "They've had her for two months. They could have done anything to her. She could be anywhere. Suffering. Tortured. Experimented on."

Maizie said, "Jax," her voice strained.

"She could be pregnant." Jax blew out a long breath.

"I have their files," she said. "I'm in the records. If they treated her, I can find out."

Zeyla said, "I'll help her. You guys keep searching."

Jax stood, unable to take his eyes off the image. It was probably not even Kenna who had been seen here. This could be a picture of anyone's child.

Just because he happened to find it didn't mean it was his. Or his wife's.

Dominatus regularly took women and impregnated them. That was where Kenna had come from, a product of their genetic experimentation. They'd want to use her to continue their research and further their agenda. If they wanted it, he would never find her. Never get her back.

That was simply how powerful they were. Nothing Jax could do on his own would bring them down, not with a lifetime of trying.

He slipped the ultrasound in his pocket, knowing what he was fighting for.

His family.

Ramon stepped out, his demeanor switching in a split second. He drew his gun. "Hey!"

Jax rushed out of the room, his gun out. He spotted an older man at the end of the hall. "Four! Do not move."

The older man, wearing coveralls so he looked like a repair guy, didn't move. He stood straight, but with no tension in his body language. Hands up, palms facing them.

"He was coming toward us," Ramon said. "Trying to catch us by surprise."

Four's expression shifted, and he almost rolled his eyes. "I'm not here to kill you."

"And if we're here to kill *you*?" Ramon stalked forward, grabbed Four, and shoved him up against the wall. "Anything in your pockets I should know about?"

"Just a phone and some other incidentals. I'm unarmed."

Ramon huffed. "I find that hard to believe." He held the guy against the wall with one hand and patted him down with the other. "He's clear." Ramon held the phone with one hand and drew his weapon again with the other. "Where is Kenna?"

The older man turned, his back now against the wall. "Ask me something that won't get me killed if I answer."

"You think we care about your longevity?" Jax yelled. "You've lived years, done more than most people dream of, and become a nightmare thing that should be eradicated."

"So kill me." Four shrugged. "But then you'll never know what I came here to tell you."

Jax didn't want to compromise what he knew was right to win at this, but it might happen. The battle between who he was and who he wanted to be raged inside.

Ramon huffed. "We aren't interested in being strung along. You know where she is." He surged forward and slammed his forearm against Four's chest, high enough his arm lifted the man's chin.

Four struggled for breath.

"Tell us where Kenna is. Now."

"You'll never reach her." Four gasped. "Even I don't know. They have so many layers of security, misdirects, and covers."

"You know." Ramon pushed on the older man's chest.

"I know your computer whiz friend will die if you kill me."

"Zeyla!" Ramon called.

Jax wasn't messing around if someone was threatening Maizie. "Check in, Maze."

"We're good," the young woman said. "We can hear you. Zeyla has me covered."

As long as he could trust Zeyla, that was fine. "Four, you'd better start talking or we're going to have a serious problem."

"You think you don't? You've been left alone so long as your childish attempts to cause problems haven't caused us issues. But your boldness will be repaid swiftly."

Ramon launched in. "If you even touch Maizie—"

Four cut him off. "My employer doesn't negotiate or respond to threats."

"Neither do we," Ramon said.

"What do you have to tell us?" Jax needed this over with, because the threat level had just gone up substantially. Clearly this man wanted to convey something more than a not-so-veiled threat.

Maizie wasn't going to be sacrificed in the fight to get Kenna back. He wasn't willing to allow her to give herself up any more than he would dangle her out as bait. He wanted his wife back, sure. But the person he would be if he lost everyone he cared about in the process wasn't the kind of man who could find that peace he'd been talking to Ramon about.

It didn't matter if he was FBI or a freelance investigator, a construction worker or an architect, he was going to be the man who did everything he could to save his family.

Every member of his family.

Four swallowed. "Call your dog off."

"He doesn't work for me. He works for the woman you kidnapped."

Ramon stepped back, but didn't go far.

"Your father made a bad deal. He's on the run." Four blinked. "*Dominatus* is offering you the chance to bring him in before they send an operative to take out your father."

"What deal?"

"Above my paygrade," Four said. "But his time is running out."

Just another of their distractions. "I want my wife back."

"So you'll sacrifice your father to get her?"

"Of course not. *Dominatus* is running on borrowed time. You all can't keep ruining people's lives. I'm not living the rest of my life always looking over my shoulder, wondering when one of your operatives is going to show up and take my children from me or take my wife."

"You think any of us have a choice in this?"

"Then make a choice." Jax was going to offer him freedom. "Leave with us. Get out and stay out."

"Live my life on the run?"

"We can protect you," Jax said. "It's not foolproof, but it's better than being their errand boy. Isn't it?"

"You wanna give me a life, a place to retire, and set me up like it's witness protection?"

Jax nodded. "It's up to you."

"The only way this ends is with blood and pain. For any of us."

Ramon said, "We've had our share, so you aren't going to scare us with that. It's time to rewrite the ending. For you. For all of us. And for Kenna."

"There's nothing you can do for her," Four muttered.

Jax wasn't going to accept that.

Not ever.

Chapter Nineteen

Jax stared at the older man, a guy *Dominatus* had sent to tell him that his father was in trouble. To get him to go after his dad before they did. Which didn't make sense. He wanted to end this conversation, but without more information than he had, he couldn't do much.

"Explain how that doctor, Marcus Buzard, is in a photo and video when Kenna killed him months ago." Jax had an idea what the answer might be, but he wanted to hear it from this man.

Four shifted his stance, impatience in his movements. "Who knows how many of him there are?"

"So they're cloning people?"

"More like identical twins," Four said. "They figured out how to introduce the gene for twins and fertilize one egg to split into two." He started to stammer. "Keep the other one for later, or implant it in someone else."

"Above your pay grade?"

"I don't wanna be a higher-up. Kind of like you guys shouldn't do things that get on their bad side. That's like walking into a hornet's nest."

Ramon snorted under his breath.

Jax said, "I'm not even going to explain how backward that is."

Ramon probably wanted to threaten him with what would happen to *Dominatus* now they were on *his* bad side. Jax didn't blame the guy. In fact, he could almost see why Kenna appreciated him. Even if Ramon was the antithesis of everything Jax stood for—the way his life would've gone if he hadn't stayed with the FBI for so long—he still respected this man.

Jax continued, "Do you know if they did that with Kenna? Is she an identical twin?"

"Sometimes babies grow up, and a couple will look like sisters or brothers, even the ones that aren't twins. It's hard to tell some apart."

"So she has a double out there somewhere." And their enemy was making it look as if Kenna was free and healthy, and that she'd simply left Jax and their marriage of her own accord. "This game they're playing isn't going to work."

Four shrugged. "How would I know what they're doing?"

"It's above your paygrade. We get it."

Ramon said, "'Cept you have a lot of information for a low-level guy who knows nothing."

Over their comms, Maizie said, "Things are getting tense here. Zeyla is about to snap."

"Am not." But her voice was tight. "There are six of them. Two women, four guys. They look like a Spetsnaz team who left to be mercenaries. Which means already terrifying becomes significantly more terrifying."

Jax glanced at Ramon, whose expression hardened. "Go."

Ramon strode away.

Jax faced the older man, hand close to his gun. "Why are you threatening my family? What does *Dominatus* want with Kenna?"

"I can tell you where we suspect your father will go and what he's planning to do there."

"How is this not a distraction?" Jax asked. "Everything they do is about misdirection, or some other form of psychological warfare. There's nothing straightforward about any of it, except when you send an operative to eliminate a loose end.

"Buzard was working on his own for years, and that was a surprise, wasn't it? They didn't know that the Phoenix Buzard, the one with his own research silo, was working on a plan to eliminate most of the world population."

"He's done, so it doesn't matter, does it?" Four shifted away from the wall.

The guy was dead—Kenna had killed him. But that didn't mean the threat represented was close to over. "What does 'offshore' mean?"

"Like a bank account?"

"You tell me." Jax shrugged. "I asked where Kenna was, and that was the answer I got. Maybe it's a place. For all I know, it could be anything. What I want to know is what *you* know."

Four mimicked his shrug. "Unless you want the threat to materialize, I suggest you let me go." He dug in his pocket. Hadn't Ramon searched him?

In his ear, Maizie said, "I see Ramon. Zeyla is getting up."

Jax palmed his gun, unwilling to be the victim here. Just in case this was another method of distraction, threatening the two women and drawing Ramon away so they could hurt Jax.

Before he could see what Four pulled out, and before he could aim his gun, someone moved behind him. Jax heard the shuffle of shoes on the floor behind him and started to turn.

The electric snap of a stun gun crackled, and the prongs' fire slammed into him. Electricity coursed through his body, spasming every muscle. In the distance he heard the gun drop to the floor as his fingers shifted and flexed. He couldn't stand up any longer. The sensation of falling shifted over him briefly, and he hit the floor on his shoulder.

Jax couldn't cry out. The moan pushed out between clenched teeth. He tried to fight against the voltage relentlessly traveling through him.

"All right, that's enough." Four crouched, a needle in his hand. "Let's do this quick before the other guy comes back."

"Should've just stunned both of them."

Jax wasn't sure if he recognized that voice. He couldn't turn and look at the guy. He could only lie there while they wrapped a strip of rubber around his bicep and tied it tightly.

"How much do we need to take?"

Four said, "I've got three vials."

"We could just kill him," the companion muttered. "They can get a genetic profile from a dead guy."

Four shoved Jax's shoulder, and he flopped to his back, the prongs of the stun gun still embedded in his back. Fire of a different kind burned in his shoulder. Jax winced in his mind. He didn't know what happened to his face but was pretty sure he had zero control over his features.

At least he hadn't blacked out.

Four inserted a needle in Jax's arm and started taking his blood. *Genetic profile.* That's what the guy had said.

As soon as they'd zapped him, the comms channel

likely went dead. Maizie and Ramon would know something was wrong, and they'd come over here as soon as they could.

Four pulled the vial out and replaced it to fill another, lifting it and looking at Jax's red blood contained in that small tube.

The other man moved into view above him. Jax had seen the guy before, at the retirement home. This one was Five. At least one of them had murdered Two when he'd been about to defect and tell Kenna everything. Just a few months ago, and yet it seemed like a lifetime. Back when he had her with him and their lives were good.

"Geez, you see this? The guy is crying." Five huffed. "That's worse than when they fight back."

Four said, "Shut up. Let's just get this finished." He switched out the tube again.

Five ignored the order. "Once we get dad here's blood back to the rendezvous, we can get a new assignment. I'm thinking Florida."

"Sure, that always works."

"Actually, Florida is way too hot this time of year. Maybe somewhere north is better."

Four shot him a dangerous look Jax didn't miss.

"Come on. I feel bad for the guy. He's missing his wife, missing all those pregnancy things that saps like him want to be around for."

"Not like me and how I didn't see any of that with Dana?"

Five said, "I didn't mean that. You did the best you could with her, and when it didn't work out, you ended it peacefully. She's in a better place and all that."

Jax's stomach clenched, and his arm moved. Both men reacted immediately.

"Hold him down," Four said. "And don't let him bite you."

"Give...ideas." Jax managed to get the words out. If they gave him the chance, he might be inclined to bite one of these men. Then he would smash the vials of blood so that *Dominatus* couldn't have his genetic profile. They had already taken far too much from him.

His thoughts stuttered. What if Kenna was hurt? What if there was something wrong with the baby? What if...?

Four pulled out the last vial, then extracted the needle from Jax's arm.

Jax gritted his teeth and swung out with his hand. He grabbed Four's wrist.

The other guy swore, but Jax refused to let go—now that he had a good grip on the guy and was regaining his ability to control his own body.

Jax managed to bite out the words, "Where...is...she?"

"Tough, this one. Kind of like her," the other guy said. "Want me to hit him again with the stun gun?"

Four didn't take his attention from Jax. The vial of blood in his hand, Jax grasping his wrist. "We need this so we can help her," Four said.

"What's wrong?"

"Why are you talking to him?" The other guy reached for the blood and took the vials. "Cut your losses and let's go before the crazy one comes back."

Jax snapped the wrist toward him, pulling the other man down in a jerky move. The older man's head swung forward and cracked into Jax's forehead with as much force as if Jax had slammed his head into Four's. The older man fell back, swearing a blue streak.

The other guy snatched up the stun gun, and Jax heard

him messing with a new cartridge. Getting ready to hit Jax again with another round of electricity.

Jax swung around and slammed his elbow into the man's chest, and he fell back. Jax found the room to scramble across the floor to where his gun had landed close to a flash drive. He snatched up the gun, rolled onto his back, and saw the two men already running down the hall.

He squeezed off three shots, his aim all over the place so that he fired wildly at the hallway walls and the ceiling. The men ducked as they ran and disappeared around a corner.

All Jax could do was slump back onto the floor, breathing hard. He lay there, staring at the ceiling, and realized he could hear someone headed this way from the other direction. He managed to roll again, lying on his stomach and aiming at the man who rounded the corner.

Ramon lifted his hands. "Whoa, just me. Us."

Behind him were Zeyla and Maizie. Jax moved his finger off the trigger and laid his forehead on the ground. Breathing hard, trying not to throw up.

"Jax." Maizie touched his shoulder.

He turned his shoulder first and rolled to his back with his eyes closed. "They took my blood. Said they needed my genetic profile. For the baby."

Maizie touched Jax's chest, and he reached up to lay his hand on hers. "I found her medical information in the computer system here. It looked like they deleted all the files, but nothing is ever really gone, so I recovered it. I think it's her, and if it is, then she's definitely pregnant."

Jax opened his eyes. "She was here?"

Maizie nodded. "A few days after she was taken, they checked her in here."

Ramon said, "You can have this conversation on the move. I'm driving."

Zeyla nodded. "That team will be right behind us."

Jax shifted and sat up, but there was no strength in him. "You'll have to help me."

Ramon hauled him up, Jax's arm across his shoulders.

"This is ridiculous," Jax said.

"Deal with it." Ramon led him back to the breezeway between buildings.

"They'll know we came this way."

Zeyla stepped around him and Ramon. "We'll deal. You just worry about walking." She opened the door at the far end and checked on the other side. "It's clear." She frowned. "Why is it clear?"

"They didn't follow us," Maizie replied.

"Maybe they left with Four and Five." Jax could carry a little of his own weight now but was still shaky.

Leaning on these people, and Ramon specifically, wasn't somewhere he'd ever thought he'd be. At least not without Kenna. Jax didn't even want to think about the fact his wife was pregnant.

He needed their help to find Kenna now more than ever.

"Maizie." He couldn't see her, but she'd hear him. "Can you hack the surveillance? Find out where Four and Five went. We need to follow them back to the source."

"They might lead us to Kenna?"

"We have to try." They needed to know where *Dominatus* had their hideouts. Uncover every one until they found where she was being kept.

Zeyla hit the button for the front entrance to ease open, which it always did far too slowly.

"Careful," Ramon said.

"Why hasn't that team come at us yet? They were right here, and they followed us to the other wing." Zeyla shook her head. "Maybe they went with Four and Five to protect them from us? Or they're watching to see where *we go*."

Maizie grasped a handful of the back of his shirt, holding on tight.

They moved as a unit to the car, where Zeyla said, "Don't leave until you see me. I'll follow you."

Ramon nodded. "Be fast."

She sprinted away, presumably to grab her own car.

Jax slid into the back seat. "Maizie, take the front. Find where they went."

"If you can," Ramon added.

Jax caught the man's gaze in the rearview and nodded. They were all feeling the pressure of this one. Maizie most of all.

"This was on the floor beside where you were lying." Maizie held up a flash drive.

"I think Four was going to give it to me. Even despite his mission."

"I'll look at it after I check the cameras. But we can't go too far away from the building, or I'll lose access to their system."

"Do what you can, then we get out of here." Ramon turned the airflow up and the radio to a different channel. As long as he didn't change Jax's preset stations, they would be fine.

Jax watched Maizie race through command line after command line, typing at a frantic pace until she said, "They don't have surveillance in or around the Edward Russell Jaxton wing." She sounded frustrated. "There aren't any cameras inside. Which makes sense for an ambush like that."

Jax tried to get his head to stop swimming. He didn't

like being useless—he'd rather be at full strength to face whatever came next.

Finding his father and discovering what he knew about *Dominatus*. What was the bad deal his dad had made? Maybe all that had been a false lead designed to send him in circles.

The fact *Dominatus* wanted Kenna—and presumably the baby—healthy and alive was a good thing. But it wasn't as if he was about to find peace leaving them in the enemy's hands.

It seemed as if that enemy didn't want a war with Jax. They wanted him distracted, or convinced he'd never get her back. They didn't want him looking for her. Jax was supposed to find his father before they sent someone to kill him, apparently. Or so Four said.

If he did that, they'd have leverage over him. A way to use his father to make his life miserable, just like they were doing with Amara...and maybe others.

Jax wasn't going to be their pawn.

He also wasn't going to leave his dad to face a trained killer.

Chapter Twenty

J ax jerked awake in the front seat of the car. The inside of his arm stung. The outside of his arm stung. His head felt like cotton had been stuffed inside it.

"Hey." Ramon glanced over from the front seat.

They were on the freeway, but Jax didn't bother trying to figure out where. He scrubbed his hands down his face. "Hey."

"Gas station up ahead." Ramon switched lanes.

"Maizie?"

From the back seat, the young woman said, "I'm good. Just working through the flash drive you got from those guys. You might wanna take a look when you're all the way awake. It's corporate stuff I don't understand."

"Okay." Jax looked at Ramon. "How long was I out?"

"Only a few minutes," Ramon said. "Not entirely surprising considering."

He checked the side mirror and saw Zeyla's car behind them. He didn't want sympathy, or for his weaknesses to get explained away. His mind wouldn't quit going over his father, and Kenna, and whatever that had been at the hospital with some tactical team threatening Maizie and Zeyla.

Jax rubbed the inside of his arm with his thumb while Ramon pulled into a truck stop and parked near the door.

"Pit stop," Ramon said.

Jax stowed his gun in the pocket behind the driver's seat and pushed the door open, then got his phone out. Dialing Stairns, he leaned against the outside of the door with his face turned to the sun.

Zeyla wandered over from her car, a couple of spaces down. She lit a cigarette and stood by the door, near a smoker's pole off to the side. It didn't quite look natural, making him wonder if it was just a good cover for her watching their backs.

Stairns answered, "Yeah."

"It's Jax. Any word on my father?" He explained what Four had said about his dad making a bad deal, and their offer for him to locate his father before they sent someone to take him out.

"That doesn't make sense."

"Maybe they just don't want a war," Jax said. "That's all I can think of. They want us to bring him in, and we feel like we've won something. Then we're more willing to accept concessions or make deals when they're ultimately going to refuse to turn Kenna back over to us."

Ramon walked into the gas station store.

Jax checked and saw Maizie in the back seat and opened the door. She put her feet out and turned to the door but stayed on her computer. She glanced at him. "Why does Ramon keep it so cold?"

Jax managed to smile.

Stairns said, "I dug in your old man's office computer and his safe, went through all his papers."

"Mom gave you access?"

"There's got to be more he never told her about. All this is way too neat. Does he have any business partners that you're aware of?"

"He worked with a guy back in the day. They had a finance company together, but he sold his half and went off on his own."

"Good place to start. I'll ask your mom."

"Thanks."

"Elizabeth and your sister are taking care of her. If your dad really did take off, there's no need for you to come here."

Jax said, "He might even be coming this direction. It's where I would go if I was gonna run. He'll be far enough away from home, but not totally cut off if he needs my help."

"The old man doesn't think like you, Son. You can't figure he'll do what you would." He said it gently, but the words still stung.

"No, I guess not." Jax watched a semitruck pull out. "Thanks for being there."

Jax had ordered him to do it, for all intents and purposes, dividing up team tasks and giving the most important one—after Maizie's protection—to Stairns, who he trusted the most.

"You think it could be a distraction?" Stairns asked. "Maybe they captured him, and getting you to focus on your father means you're not looking for Kenna as hard."

"I don't want to, but I wouldn't put it past them." Jax winced. "While you're going through his business, look for anything 'offshore' in the files. Money, locations. I don't know what it means, but it's the last thing Samuel Chistane said before he died."

"The guy is dead?" Stairns paused. "What did Bruce do?"

Jax told him the whole deal, and how Elliot was on the run. Whatever the special agent did next, he hoped it involved the truth coming out for the FBI. Someone had to realize a conspiracy had occurred. Otherwise, it would continue unchecked. The FBI could use a little of Kenna's brand of justice, but Jax was going to have to settle with what Elliot managed to achieve. And if there was anything he could do later, then fine. But it was hardly his priority.

Part of Jax couldn't really believe that was true. For so long, the FBI had been his focus, and their integrity was sacrosanct as far as he was concerned. Now that he lived more on Kenna's side of the aisle, he had way different priorities. And it had only been a few days since he handed over his badge and gun.

"There you are." Maizie's fingers flew across the keys. "But not for long."

Stairns said, "I'll check in with Bruce. See how things are going."

"Thanks." Jax hung up. "Maizie?"

"The flash drive has a virus on it, but that's hardly surprising." Maizie had all her focus on the computer screen. "Because I was expecting you."

Jax crouched by the open door. "They're infiltrating your computer?"

"This one is air gapped. They aren't getting in the Banbury Investigations network."

"Smart." Jax nodded. She'd kept the flash drive and anything on it from connecting to the computer system she'd set up for Kenna. "You need me to do anything?"

"Yeah." She bit her lip and reached to the side to hand

over her phone. "Look at what that notification is. I don't recognize the chime."

He showed the phone to her so face ID could do its thing and then pulled down from the top. "It's from the bank. You have an appointment reminder."

"No, I don't." She tapped across the keyboard.

"What's going on?" Ramon wandered around the back of the car, a plastic bag rustling against his leg. He dug inside it and handed Jax a sugary soda. "Drink this. It'll wake you up."

"Thanks." He sipped and scanned the email. "Kenna made an appointment at the bank. It's for today." According to the time... "We have an hour."

"Which branch?" Ramon unwrapped a sub sandwich and took a bite.

Jax shook his head. "Does it matter?"

"Yes," Maizie said. "Because it wasn't Kenna."

He looked at her, wondering if he wanted to question aloud if that was true. In the end, he said nothing and looked at the notification. Then went back into Maizie's inbox to see if he could find the original email. "Here we go." He tapped it. "Three days ago. Looks like that's when the original email was sent."

"Like I said"—she let out a frustrated sound and slammed the lid of the laptop closed—"they're giving me the runaround because I want to know what's on that drive."

"It should've been information about my father. Instead, it was a virus?" He didn't really need an answer to that question. "Because they want to distract us."

"They wanted something important from you," Ramon said around a bite of sandwich.

"That part probably wasn't a distraction." Jax closed his

eyes for a second. "They said they needed the father's genetic profile."

"She's pregnant." Zeyla blew out a long breath.

Maizie looked like she was about to cry.

Jax looked at Zeyla. "You knew?"

"Mom and I suspected." She looked like she wanted to shrug, but her body was far too tense. "It's what they do."

"But it's not their baby. It's mine."

She nodded, her jaw tight. This was the kind of woman who didn't fit in suburban America. She was more suited to international travel, and covert operations. Even wearing wide-leg jeans and a cropped T-shirt, she still came across as deadly, as if the clothes were a ruse meant to disarm a person.

Since he'd met her, Kenna had softened. She'd let people into her life and her heart. She'd become a believer in Jesus.

Zeyla was the person Kenna would've been if she'd been raised in a family controlled by *Dominatus*.

Maizie said nothing, that sheen of tears still in her eyes. Ramon had quit eating and looked a little sick.

Zeyla pressed her lips together. "I can call Mom and see if she and Bruce figured out anything new."

"We have an appointment at the bank." Jax needed something else to focus on or he was going to lose it. Maizie, and even Ramon, needed him to keep it together so they could help him work the case rather than being focused on supporting him. "Maizie, are you authorized on the account?"

She frowned. "Why would someone make an appointment at the bank?"

"That's what we need to find out. It could be what *Dominatus* is trying to distract us from."

Her eyes widened. "You think whoever it is, that woman who looks like Kenna—you think she's the one who made the appointment?"

"Her, or Kenna herself." He didn't want to get his hopes up, but there it was. The rush of possibly seeing her today. Getting her back. After all, it might not be the lookalike. Or it could be Kenna herself going to the bank.

Maizie tucked her legs back in the car and grabbed an iPad from her backpack. "I'll check all the accounts. I haven't really been paying attention to them."

Ramon said, "Maybe they're trying to clean out her money, since they believe she won't need it. It's probably where they get their cash from." He made a face like saying that left a bad taste in his mouth.

"I'll follow you guys and make my call." Zeyla headed off to her car.

Jax slid in the front seat.

"Feeling okay?" Ramon cranked the car.

"Thanks for the soda."

Ramon nodded even though Jax hadn't answered the question. It didn't really matter how he felt. What mattered is that they kept moving, overturning every rock in their path until they found the one whoever took Kenna had crawled under.

His father knew something about what was going on. *Where are you, Dad?*

Maybe he had this whole time and simply refused to admit it to Jax. Because it was safer for him, or for the whole family, if he kept his head down and avoided the fact he was in this whether he liked it or not.

Jax looked up the branch of the bank where Kenna had all her accounts. They'd combined personal finances when they married, but her business was separate. So was her trust fund from her dad's book and movie sales. Every two weeks, she moved money into their joint account that represented the paycheck the business she ran gave to her. She'd also told him she paid Maizie more than what she paid herself to cover bills and incidentals.

Maizie tapped his shoulder. "Nothing in these messages says what the appointment is for."

Jax turned to look at her. "What about activity on the account since she's been gone?" He tripped over the last word, even though he tried not to. He cleared his throat, and his phone buzzed with a notification—the verse of the day from his Bible app.

A man's heart plans his way, but the Lord directs his steps.

Jax nearly laughed, muttering to himself, "That's super subtle."

Even if it wasn't God blatantly trying to get his attention, it was still a good message he needed to remember. Whatever happened, the Lord was sovereign. Jax didn't really understand how free will intersected with the things God ordained, even with how long he'd been a believer. But he did know this was only going to turn out to be a victory if God directed the outcome.

It was the one thing he could count on versus the option of relying on his own fallible strength. Jax might not succeed if it was all up to him. The question was whether he could afford to trust God if the answer was one he didn't like. That he might not get Kenna back.

If he lost her...and their baby.

A lump rose in his throat.

He blinked back tears and stared out the window, trying to decide if he could take the leap and fully trust God. Sure, he was praying constantly for Kenna. He could trust God to take care of her and their baby right now, because he couldn't do anything to help until he found them.

But with the things that Jax *could* control, he found it far easier to rely on himself because he could affect the outcome.

Ramon pulled into a parking space downtown, in front of a jeweler. Towering over the jeweler was a high-rise of apartments. Across the street, the bank branch had its offices above, a huge international company that might be connected to *Dominatus*. Kenna wouldn't want to discover that about her finances—but she would want to know.

Jax holstered his gun and flipped the back of his shirt over it.

"I'm coming with you." Maizie opened her door and climbed out. "I'm not staying in the car."

Zeyla strode along the sidewalk toward them. "Mom hasn't received anything from you-know-who about Kenna since their operative was killed."

It wasn't only the woman sent to murder Samuel who had been killed, but also Sandra. So much death and destruction when all he'd been trying to do was run the Phoenix FBI office and enjoy married life.

Jax shoved away those unhelpful thoughts and focused. "Does she know where Kenna is, or what 'offshore' means?"

"She doesn't know where Kenna is," Zeyla replied, "but in the pictures it's clearly a facility. That much you can tell from the images they sent. But they have places all over. She could literally be anywhere in the world."

"And if we narrow it down to places that are on coastlines—or 'offshore'—then what happens to our search results?"

"I have no idea where they are. I just know they exist." Her gaze drifted to the side.

"What?" Jax wanted to pressure her, but they were all about to break.

"The only way to get a list of every facility is to get into one and access their server." Zeyla paused. "But we aren't doing that. It's a death sentence if we get caught. And that's the best-case scenario."

"I'll go." Maizie hugged her iPad. "Tell me where it is, Zeyla. Or take me to one like you're turning me in. I can get into the server and find the information we need."

"No," Jax replied, in unison with Ramon. "Kenna would never go for that." Jax walked a step away from the car and turned back, needing to do something.

"She isn't here." Maizie lifted her chin. A tear trailed from the corner of her left eye, and she swiped it away. "This is how we get her back."

"Actually"—Jax motioned with his chin across the road, where he spotted the Kenna lookalike approaching the bank —"that's how we get her back."

Ramon said, "Let's go."

Chapter Twenty-One

Jax went in the bank first, the others behind him. The lunch rush appeared to be in full swing, and the line for the tellers snaked almost to the door. High ceilings and an old money feel made this place appear like a hotel lobby. He scanned the crowd for the Kenna lookalike.

"We're sure it's not her, right?" Ramon asked.

Maizie said, "She dresses a little like Kenna, but not completely. And she doesn't walk the same."

"She walks like an operative." Zeyla's expression darkened. "Which means she's mine."

Jax wasn't so sure a fight in a bank lobby was the way to go. "I have an idea. I mean, she is here pretending to be my wife. In fact, the whole company is here. So let's go join her for her appointment."

Maizie grinned. "Yeah. Let's go."

Jax frowned, but he weaved through the line over to where the Kenna lookalike was waiting in a seating area. The hum of conversation drifted around him, and a phone rang in the corner of the lobby. This place smelled like the floor cleaner they used and coffee that had sat on the burner for a few hours. Someone cut in front of him, a familiar male making a beeline for the same dark-haired woman he was headed for.

Surely not here to meet her.

But who else would it be?

Jax took the chance to study the Kenna lookalike while she leafed through a real estate investing pamphlet and waited for her appointment. She didn't look like Kenna to him, though he supposed some people might be confused. She shared some features with his wife, as well as her height and build. But that was where the similarities ended.

This woman had a longer nose, and the whole demeanor was off. Kenna had softened over the past few years. This woman came across more like Zeyla. On edge. Ready for what was about to happen.

They were twenty feet away when she looked up and pinned him with a stare. *Busted.* She might think she had the upper hand here, but that wasn't what was happening.

The man who'd cut in front of him sat beside her.

She didn't look at the other man, and she spoke too low for Jax to hear, but he could lip-read. "Elliot, what do you want?"

Elliot looked haggard, talking quickly to the Kenna lookalike while she stared at Jax, watching him approach like a predator, barely paying any attention to the desperate man beside her.

Jax sat across from her, and Maizie settled beside him. "Good thing I'm not late for our appointment."

Maizie eased her iPad down and tapped the screen a few times.

Elliot whipped around, surprised to see them. His mouth opened, but he just stared at them.

"Special Agent Adams." Jax nodded. "Good to see you're all right. I was worried."

Elliot swallowed. "I just..." He looked at the woman beside him, then back at Jax. He twisted to her. "Just tell me where to meet you."

"It's over, Elliot. Sandra is dead, and you aren't an FBI agent anymore as far as I can see. So what use do I have for you?" She had no emotion in her tone. Even her expression gave away nothing.

As if she had no feeling at all.

But the voice... Oh, the voice was almost an exact match for Kenna's. Enough it made him wonder if she'd had corrective surgery to make her sound like his wife. The sound of it caused that squeeze in his chest again, the persistent pang of heartache.

Elliot blurted, "Kenna—"

Jax flinched. Maizie was the one who said, "That isn't Kenna."

Elliot frowned. "Of course, it's Kenna." He swallowed. "It's good you guys found her. I know you were pretty worried." He shifted in the seat.

Nervous? "Why are you here, Elliot?" Jax didn't take his attention from the woman, but he watched Elliot as well. "Why did you come to this bank?"

The Kenna lookalike seemed bored more than anything. She had either not noticed Zeyla and Ramon standing guard, or she didn't care one bit for this confrontation and what might happen.

"I need to know what to do." He clutched his phone between his hands. "I need orders, and Kenna is the one who gives them to Sandra and I."

"Since when?" Jax shook his head. Elliot seemed surprised his sister was an operative.

"Since you first brought her to the FBI. Everyone knows who she is. I got into my sister's phone account and read through her messages. She's been getting orders from Kenna for months." Elliot motioned to the woman pretending to be Jax's wife, who'd gone to that bar and "bought" a particular girl, and starred in a video that made it look like Kenna was having an affair with a dead man. Realization registered on his face. "In the messages, she said you knew." He shifted in the seat, suddenly self-conscious. "She said you were part of all of it."

"And when you were captured by Amara?" Jax asked, because Elliot had been in Amara's "care" for weeks.

Elliot glanced at the Kenna lookalike. "I didn't share anything Sandra knew with that woman. How could I when I had no idea?"

"That doesn't change the situation," she said.

Jax clenched his stomach, steeling himself against the voice. "You might not have told her, Elliot, but you're going to tell me."

A bank employee in a suit, his stomach distended between the sides of his jacket, wandered over. Slicked-back gray hair. "Ms. Banbury?" He glanced at the rest of them, then his client.

Jax stood at the same time she did, trusting that Ramon wouldn't let Elliot leave. "This is my wife. I'm glad I made it here in time for the appointment." Jax stuck his hand out to the guy, and they shook. "Oliver Jaxton. I work for the FBI." He didn't give either of them a chance to speak. "What are we meeting about?"

The manager seemed a little confused why Jax was there—or why Jax looked like he'd been in a fight. "I'm Brian Holder. It's nice to meet you both. I saw in our system that you've been a client of ours for years, Ms. Banbury."

She started to speak, but a gunshot exploded behind them.

Jax expected someone to drop to the ground, and his mind eclipsed with dread as to who it would be. But Elliot had his gun pointed at the ceiling.

"This is a robbery!" Elliot yelled. "Nobody—"

Ramon launched himself at Elliot and tackled him to the floor.

The Kenna lookalike darted away, but Zeyla intercepted her, and they tumbled to the floor, screaming at each other. Bank security raced over, looking around as if they weren't exactly sure where to begin.

Elliot's gun skittered across the floor and a security guard swept it up. The manager looked around, panic in his expression. Jax checked on Maizie, but she had her head dipped to her iPad. "You good, Maze?"

"Mm-hmm. I accessed her phone through the Bluetooth. I'm cloning it."

"You want to let her go?"

She looked up at him. "Should we?"

Jax realized the manager had backed up. Beyond where they stood, Zeyla caught an elbow to the face but rallied and slammed the other woman's head on the floor. She slumped on the tile, out cold. Zeyla stilled, breathing hard. "Ramon!"

"I'm good. You?"

"Clear." She flipped "Kenna" to her face and pulled zip ties from her back pocket.

Ramon did the same, securing Elliot's hands behind his back.

"Someone explain what's going on," the security guard demanded.

Ramon spoke to him, so Jax moved with the manager,

who was trying to retreat in a panic even though the danger was over.

"I have questions," Jax began.

The manager slumped into a chair, one hand on his chest.

"Breathe easy." Jax stood near him.

"You just... You all..." The manager gasped. "They were going to rob this place!"

"I need you to tell me what that woman's business here was." If he had to, Jax would explain she'd been impersonating the account holder, but even the police weren't going to believe it. At least no one had so far.

The bank manager looked up at him. "FBI, you said?"

"That's correct. This isn't a case I'm working, though. That woman is impersonating my wife and trying to gain access to my wife's accounts." He needed to sound official though, not like some crazy person with a story no one would believe.

"I assure you, without the right credentials she never would have been able to."

Zeyla was rummaging in the woman's pockets. "She has ID. A driver's license. And a bunch of numbers on a paper."

Jax took the paper. The bank manager seemed stunned and didn't appear to be snapping out of it anytime soon. Other employees ushered the customers to one side, away from their group, and someone had called this in to the police. That meant they were going to lose Elliot soon to cuffs and custody. Not only that, but the second the cops heard that Zeyla tackled the Kenna lookalike for trying to run, she was going to be released because she hadn't actually done anything—yet. Zeyla might even be arrested for assault.

Jax shifted his attention to Zeyla and saw her attention

was on him. He tipped his head to the side like, *Get out of here.*

She hauled the other woman to her feet and walked her to the side of the room into an alcove. Maizie hurried after them.

Jax refocused on the bank manager. "Brian, I need you to tell me what that woman came here for. Did she explain the reason to you prior to the meeting?"

"Uh..." He pinched the bridge of his nose, thinking about it. "I think it was to close all the accounts. I had a whole pitch planned to convince her to stay on as a customer, products I can offer that might convince her not to close everything."

They were going to take all Kenna's money.

No way.

"Did she tell you if she wanted to walk away with a check, or was she going to have you transfer the money into another account somewhere else?" Jax glanced at the numbers on the paper, then showed Brian. "Like this?"

"That's a SWIFT ID, like a bank identifier, and an account and routing numbers." Brian stared at it. "That's a US bank, but I'm unfamiliar with the abbreviation for the name of the bank. After the bank code and country code, there's a location and the branch code."

"So we can ascertain where this bank is?" Sounded good to him.

The information would tell him more than the impersonator likely planned to. She was a trained operative, and he didn't agree with enhanced interrogation. Causing someone so much pain that they talked didn't get them to tell the truth—it only got the person to tell you whatever you wanted to hear. Not exactly reliable. There wasn't any available truth serum on the market that was any more effective than torture. Which meant she had to have a genuine reason to tell them the truth that was more powerful than her drive to follow orders.

Maizie would be able to trace the account.

That made him wonder if they shouldn't allow the money to move out of Kenna's accounts and then put some kind of tracker on it so they could see where it went. Into the *Dominatus* coffers, surely.

Hopefully, the paper that woman had on her were the correct numbers, not a set of fake ones in case she was caught.

The bank employee nodded. "If you—" Whatever Brian had been about to say was cut off by a crash.

A hoard of FBI agents strode into the bank in bullet-proof vests with their weapons drawn. From this side of things, they looked kind of...obnoxious. Was that how people perceived them? Could just be because he was at odds with them.

Leading the charge was Special Agent Andrette Herron.

Once the "FBI!" and "Everybody freeze!" had died down because no one was doing anything, she said, "Ladies and Gentlemen, take a load off. Nobody leaves yet. Once you've talked to us and we've cleared you, then you can go. We'll try and make this as quick and painless as possible."

She strode over to where Ramon had Elliot facedown on the ground. "Special Agent Adams?" She seemed genuinely surprised to see him.

Elliot said nothing, still secured with his hands tied behind his back and his head turned so he could look at them. Until he gave up and slumped to the floor, evidently exhausted.

"He didn't transfer out of the Phoenix office," Jax said.

"He was kidnapped. Someone murdered his sister, and it's all connected to my wife's disappearance." Maybe he should've said that Elliot was put in protective custody.

Too late now.

Andrette holstered her weapon, and the other agents disbursed around the room. Ramon backed up from Elliot, and a couple of agents helped him stand.

"No!" The Kenna lookalike rushed out of the room, twisting her shoulders to avoid Zeyla's grasp. "Jax!" She found him. "How could you do this?" Actual tears rolled down her cheeks.

Andrette said, "I thought she was missing?"

"What?" Jax frowned, looking at the woman pretending to be Kenna. "What!"

"You know how I feel about Mark!" She gasped. "All I'm trying to do is leave you, and you're making it as hard as possible for me to be free of you. Don't you get it? It's over! We're over!"

The vibe in the room shifted, and it wasn't positive.

Before he could argue with fake Kenna, she continued her tirade, "Just let me go. I don't want to be trapped anymore."

Jax's jaw ached he clenched it so hard. "That's what you want everyone to think? These people have met you. They know you're not my wife."

"Then why aren't you letting me leave you?" she wailed. A second later, she spun around. In a moment, she drew Zeyla's weapon from the holster at her back. She pointed it at Jax. "Let me go!"

The agents in the room whipped their guns out and aimed at her. "Put it down!"

"Put the weapon down, Kenna!" Andrette walked toward her, taking the lead. "Put it down!"

Jax saw the shift in her intention. She swung the gun toward Andrette, her finger on the trigger. Andrette fired. Several of the other agents fired as well, eliminating the lead that was the Kenna lookalike impersonating his wife.

Zeyla had gone from the doorway, and Jax heard her scream.

Jax yelled, "Stop!"

Their target was down.

Jax ran past Andrette and shoved the barrel of her gun down, wincing when he found it hot to the touch. He raced by the dead woman into the room. Zeyla lay on Maizie, blood on the back of her shoulder.

"Zeyla!"

She groaned. "Ouch!"

He turned back. "Get a medic!"

"I don't want a doctor." She shifted up, and he helped her by the elbow.

Ramon reached the doorway. "You're hit?"

She moved off Maizie. "Ouch."

"Maze?" Jax brushed back hair from her face. "You good?"

"I think Zeyla broke my iPad." She shifted up from the floor, moving back to sit on her behind. "I feel like I got hit by a truck."

Zeyla lifted her fist, and Maizie tapped it.

"Ouch." Zeyla slumped back to the floor. "That hurts."

Ramon crouched behind her, touching her shoulder. "Pretty nasty graze."

"No doctors." She looked over her shoulder at him. "You take care of it."

Ramon's jaw shifted. "Fine."

Jax shook his head. "Elliot has a lot to explain."

He looked around the bank at the ocean of FBI agents

and the dead woman on the ground who'd pretended to be his wife. And apparently done well at it, given his colleagues were now looking at him with some serious pity.

Great.

"Forget it," Jax said. "Let's get out of here."

Chapter Twenty-Two

Jax opened the kitchen cupboard and found the spray can marked Dermoplast. Maizie had set up her workstation at the breakfast bar, using the stool Kenna tended to occupy. He didn't want it to be bittersweet that she sat in the same spot but couldn't help how he felt.

Maizie had Jolene the cat on her lap and absently petted her with one hand while she clicked the mouse with her other.

Jax glanced at the screen as he passed her. She navigated to another window via the desktop, which had an image of Cabot, Kenna's dog, on the screen. He didn't react, even though she'd covered what she was really doing and didn't want him to see.

"Jax?"

He stopped by the end of the breakfast bar. "Yeah, honey."

She glanced at him, surprise on her face.

"Sorry." He didn't know what her abuser had called her, and he didn't want to know. But he also didn't want to bring up old wounds by using a name attached to her trauma.

Maizie shook her head. "I actually...liked it. It sounds nice."

"All right, *honey*."

She rolled her eyes. "Don't make it weird."

Jax chuckled, surprising himself. "What's up?"

"I'm going to pass some of this to that financial analyst you sent me to a few months ago."

"Who did I send you to?" It had been so long he couldn't remember what name he'd given her.

"Samantha Littleton."

"Right." He nodded. "She did a good job?"

"She gave me a full report and got on a video call with me to explain it all," Maizie said. "She's great. She showed me her house, too. She lives on a ranch in Wyoming and has chickens, goats, *and* a cow."

It probably sounded more enjoyable than nearly getting shot in a bank. "I need to give this to Ramon. I'll be back." Jax got up.

"I'm good, *honey*."

He walked away with the spray antiseptic. "Don't make it weird." He smiled as her laughter chased him down the hall, then knocked on the bathroom door.

He heard, "Come in" and eased the door open.

"I brought the stuff." He waved the spray can.

Zeyla sat backward on one of his dining chairs, holding one of Kenna's T-shirts over her chest while Ramon wiped her back. Jax was interested to see how bad it was. But in these close quarters, he didn't want to overwhelm Zeyla with two big guys crowding her in the bathroom. He could see lines from old scars on her back.

Ramon took the numbing spray. "Thanks. That'll help on the edges."

Zeyla didn't look at him. She stared straight ahead, tears edging her eyes.

Jax slid the shower curtain open and sat on the edge of the bathtub. He kept as much distance as he could. "You okay?"

Her lips pressed into a thin line. "Fine."

"Need something for the pain? I don't keep narcotics in the house, but I have something strong you can drink that will take the edge off."

She shook her head. "I'm good."

"Almost done." Ramon caught Jax's gaze, tension in the lines around his eyes.

Jax sighed. "Reminds me of the time I went to the San Diego County Fair. I think I was twelve."

Ramon frowned. "Did you get shot?"

A fraction of the tension in Zeyla's gaze eased, and Jax knew he was on the right track. He shook his head. "The Ferris Wheel broke down, and they were repairing it. But it was taking forever, so this kid decides to climb down from the top."

Ramon said, "Uh-oh," his attention on the bandage he was putting on Zeyla's back.

"I've never been on a Ferris Wheel." Zeyla held her breath.

"We can rectify that, if you want," Ramon told her. Had Jax interrupted a moment that could be the beginning of something between them?

"What happened to the kid?" she asked.

"Everyone was screaming at him to quit climbing down. Mom is on the ground going ballistic like he's gonna fall and die. The kid swings like its monkey bars, then jumps to the next rung, catches it, and keeps going. By the time he was down, everyone was clapping and cheering for him. She put him in gymnastics. He was in the last Olympics, won a silver medal."

The corner of Zeyla's mouth curled up.

Ramon eyed Jax. "What does that have to do with a gunshot graze?"

"Uh...something, I'm sure. Maybe there's a metaphor in there about giving it everything you've got."

"Like a motivational poster?" Ramon asked.

Zeyla said, "I don't think I want to try any rides at the fair. Sounds terrifying."

Jax smiled. "I thought you were some kind of trained operative."

Ramon straightened. "I'm done."

"Thanks." She backed up from the chair and stood, her head bowed, not looking at either of them. The shirt clutched to her front as she hurried out.

Ramon watched her go.

Jax didn't glance at her back, deciding to give her privacy instead. "You good?"

The other man's jaw flexed. "Trying to resist the urge to kill them all for doing that to her. And she didn't even let me see the aftermath of them removing half her liver, one of her kidneys, and taking eggs from her ovaries so they can freeze them."

"I don't know if it's better or worse that Kenna is already pregnant." Jax wanted to kill them all as well.

"Zeyla thinks I should be more scared of them than I am. She won't even say the name *Dominatus* most of the time, because she's been trained to fear hearing it aloud."

"She's been through a lot," Jax said. "Maybe enough that we should give her some trust."

Right now, he was thinking he trusted her more than he trusted Bruce, though maybe that wasn't fair. Still, when the bullets started flying, Zeyla had jumped on Maizie and taken the hit. That counted in his estimation.

Ramon nodded. "She saved Maizie. She didn't even think about it, she just dove. I saw her do it."

"If Maizie is good, I'm good."

"Agreed." Ramon shoved all the medical packages in the trash, and Jax left him washing his hands.

Zeyla stood in the hall, her shirt back in place. "I'm not strong like her."

At first, he thought she might be talking about Maizie, but he said, "Kenna?"

Zeyla nodded. "I'm not a survivor."

How could that possibly be true? "You've been through more than most people, and you're still here." He shifted to let Ramon exit the bathroom, then leaned against the wall. "No one else can judge what we've been through unless they lived it with us." He motioned to Ramon, then himself. "We have our own vices, our own nightmares, and things we'd love to forget, but we never will."

She stared at him as if she didn't know whether to scream or burst into tears.

"I'm an addict," Jax admitted. "Maybe I've been trying to forget that for so long that I'd forgotten there might be something else out there for me than the FBI. Being a fed was a safety net, a way to make sure I was the man I needed to be. Walking away might not be my choice necessarily, but I should be able to be the best version of myself no matter the circumstances. That's how I'll know I've really beaten the addiction."

"I wanted a sister."

Jax said, "So did she."

"I found one. She's in the kitchen." Ramon cleared his

throat. "And I have Kenna, too. Because I need the safety net still. I'm not ready to be out there on my own."

Zeyla sniffed.

"You had your mother," Jax pointed out.

"My mother isn't someone you *have*. Bruce needs to realize that." Zeyla slid her hands in her pockets, her arms tight to her sides. Nervous, and unsure of herself. "But she wants to destroy *Dominatus* as much as I do. We just don't know how."

"We're gonna figure that out," he told her. "As a family. Together."

Zeyla stared at him, something like wonder on her face. "Together."

Ramon nodded. "We get Kenna back, and we take them down."

Jax pushed off the wall, but before he could say something, the house alarm chimed. "Someone is here." He went to the front door while the others gathered with Maizie in the kitchen, moving out of sight.

Jolene wandered across the hall behind him, unbothered by what was happening.

He checked the peep hole. "Someone order a pizza?"

But he knew the answer.

Jax slid open the entry table drawer and grabbed the revolver Kenna kept there. He checked it was loaded, then cracked the door an inch. "Can I help you?"

"They're watching." It was his father. "Let me in."

Jax swung the door wide. "Come in. I'll grab some cash."

As if he would ever do that with a pizza guy, but if someone was listening or watching them, it made more sense. Until the pizza guy didn't leave and they'd know something was going on.

His dad stepped in, and Jax shut the door behind him. Edward Jaxton slid the branded pizza ballcap off his head, sending his gray hair all over. It curled around his ears on the sides, and down on his forehead in an odd way. But the old man didn't fix it, which told Jax a whole lot about how he was doing right now.

His dad followed him to the kitchen, putting the pizza on the counter. "It's hot, and I paid them a whole lot for it. We probably don't have much time."

"Edward Jaxton, my father." Jax motioned. "This is Maizie, Ramon, and Zeyla." His daughter, his friend, and his wife's closest relative.

They all shook hands, except Maizie. She slid her laptop across the breakfast bar and turned it toward herself so she could work without anyone checking on her.

"What's going on, Dad? An operative from *Dominatus* talked to us," Jax began. Then something held his tongue, and he stopped short of explaining what Four had said about his father having made a bad deal. They were going to send someone to kill him, unless Jax found him first.

None of it sounded right.

"I didn't know where else to go." He slumped onto a stool, looking exhausted but also ridiculous in a pizza delivery outfit. The man lived his life in tailored suits and silk ties.

Ramon grabbed a few bottled waters out of the fridge and handed them out.

Jax's dad probably wanted something stronger, but Jax wanted to hear what he had to say first. "Did you make a bad deal with them?"

"My debts have come due." He fiddled with the lid of the water but didn't open it. "It's a long story, and there's nothing I can do about what is going to happen."

"So why was I supposed to find you?"

His father frowned at him. "They told you to find me?"

"I had no idea where to start looking, but they said I should find you before one of their operatives did."

Ramon and Zeyla headed out of the room, and Maizie grabbed her laptop. She followed them to the living room, leaving him alone with his father.

"I want to help you," Jax added, "but my priority has to be getting Kenna back."

"Then you can guarantee I won't be able to help you with that. Otherwise, they'd never have told you to find me." His dad let out a breath. "They have to believe that you helping me will detract from finding her."

"I think they believe I'll never find her. Not even when they send men to take my blood so they can have my genetic profile."

His dad whipped around to face him. "What?"

"Kenna is pregnant."

The color drained from his father's face. Jax wandered to the cupboard above the microwave and poured his father two fingers of whiskey. The old man knocked it back in one gulp. "You need to find her."

He'd been saying the same thing over and over to himself, but now he couldn't bring himself to echo his dad's words. He couldn't find her. They had no leads, and if he was going to get her back, wouldn't he have done it already?

You could have led me to her by now, but You haven't.

He didn't want to be angry at God, but the situation seemed so hopeless that he wasn't sure what else to be. It might not be fair, like taking his frustration and fear out on his friends wasn't fair. But if anyone could handle his anger, it was God.

"What was the deal you made?" Jax stared at his father

across the breakfast bar, entirely too much history between them. They lived different lives in different worlds, but right now they had to bridge that gap and figure out what was going on.

His father poured himself another drink. "Little things at first. They needed favors, like a delivery that had to be accepted with no questions asked. Customs forms and shipping manifests. In return, your mother and I went on trips that were paid for. Then it was bigger, and they offered to pay down the mortgage. Your mom had surgery, and they brought in the best doctor. An expert in the field."

"Probably seemed like it was worth it in the beginning. Like it wasn't a big deal."

His father nodded. "My business partner was stealing from me. Suddenly he's gone and isn't a problem anymore. I wind up with a silent partner and an influx of cash, and we're expanding to more locations up and down the West Coast. We got a contract with the Port of Los Angeles, which was a huge win considering it's the busiest port in North America."

Jax wasn't sure that random fact was relevant, but his father needed to explain it his way. If Jax interrupted or steered what his dad was saying, he could shut down or forget something.

His father continued, "I didn't realize how deep in I was getting until it was too late. Then when I wanted out, it was impossible to untangle myself from their business."

"What about cutting your losses and walking away?"

"First, I tried to push back. When that didn't work, I put my half of the business up for sale. They should've just taken the offer and bought me out. Instead, I started to get threats. Adrielle, Laney and her family, even you. They were watching me. Following me."

"When was this?" Jax asked.

"Years ago."

"So you stayed?"

"I tried to retire, just in case stepping aside as the figure-head of the company was going to work. Tried to put someone else in my position. They wanted you to quit the Bureau and take over the company, but I told them you'd never do that."

"Why me?"

His dad shrugged. "They always think in terms of lever-age. I'd have a reason to want you alive, and cooperating. You would have a reason to want the same for me. That meant they could use us against each other." He winced. "I didn't let them do that. I pushed you away, and then I let you go."

Jax might owe his father a thank-you. "You protected all of us, even though it meant you were trapped."

"You have a family now, Son. You know that's how it works."

Jax stared at his father, his eyes burning.

From the living room, Maizie yelled, "Jax!"

Ramon rushed in. "We've got incoming."

Jax pushed off the counter. "Gun safe is in my closet."

Zeyla yelled, "It's that team from the hospital!"

His dad backed up so fast he nearly toppled off the stool. "They found me here. They know I came to see you, and they're going to kill all of us."

Maizie rushed in, clutching her laptop, with Zeyla right behind her. "They're approaching the house from all sides, and they're armed."

Jax nodded. "We can't stay here."

"We can't get out." Zeyla's voice shook. "Not without

someone getting hurt. And digging in to defend ourselves will only prolong it. They're going to kill all of us."

"So what do we do?!" His father's gaze darted around. "I'm sorry. I didn't come here to die or get all of you killed."

"Has to be why they wanted you to find him."

Jax glanced at Ramon. "So we could all die?"

Ramon only shrugged.

Jax looked at Maizie. "Grab Jolene."

"The RV?"

He nodded. "The RV. It's our only way out."

Chapter Twenty-Three

J ax held the wheel with both hands, a vest on just in case they fired through the windows. Everyone else hunkered down in the back. He hit the gas and let the RPMs build before he put the rig in gear and released the emergency brake.

The RV lurched forward and splintered the garage door as it burst onto the driveway and slammed into Ramon's car.

Jax held the gas pedal down, moving the compact off the drive until he had enough clearance to pull between it and the pizza delivery vehicle at the curb.

The side window shattered.

Jax ducked down, holding on as he turned the wheel in an arc, and they almost toppled over. The giant RV roared down the street, and he blew the stop sign at the corner. With no other traffic around, he sailed through the intersection and away from his house.

In the rear of the RV, Jolene screeched.

Bullets slammed into the back of the RV, and he prayed they didn't hit the gas tank. Then he felt like a hypocrite for praying at all considering how things were between him and the Lord right now. He should've been going to Bible study the past few weeks and reading his Bible in the morning. But the minute he had even an inkling of a lead on the search for Kenna, all that went out the window, it seemed.

Why was it far easier to nudge Ramon toward faith than it was to work on his own journey?

He turned west out of the neighborhood, unsure of where he was going. At some point, they'd need to stop for supplies. They only had the go bags Kenna had insisted he pack and leave in the RV. Just in case. First, they needed to get far enough from the team behind them to lose their pursuers.

Jax kept his speed at a level where he was pushing it, watching for them tailing him. With the limited view from the side mirrors, it was hard to see. "Ramon!"

The guy crouch-walked up the aisle to the front. "She's gonna be mad we got bullet holes in her rig."

"I'll take that any day if we can have her back."

"Good point." Ramon nodded. "What do you need?" He eased into the passenger seat and checked the mirror on his side.

Jax couldn't even begin to articulate what he needed. Focusing on the rest of them was a far better anchor. Distraction. Whichever it was it didn't matter. "Everyone good back there?"

"Yeah, we're all hanging on."

A phone rang in the rear of the RV.

Ramon said, "That's Zeyla's cell."

"You think *Dominatus* can track us?" Jax said. "We might not be able to escape this team if we're giving away our location."

Ramon shot him a look.

Jax turned his focus back on the road in front of them.

They were coming up on the freeway entrance, and they were going to take it. He wanted as many miles between them and their pursuers as they could get before they had to stop for gas and cat food.

"You think they can't locate us?" Ramon scoffed. "They're one step ahead, and they have been this whole time. Every lead we get is a trap, and there's nothing we can do about any of it now. We've got a team in pursuit, you just wrecked your house, and now we're babysitting your father."

"Excuse me, Son."

Ramon glanced back, but didn't apologize for saying *babysitting,* even though Dad objected to it.

While Ramon seemed completely unfazed, Jax focused on the road, listening to Zeyla on the phone. Trying to save their lives was a higher priority than whether Ramon got along with his father. Having the old man here was weird enough without this being about relationships.

Zeyla said, "Okay, I'll tell him." Louder, she said, "Jax! My mother got another video. She's sending it over."

Ramon twisted in his chair while Jax hurtled around the on ramp that circled in a giant bend and dumped them out on the freeway where he was already going top speed. "I don't see anyone behind us." He looked out the front.

Jax spotted someone on the bridge above, looking down at them. "We're not exactly inconspicuous in this thing."

Focusing on the road helped keep him from thinking about whatever Amara had received. Or why *he* wasn't the one who was receiving these videos and photos. They were using them to get Amara to do what they wanted.

"But if we need somewhere to sleep," he continued, "it'll do better than being cramped in a car. And I'm pretty sure she's got coffee tucked away somewhere."

Maizie said, "And microwave popcorn."

Ramon said something to her in Spanish, and she chuckled.

Zeyla said, "You speak Spanish?"

"Only a little," Maizie replied. "I'm pretty sure Ramon dumbs it down for me. And speaks really slowly."

Jax wanted to be glad they were all getting to know each other, but the threat here was real. He watched the mirrors for that team and drove for an hour before he was willing to pull over. They'd switched back and forth along highways and wound up at a gas station in the middle of nowhere with two pumps and metal bars on the windows.

As soon as he pulled over and put the RV in Park, he turned to Zeyla. "Can I see the video?"

Ramon moved his hand toward Jax's shoulder, but didn't touch him. Which was good, considering how tightly he was wound right now. Like a rubber band pulled so tight that the slightest thing might make him snap.

Beyond Zeyla, his father touched Maizie's arm. Probably to help her up. She made a noise in her throat.

Ramon nearly knocked Zeyla over getting by her to Maizie and Jax's father. He spoke to her in Spanish and helped her slide onto the dinette seat. The young woman had paled.

Meanwhile, his father backed up to stand by the door. "What did I do?"

Jax shook his head. "We're all tense and on edge right now. Don't worry about it."

"Sorry," Maizie said. "I'm fine."

Ramon flinched. "You don't apologize. Ever."

Jax wasn't sure that worked in *every* situation, but right now he'd have to say he agreed with the sentiment in general. He squeezed his eyes shut for a second.

"I have it." Zeyla held out the phone. She'd taken Ramon's seat in the front and now looked at the Hispanic man with a curious expression on her face.

Jax looked out the windows. "Ramon, check out the back. Make sure no one is behind us."

"Got it." Ramon shot Jax's father a look, then went to the bedroom in the rear.

Maizie said, "I can turn the cameras on. We'll know if someone approaches on foot, but it won't help us see a vehicle. You have to be within a couple of feet of the rig for the sensor to turn on."

Jax nodded. "Get it activated, Maze."

"You're stalling."

He looked at Zeyla. "Because I don't want to see her like this. Whatever it is."

"It's proof of life, right?" Zeyla said. "So, no matter what, you know she's there for you to rescue. She's *alive*."

Jax looked down at the screen. The dark image looked gray and grainy like surveillance video. He didn't think this was some kind of plea from Kenna, like a hostage video or the kind where someone confessed to crimes they were forced to take credit for.

He tapped Play.

A door opened on one side of the view, and he realized rain streamed from the sky. Someone in a dark jacket, bare legs and bare feet under it, darted out of the door onto the walkway. Barely an aisle, before there was a railing.

His whole world tunneled, and it was just him and Kenna, making a run for it along the railing.

Someone in dark clothing and carrying a rifle followed her, and another person with a weapon approached from the other side. She climbed up onto the railing as if intending to jump. Beyond it was only black, like the night sky.

His breath caught in his throat.

Jax's father came over. He put his hand on Jax's shoulder, but he shrugged off the old man and kept watching.

The two men dragged Kenna down off the rail, and she fell to her back. The coat fell open, and he strained his gaze, trying to see a bump on her abdomen.

"It might be too early to see," Zeyla said quietly. "But she's alive."

The video stopped and text showed on the screen.

You'll never find her.

Jax watched it two more times. He wanted to lock himself in the back room and cry for an hour. Just break down and lose it, seeing his wife in that situation. Knowing she wanted to escape, but in the end had no way to get free.

His father stayed where he was, by Jax's side.

Maizie sniffed. Ramon came back in from the bedroom where he'd been looking out the back window, and they spoke low to each other. Jax figured if there was a reason to tear out of here in a hurry, then his friend would tell him to put the phone down and do that.

Jax pulled in a choppy breath and pushed it out slowly.

Staring at the screen.

Dad gasped. "I recognize that place, Son. I know where it is."

Jax looked up at his father, wanting to find words, but there was nothing.

Zeyla said, "My mother didn't recognize it. How would you?"

"Because I visited that shipyard twice a month for years." His dad lifted his chin. "I owned it."

"Where is it?" Maizie asked.

His dad looked at her. "Canon Marine Shipyard. It's on the northwest coast of Washington State."

Maizie's fingers flew over the keyboard. "Found it. Give me the video, Jax. I'll match it to the location if I can."

Jax handed the phone back to Zeyla. "Send it to Maizie, please."

She dipped her head to the phone and tapped away. "Just as long as we realize that there's no way they'd send us video if there was any chance we'd be able to use it to find her."

"And if we do," Ramon said, "then it's for sure a trap."

Jax didn't want to admit they were likely right. He wanted to find his wife. After all this time, he needed her back in his arms so he could protect both her and the baby.

His dad said, "The timing is a little coincidental."

"Considering your arrival, I'd say so." Ramon folded his arms.

"What is that supposed to mean, Son?"

"I'm not your son." Ramon lifted his chin, motioning toward Jax. "He is. I'm the one watching his back while he does everything he can to find his wife. And what are you doing? Seems more like trying to save your own skin."

"I've done what I've done to protect my family."

"And save yourself," Ramon shot back.

"Why wouldn't I ensure we all survive? I don't have to surrender myself to keep the people I love safe. This isn't some contest of nobility where the one who is determined to die heroically is the winner."

Jax turned around and started the RV engine, then pulled out of the gas station whether everyone was ready or not. They still had three quarters of a tank worth of gas remaining. "Buckle up. Washington is a long way."

Zeyla clicked in her seatbelt. "What if my mother and Bruce want to come?"

"They can meet us." Jax dug out his phone and called a number he hadn't used in a long time. When it went to voicemail, he said, "I have updates. I've been expecting a callback for weeks, but no one has contacted me. So I'm making alternate arrangements."

It wasn't going to go down well, but he had priorities, and those of the group didn't align right now.

He might apologize later, but he wasn't going to mean it. The taskforce the president had set up wasn't working. They weren't achieving anything, or they'd cut out Jax. Instead, he needed good-quality, professional help. The kind that didn't come cheap.

Jax hung up and called another number.

"Lightwood."

"Preston, it's Jax."

"Wow." The guy paused. "Didn't think I'd hear from you."

"I figured you might be in a position to help me out."

Preston had spent time in prison for a murder he didn't commit and found Jesus through a ministry that served inmates. He'd known Kenna's father as a friend and considered Kenna the same. They'd helped each other out, and Jax had been involved for some of it.

But when Preston aligned himself with Miami Security International in keeping secrets about Kenna's history from her, it had driven a wedge between them. Not that it stopped her from rescuing him and two MSI operatives from *Dominatus* captivity in France. Something that was only months ago but felt like years now.

Preston said, "Whatever you need, I'm there. No question."

Jax fought the lump in his throat.

"Did you find her?"

"We have an idea where she might be," Jax said. "I know you have a house in Washington State."

"Just outside of Seattle."

"And I know you're in contact with MSI."

"You need a tactical team, just say the word."

Jax flexed his fingers on the steering wheel. "I'll have Maizie send you the information."

"I'd love to hear from her. It's been too long."

Jax gave him some details about how long they were going to be, driving up to Washington. Preston didn't seem to think it presented a problem getting the MSI team there, probably before Jax and his family arrived.

Jax hung up the phone, clearing his throat. He busied himself settling it in the phone holder clip. Ignoring the way Zeyla glanced at him and how he could see the others in the rearview. All of them were here to support him, making sure he didn't lose it. They would step in if he did, and probably wouldn't care if he broke down, but Jax didn't want that. He needed to hold it together and be their support.

Ramon and Maizie cared about Kenna as much as he did. She was a hugely important part of their lives. Zeyla had pitched in, wanting the chance to get to know her sister. His father had some amends to make.

"If we go up against them"—he glanced at Zeyla—"will you be okay? Will you stick with us?"

"I'm in this until we get Kenna back," Zeyla said. "We all are."

Chapter Twenty-Four

Almost a day later, Jax drove the RV through a rolled-up loading bay door, into an expansive warehouse. The rain that had been incessantly hammering on the windshield—and driving him crazy—quit as soon as they were under cover. After hours of driving, during which he'd switched off with Ramon so he could get some rest, they were finally in Seattle.

He turned the dial on the lever and shut off the wipers, easing his foot down on the brake. Inside, the warehouse was lit up with bright fluorescents thirty feet above them. Whatever this place had been once, it was a good choice to hide an RV and stage a standoff.

Jax put the RV in Park and shut off the engine, breathing hard. "How long do we have?"

"Probably not long." Ramon strode down the middle aisle to stand between the front seats. Before he could say anything, Zeyla came awake fast in the passenger seat, swinging her arms. Ramon said, "Whoa," catching her flailing. "Easy."

Zeyla blinked. Terror flashed in her eyes until she focused on Ramon. "Let go."

He loosened his grip. "Good?"

"Sure." She passed him and stepped out of the RV after Maizie.

Jax's dad glanced at him, then followed the two women. They'd been in a kind of silent standoff the past few hours, since there was nothing more to say and everyone had been focusing on resting. Only stopping for gas had taken its toll on them. Kind of like sleeping on the floor in the aisle because they'd given the women use of the bedroom.

Ramon glanced out the windshield. "Looks like Preston and MSI have already set up for us. Come on."

Jax followed him out of the RV into the middle of a tense standoff between the people he'd brought and the men waiting for them. He spotted Preston in the middle, dressed in jeans and a sweater, looking nothing like the man Jax had seen in Arizona at that resort, either before or after he'd been shot in the shoulder.

Kenna had spent time at his house in New Orleans, getting into several situations with Ramon and these people, who were operatives for Miami Security International. Then there was the whole deal in the UK where Preston and a couple of MSI guys had been kidnapped.

Jax spotted their boss, Earl Jonas. He'd brought a team with him, and they were all geared up. Mostly ex-military.

Maizie smiled widely. "Bear!" She stayed where she was, next to Zeyla, who had shifted into a protective stance.

One of the guys in tactical gear grinned at her. "Hey, Maizie. Good to see you."

Ramon wandered over to the guy. "Bear." They shook hands. "It's good to see you back with the team."

The move diffused a lot of the tension, but several of them regarded both Zeyla and Jax's father with suspicion.

After a member of the MSI team, Allison Moore, had been killed in New Orleans, Kenna said that Bear dropped off the map. And Maizie had been the only one who kept in touch with him—so she didn't have to hunt him down. For a few months, Maizie had been his only contact with his life while he went off grid. Even his company hadn't known where he was, but the young woman saw fit to make sure he knew people cared about him.

Now he was back.

Jax said, "We don't have much time. That team of operatives has been behind us for the past three states." He was so exhausted he was seriously dragging but apparently had to manage this. "Dad?"

His father came over with him to Earl and Preston, both of whom eyed his father with suspicion. "Edward Jaxton, this is Preston Lightwood and Earl Jonas." Before his dad could point out that Preston was a murderer—even if he had served his time and been released—Jax explained, "Preston is a friend of mine and Kenna's, and Mr. Jonas runs a security firm who have saved our lives in the past."

His father couldn't argue with any of that.

Mr. Jonas said, "Interesting company you keep." Glancing specifically at Zeyla.

"Yeah?" Zeyla fired back. Jax didn't turn, but given the tone in that one word, he figured she had a hand on her hip. "I'd have to say the same about you, *Mr.* Jonas."

Maizie said, "Kenna and Jax got a cat. Her name is Jolene. I'd show her to you, but I had to secure her in the bathroom so she doesn't get hurt."

Jax figured she learned from Kenna to diffuse any

tension with humor, and he was more than proud of her for all of who she was becoming, but they had to focus here.

Preston grinned. "A cat?" He started laughing. "What happened to the dog?"

"She's in California with Jax's niece and nephew."

"Guys," Jax said, "we have a team incoming who are probably going to try and kill us all. We should make a plan."

Bear came over, offering Maizie a wink. "Jax?"

He nodded. "Good to meet you. Again?" The guy offered a hand, which Jax shook. "I know you were in Mexico, but I'm pretty sure I was unconscious at the time."

Bear grinned. "We're all set up. My team can show your people where to position themselves." He glanced at Zeyla, then Ramon, and finally at Jax's dad. "Depending on whether you have them here to fight or if you want them protected."

Jax turned to his dad. "Go with Preston. Do what he says."

"I think I could—"

"Go with him." Jax looked away. "Maizie?"

"You're giving me a choice?"

He needed about six cups of coffee for this conversation. "You're an adult, and you've pulled your weight so far. What do you want to do?"

"Bruce has been teaching me how to use guns, but..." She bit her lip.

"A pistol?"

"I just want to be able to defend myself if I have to." She seemed nervous.

Jax cupped her face with his hands. "Honey, you get scared, you shoot whoever you want. Okay?"

Someone off to the side laughed.

She smiled up at him, still somewhat unsure. "Okay."

He kissed her forehead.

Ramon came over. "I'd say stick with Zeyla, but she's already taken a bullet for you once this week." He smiled the kind of sibling smile Jax had come to expect when the guy looked at Maizie. "Wanna stay by me and Bear?"

She nodded.

Bear said, "Someone get these ladies pistols."

One of his guys jogged over to a crate. They'd set up plenty of pallets and stacked them high so they'd have defensible positions. Preston walked away with Mr. Jonas beside him, limping on his cane, and Jax's father following them.

"I don't like this." Zeyla glanced around. "Who are these guys?"

"I'm sure they're asking the same about you," Jax pointed out. "Bottom line? They've helped Kenna and I before on more than one occasion, and they're here to help us face off against this team. They're pros, mostly ex-military. The kind of people who show up when you call, no questions asked."

"Fine." She looked up at the windows, high at the top of the wall just before the ceiling peaked under the eaves of the roof. Rain hammered on the glass and in a few places ran down the wall on the inside. "Washington sucks."

"You prefer the heat?"

"I don't like being cold." She hugged herself with one arm.

Jax said, "That's one thing that you and Kenna don't agree on."

An alarm went off across the room, not loudly, but loud enough to pause the conversation. One of the MSI guys said, "Someone tripped the perimeter."

Bear handed Zeyla a gun and said to Jax, "You take position over there."

Jax crouched behind the pallets, unsure where to focus his attention. There were a couple of doors around the room, front and back. Probably entrances on the sides. The windows above were vulnerable points. Hopefully, someone on the team had been assigned to protect his father and the other two older men, even if they were capable of defending themselves. There was a reason they weren't out here helping with the fight.

With this team and the resources MSI brought to the table, they had a much better chance at finding Kenna. As soon as they got rid of this squad that had been chasing them up the freeway incessantly for days, they could get to the shipyard his dad had recognized in that video.

Kenna seemed to be closer than ever—but still too far away to grasp. His heart echoed the hammering of the rain on the window, fat droplets that hit the glass and dampened everything. The slow creep of hope faded, trickling away out of reach. Leaving him with an empty ache, tempting him to give up the search. To surrender his wife to their enemy because it looked far too impossible to get her back, and at least they were keeping her alive.

They still had an idea where she'd been, but no idea where she was now.

The slim lead of one word, *offshore*, and a shipyard in Washington State weren't good. If she'd been put on a boat from here, she could be anywhere in the world now.

"Pizza delivery!"

Jax flinched, but he recognized the voice. Reminiscent of the way his father had shown up at his house—something Bruce hadn't been present for—it was a decent way to announce himself in a situation like this. Anyone with their finger close to a trigger would hesitate, suddenly thinking about melted cheese and the scent of hot pepperoni.

"It's Bruce!" Maizie yelled loudly. "Nobody shoot!"

"And Amara!" the pizza guy called back. "We're coming in, so don't blow our heads off."

Zeyla came out from behind cover. "Mom!"

Jax heard Ramon say, "Stay put" and agreed with him. He wanted Maizie to remain where she was. Zeyla crossed the warehouse floor and went out of sight for a second when she passed a stack of pallets.

As she stepped into view, a gunshot rang out from high in the rafters.

Zeyla hit the floor and rolled out of sight. He didn't think she'd been shot but couldn't be certain without looking for himself.

Jax spun and saw a guy climb through the window. He aimed at the shock of nearly white-blond hair at the same time several other people fired their weapons. The guy's body jerked, and he tumbled over the railing to the floor not so far away from Jax. He hit with a sickening thud, and Maizie yelped.

"Keep your eyes open!" Bear turned, assessing all corners of the room. "They're here."

Amara yelled, "Bruce, this way! Help me!"

The two of them moved with Zeyla to the side of the room out of sight. Jax kept an eye on the windows he could see, covering that entrance just in case. Making sure no one from the team got the upper hand on them.

He saw movement behind the glass, and the window began to tilt. In a second, whoever it was would step inside.

Jax would've preferred a rifle, given the distance, but braced his elbows on the edge of one pallet and squeezed off two shots. The window shattered, and the person never stepped inside. If someone had been out there, they weren't anymore.

"I have two coming in the front," one of the MSI guys said between the sound of gunshots. "Another at the back."

Two MSI operatives raced to the back of the warehouse. Everyone else braced for the front entry.

Instead of gunfire, the front of the building exploded. Jax hunkered down, ducking his head at the smoke and debris that rained down. His ears rang with the concussive force of the blast.

He checked the windows again and saw someone lowering himself to the ground on a rope. The second the guy's feet touched the ground, Jax wondered if it was already too late. He ran at the man, tackling him to the ground. The rope caught between them, twisting both as they fell. Jax landed on his shoulder and cried out as pain whipped through it like lightning.

He kicked out at the guy, unable to move his arms for a second as the pain vibrated through his upper body.

The other man rolled them and slammed Jax's head against the floor. Jax got one leg up and kicked him back, lifted his upper body off the floor, and squeezed off two shots.

His opponent fell back, dead.

Jax slumped back to the floor and hit his head again. He winced, breathing hard. Awareness coalesced around him, and he realized the others were in a firefight with whoever had come through after that explosion.

He stayed low and made his way to where Bear and Ramon fired over a short stack of crates, and Maizie hunkered down on the floor between them.

"You good?"

"You killed that guy." She whimpered. "I saw you."

Jax nodded, unsure what she needed him to say. "They aren't going to get to you."

"I might not be the target. Maybe they don't care about me at all."

He found that hard to believe, but it wasn't going to be reassuring to her. Beside him, Bear quit firing. "They backed off. One dragged the other out."

"Injured and on the run?" Ramon turned to them. "Sounds like fun." The Hispanic man touched Maizie's shoulder with his offhand. "Stay with Jax." Then he hurried away, and Jax heard him call out to Zeyla.

Bear gave orders to his guys, and they ran after Ramon, giving chase to the team who'd tried to infiltrate this warehouse.

"Should we go tell the others it's safe to come out?" Maizie asked.

He shifted so he could put one knee down.

She tucked her legs closer to her chest, her knuckles white from gripping her knees.

"In a minute," he replied. "It's over, but we need to be sure."

She nodded. "That was intense, but it was over quickly."

"It always goes faster than you think." He touched her shoulder. "You good?"

"I wasn't in any danger." She considered what she was saying. "I might ask Bear if I can do some training with his team."

"It would help you to know what they're thinking, and how they approach problem-solving."

She bit her lip. "There's something I need to tell you, and you aren't going to like it. But it wasn't worse than those people coming to kill us, and Zeyla said I should just let you know later. So you could focus."

And now that the situation was resolved, she could say it. "What's going on?"

Maizie lowered her knees, her backpack beside her. She probably felt odd not having her laptop or iPad in her hands.

She started to speak, hesitated, then said, "Elliot Adams was killed a few hours ago. The transport was ambushed, and he was executed."

"Were any other agents killed?"

She shook her head. "But..."

"What is it, Maze?"

Chapter Twenty-Five

Earl Jonas stood at one end of the huge conference room. "This presents a considerable problem."

Jax wasn't so convinced. "I don't show my face in public until Kenna is found. Problem solved." He pushed off the wall, antsy to get this thing going.

They'd left the RV at the warehouse but brought Jolene. She was now the office mascot at the MSI facility in Seattle. Though, here they didn't call it Miami Security International. The doors had another far more generic name on them, and the place had no online presence.

Bear and a couple of his teammates were absent. They'd captured one of the people that attacked the warehouse and had the guy in an interrogation room. Jax was surprised that Amara and Bruce had opted to join the meeting. Then again, Amara had spent most of it talking quietly to Zeyla and earning heated looks from Ramon.

Maizie had been distracted by the walkthrough of the tech lab and decided to stay there after being introduced to the office technician—a tall and stocky dark-haired woman with a pixie cut that included shaved sides and three cut-in stripes above each ear. It hadn't hurt that Earl Jonas had given her carte blanche access to the MSI system, and the technician, Hazel, had taken a shine to her.

That, more than anything, told him these people didn't have anything to hide.

Amara was the one that concerned him. Especially considering the look she'd given Maizie at the warehouse.

Preston said, "Speaking as someone who has been arrested for murder and spent years in prison, it's worse when you didn't do it."

Someone said, "I bet the payday is better, though."

"I don't want to find out." Jax shifted his weight and folded his arms. "It doesn't matter if the FBI is gunning for my arrest. I didn't kill Elliot Adams and I didn't order the hit. Any proof they come up with is going to be fabricated. So all we've got to do is prove them wrong, starting with the GPS location of my phone, and the fact I've contacted no one using it to order a hit."

"We've got more important priorities." Ramon leaned his chair back, tipping it onto the two back legs.

"Exactly." Not that Jax wasn't worried, or didn't think he could end up with a serious fight on his hands if he was forced to prove his innocence. It's just that he didn't consider it more important than finding Kenna. "It's all just more of a distraction. Ways for them to slow us down, get us hung up and occupied by nuisances rather than focused on finding her."

"That's why I sent a couple of my guys to the shipyard." Jonas leaned on his cane. "They should be back soon."

"You weren't going to tell me?"

"You can't be seen in public. We know what we're doing."

Jax clenched his back teeth.

Ramon and Zeyla both glanced at him.

"What about the man you have in custody?" Jax asked.

"So far he hasn't been cooperative."

Ramon said, "I'm surprised they don't have cyanide capsules in their teeth for just such an occasion."

"It's not unheard of," Zeyla said. "But if you screw up or get caught, you're cut loose. It won't be long before they send someone to take him out." She looked from Jax to Mr. Jonas. "They'll dispatch an operative to kill him."

One of the MSI guys said, "Do they have tracking devices on them?"

Zeyla looked distressed. "Even if this one doesn't, it won't be long before they find him. Just like they found Samuel Chistane."

Ramon tipped his chair back down. "They're probably kicking themselves they didn't take out Elliot then. Or at the bank."

Jax had thought about that a whole lot during the hours of driving, talking it through with Zeyla while Ramon slept. They'd concluded that Special Agent Herron had to be more than just someone they were using for their ends. She came across as more deeply embedded than just being coerced into losing evidence or giving orders that suited them.

"We know who they're targeting," Jax said. "So it's worth checking in with everyone in this building."

"Like a lie detector test?" Preston asked. "Because just asking the question doesn't mean you're going to get the truth. These people are under duress."

"A lie detector test sounds like a great idea," Amara said. "I'm sure they have tech that can function as one. Everyone should be questioned."

Jax shrugged. "Or that's just more distraction, and we should go."

But then the door opened, and his objection was swallowed up by the appearance of Hollace, who Jax had met briefly in France, and a female operative with blond hair and a wedding band on her left hand. Hollace was ex-military and had a command presence that filled the room. "Sir?"

Mr. Jonas nodded. "Go ahead."

"We performed a thorough search of the location Mr. Jaxton gave us and walked through the entire shipyard. It appears to be the location from the video showing Kenna trying to escape them, but if there was ever any evidence she was there, it's gone now. They cleared out."

Jax slumped into a seat.

It was for the best that they hadn't taken him with them, if his presence was only going to enable the FBI to find him and arrest him for a murder he hadn't committed. But Jax still would've wanted to go—to stand in a place where Kenna had been and see for himself what was there.

Hollace continued, "We took a look at the security archive and found buried files that Maizie and Hazel managed to access. They found a day several weeks back where there was unusual activity in the middle of the night. A helicopter landed in the parking lot and took off twenty minutes later. We think Kenna was transported away from there."

"And now she could be anywhere." Jax ran his hands down his face, trying to tamp down the frustrated anger swelling up in him.

"Do you want me to tell you that helicopters don't have that much range?" Hollace paused. "That puts the search parameters at a restricted mileage."

Jax lowered his hands, not looking at anyone else. "And if they landed at an airport and put her on a plane? Like I said, she could be anywhere."

"They brought her up here. It wasn't the final destination. Accept that we're at least another step closer to her."

"I've been another step closer to her for months, and I'm not there yet. Eventually I'll run out of road."

His dad turned to him. The old man had been quiet so far and kept to himself. Now he said, "You can't lose hope. That's what they want."

"I don't need any of you to tell me how to feel. I need you to find my wife."

Preston stood, moving to the front of the room while Mr. Jonas sat to the side. "That's why I bought a house in Seattle."

Jax frowned. "You had that house way before Kenna was taken hostage, so don't try to convince me it was so you could be up here to find her."

"Right." Preston nodded. "What I meant to say is that *Dominatus* is why I moved up here." He looked around. "Each of you is here because we've cleared you sufficiently to include you in this. But MSI and I have been working together for years to try and identify how to dismantle *Dominatus* in a way that will finally put a stop to them." His attention settled on Amara and Bruce. "We know you've tried, and had some success, but our goal is to find their main locations and hit a few simultaneously. Knock them back a step."

"Great." Jax figured Kenna might be at one.

"We can't do that if destroying a facility gets everyone inside killed. Either because they see us coming and execute all personnel, or because we level the place." Preston leveled a steady gaze on him. "So we need to find Kenna and get her out, which means the plan is on hold."

Because they had the armaments to destroy facilities.

"You know where they are?" Ramon asked the question that had been on the tip of Jax's tongue.

"We're in the process of narrowing it down. What we know at the moment is that *Dominatus* has a presence in both Alaska and British Columbia. There are some out of the way places, islands, and isolated communities between. We believe they have a facility, or several, in the area."

Right. That was an "area" that covered hundreds of thousands of square miles. Not an easy task to search without even knowing what to look for.

Preston turned to Mr. Jonas, who sat in front of a laptop. "Go ahead." The screen on the wall flickered on, showing an image of an island covered mostly with trees. "This is a location we are currently investigating, a protected island populated with Indigenous Alaskans. Their tribe is believed to have been undisturbed for centuries, but our satellite scans show evidence there is a massive power plant on the island."

Jax said, "Why haven't you gone in yet?"

"Our goal was to get a man on the inside in order to gather intelligence." Preston looked a little disappointed, so Jax figured it failed.

Hollace glanced at Jax. "You know as well as anyone that going in a situation totally blind is nothing better than a suicide mission."

Preston said, "So we can't get a man in. And we can't destroy it if there's a chance Kenna is there."

"I'll go," Jax said. He was here to find her. Why sit around and wait for evidence?

"It's a one-in-a-thousand shot." Preston hesitated, looking at Jax. "We have no idea that's where she is."

"I'm done doing nothing."

"I'll go with you," Ramon said. "Watch your back."

"We have more images, but not much." Jonas clicked the mousepad, and the view changed to a shot of the shore that had to have been taken from a boat.

Zeyla let out a noise and jumped up from her chair, which toppled over behind her.

Amara shot up beside her. "What is it?"

"I've been there. I know I have." Zeyla gasped. "I remember it."

The room electrified. Preston looked at Jonas with a whole lot of hope in his expression. Ramon dropped his chair back down again and stood. Even Bruce huddled in. The MSI people stayed back, letting her have those she was close to around her. But Jax could see in their expressions, that this meant a great deal to them.

"Those places are impenetrable," Amara said to Preston. "You'd never get someone inside without them being discovered. But I can get you in."

"I'd like to hear about your daughter's experience." Preston folded his arms. "If she'd like to share. Zeyla is the first person we've met who has come out of one of these places and lived to tell about it."

Ramon glanced at Jax.

Preston winced. "I'm sorry. That isn't going to happen to Kenna. We *are* going to get her back."

"I didn't get this far by believing I'll never get her back, or by quitting." Jax touched Zeyla's shoulder. "What do you remember?"

"Not much." She winced and shook her head. "It's foggy. I'm pretty sure I was drugged at the time. I remember that tree line, though. And wind. It was freezing. I was shivering, and I could feel the spray of the ocean on me."

"That's really good," Hollace said, his voice soothing. "Do you remember any buildings?"

She closed her eyes. "Maybe a tunnel? There were lights flashing overhead."

Jax said, "You were moving, being pushed like on a gurney. The lights overhead would seem like they were flashing."

She nodded, then opened her eyes and looked at him. "I don't even know when it was, or how old I was, or anything."

If they'd done something to her, she didn't remember. "That could be a good thing. Better than the memories."

"They've taken too much from me. How could there be more that I don't even remember?" Tears filled her eyes.

"I'm sorry." He had to clear his throat. "I know someone who has been through too much as well, and she's the kind of person who could walk you through how to move on. How to build a life."

"We're going there tonight," Ramon said, only looking at Jax. "If Kenna is there, we'll get her back."

Jax agreed that it would be just the two of them. "Let's do it."

"This island," Preston said, "is one of a half dozen we've got under watch by the satellite. And we only get a picture once every few hours. You'll be going in blind."

Jonas flicked through more images, and Zeyla sank into a chair.

"I know how to find Kenna," Amara said.

Bruce reached up and scratched his jaw. "I told you they won't go for it."

Amara shot him a look. "They need someone inside. I can do it."

"I'm not going back." Zeyla spun to her mother. "I'm not just going to walk into one of their facilities and submit to their—" Her voice broke.

"Not you," Amara cut in, avoiding eye contact. "Maizie."

Ramon exploded. "Are you kidding?! No one is going to walk in there. *Especially* not Maizie."

"Except you and Jax. Because you're big strong men," Amara taunted. "And you can protect yourselves."

"You aren't taking Maizie." Jax folded his arms across his chest.

His father said, "That's right. We safeguard the people under our protection. We don't send them into the lion's den."

"She's an adult. At least she was the last time I checked." Amara wasn't backing down. "She's also the innocent who can get us in if we pretend like we're handing her over."

Jax looked at Bruce. "Care to talk some sense into her?"

Bruce shook his head.

Zeyla and Amara looked at him with identical expressions. Amara said, "Because he's the voice of reason and I'm an irrational woman, is that it?"

Jax sighed. "Maizie stays where she's protected. No exceptions."

"Maybe you should ask her why *Dominatus* doesn't seem the least bit interested in her." Amara lifted her chin. "Ask her why she's untouchable."

"This is ridiculous." Jax shook his head. "Whatever game you're playing, Amara, I'm not interested. Maizie isn't going into one of their facilities, no matter how you goad us into agreeing with you."

He knew she'd been tested years ago, as a child. The man who'd held her had taken her to a house in England where she'd been assessed. Whatever their criteria, she hadn't met it. That was the simple reason why *Dominatus* didn't want her as one of their captives, the ones kept to give birth to a child they augmented in a lab.

"You don't know anything about her," he added.

Zeyla turned to her mother. "You can't take Maizie in there just to get intel."

Amara backed off and sat down. Still, her words echoed in his head. She'd successfully planted a seed of doubt, and he wasn't sure how to uproot it. There was a chance Kenna was out there on an island in Alaska. That was all he knew.

And he was finally going to find her.

Chapter Twenty-Six

"Gear up and get going?" Ramon's jaw flexed. "We need a boat or a small plane."

Hollace went to the door ahead of them. "We have a helicopter that can get you to the airport. Pretty sure you already know that since we picked you up in Mexico."

"Right." Jax stepped into the hall, where he could hear raised voices. A man and a teenage young woman.

"Is that Maizie?" Ramon asked, walking faster.

Jax headed for the source, down the hall where a set of double doors opened into an expansive room. Computer screens covered the walls. In the center were long metal tables and white-coated technicians performing forensic testing. "You guys have your own lab?"

Hollace looked around. "Fully state-of-the-art. The largest private lab on the West Coast, actually. Preston and Mr. Jonas didn't mess around. We're funded for whatever we need, and we've been taking cold cases, along with privately contracted investigations. A lot of it was inspired by Kenna. She's done an amazing job closing cases over the years, bringing down dangerous criminals and saving victims who fell through the cracks."

Across the far end of the room, Maizie yelled, "Don't touch that!"

Jax strode down the aisle and saw an MSI guy facing off with her. She held her tablet to her chest.

The guy said, "You'll get faster results if you connect to our system."

"Give her some space, yeah?" Jax ushered the guy back, noting the tension in Maizie. Not so different than how she'd been for weeks, but the addition of what Amara had insinuated was making his head spin with implications. "Maizie?"

"I don't have to connect to their system if I don't want to."

"Why would you not?" the guy said.

Hollace spoke from behind Jax, "Richards, why don't you give us a second?"

The guy wandered off. "Whatever."

Hollace sighed.

Jax hadn't taken his attention from Maizie, but just then he glanced at Ramon. His friend met his gaze, shaking his head very slightly. Exactly. She wasn't okay. He'd figured that had a lot to do the fact none of them were. Kenna was gone, and they had no idea what was happening to her—which for Maizie would bring up some pretty serious memories. Maybe even flashbacks.

He wondered if she hadn't been okay since they'd discovered Kenna was gone and she'd hidden it better than he realized.

"Maze?" he said, gently.

Her eyes remained unfocused.

"Look at me, honey." He'd always been so cautious of

not triggering her, leaving getting in her face to Kenna so he didn't trigger any of her trauma. "I need you to look at me, Maizie."

She sucked in a breath, but her eyes found his.

"It's just me and Ramon." Jax was aware more people had come in. Maybe Amara and Bruce. Preston and Earl Jonas, or Bear. He didn't know who, but they had an audience. "Focus on me."

"They know something is going on with you, Maze." Bear came around and stepped between Hollace and Jax.

The move made Jax wonder if she was going to get overwhelmed with the proximity of males around her. He couldn't help it, though. He needed her to talk to them.

Bear continued, "You're shutting out people who care about you. But do you know what? When I didn't want to talk to anyone, you hit me up and kept tabs on me. You didn't let me lose myself, making me tell you where I was."

"It was just a ping." Her voice sounded hoarse.

"You probably saved my life. That means I owe you, and I'm choosing to repay that favor right now. You haven't contacted me in months."

"I've been busy." She scrunched up her nose for a second. That response had been far too quick. A defensive reaction.

Jax said, "What was going on in here when we came in?"

"Nothing."

"You're lying." He needed to get moving but wanted this out in the open before he left. "Cards on the table, Maze."

"It was *nothing*. I don't have to connect my stuff to their system. They'll be able to see everything."

"And you'll be able to see all of ours," Hollace said.

"Full access. Because we have nothing to hide." The implication being that Maizie *did* have something to hide.

A machine at the other end of the room beeped.

"No one gets in Kenna's system." Maizie shook her head. "I promised her that her stuff would be secure."

Jax caught something in what she wasn't saying. "Did you break that promise, Maze?"

Maybe it was redundant to keep using her name, but he needed the personal connection. She needed to be the person she was with Kenna—strong and capable. The woman she was becoming, not the scared child with no power in a horrible situation.

She flinched, and her face scrunched up.

"Told you." The words were quiet and came from somewhere behind him. Amara.

Bruce sniffed. "You and I are going to talk about how you chose to reveal that."

Amara said, "I don't owe you anything."

"Guess not." Bruce didn't sound happy.

Jax glanced over his shoulder and tipped his head for them to get out of the room.

Bruce shook his head. "I'm not leaving Maizie until I know she's okay. Amara can go."

The older woman stomped out, past Zeyla, who stood at the door looking unsure of what to do.

"I'm fine." Maizie shook her head, lifting her chin. Trying to convince them.

It didn't work.

"We know you aren't, and you haven't been since Kenna was taken." Jax had to swallow against the lump in his throat. "I know that because none of us are okay."

"No one's getting on anyone else's case. Just mine," she said. "Because I'm 'poor Maizie' who can't function like a normal person. Who gets—" She caught herself and stopped talking.

"What?"

Ramon said, "Tell us what's going on."

"It doesn't matter. I'm dealing with it just like Amara did."

Jax frowned. "Either it doesn't matter, or you're dealing with it. Not sure it can be both. But either way, we want to know what it is. We need you to let us in, Maizie."

"Or what? You'll force yourself in." She stared at him, defiance in her eyes. "Been there. Done that."

Someone gasped, and he thought it might've been Zeyla, but didn't look.

"You know the kind of men we are," Jax said. "You know you're safe with us."

"Then leave me alone."

"Plug your iPad into their system." Jax wasn't backing down. "And your computer." Because that was what had started all this.

"No."

"Why not? What don't you want anyone to see?" He took a step toward her, knowing she understood how he would act in her personal space but not touching her. "Maizie, why does *Dominatus* seem to not care about you at all?"

"You don't know that," she snapped.

"Tell me."

"It isn't a big deal. We're not even at the FBI anymore, so it doesn't matter."

Jax lifted his brows. "The worm in their system?"

She sniffed, glancing away.

"You put it there so that *Dominatus* had access to the

Bureau's computer system, likely giving them access to other systems and national databases in the process."

She didn't deny it.

Jax's mind spun with the implications. It had been her. "So they've infiltrated the government because of your choices." He folded his arms. "Which means the president's taskforce might have been burned because of you."

Her features flashed with anger. "You don't know that."

"I know that Samuel and Sandra, and now Elliot, are dead because our enemy can track your every movement. And if you plug your stuff into the system here, MSI gets hacked by the people they're trying to stop."

"We need to destroy her system." Hollace took a step toward her.

Maizie backed up.

"Why did you give them access, Maizie?"

Ramon took a step forward. "*Hermanita?*"

She whipped around to look at Ramon. "Don't."

He lifted his hands.

"What did they send you?" Jax asked. "Pictures of Kenna, or something else?"

She scrunched up her nose.

He took another step toward her. "Pictures of you?"

"I got rid of them all." She gasped. "I wrote a program that went through every website, whether it's indexed or not. Even the deep web. I took down every terabyte of data that had to do with me. I got rid of all of it. But they had—" Her breath caught in her throat.

"I'm sorry." He didn't want to tell her that it was unlikely she'd have ever been able to delete electronic pictures or video of the time she'd been held and abused. "I'm so sorry, Maze."

"They said they'd publish it online and tell everyone I work for Kenna, and all kinds of—"

"They were going to ruin all of us?"

She nodded sharply. "And they sent me this." She tapped the screen of her iPad and turned it so he could see the screen. Audio kicked on, and he heard a heartbeat.

The sound of an ultrasound machine reading the heartbeat of a baby.

Thump-thump, thump-thump.

Faster than he'd have thought it would be. Stronger. He stared at the image of his baby, kicking and shifting in the womb. The baby's head, and the little prominence of the nose. He could see the limbs and a couple of places where it looked translucent.

Jax sucked in a sharp breath.

Ramon squeezed his shoulder. "Did they threaten the baby?"

Jax stared at the video, unable to speak. They'd sent this to Maizie and not him. Because this life was a weapon they could use against people who cared about Kenna and wouldn't allow anything to happen to her and her unborn child.

Maizie probably nodded, because Ramon squeezed Jax's shoulder. Pain roiled through him, but for the first time it wasn't something he thought about getting rid of with the right substance. He thought about Kenna and what she must be going through alone, and how he had their friends —their family—around him. He wasn't going to give up, because he wasn't alone. He was part of a team.

"They can't know I told you." Maizie backed up and slumped into a chair. "They'll kill her."

Jax tore his gaze from looking at the baby. "They won't

kill her. They need Kenna alive. That's why they're working so hard to divide us to keep us from finding her."

Maizie's gaze widened. "I meant they'll kill *her*." She pointed at the iPad.

Jax stared at the young woman.

Ramon said, "It's a girl?"

Maizie nodded. "I'm sorry. I should've told you, or Elizabeth, or someone. But they said they'd destroy everything. They said Amara couldn't be trusted and that your father was one of them." She swallowed. "They said I would destroy everything."

"Their goal is to divide us. To get us to doubt each other's loyalty, split us up, and keep us from working together. Because they know that if we act as a team, we'll find her." Tears burned in his eyes. "We won't stop until we find her."

Maizie looked around, nervousness in her stiff movements.

Jax took the iPad and went to a chair so he could watch the video again. He found the Share icon and sent it to himself as well. The fact everyone else had information about his wife and he'd been sent nothing wasn't lost on him. It made him want to rage that they'd been keeping all this from him, knowing he would want to see it. That the life of his wife and child were being threatened and he had no idea.

His stomach clenched.

They're alive. Dominatus *wants them alive.*

He had to remember that, or it would kill him wondering if, when he found her, it would be too late.

Hollace and Bear came over, dragging stools to sit. It put them at eye level with Maizie and made them less imposing so they weren't towering over her.

Hollace said, "I understand why you don't want us to access your system. Thank you for protecting MSI from a cyberattack. But if you let us, we might be able to connect your laptop to an independent system that's air gapped from our network. We can watch what *Dominatus* looks at. We might be able to feed them incorrect information or even trace back their location. Find the source."

Maizie stared at him. "I couldn't do that because they would've seen me. But I wanted to."

"I know," Hollace said. "And thanks to you, they won't see us coming."

"They'll find out. They'll hurt Kenna's baby." Maizie sniffed.

"I need you to trust me. This could help us find her. It could help us take them down. For good." Hollace kept his voice steady, his tone even. "We know what we're doing."

Jax looked at her. "Maizie, I'm asking you to let them do this."

She pressed her lips together for a long moment, then finally said, "Okay."

Jax set the tablet aside and started for the door. Ramon walked with him. They were in the hall when she called out, "Jax!"

He turned back and saw Maizie in the doorway, Zeyla beside her.

"Ramon and I need to go check something out." He needed to fill her in on some of it, though. "Amara doesn't take you anywhere. No one does. You stay here and you don't leave without me coming back first. Got it?"

Her lip quivered. "I'm sorry I couldn't tell you."

"I know they threatened her and you felt like you had no choice. I understand that."

She stared at him.

Jax didn't like the cold feeling inside him, but what else could he do? She'd made her choice and didn't allow him to be part of it. Thinking that would keep him safe.

"You hate me."

Jax unclenched his jaw. "Thank you for telling us the truth."

She sniffed. "You do. You hate me."

He shook his head, but there weren't words to reassure her when it was all too close, too raw. "I just want to find Kenna."

But the bottom line was, she hadn't trusted him and she'd lied to him. Yes, she'd been scared and coerced. That was why he wasn't fuming at her. Their enemy knew who to manipulate and how. Which meant Amara cared about Kenna enough to do what it took to keep her alive—because that was what they'd threatened her with.

They'd used Maizie to infiltrate government servers and undermine efforts at the highest level to take them down.

Dismantling the fight against them the way they'd dismantled Kenna's team.

"We'll be back soon, I hope," he added. "We need to check something out."

"Okay."

Jax gave her a hug, because she needed it. "See you when we're back." He looked at Zeyla. "She doesn't leave. Not for anything."

Zeyla nodded. "Understood."

Jax strode away, around the bend in the hall to the elevator. Bear passed him, handing over a watch identical to the one Jax wore. He took off his own and traded with the other man.

Bear started to speak, but Jax turned away. He jabbed

the button for the elevator, feeling the anger in him release. Pain echoed through his shoulder.

He planted his palm high on the wall and tried to breathe through it, but the anger rose in him, and he pulled his arm back. Swung his fist and punched a hole in the drywall.

Ramon's arm snaked around his waist and pulled him back. "That's enough. You save that for *Dominatus*. Because they deserve it."

Jax shoved him away as the elevator doors opened.

Ramon said, "Let's go get your girls."

Chapter Twenty-Seven

Cold sea spray arced across the bow of the little boat they'd rented, thanks to the MSI expense account. In fact, Jax owed them a whole lot right now. There was so much riding on this that he felt like he was being tugged in a hundred different directions, and he needed everyone to do their part or it would go sideways far too quickly.

"She's gonna tie herself in knots making it up to you and Kenna."

He didn't look at Ramon, not really wanting to yell in reply to his friend over the sound of the boat motor and the water cutting under them. Not wanting to talk about Maizie, not even with Ramon.

The sun hung low, almost to the horizon, because it was after midnight in this part of the world where day and night seemed to be off-kilter most of the time.

"You can't let her do that," Ramon added.

Jax gripped the wheel, steering the boat to a dock he spotted on the west side of the island. One in a chain of islands that dotted this stretch of southern Alaska coastline. "I know."

"You and Kenna, you're better at forgiveness than most people."

Jax glanced over, wondering if Ramon was ready to hear why that was. He figured the guy already knew, because Kenna had told him about her faith. In the quiet moments between cases, she had been steadily approaching the subject with him.

Ramon continued, "She needs to get that from you guys. Learn it. Live it."

"You sound like a motivational poster."

Ramon almost grinned but didn't. "But if Maizie forgives the wrong person, it'll be on you."

"I got it." Jax didn't need his friend to tell him how much was riding on him and all of this.

Right now, Jax wasn't exactly focused on what Maizie needed to learn as she matured. He was really only worried about her physical safety—which he'd entrusted to Zeyla. Jax had figured Zeyla was inclined to stay behind rather than face her nightmares for a woman she didn't really know but wanted to. Zeyla knew how they all felt about Maizie, and if anyone might be able to stop her mother, then it was her.

"I'm sure you do, once you've found Kenna. Only then, you'll be focused on your wife and her pregnancy, right?" The implication being that until he found her, Jax only cared about one thing. And the "I got it" was a maybe at best, and didn't include Maizie.

He wasn't sure he agreed with Ramon's assessment of that.

Jax slowed the boat and came alongside the dock slowly, saying, "How about I explain it to you? You learn what forgiveness truly means. What surrendering your life to God simply out of gratitude for everything He saved you from really means. And then you don't need to worry that you can't teach her. You don't have to worry that I'll miss something because I'm focused elsewhere."

"I'm not her parent."

"You're the closest thing to a brother she'll ever have."

"I'm an adult male who isn't a blood relative."

"The fact you pointed that out is *exactly* why Kenna and I have no problem with you and Maizie being close friends and acting like siblings. Because you aren't going to do anything to hurt her."

Ramon scanned the shore. "If someone does hurt her, I'll string them up by their—"

"Got it," Jax said. "Bruce will probably help you. That way I'll have plausible deniability when the cops come and knock on my front door, asking questions."

"Just make sure you tell them Kenna was with you the whole time."

Jax managed to laugh at that. "Let's go find her."

He was echoing Ramon's sentiment when they'd left the MSI office hours ago, making their way north first by plane and now by boat. He grabbed a shotgun out of the hold, a pistol in his belt holster, and extra clips in the pouches on his vest. Among other things they'd pre-planned. No point giving away all the tricks they had up their sleeves.

Ramon tied up the boat, and they headed down the dock. "This is weird in broad daylight."

"Waiting for dark in Alaska this time of year isn't worth it. Keep your eyes open."

"You're supposed to say 'head on a swivel,' aren't you?"

"I thought it was 'stay frosty.'" And all those other sentiments tough guys shared with each other. Did it actually help?

Ramon chuckled under his breath. "I thought you were a real stiff. Turns out you're okay."

"Thanks, I think." Jax figured that was the ultimate sign of respect coming from this guy. He nearly rolled his eyes, but doing that was ridiculous and reminded him too much of his sister in high school. *What-ever. Talk to the hand.* As if his middle school years hadn't been traumatizing enough.

Ramon stepped off the deck onto sandy grass, followed by Jax. Another boat pulled up to the dock behind them. Amara and Bruce.

The chilly night breeze—Jax wasn't going to call after midnight "evening"—cut through his shirt and cooled the sea spray on his face. His whole body ached. The cut on his forearm stung, his shoulder throbbed, and the ibuprofen-acetaminophen mix he'd taken had worn off hours ago.

Ramon scanned the shore. "Something is up."

Jax had the same vibe, a kind of hum in the air, making all his senses fire. "This is going to go south any second."

Armed men stepped out of the trees, all of them dressed in black fatigues. Comms earbuds in, sunglasses up on the top of their heads. At least six of them. Hardened warriors who didn't look like they were in a mood that was open to visitors they hadn't been expecting.

"They didn't bring me a drink to welcome me to the island?" Ramon huffed. "I'm hurt."

"Weapons down!" the lead guy yelled.

They spread out, each of the armed men fanning to the sides so they could eventually circle around Ramon and Jax and cut off their retreat. Jax held one hand up.

He muttered, "I don't like this," under his breath. Even though it wasn't exactly surprising, and they'd been expecting something to happen as soon as they showed up.

Had planned for it, in fact. Because there was no way they'd have been able to sneak into a *Dominatus* facility.

Jax lowered to a crouch and set his shotgun on the dirt.

When he stood, one of the men closed in and slid the pistol from Jax's holster. He clenched his stomach and kept from reacting to being disarmed that way. He whipped his head around to look at Ramon and said, "Don't."

The last thing he needed was for his friend to run his mouth or start a fight just to make the point that he could defend himself. The odds were stacked against them.

A tendon flexed in Ramon's jaw, a fiery look of defiance in his eyes. "Wouldn't dream of it."

"Right." Jax looked at the leader. "You're in charge? How about you take us to whoever gives *you* orders." The guy sent to scoop up trespassers wasn't the boss.

The guy chuckled under his breath. "Don't worry, you will be coming with us."

He didn't like the dark tone of voice this guy had. Or the dead look in his eyes. If he said they were all hired mercenaries, the kind of guys who would do anything for money, Jax would've believed it.

He spotted Amara emerging from the tree line, Bruce following her. The older man had his hands secured behind his back, and another armed man in black fatigues followed Bruce. Holding a gun on him, presumably to keep him from escaping. Amara didn't have any fear that she would be shot in the back. In fact, she walked as if she had a position of power here.

There it is.

Ramon twisted around to Jax. "Take me to your leader? Really? We were supposed to sneak in here to steal all their secrets and that's all you say?"

Jax shot him a look right back, just as planned. "You're

the one who said we steal a boat from those meatheads. Figures *your* plan is what gets us caught."

"That's enough." The gunman closest to Jax dragged his shoulder, turning him around. "Hands behind your back."

Both Jax and Ramon had their hands secured behind their backs. Jax's shoulder burned with his arms pulled back like that. "I have a shoulder injury, if you don't mind." It was dangerous, but just in case the guy would ease up...

The gunman chuckled. "Guess it isn't your lucky day, then." He dragged Jax by the elbow.

His foot caught on a rock, but he caught himself and stumbled instead of falling to his knees in front of these guys. Tumbling on a rocky beach wasn't going to feel good. He didn't need a smashed knee on top of everything else.

Teeth gritted against the pain blossoming in his shoulder, the heat there growing into a furnace until he had to bite his lip, Jax forged ahead.

The trail stretched about a mile, winding between the trees. A deer trail, or some other wild animal, and these guys had tramped back and forth until it was worn into a full-fledged path. He ignored Amara and Bruce, tied up like they were, accompanying them. And the incessant comments from Ramon, directed at him.

All he could focus on was whether Kenna had been brought here.

Was he about to find her?

I don't have any right to ask. I've lost my grip on who I am. Don't let me lose what I have.

At the center of the island in a clearing about half a mile wide, someone had built a structure many years ago. The windows were yellowed now and shattered, the roof missing in spots and secured with tarps to keep the weather out. A worn-down and weather-beaten former homestead that had hopefully been abandoned decades ago.

On either side, someone had erected huge military-style tents that flapped in the evening breeze coming off the ocean, racing over the trees and dipping down into the clearing.

People in heavy sweaters, beanies, and what looked like insulated jeans walked back and forth, their heads down. Carrying heavy bales of hay, big bags of rice or flour, and boxes with canned goods logos on the side. Unloading—or loading.

"Keep walking." The gunman jabbed him in the back, between his shoulders.

Jax set off again and was steered toward the tent on the left side whether he wanted to go there or not. All the images they'd been sent of Kenna, she'd looked to have been in medical facilities or the like. Okay, so *he* hadn't been sent any.

A fact that Jax was trying not to think about because he didn't want to contend with the fact everyone else seemed like they'd been sent videos or pictures, and Kenna had been threatened if they didn't act. But did he get any pictures of his wife?

No.

Whether they thought they could manipulate him...use him...or not didn't matter. They weren't using him.

"This way." The voice behind him wasn't the one who'd ordered Jax left.

He twisted to look over his shoulder, which didn't feel good at all. Ramon was being walked in the other direction, along with Bruce. Amara followed the two men with Jax.

"Keep going."

Jax was shoved, so he breached the front of the tent mid

stumble and this time landed his knee on the tarp under his feet.

Amara strode past him to a folding table and metal folding chair, where she sat and opened a file on the table. "What's the timing on the next delivery?" When she got no answer, she said, "You think I don't know this is a holding point? When is your next trip to the facility?"

The team lead for the gunmen strode over and closed the file before she could read much. "We have a few hours. Let's get this done." But he didn't turn to Jax. He stayed where he was, both fists planted on the table. Entirely focused on Amara. "Wanna tell me why you brought three of them?"

"They do all this together. Like a team." She made a face like she thought their efforts were little better than children playacting and chuckled. "They thought they were going to simply walk in your front door. Of course, you want all of them, Roberts."

Why she chose to use his name then, Jax wasn't sure. Did she want him to have their designations?

Roberts huffed. "Back to make a habit of ordering people around, I see. That'll be a nice change."

Someone behind Jax snickered.

He started to get up off the floor, but the man behind him slammed a hand—and all his weight—on Jax's shoulder and pushed him back down to his one-knee stance on the floor.

Amara sat back in the chair. "I delivered the goods as promised. I get to escort them to the facility. After all, I wouldn't want you taking all the credit because I wasn't there."

Roberts said, "Good thing you're nice and early."

"What is there to do? Wouldn't hurt to be early."

Roberts shook his head, pushing off the table and setting his rifle aside. "Stick to the timing. We do not deviate from schedule. So sit tight, shut your mouth, and let us do our jobs." He glanced at one of his guys and lifted his chin, then went to sit behind another table.

Amara rolled her eyes and left the tent in a huff.

Jax lifted his chin. "Is this when the interrogation starts?"

"Wrong tent." Roberts lit a cigarette and blew the smoke to his left. "That one has a plastic sheet on the floor."

One of his men wandered into the tent with a laptop and a webcam. He hooked them up so they pointed toward Jax, then got the chair Amara had been using and set it in front of the table facing the laptop.

Jax wanted to ask if this was a meeting he hadn't prepped for. But the fact they might be about to put him in contact with Kenna drew him with a promise he hadn't felt in months. Seeing her again—alive.

He could practically taste the anticipation on his tongue, coppery with blood.

The man behind him dragged Jax to his feet and shoved him into the chair. The laptop screen showed his face, and a green line ran across the screen moving from top to bottom. As if it was scanning his face.

Scan complete.

"What's going on?" He looked at Roberts. "What is this?"

"Business." Roberts turned the laptop and clicked the mousepad. Typed on the keyboard. "Okay, capture complete. Not bad, actually. Pretty impressive tech."

A deep fake.

They'd seen it before with *Dominatus* assets.

"What are you going to do with my face?" Jax asked.

"You're about to tell that taskforce of yours that you've switched sides. Become a true believer."

"No one will believe it." Jax shook his head. "I would never join *Dominatus*."

"No?" Roberts tipped his head to the side, studying Jax. "First, you walked away from your cases, then your job entirely, and now you've come here. You walked right in the front door. You're one of us now, and everyone will know your allegiance now lies with us. After all, it's the only way to get your wife back."

Chapter Twenty-Eight

I've made up my mind. Jax's voice came through the computer speakers. Roberts typed on the keyboard. *I won't be standing against* Dominatus *anymore. The fight is over.* The computer program looked like Jax and sounded like Jax.

Jax sniffed, his entire body taut like a livewire. He'd listened to the whole conversation between Roberts—using their software so he could pretend to be Jax—and the director of the FBI. Jax hadn't even known the guy was a member of the taskforce the president had put together to fight against *Dominatus.* Jax had been connected all the way to the top after meeting with the president in London.

It seemed his enemy had been one step ahead this entire time...and then some.

They were so far ahead it wasn't even a contest. His head was still spinning with the ramifications of how much they knew, how connected they seemed to be to any attempt to come against them. No wonder they'd so efficiently taken Kenna after infiltrating the FBI with fake badges. He figured it wasn't outside of possibility that they had assets in multiple government agencies.

And no one had any idea.

Roberts typed and the Jax-like voice continued, *It's the only way I'll get my wife back. I'm sure you understand why I have to give it all up. For her.*

At least they got the sentiment right, because he was feeling the need to burn it all down to save Kenna. But not to join *Dominatus*. Not even if he had a gun to the back of his head, which was effectively where he was at right now. He couldn't take more than a step or two without being gunned down.

Then the fight really would be over.

Right now, he had to watch this man, this agent of his enemy, destroy everything Jax had worked toward for years. In the space of a few minutes, he was tearing it all down and making sure Jax had absolutely nothing to lose. Which was absolutely going to backfire.

First his job, then his career when he walked away from the FBI just days ago. They'd taken his friends from him, too. Now they were going to destroy his reputation and any chance he might have to get his standing as an agent back. After this, they'd believe it had been him in the video call.

His boss, the director of the FBI, sighed over the connection. "I'm sorry to hear that, Special Agent Jaxton. You understand what this means."

He wanted a way to tell the director that it wasn't him. Some kind of code word that would indicate he was under duress, let alone that it wasn't even him. They'd told him there was no point yelling. The mic wasn't going to pick up anything, so the director would never hear it.

I made my choice. Roberts hit a button, then closed the laptop lid.

Jax said, "Where is Kenna?"

He heard a breathy laugh behind him. Jax wanted to punch whoever it was in the face, but it wasn't going to solve his problems right now.

He lifted his chin. "I am getting her back."

"Why not let's go see her for yourself?" Roberts stood. "Isn't that what you want?"

Jax had to assimilate that question and what he meant. "You're taking me to her?"

"We leave with the next shipment. Wasn't that the deal?"

Whatever that meant, it was definitely a trap.

"Where? Where is she?" Jax nearly jumped out of the chair.

Months. It had been *months*, and he hadn't been able to find her. Now he was going to be able to hold her. He'd get to see how much she'd changed with this pregnancy, things she'd experienced all alone. She could tell him everything that had happened to her, while he could share what had gone on in the outside world.

Roberts said, "Guess you'll find out" and walked to the tent flap.

Someone shoved it open and pushed him back.

Ramon entered first with a rifle in his hands. He squeezed off two shots, and Roberts fell back. Another of the men dove out of the way, or was shot, Jax wasn't sure. Bruce barreled in with a gun as well.

Someone fired into the tent from outside.

Jax tipped the chair to the side and landed on his good shoulder, clenching his abs to sit. He pulled his knees in and kicked at the man closest to him. Aiming to shoot at one of his friends.

Jax slammed his boots into the back of the man's knees, and his legs buckled.

He pulled his knees in again fast and kicked the man's shoulder and the back of his head right before he hit the ground, the motion shoving the guy forward.

Jax rolled over and stood up, which made him a target for any gunman. Not good. He ran to the table and kicked it over, sending the laptop flying. It wasn't going to provide much cover, but it would be better than nothing.

Ramon kept going, unfazed. A gunman over on the side of the room lifted up and fired across a table. Ramon fired at the same time, his aim arcing up as he fell back, blasting bullet holes in the ceiling. Crying out in a way that sounded more like anger than pain. He'd been shot.

Bruce fired at the shooter.

Several other men ran into the tent. One of the men slammed into Bruce and tackled him to the floor.

Amara came in after them. "Tie them all up," she ordered.

For a second, Jax thought she was ordering him and Bruce to tie up the men, but he quickly realized the opposite was true—she was telling these guys to tie up him and his friends. But Jax still had his hands secured behind his back.

He rushed over to Ramon but couldn't even put pressure on the wound.

Amara walked over to them, all high and mighty. An expression on her face like she didn't care one bit about any of them. They might as well have been dirt on the bottom of her shoe. "What was the point in that show? You had to know it would be over quickly."

Ramon had a bullet hole high on his chest, just under his collar bone. It was probably the best place it could've hit.

Thank You, Lord.

The Hispanic man breathed hard, clutching his chest with his teeth gritted. "Ow! That hurts."

"We'll get you help," Jax told him. "Sorry, but I can't put pressure on it."

Ramon shook his head, as much concession as Jax was going to get.

Amara said, "I should kill you now. Just put a bullet in your head and put the world out of its misery having to deal with your sorry self still existing."

Fire flashed in Ramon's eyes.

Despite the plan, and Amara making it look good with her overacting, he could see the words hit home for the guy. Jax wanted to chide her, but the men here had to believe she was on their side.

"Enough." Roberts clambered to his feet, fury in his eyes and two silver bullets embedded in the vest he had on. The look on his face wasn't an expression Jax wanted to see late at night—or ever. "No one shoots anyone else." He looked at one of his men. "Take the wounded to the medical tent to be shipped back to the mainland, and the rest go on the transport."

That meant Bruce was going with Jax, while Ramon went to get treatment.

Jax could deal with that.

Amara swung around to him. "What kind of farce is—"

Roberts swung around and punched her in the face. Amara dropped to the floor, crying out with her hand to her cheek.

Jax's stomach clenched. "Enough!"

He couldn't let on that she might be on his side, though. It had to be purely because this guy had hit a woman.

"Yeah?" Roberts pointed his gun at Bruce, talking to Jax

when he said, "Turns out the only one I need is *you*, and even that is debatable. Means I don't need this guy."

"We all have orders to follow." Jax shifted and stood, leaving Ramon clutching his gunshot wound. "But that doesn't mean anyone needs to die. Everyone has their uses, don't they?"

His friend was out of this fight. Ramon needed help, and Jax needed to not have to tell Kenna he had been killed. Okay, fine—he didn't want to lose the guy. He needed to make a good case.

"Killing too many people will draw attention to you," Jax continued.

Roberts' lips curled up. "But it's fun."

Someone slammed into Jax from behind, shoving him forward so that he hit the ground. Before he could get back up, the guy stepped on the back of his shoulder and with a hand grabbed Jax's elbow.

Someone cried out.

Maybe it was him. Or one of the others.

The fire that erupted in his shoulder told him that all the healing he had done so far was being undone.

Eventually he passed out.

He didn't know how long it was before he woke up. Face smashed against cold metal, the smell of rust and dirt all around him. The temperature in here far colder than it had been before.

He shivered and found his hands now secured in front of him. His feet had been tied together as well, which meant moving wasn't going to be easy. As soon as he was... Soon as he could process through the situation... He'd take stock of what weapons he still had on him. *Come on, think.*

He'd gone full Kenna, hiding weapons all over him, hoping that if they found a few, they would stop before they discovered the rest.

Jax used his left elbow to shove himself up. His right shoulder was almost twice the size on the front side, and he had to fight to push his awareness of the pain to the back of his mind.

Nausea snaked up his throat.

Yeah, he couldn't ignore this pain.

Jax leaned over and deposited the last thing he'd eaten on the floor beside him. He leaned back against the wall, and when he looked around, he discovered he was in a shipping container.

"Did you just barf?"

"Bruce?" Jax looked around and found the guy in a heap on the far side. "You okay?" He wasn't going to admit he'd just thrown up.

The older man groaned and moved his legs, but didn't sit. "I'd get up, but it sounds like effort."

"What did they do?"

"What didn't they do? Apparently, Samuel Chistane was a friend of theirs...and that asset sent to take him out. Real close neighborly type friendship between the two of them and these guys up here. Guess I was due for some payback."

"A friend?"

"Or the kind of boss they worshiped like he was a cult leader." Bruce coughed, and it turned into groaning. "That's who these people are. Blindly following their superiors because that's what they've been conditioned to do. I'd rather think for myself."

Jax waited until he was done with his whole rant, then said, "How long was I out?"

"Hours, days—who cares."

"Bruce."

"Fine." The older man sighed. "I'll quit feeling sorry for myself."

"That would be helpful, thanks." Jax had enough of that going on in his own head, so Bruce adding to it would be a real drag. Okay, fine. Instead of Jax feeling sorry for himself, he was projecting onto Bruce. "Sorry."

The guy probably didn't even know what Jax was apologizing for.

"Don't worry about it," Bruce said. "You just wanna get your girl back."

Jax couldn't keep using it as an excuse to be a jerk. The plan had gone haywire. Not that most plans really went... well, as *planned*. He still had his watch on. It lit up with the display that showed the time when he lifted his wrist, but was it transmitting? Maybe this shipping container blocked the signal. Or a million other things that meant this all had gone wrong.

Jax shook his head like it actually dislodged the thoughts. "What about Ramon and Amara? Assuming these guys aren't listening to us talk."

"I doubt it. That's why they shut us in here." Bruce managed to sit up. "They carried Ramon off, supposedly to the medical tent. Which probably means they'll shoot him and leave him in the woods. Amara is hopefully sticking to the plan."

Jax lifted his gaze from his shoes. "You have doubts?"

"Wish I didn't, but it's hard to tell in our line of work. You rarely tell the truth, and it gets to be a lifestyle."

"Bruce, are you an agent for *Dominatus*?"

"Of course not." He shook his head. "They wanted me in the fold, then they came to kill me. Guess we had a truce for a while there, but I'm also guessing I'll find myself in their crosshairs again pretty soon." He sighed, as if that wasn't surprising at all but a regular part of their lives.

Jax felt moisture burn in his eyes. "I just want Kenna back."

"That's all any of us want. But if you're gonna be safe after that, means we've gotta take them down." Ire rang in his tone. "For good."

"It's impossible."

"Isn't that why you believe in God and all that stuff? Because He pitches in when things are impossible."

Jax groaned, leaned his head back, and closed his eyes.

"What? I was paying attention," Bruce said. "And I listened to some videos and stuff online. I like the idea of having God Almighty on our side."

"Doesn't mean we win. It means He wins."

"Okay, but that could come out good for us, right?"

Jax swallowed, still tasting the sick in his mouth. "Not if I'm supposed to learn to trust Him through losing her."

"Does God do that kind of thing?" Bruce asked. "Make you lose people just to teach you a lesson?"

"Not in the bad way, like I deserve it. But in a way where I have to grow through that to do the things He wants me to do. To be the person He's making me into. Someone more like Him."

Jax had to face what he'd been avoiding since he first realized she was gone.

That he might have to walk the road where he didn't get her back. That he was being called to trust God despite not getting what he wanted most.

He'd have to become who Kenna used to be.

Chapter Twenty-Nine

It started as a dark spot on the horizon. The water reflected the morning sun, which he'd watched rise after it made its lazy descent down and started to ease back up almost immediately, not even really setting. Lightening the sky with a promise Jax didn't feel.

Rain and gloom would have matched his mood far better than this. Not just the spray of the ocean as they raced across the surface of the water to the platform out in the stretch of ocean between Alaska and Russia, down to the south. Out of the main shipping lanes, and areas fishermen frequented.

Bruce lay in the back of the boat, the daylight giving Jax a full view of the bruises on the man's face and neck. He'd understated what they did to him.

Jax's head swam, his body a mass of pain and his arm limp by his side. The plastic ties securing it to the other hand put his shoulder at an angle that made him want to throw up again, but there was nothing in his stomach.

Three speedboats in a V formation, the one they were in at the lead.

Roberts piloted theirs, a coat on now instead of the vest over his shirt—with those two bullets embedded in it. They were all dressed for the weather out here, except Jax and Bruce. But if they were only bringing them out here to be killed, they'd surely have done it already.

Water ran down Jax's face, and he didn't know if it was sweat or sea spray.

The boat eased to a stop at a dock at the bottom of the platform, thirty or maybe fifty feet below the main level. Far above the swell of the icy waves, so cold the temperature numbed a person before they even realized they'd fallen in. His head swam trying to gauge the distance.

Right now, that sounded good. His shoulder would certainly stop hurting.

But this close to Kenna? There was no way he was going to do anything to jeopardize what happened next. He had to get her back.

I trust You.

The balance was there, his flesh versus his spirit. A husband's need to find his wife coming up against the desire God had placed in Jax to surrender to His will no matter what happened next.

He had to balance the two, admit what he wanted whether it was right or not, and decide to trust God for the outcome. Faith would come in the mix. Soon enough he would have his answer, and no matter what, he would do his best to give glory to God.

Your will be done.

He knew what he wanted, but that was going to be given to God as well.

Surrender.

Two men lifted Jax by his arms. The world swam around him, and he dropped to his knees.

"Geez, you guys really messed him up."

Jax got his orientation settled without falling into the water and followed Bruce down the dock, then to a walkway that led to a set of stairs. The stretches of steel steps doubled back on each other again and again until they were at the top.

"This way." Roberts led them down a walkway, the building on one side looking a whole lot like a warehouse and on the other side a railing and nothing before a person hit the frozen water below. The impact would feel like jumping from a thirty-story building onto concrete.

Roberts slid a key through a card reader, and the display turned green. He pushed through a set of double doors into a white corridor lit with overhead lights so bright it was like San Diego in July. Jax winced against the intense glow and trudged after Bruce, keeping his focus on the man's back with every step.

One foot in front of the other, over and over.

Each step one closer to Kenna.

Another set of doors led them to a lab. A man turned from his work, rows of test tubes in racks in front of him. To the side, he had microscopes. Jax even spotted a mass spectrometer. He was a man that Kenna had killed months ago.

"Last time I saw you," Jax said, "you were a stiff at the morgue. A bullet in your chest. Lights out."

"I'm aware." Marcus Buzard removed his glasses and tucked them into the breast pocket of his lab coat. "After all, I've seen him for myself."

"Right. You guys steal bodies a lot?" Jax looked around.

"She isn't here."

"Where is she?"

Buzard waved his hand. "All in due time."

"No." Jax stepped forward. "Now."

Buzard seemed to find that amusing, while no one else said anything. "Have a seat, I'll take a look at that shoulder."

"No, thanks." He glanced at his friend. "Bruce, how about you?"

"I'm the picture of health."

Jax looked back at Buzard. "We're good."

"Seems difficult patients is my lot right now. And our dear Zeyla isn't even here." He scanned Jax's face. "She was a firecracker, that one."

"We're not talking about the sick things you've all done to my sister-in-law. You're going to tell me where my pregnant wife is, and then I'm leaving with her."

"You really should let me look at that shoulder before you go. There isn't any good healthcare for hundreds of miles."

Jax yelled, "WHERE IS SHE?"

Buzard flinched. "We're currently running another test. I've been so pleased with the results thus far. I'm sure they'll come through this one hale and hearty, as they say."

"As who says?" Jax might have read that in a book somewhere, but not one from this century. "Because I've never heard anyone say that."

"If you'd gone to a *Dominatus* school as we advised your father, you would have received an adequate education. But we got here in the end, didn't we? Your baby in the womb of one of our children. It's almost poetic the way things worked out."

Jax sucked in a breath. "Excuse me?"

"It's the way things were always supposed to be. There's really no point arguing with it." Buzard sank onto a rolling stool with no back. "We try and things don't always go the way we plan. We try again in a new location, with a new version of us. Sometimes it works out and other times it doesn't. Life goes on. We make new plans."

"Is this going to make sense at any point?" Bruce asked.

"Escort our friend here to be assessed." Buzard motioned. "I'm sure there are some worthwhile parts in there we can use."

Two men came over and grabbed Bruce by the arms. He yelled as they dragged him away. Jax started to go after them, but Buzard grabbed his shoulder.

Jax cried out, and one knee hit the floor.

"Like I said, let's get that shoulder looked at."

A sharp burn touched the side of his neck. Jax cried out, knowing exactly what had just happened. They wanted him to pass out. Unconscious so they could do anything to him, and he'd have no way to fight back.

He launched up, refusing to go down like this. Determined not to pass out.

Warmth spread through him. "No, no, no."

"Just something to make you feel better," Buzard said. "My own recipe."

"You gave me pain meds."

"Even better, you'll need another dose within an hour, and if you don't get it?" He whistled. "You think it was rough getting off the meds last time."

Jax stared at him. "Your own recipe?"

"You're welcome."

"The other you said that to Kenna. Seems like it runs in the family."

Buzard stared at him, his assessing gaze entirely too clinical. Sure, he was a doctor, but he also came across like some of the serial killers Jax had met over the years as an FBI agent. This guy just had that look about him. Above the law, to the point he considered the law irrelevant. It definitely didn't apply to him, so much so that he rarely even thought about considering it a boundary for living an upright life.

Then Buzard laughed, and it sounded hollow. "The other me. He was a nut job, wasn't he?" He glanced down the long room, with rows of hospital beds.

Jax said, "She told you about how she killed him, right?"

He needed to goad the guy rather than contemplate the feeling that seemed to be spreading through him, reaching the tips of his fingers and his toes. Whatever Buzard had given him sent the pain packing somewhere else. Not that he was going to thank the guy, since he'd implied it was even more addictive than narcotics.

"He was working to release a deadly contagion that would wipe out most of the world's population," Jax continued, looking around as if interested. "Is that what you're doing here?"

Buzard sat stiffly, so pale he might as well be dead. "A pandemic." He shook a little, as though laughing. "A little on the nose, isn't it? Release a disease and show up with the cure so you can be the savior of the world."

"That position has been filled." Jax wanted to roll his shoulders. It was like an itch, but he knew it would be excruciating if he tried.

"Let's get him on the scanner. We need to find out what's going on with that shoulder." Buzard lifted his chin.

Jax spun to whoever was coming up behind him, spotted Amara at the door watching everything, and was too late to stop them from grabbing him. His head spun. His reflexes seemed like they were under water.

Then his back hit a hospital bed, and he realized they'd lifted him and dumped him there. Pain echoed in his shoulder, but he couldn't quite feel it.

Leaning over him, Buzard palpated Jax's shoulder joint, sending white-hot shards racing through him on the inside. But without the pain receptors functioning, he could barely feel it. "Not good. He may need surgery."

The bed moved, and lights flashed overhead.

This was what God wanted him to submit to? He could fight tooth and nail, but what would that achieve? Right now, he could barely lift his head, let alone swing a punch with his off arm.

The world rotated around him.

More lights overhead, him being pushed along on the bed underneath them. Only able to lie here and stare at the ceiling as it passed.

This is what You're asking?

Sure, Kenna had suffered for years with painful forearms, and the other Buzard had "fixed" her as if she'd asked him to alter her genetics. Whether he liked it or not, they had been drawn into this because *Dominatus* saw them as meeting some kind of quota.

Which his father had apparently neglected to tell him.

Not entirely surprising. Jax didn't have the energy to be angry about it. Not when he was far more concerned with the IV being inserted in the inside of his elbow.

When he'd talked through it with Bruce, Jax hadn't even been thinking about something like this. He'd wondered now if God really did want him to trust, even if it meant losing Kenna.

Would they both be at the mercy of their enemy for the rest of their lives?

He didn't want to raise a child in this.

He wanted the RV, a shot at disappearing, and years of peace to be a family. Not the FBI career he'd thought he would always have, because it's who he had become out of necessity—for his own survival.

Eventually, he'd lost the place where who he was ended, and he'd become who he needed to be. Without that part of his life there to hold him together, he had to rely fully on the Lord for a shot at keeping it together. He couldn't rely on himself. That guy was far too human, too fallible. Too much of an addict. Kenna needed the man God was making him into as the man with her, standing by her. Supporting her. Saving her from their enemies.

Jax's arm shifted, and someone took off his watch.

That was the last shard of awareness he had.

He didn't drift to the surface. He clawed his way up, grasping for every ounce of consciousness he could get before he found himself blinking and opening his eyes. Trying to get the room around him to come into focus.

She sat beside his bed. Dark hair, and slender shoulders. Tall enough to fit just right.

"Kenna."

She moved, coming over to stand beside the bed. "Sorry. It's just me, Amara."

He sighed out a heavy breath.

"Like I said. Sorry." She shook her head. "I can't find her. They only said she's 'out there' somewhere and it's an experiment, but I don't know what. They won't give me details, and it would be too suspicious for me to keep asking.

He managed to nod, understanding but not liking it. "What about—"

"They saw the chopper on approach. They shot it down." A tear ran from the corner of her eye. "Everyone on board is dead. It crashed into the ocean on fire."

Jax squeezed his eyes shut.

"The doctor said the surgery went well."

He didn't open his eyes.

"They replaced your shoulder with some kind of cutting-edge technology with their proprietary material that's supposed to mimic bone. And it interacts with your body and your bloodstream the way real bone would. It's kind of amazing what they can do."

Jax looked at her. "Yeah?"

"Yes, because it means that my grandchild might be born healthy." She sounded tentative, unsure how he would react to the cold reality of the situation.

"She will be born into this nightmare. Raised not knowing any other way. A victim, like the rest of us."

Tears filled her eyes. "I take what I can get. That's all I've ever been able to do." She reached for the hospital blanket over him but pulled her hand back. "You'll be together again, at least."

"Living here? For the rest of our lives?" He refused to believe it was over. No way was this fight finished. He would never quit and accept defeat.

Don't take me to that edge, Lord.

And yet, that was exactly what might happen. That same surrender might look a whole lot like submitting to *Dominatus* on the outside, while in his heart it was about yielding his life to what God wanted from him. No questions, just surrender. Just faith that God had it all in His hands, and He'd work everything for good for those that love Him.

No matter what.

Chapter Thirty

Voices drifted through the door, solid white with a tiny window crisscrossed with metal lines. "...total carnage. No one left alive, we didn't even find remains floating on the surface. The whole thing was burning."

"Burned alive is a nasty way to go."

"Better than drowning."

Two men walked by the door and continued down the hall.

"Out here?" one said. "You'd never feel it you go cold so fast. Get numb. Drift off and start to sink. Better than flames, and your skin melting."

Jax stared at the window. As soon as the two men were out of sight, he tried the door handle again. He had no idea how long he'd even been in this room—whether hours or days—since the surgery. His limbs were dragging a little, as if the signals from his brain needed a second longer than normal before they activated.

He had white scrub pants on, and canvas shoes he'd found under the bed that were a little too small. No socks. His own underwear still, thank you very much. A white tank top, muscle shirt so that the bandage on his shoulder was more visible. Or it had been, until he'd taken it off so he could see the wound underneath. With no mirror in here, it had been hard to look at the back of his shoulder and the extent of how they'd carved him up.

Still tender. The shoulder joint felt better than it had in a long time, if he was honest. But it felt more like having some foreign thing inside him and he wanted it out.

Captured.

Experimented on.

Shut in a cell with no way out.

He was living the life Kenna had lived for the past few months—and even longer. Ever since Colorado she'd been at their mercy, whether either of them had wanted to realize it or not.

Thank You.

He knew now what it felt like for her, being here. What it was like to live through everything they'd done to her. *I get it.* What she was currently going through, and what she had been forced to endure. He understood what it felt like to have no power.

If she'd told him what it felt like, he'd have said he understood. But he never would have. Not really. Now *when* he got her back, he'd be able to empathize.

Because he'd lived it as well—even if it was only for a short time.

Jax tried the door handle again. Still locked.

Thank You for giving me this understanding.

Gratitude pushed anxiety out of the brain. In fact, the two couldn't coexist inside a person's mind, so he'd fight fire with fire and keep saying thank you for anything he could think of. And he'd keep doing that until this was over. In between, yes, he was asking for what he wanted.

Laying his desires down and trusting God for what happened next.

He had no other way to fight this than to ask for God's intervention.

Thank You that MSI had a plan.

Maybe it had only been Bear, but regardless, things were still going to plan. Sort of. At least the highlights were on track.

He hadn't seen Kenna yet.

Jax went to stand on the cot mattress and tried the ceiling tiles, just in case one wasn't securely fastened. He might be able to climb up there.

Sure, he'd purposed in his heart to trust God no matter what, but he was still going to do everything he could to get out of here. Surrender wasn't about giving up and quitting.

A dull thud echoed down the hall.

Jax jumped off the cot and went to the door so he could see out. So what if they saw him watching.

But it wasn't any of the gunmen or medical staff who worked here.

He spotted a guy in black fatigues, dressed a lot like one of the gunmen from the island but with a couple of distinct differences. It was his friend.

Bear scanned each room as he came down the hall, looking in the little window at every door. Jax knocked on his, drawing the man's attention.

I guess the plan is working.

Bear rushed over, his gaze scanning the four corners of the door. Then he signaled Jax to back up. He reached up on the side with the hinges. Attaching explosives to the door?

Jax backed up farther, hugging the wall in the corner.

He heard three knocks on the door.

Then two.

Then one.

A long second later, the door popped. Smoke blew from around the frame on the far side from the hinges, and through the lock. Jax rushed over and caught the door as it fell in, making sure it didn't land hard on the floor and make a lot of noise.

He laid it against the end of the bed. "Got another of those guns for me?"

Bear grinned and held out a pistol. "Thought you were going to complain I took so long."

"Take as long as you like." One way or another, he was getting out of here. "Have you found Kenna?"

"Sounds like she isn't back yet. I've got my guys spread out all through the facility finding Amara and Bruce and looking for Kenna. One of them shot the breeze with a couple of *Dominatus* guys who are waiting for orders to go get her." Bear stopped at the end of the hall and whispered, "Bro..."

"Say it."

Bear winced. "Sounds like she's out in the ocean on some kind of dingy. They want to know how she responds to cold exposure, and hunger, so they've left her there a few days with nothing. Like a stress test for her and the baby."

"I'm going to kill these guys." Jax's stomach clenched. He checked the weapon and confirmed it was loaded, ready to fire. Safety off. Suppressor screwed to the front to mute the sound of a gunshot at least somewhat. "How did you get in without being discovered?"

Even walking down the halls trying to escape was a risk.

"Orders from on high. Half the staff went to the mainland." Bear quick-walked down the hall, his steps almost silent. Which for a big man was pretty impressive. "The other half haven't realized the security system has been tampered with." He winked over his shoulder, then proceeded around a corner. He said, "Copy that," to whoever was on the other end of his comms.

"Where is Bruce?" Jax wanted to ask about Buzard, just to make sure the guy didn't disappear and manage to escape.

"Sedated and being prepped for surgery since they were done with yours. Looks like they were going to take most of his organs." Bear muttered under his breath. "These guys are sick. Carving people up. Zeyla told me some of what happened to her."

"She and Maizie are good?"

Bear nodded. "Tucked up safely back at the office. They're digging into their whole computer system. Giving them a little payback. So far, they've backtracked the worm in Maizie's system and dug out what was in the FBI network. They wrote a program that erases the worm and everywhere it's been, repairing all the damage that was done. Don't ask me how they're able to do that. And they said it might take weeks to complete the job because it goes slow through each byte of data, backtracking what the worm altered or restoring what was deleted."

Thank You.

Maizie had managed to salvage the damage their enemy had done to the FBI network, destroying the chance for real justice for too many people and bringing in their own agenda. The young woman could repair what she caused, even if it was originally done to save Kenna's life.

He needed some time with Maizie so they could talk it out and get to the place they were good with the fact she'd withheld all that from him. Probably they both needed to forgive the other as part of it. But it seemed as if they would get the chance and Maizie would have a clear conscience. So one way or another, it would be resolved. Jax could teach her about forgiveness like Ramon had suggested.

Beyond that, he wanted them to deal a blow to *Dominatus.*

In fact, an idea began to coalesce in his mind. Jax had been fighting being two steps behind their enemy this entire time. But what if they could get a chance now to reverse that and finally be a step ahead of *Dominatus* for once? Like a punch their enemy didn't see coming. Or a virus they didn't notice had infected them until it was too late to repair the damage.

Good idea. *Thank You.*

He wasn't going to quit being grateful to God for anything. Not until the day he died and couldn't be thankful anymore. And after that, he would spend eternity being thankful, so it wasn't really as if he was going to stop ever.

No matter what happened.

Jax checked the hall behind him and followed Bear. "Let's get out here and go find Kenna." Once they were clear, he told Bear his idea.

"Exactly what I was thinking." He moved down hallways, around corners, until Jax had no clue where they were.

He'd been unconscious when they left him in that room. How was he supposed to find his way out now? The futility of it hit him in a way he knew Kenna had felt the same emotion. Yet another way God allowed him to understand what it had been like for her.

"This way." Bear headed through a set of double doors, in front of which was a desk to the side.

Jax spotted a guy behind the desk, a hole in his forehead.

As he stepped into the room, smaller than his office at the FBI, Jax pulled up short. Doctor Buzard sat behind a desk, both hands on the surface. Palms down. Sweat on his forehead, and over that bald dome. Jax wondered that it only took two trained private security officers to make the guy sweat.

Apparently, he wasn't as unflappable as Jax had thought.

"Figured you'd want to do the honors." Hollace took a step back.

Buzard eyed him. "After everything I've done for you?"

"Shoot him and let's go." Hollace turned away from the desk, disgust in his expression. "I don't wanna be here any longer than we have to be."

The idea that had been assembling in his mind clicked into place a little more. "You know how much intel is locked up in that mind?"

"He isn't gonna talk." Hollace shook his head.

"Maybe not for a while. Depends how long you keep him. Who knows what he'd be willing to trade in exchange for concessions, or a sweet deal in protective custody?" Jax shifted his stance, aware this needed to be wrapped up quickly but unwilling to lose a golden opportunity.

Bear took a step closer to Jax's side. "Shoot him, or I will."

"Everyone step back." Jax looked around. Two men, one of them Hollace, and Bear. He had to convince them. "Take a breath. Killing assets to tie up loose ends is what they do. That's not who we are. We're supposed to be better."

Hollace said, "You wanna let him go so you can feel

good about yourself? Clearly you don't understand what they're capable of."

"You think I don't know?" Jax shot the guy a look.

"If you'd suggested we bring him before a court, maybe I'd have believed that. Or if you said to torture him until he squeals because it's what he deserves. If you'd said *that*, I might have gone along with it. But altruism? No way. The moral high ground doesn't make us the winners here. It leaves us with nothing."

"How about this, then," Jax began. "None of what happened here gets out. You guys settle in and take over operations—at least as far as *Dominatus* is concerned. Keep things running at this facility. Check in, file reports. Do whatever he does to provide evidence of what he's doing to the higher-ups. Feed them information like nothing has changed."

"Take over and pretend nothing happened?" Bear looked intrigued. "We could tell them whatever we wanted. Find out information we never would've known otherwise."

Buzard scoffed. "That will never work."

"I'm not so sure," Jax said. "I think you know it could work. And if you want to stay alive, you'll explain to us exactly what to say to report in, so they never suspect a thing."

Buzard's jaw flexed.

Nothing to say to that? Jax figured that meant he was onto something. Especially when these people had a computer program that could let them pretend to be this guy, or anyone else they wanted. That's what they'd done with Jax, undermining what he'd built. Trying to strip even more from him.

"Buzard goes with us." Jax motioned to the guy. "Everyone else stays and does what they're told. They're used to it, after all. And MSI is now the proud owner of an offshore platform."

"I'll call it in to Mr. Jonas," Bear said. "Get approval from him and Lightwood."

Interesting that Preston was now an authority figure at the office. But not interesting enough to ask about it. While Bear pulled out a satellite phone, Jax turned to the others. "You guys are good with it?"

Hollace nodded. "As long as they pay for what they're doing, it could actually get us a win."

"Did you get Maizie in this system already?" Jax lifted his chin, indicating the computer on Buzard's desk.

The doctor sneered. "Soon as we got here. She got into the surveillance and helped us move through the facility without being seen."

"Good."

Hollace started to speak, but Bear cut him off.

"Green light," Bear said. "Pack it up, and let's get Buzard out of here."

Jax didn't move. "Tell me where to find Kenna."

The doctor only chuckled. A hollow sound, the satisfaction of a man who thought he could do whatever he wanted, and no one would ever hand him the consequences of his actions.

Hollace said, "I'll find out." He pressed the button to speak into his comms. "Base, this is three. Do you copy?"

Jax didn't take his attention from Buzard, not for one second, the entire time Hollace spoke to the office—presumably to Maizie, in the computer network. Scouring the files for information about Kenna, most likely.

Jax stared down Buzard. "You don't realize it yet, but you're done. These guys are going to decide what happens to you next. And I doubt they'll take my advice."

"She wants to talk to you." Hollace lifted his chin.

Jax stared at the MSI guys. Bear's satellite phone rang, and he handed it over.

Jax answered the call, "I just need to know where she is." He didn't want small talk, and this wasn't the time for them to process how they were feeling. The sense that time was running out had grown until he was antsy with the need to move.

"I know," Maizie replied. "But *I* just need to know that we're good."

He heard the fear and hurt in her tone.

"We aren't right now, but we will be. That's what families do," Jax said. "They stick it out no matter what. They get through the hard stuff together."

"Okay." Her tone sounded stronger. "There are eight buoys spread out around the platform, at various points, like a boundary line. All about a mile apart. They have codes, and one matches the record of Kenna's testing." Her voice shook. "Jax..."

Dread washed over him, cold like the ocean had sucked him under. He wanted the numbness, but it never came. "What is it?"

"She's been out there for three days."

Chapter Thirty-One

The speedboat cut across the water, bouncing. Drowning everything out.

Jax had run down to the dock so fast that only Bear managed to get on the craft with him. Now he pushed the engine as hard as it would go, unwilling to waste even one second getting out there. *Three days.*

She'd been out there, exposed to the elements for that long. No food and limited water to drink.

He'd nearly strangled Buzard with his bare hands, but that would have taken a few moments he hadn't been willing to sacrifice.

Bear glanced down at the screen in his hands, then yelled, "Keep it straight! We should be seeing it in a second."

Jax's eyes burned until he had to blink from staring so hard at the horizon, trying to find the spot indicated on Bear's GPS. Transmitted to him by Maizie.

He hadn't been surprised she wanted to know if he forgave her. Their relationship might be vulnerable for many years to come as they navigated resolving conflict, but he wasn't worried that they'd figure it out. First lesson: trust. Which didn't surprise him given that's what he had been learning from the Lord.

He spotted it and pointed. "There!"

The buoy was tiny. He gripped the steering handle and kept the military-style inflatable gliding across the water, jumping waves.

Apparently, the whole helicopter-on-approach thing had been a ruse, since they'd known it would be shot down. It had been unmanned and controlled remotely.

Bear and his friends had then approached the platform using underwater single-person submarines, retired equipment they'd bought from the US Navy. They'd come up underneath it in diving masks and snuck on board from there, quickly subduing the skeleton staff remaining.

There was a sense of satisfaction in saving Kenna using a *Dominatus* boat.

Jax prayed for Bruce as he approached the buoy. That the guy would recover quickly. Jax thanked God that they'd found him before Buzard and his men did their sick surgery. Taking what Bruce had never agreed to give.

Then he prayed for Amara, wherever she was—whatever she was doing. Hopefully, she'd be able to aid them in convincing their enemy that the platform had remained in *Dominatus'* hands after MSI took control of it.

Because once he had Kenna back, he wasn't going to be thinking of anything else.

Eventually she'd want to spend time with her mother. Jax would deal when the time came, but he wasn't sure he would ever fully trust Amara.

"Okay, slow it down," Bear ordered.

Jax didn't want to, but he followed Bear's advice and came up to the buoy without jostling it, scanning the surface for her. The buoy had a platform chained to the back. Jax circled the boat slowly around the bobbing flotation blinking with a yellow light on it. Transmitting data back to the platform.

"Kenna!"

She lay facing away from him, curled up on the flat boards undulating with the surface of the water.

Bear grabbed the handle and took control of the boat. "Go. I've got this."

Jax scrambled over to her, ignoring the heavy feeling in his shoulder. So far, he hadn't felt the effect of the drugs wearing off. In fact, he felt pretty good. Which was a serious problem considering Buzard had dosed him with...whatever that had been. So soon after surgery, he should still be laid up. He certainly shouldn't feel as if he was back to full strength and using his arm.

He steadied his weight on the platform, barely six by six if that. A prison cell with no walls, floating out here in the middle of the freezing ocean. He would've been terrified left out here all alone, wondering at any minute if he was going to be eaten by an Orca.

"Kenna." He rolled her to her back, wondering for a split second that his hopes would be dashed and it wasn't going to be her.

She flopped to her back, her face pale. Lips chapped. Her skin sunk into her eyes and cheekbones. Her skin cold.

Tears rolled down his face. "Kenna."

He had to do it. *Just do it.* Jax pressed two fingers to her neck, feeling for a pulse.

Bear called over, "Is she alive?"

The question thrummed through him, a hollow echo of defeat that resonated in his bones. And then he felt it.

"Faint. It's there, but it's faint." He glanced at Bear. "She's alive, but she needs medical attention. *Now*."

"I see them!" Bear lifted a hand and pointed at the sky. The call he'd made as soon as they found the location and were able to ask for help.

A coast guard helicopter—with an orange nose, and orange striped with white down the body—approached them, still a minute or so away.

Jax leaned over his wife, protecting her even though he was freezing and soaked by the spray of the sea. "Kenna." He touched her face. "Don't let go. Hang on. You're almost home."

She had a jacket on, at least. A lined overcoat zipped nearly to her throat. The bump of early pregnancy would be under the big coat, at her middle. He wanted to look but wasn't going to let cold air in right now when she'd been out here facing exposure for days. He'd keep that baby protected where she was.

He took Kenna's hands, as icy cold as his own. Her feet in canvas shoes like his, and wearing the same white scrubs. Her toes were probably as cold as his as well.

"Hang on." He leaned down and pressed a gentle kiss to her lips, shivering with the cold. Fighting back the rush of emotion at having her here, finally in his arms. *Safe.* "You're safe now. I've got you."

The chopper whipped wind and ocean salt against him, and he protected her face, because that was the only thing he could do. The sound of it swelled around him, filling his ears until he couldn't think through the disorientation of the noise. Helicopter motor. The boat, which Bear circled around. That steady beep of the buoy he hadn't even noticed at first.

He twisted and saw a US Coast Guard rescuer in an

orange jumpsuit lowering down to them with a basket the length of a stretcher. The spin of the rotors pushed the water away from them and whipped his T-shirt against his chest.

He turned back to her, holding her cheeks with his hands. "You did it. You beat them. You're almost home."

Her eyes fluttered.

"Kenna, can you hear me?"

Her lips parted.

He leaned down and put his ear in front of her mouth. He heard her whisper, "Dream." Or, at least, that's what he thought she might've said. He wasn't sure, and he didn't want to ask her to repeat it. She needed to sleep—to heal—and that started now.

Jax took her cheeks in his hands. "This is real, it's not a dream. You're going home, Kenna. It's over."

Her eyes fluttered, and he spotted white in the open slit when her eyes rolled back in her head. Then she was unconscious again.

It felt like hours waiting while the guy loaded her on the basket, covered in blankets, and lifted her to the helicopter. He said his name was Kevin, and that Jax would be next. He said more things, asking questions, and Jax nodded or shook his head in reply.

Jax watched Kenna ascend the rope to the helicopter, then looked at Bear.

"Go," the big man said, motioning to the helicopter. Then he yelled, "I'll take care of everything else!"

They both knew what that meant.

Jax didn't even care that the MSI guys could veto his idea, kill everyone on the platform, and set the place on fire. They could do whatever they wanted. The idea to keep it going and trick their enemy had been a good one, but it wasn't the only option. Crafting a ruse so that *Dominatus* had no clue they'd taken over the platform would be tricky —and it wouldn't last forever.

Kevin, the coast guard rescuer, clipped Jax roughly into a harness, and they rose, winched up to the chopper. He let them unclip him and moved the first second he was disconnected. Sliding onto a seat so he could be near her, leaning over and taking her hand. "This is Kenna. She's my wife."

Kevin handed him a silver blanket to put around his shoulders, and the chopper sailed over the ocean headed toward the land.

Being away from the platform and having Kenna's hand in his felt better than even the day they'd married. Standing beside her in that small country church and saying their vows to each other meant everything to him. But having her back now? He couldn't even process how he felt.

His head swam, and he shivered. Kevin had a stethoscope out and listened to Jax's heartbeat. "Kind of fast."

"I just found my wife again. She's been missing for months." He had to yell over the sound of the chopper, now able to see the coastline ahead of them. The tall peak of Denali, perpetually snowcapped. The spread of lights, illuminating buildings. "Where are we going?"

"Anchorage. They have trauma care."

Jax nodded and closed his eyes so his head would stop swimming. It didn't necessarily help. His stomach felt like it flipped over and his body flushed, oddly hot and cold at the same time. Sweat broke out on his skin.

"They can check you out as well."

He nodded again, but it made him dizzy. Their comments about Kenna flew by his awareness, a back-and-forth exchange of medical assessment terms.

Jax leaned his head back on the seat and took long

breaths while the helicopter lowered to the ground and set down on the pad beside a collection of tall buildings, another set of buildings to the right. The city surrounded them, mountains in the distance.

The door opened, and Kenna was unloaded, Jax disembarking to follow. His legs gave out, and Kevin caught him, then helped him to a wheelchair, lowering him into it whether Jax wanted to be there or not. He heard the word *withdrawal* muttered around him, along with other words he couldn't focus on with the noise of the chopper blades cutting through the air.

"Don't give me drugs." Jax gripped the handles of the chair to get up. "No narcotics."

The guy behind him laid a heavy hand on his shoulder. "You're going to sit there, and I'm going to wheel you in."

Jax slumped back down. "No meds. Tell them I don't want any narcotics."

"You tell the doctor."

They whisked him after Kenna, which was the only reason he allowed it. Not because he didn't know if he'd have been able to walk. Inside the automatic doors, where the sounds of a hospital surrounded him on all sides, he kept his focus on her but felt as if she was slipping away again.

"Go faster," Jax said. "I'm not leaving her."

"You need to be seen by a doctor," the guy said. "And so does she. That won't happen if you object every second."

"I'll take the bay next to hers."

He wheeled Jax through the opening in the curtain. Soon as they stopped, Jax jumped up and went to Kenna, pulling back the curtain between their bays so he could see her. The nurse looked over.

"I'll stay out of the way," Jax promised. "I won't interfere. I just want to see her."

The nurse looked at the doctor.

He pulled the stethoscope from his ears, winding it around his neck. "She needs warming blankets. I want a heart rate."

The nurses tugged off her coat, leaving her in a thin white T-shirt and the same scrubs pants as him.

Jax said, "She's pregnant."

The doctor barely glanced at him. "Are you the father?"

"Yes."

"How far along is she?"

Jax's skin tingled. "I don't know exactly. She was kidnapped, and I just got her back. A few months?"

The doctor frowned. "Stay back. Let us work." He turned to the nurse. "Get an ultrasound machine."

The nurse raced away.

"I don't know what they did to her." He swallowed. "Or what they gave her." Tears rolled down his face.

"Sir?" the orderly who had pushed him in the wheelchair led Jax back to the bed. "I'll leave the curtain open so you can see, but we need to let them treat her."

The doctor said a bunch of stuff Jax didn't know to the nurse beside Kenna's bed, but he understood "tox screen." *Good.* After all, they had no idea what Buzard put in her system.

"They should do that for me, too." Jax shivered. "I don't know what he gave me, but he said it was crazy addictive."

"There will be a doctor in here soon."

Jax nodded, his skin starting to prickle and itch.

"Jax!"

He reluctantly turned from watching them warm Kenna, hooking her up to monitors and an IV of saline, and spotted Ramon coming toward him. The guy had his arm in a sling. "You got out?"

Ramon nodded. "Amara had a couple of guys bring me in. But I had to wait thirty-six hours before we could move, and they cauterized my wound so I didn't bleed out."

Jax winced. "Ouch." He looked back at Kenna.

"They took me to the mainland and called me a rideshare." Ramon shifted to stand beside him. "Is she okay?"

"She's going to be."

She had to. After all, he had her back now. That meant it had to be God's will that they were together again. Her. The baby. Jax.

More tears rolled down his cheeks. He scrubbed them away, and didn't stop scratching his face.

"Whoa, *Hermano*. Ease up on that, okay?"

"I've gone through withdrawal before. I can do it again." He sniffed, his hands by his sides making fists before he straightened his fingers. "I can do it." He turned to Ramon. "Distract me."

Ramon blinked. "Your pupils are huge. You okay?"

"Nothing a few hours of holding it in check won't fix." Which was part of why he needed a distraction.

"I've been trying to contact MSI, but I can't seem to get through."

"You have a phone?"

Ramon shook his head. "I borrowed one from the nurse's station. Said I was calling my mother. Maizie never picked up."

"Could be she was distracted with the fact we found Kenna, focused on the locator beacon, but let's try again. Maybe Zeyla will pick up." He needed a phone, or his watch. "If something is wrong, you can go there, right?"

"It would take hours to get back to Seattle from here."

"I'll call Preston," Jax said. "I'm not leaving Kenna."

Ramon clapped a hand on his shoulder. "You stay here. I'll go try them all again."

"Thanks." He listened to Ramon's footsteps and was about to go to Kenna again, so he could feel how much warmer she was now, but the doctor stepped in front of him. Jax moved to the side so the guy wasn't blocking his view. "Excuse me."

"Sit on the bed."

Jax didn't want to, but he perched on the edge. The doctor shined a light in his eyes until he winced.

The doctor blanched. "What did you take, and how long ago was it?"

"No idea, and no idea."

"Tough to treat."

Jax rubbed his arms. "I know how to do this. If I know anything at all, it's how to do this."

The doctor looked at Kenna. "Your wife?"

Jax nodded. "And my baby."

"She'll be asleep for a while. It's the best scenario, giving her body the chance to return to normal levels. When she wakes up, are you going to be sober?"

"Yes, sir." Jax shook. "My shoulder will hurt something fierce. But whatever I say, don't give me anything." He looked at the doctor. "Got it?"

"I'm going to run some tests. Call it a hunch, but you're not the first person I've seen in the same state."

He opened his mouth to reply but never got that far.

"Jax!"

Kenna was awake.

Chapter Thirty-Two

"I could stay right here forever." Jax couldn't stop touching her face. Probably he should draw back, let her go so she could have some space in case that's what she needed, and let her set the pace.

Kenna reached over his shoulder and grasped the back of his T-shirt, holding him close in a way he figured she didn't intend to let go—or let him get far. It was almost like a hug, but where she needed to hold on. Desperate to keep him near. Her eyes wide. Dazed and a little in awe of the fact he was here.

"Forever?" Her gaze scanned his face. "Maybe not at the hospital. You know how I feel about those."

Jax would've smiled then, but he couldn't stop himself from leaning down and touching his forehead to hers. "Love you."

She gave a slight chuckle. "Keep talking. This feels way too much like every dream I've had recently." She shivered. "Like I'm going to wake up any moment back in that room." Her breath hitched. "With that dead man. The doctor."

Buzard. "You did kill him in Arizona. Maybe there are

more. I don't know if they're clones, or just really close copies of the genetic profile. I don't really care."

"Me, either," Kenna said. "Is he dead?"

"I suggested MSI get information from him. When I can check in with Bear, I'll find out what they decided." Jax blew out a breath, shaking his head.

There was so much to fill her in on, but at the same time, he didn't want to talk. He'd much rather curl up beside her, hold her, and just rest in the fact he had her back.

"Distract me." She squeezed his hand. "I don't want to think about him."

"Wait until you hear about the woman who looked like you, running around causing trouble. She's dead. Maybe I shouldn't thank God for that, but I want to." Jax's skin itched, but being here with her made it so much easier to fight the effect of withdrawal.

The doctor had given him something, part of the detox protocol he'd established. Someone who worked at the platform had been stealing whatever the drug was and selling it on the side in Alaska, causing enough of a problem that the doctor had not only identified the issue but found a way to treat it.

Thank You.

Again.

I'm not going to stop saying that. Not ever.

He leaned back far enough that she would be able to see his face. "You won't be waking up in that room ever again."

"I want you to tell me everything, but I also just want to shut my eyes." She smiled, the relief on her face a visceral thing that sank into him.

"You don't have to be scared about waking up back there. Nothing is going to happen to you." He smiled back.

"I want to promise that nothing will ever happen to you again, but that's not within my power to make."

"Make it anyway."

He traced his thumb over the curve of her cheek. "Nothing will ever happen to you again. I'm going to make sure of it."

Kenna drew his face down to hers, her hands on the sides of his head. She pressed a kiss to his lips, and he stayed there, enjoying that simple connection when it had been so long. When things had so much weight to them, what with the pregnancy and the worldwide scale of their enemy, and it had all been horrible on an epic scale. All he had needed for months was this small thing that so many people took for granted.

He slid his mouth to the side and stayed with their cheeks touching. Breathed. *Thank You.*

"The doctor said the baby is doing fine. Better than fine."

Jax couldn't help thinking it might be because Buzard had done something to their baby, some genetic experiment. But he still thanked God for a healthy child. "That's good."

Her hands squeezed, like a reflex. "I know."

He opened his eyes.

"Surprise."

Jax started to smile.

"It's a girl."

He let those words resonate in his ears even though he'd already known. "We're having a girl."

"Yes, we are."

There was so much for them to work through, thoughts would creep in during the weeks to come. Emotions would surface out of nowhere. Probably both of them needed to see a professional, so they could work through this separately and together. Whether that was Elizabeth or not, it needed to be someone. Just as long as they could ensure it wasn't an agent of their enemy—something they were going to have to consider with everything that happened until this was over.

Someone behind them cleared their throat.

"No," Jax said. "Go away."

Kenna started to laugh, her dark eyes flashing with humor. "Wow, I don't think I've laughed in…"

He figured he knew the answer to that. "The first of many to come. Hopefully a lifetime of it."

Even if they had the fight of their lives on their hands. If they wanted to make sure their baby grew up safe, protected in a world where there was no *Dominatus*, there was yet more work ahead of them.

He couldn't walk away and hide, knowing they were out there. His family would always be on their radar. Agents would never stop coming after them, and their children.

"Guys."

Jax reluctantly looked over his shoulder, the movement making him antsy. He shivered, rolling his shoulders, and let go of Kenna. But he stayed close so he could be near her, taking her hand when she touched his. Reluctant to let go of each other now that they were back together.

Ramon stood at the curtain. "We have a problem." He handed over a cell phone. "It's your father."

Jax took the phone and saw it was on speaker. "Dad?"

"You found her?" His father's tone rang with a tone Jax couldn't decipher. Wasn't he happy? Maybe this problem they had was overshadowing the relief.

Kenna squeezed his hand.

"Yeah, Dad," Jax said. "I found her."

"I'm sorry to do this. So sorry. Something happened." He quit talking. "I'm so glad you got her back, but things have happened here. I don't know how to fix it."

"What is it?" After his dad didn't reply for a few seconds, Jax said, "Dad?"

"Sorry. I'm in a closet, hiding."

"At the MSI office?" Jax glanced at Ramon, who shrugged.

His dad said, "Yes."

Ramon spoke quietly, "I couldn't get Zeyla or Maizie to answer. I remembered the number to one of our burner phones. He's the one who picked up."

Kenna's hand tightened in his when Ramon mentioned Zeyla and Maizie. He had so much to tell her about what happened since she was taken.

Ramon stared at Kenna. "It's good to see you."

She smiled at her friend, a sheen of tears in her eyes. "You, too." She sniffed. "Pregnancy is making me emotional."

Jax leaned over and kissed her forehead. He was about to ask his dad what was going on when the old man came back on.

"Okay, I think they're gone," his dad whispered. "I don't know how to explain it. I got a weird vibe, and things went all tense here. The security guard just finished a sweep, so I should be able to leave this closet now. Preston told me to stay put."

"Dad, where is Maizie?" Jax asked, aware of the tension in both Ramon and Kenna at the idea that the young woman might be in danger. Meanwhile, his skin hummed, and he was sweating more than he should be, his heart beating hard in his chest so he could feel it thump against his insides. *I'm fine.* Like saying that to yourself ever actually worked.

"That's part of it," his dad said. "I don't know what happened, but things got worse. The first day after you left, Maizie started freaking out because she couldn't get a signal from your watch, and Zeyla was right there with her. After the next day, when the team deployed to come after you, there were just a couple of MSI guys who stayed behind—guess they didn't make the cut. Then yesterday, Preston and Jonas were in a meeting in the conference room, talking to someone on the screen. That's when things went electric and everyone was acting weird."

Jax nodded. "*Dominatus* mapped my face and got on a call with the director of the FBI to tell them that I switched sides." He had to stop and roll his shoulders.

"Are you okay?" Kenna asked.

"I'm good."

She squeezed his hand. "Look at me." He turned his head to her, and she frowned. "What's going on?"

There hadn't been time to tell her. "It's a long story. The doctor gave me something to help." He wasn't sure there was time now. "Dad, what do you think changed? Was it that *Dominatus* made it sound like I turned? Or was it something else?"

"That definitely tripped something, the team here thinking you switched sides. I stuck with the ladies, just to make sure they were okay. One of the MSI guys was asking too many questions about how they knew each other and a bunch of personal details that might sound like small talk but was way too much like prying. Zeyla got upset with him. Maizie was working and didn't need to be disturbed. When I asked him to leave the room, he got mouthy with me until I threatened to inform Preston he was bothering us. Then Maizie told us that Kenna had been found, and he ran out of the room anyway. That's when things went sideways."

Jax frowned. Ramon looked about as happy as he was.

His dad continued, "I stepped out of the room to ensure he was going to tell Preston and Jonas that you knew where to find Kenna. It had been hours since the others left, but no one slept much, and Zeyla never left Maizie's side. Mr. Jonas came out of his office and had Preston and I wait in there. He spoke with his people, and by the time we realized he wasn't coming in, it had been an hour. I don't know what happened."

"Dad." He needed his father to quit beating around the bush and just say it.

"The men who stayed behind, and Mr. Jonas, Maizie and Zeyla—they're gone. The lab is a mess, a computer screen was smashed, and there's blood smeared on the wall."

"Where's Preston?"

"He ran to the security office to look at the cameras."

"I want to know what he finds." Jax paused. "Can you go there?"

"Of course, Son. I'm sorry, I don't know what's happening. I feel like we were all duped."

A nurse appeared at the curtain. "Guys, I'm gonna need my phone back."

Ramon said, "I can go to the store and grab one I can load up with minutes."

Jax nodded to him. "Dad, we'll call you back from a different number, okay? Try to figure out where they went and what happened."

"Are you coming here?" his father asked. "If Mr. Jonas works for *Dominatus*, and he took them..."

"I know," Jax said. "We'll figure it out."

Ramon ended the call and handed the phone to the nurse. "Thank you so much for letting us use your phone." He followed her through the curtain, asking about a nearby store where he'd be able to buy a phone.

Jax shifted on the bed, turning to face Kenna again.

"You're worried about her?"

He nodded. "I can't believe Earl Jonas might be working against us. He's been part of this fight for years. Even Preston trusted him." His thoughts stuttered. "I can't believe he might've taken them."

Jax explained about the MSI team having taken over the platform—assuming they'd followed his plan to try and convince *Dominatus* that it was still in their hands—and a bunch of other random details that dropped into his mind in an odd order. Hopefully, she pieced it together.

Kenna said, "If Jonas heard about the plan to fake it to *Dominatus*, then maybe he's going to them with the information that his men are in control of the facility. That it's fallen into our hands."

"I hope they all lose their minds." His heart started to beat harder in his chest. "I'm not leaving Maizie and Zeyla there when he's probably only taken them as a concession for how royally this has been screwed up."

"We need a way to get there. Where are they?" She frowned. "Where are we?"

"We're in Anchorage. They're in Seattle. It's too far for a helicopter."

"Charter flight? We could find a private company to take us. It'll be faster than trying to get flights today."

Jax nodded. "Neither of us is fit to travel, let alone go on a mission, and Ramon has a bullet hole in his shoulder."

"Has that ever stopped us before?"

He knew the answer to that, but the situation had changed. "I'm not putting you in harm's way."

"I don't want to be anywhere near danger right now. But I am coming with you."

"You're assuming I'm going?" He had just said that neither of them was fit to travel.

She eyed him. "Are you?"

"Of course. It's Maizie." Jax figured he could maybe get her to stay in the car with Preston and his father. Between the two of them, they could protect her if someone tried to take her again.

The idea someone might do that made him want to flip out. Stick with her every second, constantly standing in front of her. Permanently attach himself to her side. Be that stick-like-glue husband who would be overprotective and completely annoying, because deep down he was *terrified.*

He touched her cheeks. "Am I going to feel this way forever? Like at any moment I could lose you all over again, and this whole nightmare will happen a second time."

"They're still out there, and they will be unless we destroy them." Kenna held on tight to his hands. "However you're feeling, I'm right there with you. I'm as scared as you are. But saving Maizie is a job that was given to us, and we have to do it."

"Zeyla gets that as well."

Kenna said, "I want to meet her."

He'd forgotten that she'd never actually spoken with her sister. Cousin. Whatever they were to each other, it would probably grow to be more like sisters. "She's terrified that they'll capture her again, but she's tougher than she thinks and a lot like you—one of the strongest people I know."

"And everyone else? Ramon, Bruce, and Amara? Stairns and Elizabeth?"

He gave a rundown of Stairns, Elizabeth, and her dog, Cabot, all of them in California, protecting Jax's family. Ramon, and how he'd stuck with Jax the whole time Kenna was missing, even when Jax didn't want help. Bruce's presence with them, pitching in, and how Amara used all the skills and clout she had to get them access to the facility.

"You never stopped looking, did you?"

Jax shook his head.

"I love you."

"That's why I didn't stop."

Kenna squeezed his hand. "We need to go get Maizie back."

Chapter Thirty-Three

The airplane wheels screamed against the tarmac, and Jax gripped the chair handles, staring past Kenna out the window where the sun set behind the ocean off the coast of Washington. Nothing but coffee and some pretzels in his stomach. Maizie and Zeyla—then food. That was the order of priority.

"Still feels like a dream." Her voice sounded wistful, and a little sad. But both of them were on a rollercoaster of emotions right now.

"You aren't asleep." Jax motioned to Ramon, across the aisle. "He is."

The guy had been snoring since they left Anchorage.

She smiled. "Bear is meeting us on the ground?"

He nodded.

"I can't believe I missed months. So much has happened." She grabbed her bottled smoothie and took another sip. "There's so much I need to tell you. Random things that keep popping in my head."

"We have time," he said. "I want to hear all about the pregnancy stuff that I missed."

Kenna nodded, leaning her head on his shoulder while they taxied to the hangar, and the small plane came to a stop, her arms hugging his right arm. The jitters had stopped, but it wasn't as if the detox was over.

He'd been ready to throw up when the plane took off and spent the first fifteen minutes in the tiny airplane bathroom. Whatever the doctor had given him worked better than anything he'd ever taken during a detox. Last time it had gone on for days, but after the surgery on the platform and the days since, he hadn't felt too bad.

Which only made him suspicious that the doctor in Anchorage was somehow connected to *Dominatus* and it was all part of their larger plan. Because how else could the guy have figured it out?

Jax didn't have the brainpower to figure it out right now. He'd live to fight that battle another day. Right now, he just needed to get to Maizie and Zeyla, wherever they were, and not spend the next four months looking for them. The last thing he wanted was to lose Maizie when things had been so tenuous between them before he left to get Kenna back.

Kenna touched his knee, and he realized he'd been bouncing it up and down. "You're different."

"No, I'm not." Once he got over whatever he'd been given, things would be back on track. He'd start going to meetings again, figure out his job, get back to that happily ever after they'd been enjoying.

"What if I like it? You're...edgy. Or I just missed you and you're having a rough day. But you're still hot, by the way."

Jax frowned. "That's a lot to unpack."

Instead of responding to that, she said, "You are different." She eyed him. "You've been through a lot."

"How can you say that *I've* been through a lot?" He

twisted in his chair to face her. "After everything you've been through. My stuff doesn't even hold a candle to that."

"Doesn't mean you didn't go through something huge." She squeezed his knee. "I'm just processing, and I'm doing it out loud. Sorry. I'll keep it to myself."

"No, don't do that." He leaned over and kissed her. "Tell me whatever you want to say. It's okay."

"I was just realizing there's a lot we need to tell each other, and some of it might be really hard." She sighed. "It's going to take us time to work everything out."

"It'll keep." He squeezed her hand. "Elizabeth can help."

She nodded. "I haven't had coffee in months."

"What? That's insane. Those monsters."

Kenna's eyes flashed, and she burst out laughing.

Ramon sat up suddenly, groaned, and slumped back in the chair. "Ouch. What's going on?" He looked at them. "Oh, never mind. You guys need to get a room?"

"Maizie first," she said. "Then the RV."

"We could pick it up on the way," Jax suggested. "But I think they'd know it was us coming if we roll up to the house in the RV."

And that urgent feeling was back again. The sense there was a ticking clock, and they had to get moving fast or they would lose their window to catch up and rescue the two women.

Ramon looked at his phone while the pilot opened the exit door. At the door Ramon said, "Bear's here," and went first down the stairs.

Jax frowned. "He's moody in the morning." Maybe he was moody all the time, except with Maizie. He wanted to tell Kenna how he and Ramon had developed a friendship the past few months. About the FBI. All of it. Instead, he said, "Hold on to me, or the rail?"

Kenna said, "What will *you* be holding on to?"

Jax hesitated, because she made a good point.

"Geez, both of you look terrible." Bear pulled back from giving Ramon a back-slapping hug and came to the stairs. He jogged up wearing fresh tactical gear and looking like he'd been here long enough to shower and freshen up.

"Thanks a lot," Jax said.

Bear gave Kenna a hug. "Look at you. Sight for sore eyes."

"You, too. I'm glad you're back." She hesitated. "You *are* back, right?"

"It's been a while, but yeah, I'm back." Bear headed down the steps. "Come on. I have a car waiting. Thanks for the ride from Alaska, by the way. Normally I'd call in to the office and have them hook me up with transport, but in this case..."

They'd actually chartered two planes from Alaska, but Bear had been so far offshore it had mean he took a different route entirely. One that apparently got him here faster. Probably because he hadn't had to explain to the doctor they were leaving.

A huge commercial plane hurtled down the runway behind them and took off. Jax could hear traffic on a nearby road over behind the hangar and the fence beyond it. Mount Rainier in the distance, no snow this time of year.

The stark contrast between the Pacific Northwest and his home in Arizona made him want to pack up his life there and hit the road just for a change. After all, Jax had nothing waiting for him there. Not when everything he needed was right next to him.

Kenna had become nomadic after her life took a tragic

turn, and he could see the appeal of the open road. Maybe it was because his life had almost gone the same way, and all he wanted to do was never take what he had now for granted. That might mean finding a new home base some-where else, and it might mean living in the RV year-round.

What mattered was that they could figure it out together.

Bear opened the rear door. "Hop in. I'll explain on the way."

"We're meeting Preston and my father?"

Bear nodded. "Right now I don't trust anyone except you guys, but if you vouch for them, I'm okay with it."

"Thanks."

Kenna climbed in, moving to the captain's chair on the far side of the middle row. Ramon in the front seat.

Jax said, "Just tell me you know where Jonas took Maizie and Zeyla."

Bear nodded. "Get in."

That was the impetus that meant Jax could follow the order. He buckled up, and Kenna held out her hand. The tiny snack mix they'd found in a cupboard on the plane hadn't lasted long, but it had helped to settle his stomach. He wasn't about to suggest a food stop. Not until this was over.

Jax said, "Talk."

Bear hit the gas, and Jax had to grab the handle on the door. "There's been a load of turnover at MSI since I left. It hasn't even been a year since..."

Since Allie had been murdered and Bear had cut everyone off, walking away so he could heal. Keeping in touch only on a basic level with Maizie, she at least knew he was still alive even if he didn't want to talk to anyone.

"Since I left," Bear finished. "The new guys seemed

okay, but something was off with a couple of them. I didn't clock that they were the ones who stayed behind when Hollace sent the team out to find you and Ramon, and bring Kenna back in. Mr. Jonas must have planned it that way."

"I figured it was because he didn't trust them with the job," Ramon said, his head bowed to his phone. Texting.

Jax said, "But that's who we left protecting Maizie and Zeyla. Not super reassuring."

Bear turned a corner fast, swerving lanes and cutting through traffic like a pro. "Update on the platform, in case you're interested."

"Yes." Jax leaned to the side so he could see better out the front windshield.

"Unfortunately, there was a fire, and it got out of control. The whole place burned down, and no one survived. Not even the doctor."

"How do you know that if no one is left alive to tell the tale?" Ramon asked with a wry tone.

"Well, there was a similar incident on an island over by the coastline," Bear replied. "The people who escaped that, locals who were caught up in it but innocent of wrongdoing, happened to notice. The coast guard did a flyby and confirmed there's only smoldering wreckage where the platform used to be."

"Interesting." Jax glanced at Kenna. "Are you okay?"

"I'm glad it burned down." She blinked back tears and waved away his concern. As if that was going to work. He took it more that she didn't want to talk about it right now—not never.

Later was another story, alone in the RV. Safe and sound. Maybe somewhere in the mountains, by a lake. No cell signal for miles around and no way for anyone to find them except the people they loved.

He glanced at Bear. "Just tell me where Maizie and Zeyla are." Right now, Jax didn't want to know about anything else.

"Hollace has Bruce and Amara with him. He and the others from MSI—the ones we know are solid—are with your dad and Preston. The team is going to rendezvous in the parking lot of a closed-down store about a mile from Earl Jonas' mansion."

"That's where he took them?"

Bear nodded. "Maizie gave me access to a system she keeps connected, for just in case. Which I figure is right now."

Ramon glanced over. "The trackers?"

"I have the password as well," Kenna said. "But they took my watch."

He squeezed her hand. "Mine, too."

Thank You for these people and the care they have for each other.

A whole lot of forethought had gone into protecting each other. So they could find a missing team member if need be. Still, even with the safeguards they had in place, Kenna had been simply *gone* for months. And he prayed they would find the two young women quickly, so the same thing didn't happen again.

Already being pregnant when she was taken might have saved Kenna from some horrifying experiences, or it could have opened up new avenues for them to conduct procedures on her. But neither Maizie nor Zeyla was pregnant, and the latter already knew the horrible things *Dominatus* would do to her. She had missing organs and scar tissue as evidence.

As for Maizie...

We need to get them back. That means You have to move.

He'd never prayed as hard as this in his entire life. Such a simple sentence, and yet it meant the world to him that God came through on their behalf.

Bear said, "When y'all showed up in Seattle, and we put the mission together, she gave it to me just in case."

"Good." Jax nodded.

Bear merged onto the freeway and hit the gas. "Hers is transmitting from the house. Zeyla as well."

"Why would they go there?" Ramon shifted in his seat. "Makes no sense that Jonas wouldn't think we'd look for him at his house."

"Or that's exactly where we wouldn't look, so it's where he went. Familiar territory, and he can pack a bag," Bear said. "There's a flight plan filed. The MSI plane is going to Argentina tonight, leaving Sea-Tac airport in five hours."

Jax's stomach clenched. "He's taking them out of the country."

"That's what we think." Bear held the wheel with both hands, driving like someone who had graduated from every advanced driving course there was.

Jax held on to Kenna's hand. "Jonas has been working with *Dominatus* this whole time, and he's handing those women over to them? It must be because everything that happened here all went wrong. He didn't expect us to survive the island. Then we were taken to the platform, and I guess he didn't know what the plan was."

"Hollace kept it under wraps because we didn't trust those guys," Bear said. "So Jonas never knew, and we monitored communication from the platform to the office, with Maizie's help of course. All so we could figure out who was with him and who is still loyal to us. The last thing we expected was for him to retaliate and take the women. Preston and your father were left behind, but they managed to sneak into hiding spots. No one looked too hard for them. They just grabbed Maizie and Zeyla and left."

Jax was glad to hear that it hadn't been bloody, at least. "Something else to be thankful for, considering how easily they all could've been killed."

Ramon glanced over. "We need to keep them protected even after we get Maizie and Zeyla back. *Dominatus* will send an asset to take out both Preston and your father."

Bear took the off-ramp, and a street over he pulled into the parking lot of a pharmacy, closed for the night. He rolled his window down and spoke to Hollace.

Jax spotted Preston in the front seat, and his father rolled down a window in the back to listen.

A minute or so later, they pulled out. Driving in a convoy over to Earl Jonas' house. Through the streets, where headlights from oncoming traffic glared far too bright and the stars weren't visible. Ramon's knee bounced up and down, and he turned his phone over and over on his leg. Bear got a phone call, muttered a few one-word statements, then hung up. Ramon and Bear spoke quietly, and Jax didn't catch the exchange.

Jax felt Kenna shift to lean her head against his shoulder. "Losing steam?"

"Aren't you?"

"I'll rest when we get them back."

Kenna ran her hand along the top of his forearm, the resilience in her touch shoring up some of his weak places. Which he didn't mind. God had put her on this earth to be his partner. But Jax had to trust Him above anything else, so he could be the strength Kenna needed. He was the one here to keep her safe, to protect her from all the evil in the world—because that was his role.

Kind of like the role of father, and brother-in-law.

The women in his life might not have an army to keep them safe, but he was going to ensure they had what they needed.

People who cared about them enough that they put it all on the line to save them.

Kenna shifted, lifting her chin so he could see her face. "I love you."

"I love you, too." He tugged her close, planning not to let her go ever again.

Chapter Thirty-Four

"I can stick with Kenna." Ramon walked behind them along the side of the road where they'd left the car, though it was only the three of them right now. "I can watch her back while you find Maizie."

Jax wondered if this was about the last time they'd lost her. "Looking for a shot to redeem yourself?"

"Long as no one hits me with a stun gun."

Kenna glanced over her shoulder at Ramon, bringing up the rear. Why did the woman look so good in a bulletproof vest with her hair in the quick braids? She'd done her hair in the car with two rubber bands—the only thing available.

Even with dark circles under her eyes, and being thinner than might be healthy for her, she looked amazing to him.

She smiled at Ramon. "I'm surprised you haven't spent the last few months practicing so you can get hit and keep going."

Ramon saw the look he shot her. "What makes you think I haven't?" The note of humor in his eyes took the tension out of it. At least a little.

Kenna said, "No one blames you for not being able to stop them."

"Thank you." Ramon gave her a tight nod. "But that doesn't mean I won't hunt down those old guys and get some payback.

"Put that on the agenda for the next staff meeting," Jax said. "And we appreciate the offer, but both of us are hanging back. We'll watch out for each other, and *you* go find Maizie and Zeyla. We'll be right behind you."

"Copy that." Ramon skirted around them and jogged up the path behind Earl Jonas' house. A walking trail that ran alongside the highway.

The MSI boss had a house across the hill beyond the trees. Bear, Hollace, and the men loyal to them would breach the house. Ramon had the back entrance. They were his backup, hanging back but still part of it. Neither of them was a hundred percent—or even close to it—but no way were they going to sit this one out.

Preston and Jax's father were also supposed to hang back and not come in the house until it was clear. Which, if he were honest, he and Kenna should do. But when had that ever stopped them?

Jax shifted his gun to his left hand and took Kenna's with his right so they could walk through the woods down a deer trail together. Ramon sprinted the length of the trail, and some words drifted to them when he got on the radio Bear had given him with instructions to use a channel the men in the house wouldn't be on. An encrypted channel they wouldn't find the frequency for, even if they scrolled through them all.

"I guess you and Ramon became friends while I was gone."

Jax couldn't argue with her assessment. "First it was

tense. We worked together out of necessity, and he was probably in it because he felt guilty about what happened as much as he wanted to get you back. But he's more than proven his loyalty to you, and I can't help but respect the guy."

Kenna glanced at him. "Shouldn't the FBI be out here, helping you take this guy down?"

"The FBI and I...aren't exactly on speaking terms right now." He gave her a brief rundown of Maizie coming on as a consultant, the worm in their network, and Special Agent Herron. "Who knows what Andrette is doing now, and what the Assistant Director in Charge thinks. I'm not sure I really care. I have you back, and we'll have our family back together by the end of the night." He shrugged. "Even the taskforce the president put together is kaput. However it happened, *Dominatus* discovered people are trying to fight them and squashed it."

"We need a new plan."

"We need a vacation."

Kenna chuckled under her breath. "Maybe we can vacate and make a plan while we're relaxing."

"I'll think about it." Right now, he didn't want to do anything but take a month off and spend it with her. Maybe a year. Or twenty.

She squeezed his hand. "Why did we get the farthest walk from the road to the house?"

He smiled. "Because they're hoping they get the situation resolved before the injured people even get there."

"Fine by me. Bear seemed pretty...perturbed that his people worked for *Dominatus*."

"I mean, if I thought I was an Avenger, and it turned out I was working for Hydra..."

She glanced at him. "You...what?"

He shrugged. "You were gone. I watched a lot of movies to distract myself. Maizie and I worked through the entire Marvel timeline. Twice."

Kenna laughed aloud.

"Why is that funny?" he asked, smiling.

"Because I probably would've done the same if it had been months." She squeezed his hand. "Movie night sounds good."

"It's a date."

The trees came to an abrupt end, the terrain switching from backwoods overgrown brush to a manicured lawn in a stark line that delineated the edge of Jonas' backyard. Acres of grass that could've been a golf course stretched beyond them, a slight decline down to the gravel around what could only be described as a mansion.

"Why do all these bad guys have gorgeous stone houses?"

Jax tugged on her hand, and they set off walking down the hill. "Do you want one?"

"No way."

Over by the house, Ramon ducked through a door and left it open for them. Light flashed in one of the first-floor windows to the left. A gunshot.

She continued, "I want a cabin with acres and acres of hills, and mountains in the distance so you can see someone coming toward you from a long way off. The kind of place where the closest neighbor is five miles down the road and you get snowed in for weeks in the winter."

"I'll need an ATV with a snowplow attachment."

"Of course." She squeezed his hand. "Kids. Dogs. Cases we can consult on and not leave the house."

"At this point, we're gonna have a team we're coordinating who go out and do the legwork for us while we go through the evidence."

"Sounds good to me."

To him, it almost sounded like a dream. The kind of life they might've had without *Dominatus* in the picture. Something that "could be"—and if things went a certain way, that's all it would ever be. The only chance they'd actually achieve it would be after the fight of their lives, doing whatever it took to take that organization down. If they even survived the battle.

And with her pregnant... Well, he wanted to decree that they found that sanctuary of a cabin together. Then she could stay there while he took care of it for her. Kenna would never go for it, which was why he didn't voice the idea out loud. Still, now that she was carrying their baby, he needed her to stay safe rather than be a target for *Dominatus*.

For all he knew, they were both now on the radar. Targets of an enemy who would relentlessly pursue his family until they got what they wanted.

"As much as we might want to," she began, "we can't check out or bury our heads in the sand. Not with all we know and how widespread the threat is."

"I still can't see how we'd ever be able to take them down. The whole thing seems insurmountable."

Not without identifying every single member of *Dominatus* and taking them down one by one. That was a fight that could take a lifetime.

He continued, "Right now all I can see is a fight that will be so difficult I don't want to do it. I'd rather pack it all in and enjoy my life instead. But you're right—with all we've seen, that isn't something we can do. Not in all good conscience."

"So we take it one day at a time. One mission at a time." She slowed. "To be honest, this is the most exercise I've had in months."

And she was coming off an "endurance" test, where she'd been subjected to starvation and hypothermia.

"Before you say it"—she smiled—"there's no way I was going to stay in the car any more than you were."

The steps up to the back door Ramon had left open were stone and looked like they'd been imported from some-place where medieval structures like castles and churches still stood. Was Earl Jonas really the kind of guy who would ship every piece of it over, stone by stone, and reassemble it? Jax wouldn't have said so, but that was exactly what it seemed had happened.

Above his head, a window shattered and a dark form sailed out.

The man hit the gravel behind them with a sickening thud.

Kenna moved closer, and he slid his arm around her waist reflexively, even if the guy was dead. He could feel the baby between them, his family safe and sound. He leaned down and kissed her neck. "Stay behind me."

"I'll watch your back."

"That's not why."

She squeezed his waist right as he crossed the threshold of the door. "I know."

Jax couldn't hold her hand because while he could shoot with his left, now wasn't the time to sacrifice accuracy for convenience. He scanned the hallway, which was encased in wood wainscoting with pretentious paintings on the wall, listening to the faint sounds of hand-to-hand combat through the house.

A gunshot exploded, somewhere far enough it sounded like a muffled thud. Like a firework miles away.

"You think this place has basement cells like in France?" she asked.

"I wasn't there when you rescued Preston," he replied. "I was delivering a message to that publisher."

"Right. I was thinking about that in my cell. In fact, I came up with a whole story for a book. But it's so outlandish no one would ever believe it could really happen."

"Like our lives?" He had her wait at the next corner.

Someone stepped into view at the end.

"Ramon!" Jax stayed where he was, though. Just in case. There was something about—

The guy lifted his gun.

Not Ramon. Jax fired around the corner, and the guy fell to the side. He shot wide, the rounds slamming into the ceiling while muzzle flash lit up the long hallway.

"Jax!" Bear strode down the hall from the other end. "You guys good?"

"We're good. Where's Ramon?"

"This way." Bear motioned. "He found them, but he can't get through the door. Jonas barricaded himself in there with Maizie and Zeyla, and he's threatening them."

Jax followed him, Kenna by his side.

Tension stiffened every inch of Bear's body, as though the slightest thing might make him snap. Like he wanted to rant and pace or just knock someone out with one punch. He stepped through a set of doors into a pretentious study. There really was no other way to describe the floor-to-ceiling bookshelves that filled the room, complete with one of those old-world library ladders that slid all the way around so a person could climb up and get a book off the top shelf.

Ramon stood at the far end, pushing on a panel that looked like it should move one way.

Jax said, "Panic room."

"I need plastic explosives." Ramon didn't turn around, he just kept pushing.

"One of those remotes." Kenna clicked her fingers. "When was that?"

Ramon glanced at her. "New York. Look around."

She went to the desk and sat in the leather chair before she pulled open drawers. "Wish I could remember what that thing looked like. Some kind of clicker remote thingy that opened the secret drawer."

Ramon pulled open drawers on the other side of the desk, rooting around.

A man came into the room. Jax lifted his gun to protect the rest of them, but the guy's body jerked, and the sound of a gunshot rang through the room. Shot from behind. He fell to the floor, and Hollace appeared in the door. "It's clear."

"That's all of them?" Bear asked.

Hollace nodded.

Jax said, "Is there any way to communicate with Maizie, or Zeyla, or even Jonas, inside there?"

Bear scratched his jaw. "Preston might know."

"Or my father." Jax figured that was a longshot, but anything was worth a try right now. "What happened, Ramon?"

He was still thrown by the guy he'd thought was Ramon in the hallway, not wanting to contemplate how many doppelgangers might be out there. Assets loyal to *Dominatus* who would be willing to lay down their lives for the cause. That guy probably hadn't looked like Ramon, just a similar build in the dark, but tell that to Jax's racing heart.

Ramon crouched to root around in a drawer, while

Kenna sank back in the tall-backed leather chair with an audible sigh. The Hispanic man said, "He shoved them in there and hit the button inside that closed the door."

Jax heard the note in his voice. The two women had been freaked out. He turned to Hollace. "C4?"

Hollace folded his arms. "He could kill them before we clear the smoke to get in there."

"That might be a chance we have to take," Kenna said. "If we can't find the remote that will open the door."

Bear shifted and pulled out a phone. "Earl Jonas is calling me." He tapped the screen and held the phone in front of his face. "Let those women go, and I won't put a bullet in your head. If you hurt them, you have *no* leverage."

"No?" Earl Jonas said. "Seems like all I have to do is wait for backup to descend."

Descend. Interesting choice of words there.

Jax whispered, "Helicopter."

Hollace headed for the door, talking into his radio.

Jonas continued, "They'll take care of you, and I'll get to walk away. Over your dead bodies."

"That isn't going to happen," Ramon said, loudly enough Jonas would hear. "Let them go, and we might not kill all of you."

"Hmm. No thanks." The line went dead.

"We know how they're going to approach." Bear glanced around. "Let's make a stand. He'll be forced to come out eventually."

Hollace said, "Nothing incoming yet. We have no idea how many people there will be, or if it's even a chopper."

"You won't like my idea." Ramon slammed the desk drawer shut and stood.

"Try us," Kenna suggested. "We're brainstorming. There are no bad ideas."

More MSI guys came in the room, and since Hollace and Bear didn't react with lethal force, Jax figured they were on the same side.

Ramon eyed her. "He thinks we're going to fight them all. That's what he wants—he's planned for it."

"So what do we do?" Bear shrugged.

"Set the house on fire," Ramon said. "No way to get in, no way to fight them."

"With them inside that room?" Jax said. "They'll suffocate."

Ramon didn't seem worried. "Unless it's the kind of panic room that's sealed."

"He could kill them," Jax countered.

Kenna glanced at him. "Whatever we do, there's a risk he retaliates and hurts them."

"There's a risk Zeyla will hurt him, and I hope she does." Ramon folded his arms.

Hollace said, "We can blow the gas line and the water at the same time. Trip the system so there's fire and it's working on putting it out." His tone indicated it was a question.

"Can he see us?" Jax pointed at the panic room door. "Or can we fake a fire?"

"We have no idea," Ramon said. "You're no fun."

"Decide fast." Bear strode to the door. "There's a chopper incoming."

Jax glanced at the sealed door to the panic room, or hidey hole, or whatever Mr. Jonas had installed behind his study. Some firefighter tools would come in handy right now.

Dark-gray smoke drifted out of a vent, high on the wall.

He told Ramon, "Seems like someone beat you to it with the fire idea."

Chapter Thirty-Five

The door to the panic room flung open, and smoke billowed out. Jax lifted his gun, aimed at the fire coming from in the room. Zeyla came out first, an angry look on her face. "Maizie."

Jax didn't see the teen, but Earl Jonas came out behind her. The MSI boss said, "No one fires, or I kill her! We're leaving, and you're going to let us walk out of here."

Zeyla winced, hunching her shoulders, and Jax realized Mr. Jonas had a grip on the woman.

"Let her go." Jax pointed his weapon at the MSI boss but couldn't get a clear shot with Zeyla in front of him. "Put the gun down!" He said it on a reflex, all his FBI training coming to the forefront with the adrenaline surging through him. His mind cleared in a way it hadn't been a moment ago, but no doubt it would be short-lived. When this was over, he would crash, hard. But right now, he needed to ensure the safety of two women he cared about a whole lot while making sure no one else got hurt.

Ramon grabbed Kenna's chair and dragged it back,

moving to stand in front of her. Protecting her in a way Jax couldn't because he was on the other side of the desk.

"Let her go and put your gun down, Jonas." Jax pushed out a breath. Where was Maizie? "I'm going to keep telling you until you comply. These guys won't let you past. You *aren't* leaving."

The MSI guys stood more toward the door, their guns pointed at their boss. But did they have a clear shot? Did anyone?

Zeyla took another unsteady step.

Across the room a gun exploded, and Earl Jonas jerked back, falling to the floor. He nearly dragged Zeyla down with him.

Jax held out his hand, and she grabbed it. He dragged her past him, away from the door. "We need a fire extinguisher!" He ran into the room and searched around, spotting the flickering orange of flames in a pile of papers.

A cot in the corner had a blanket on it, which Jax grabbed and used to smother the fire.

"Maizie!" He searched around for her, desperate with panic that she might be hurt. He covered his mouth with his elbow and coughed. There was nothing he could do to keep himself from sucking in the flames. He coughed again and sank to his knees. "Maizie!"

Ramon shoved him aside and shined a flashlight around. "Here!" He dragged the young woman from under the cot across the floor. "Up we go." He lifted Maizie and stood, leaving the room.

Jax coughed, trying to catch his breath. In the end he simply stumbled out and followed Ramon. Kenna stood by the door.

"We can't leave." Bear stood blocking the doorway, so much intensity in his expression Jax wanted to shrink back.

Kenna reached out her hand for him, and he tucked her under his shoulder, finding solace in her being close again. "She'll be okay."

He nodded, not sure if he was quite ready to believe it. *Thank You.* They had her back, and that's what mattered. Their family was together again, no matter that their enemy had tried to tear them apart and destroy them.

Ramon squared off with Bear, Maizie still in his arms. "She needs a medic. Move!"

Bear shook his head. "Preston reported there's a chopper on the roof and men coming down."

Jax said, "What about local cops?" as Kenna leaned against him.

Bear gave them all a tight shake of his head.

"We can't stay in here. It's full of smoke." The words caught in Jax's throat, burning his tongue. "We need air."

Bear glanced at Hollace. "We'll find a place for you to hole up. Sit tight until we take care of it."

"Fine." Whatever it took to get things moving.

Keeping Kenna close to his side, Jax followed Ramon, who acted as if holding Maizie in his arms was no trouble at all, like he could walk around carrying her forever if he had to. Jax blinked away the burn of tears in his eyes and looked over his shoulder. "Zeyla?"

"I'm right behind you guys." Tears streamed down her cheeks through the ash, making twin paths of moisture on her dirty face.

Bear led them to a sitting room with two walls of windows. "All of you sit tight."

Ramon laid Maizie on a short velvet couch. "I'm coming with you."

Bear didn't argue.

The two men rushed out, leaving the others with Maizie.

Jax went to the couch and brushed Maizie's hair back from her face. "Wanna wake up for me, kiddo?"

Kenna sat by her feet.

Zeyla took a seat, running her hands down her face. "Setting a fire seemed like a"—her breath caught, and she coughed—"good idea at the time."

Jax glanced at her. "Ramon had the same one."

"That's why it seemed so crazy in my head." She sounded as if she was trying to smile, but it never reached her face.

Kenna touched the hem of Maizie's pant leg, and the girl's eyes fluttered open, her gaze distant at first. But as they waited, she focused on them. Glanced between them. Gasped—and then coughed it out, shaking the whole couch.

"Easy. We're almost out of here, okay?" Jax touched her arm.

Maizie moved her arm, and he thought she wanted him to draw away, so he lifted his hand. She grabbed his fingers and held on. "Jax." Her gaze settled on Kenna, and her eyes filled with tears. "Kenna."

"I know." She swiped a tear from her cheek. "You okay, Maze?"

The girl curled up, crying, and held out her arms for Kenna. They collapsed against each other in a hug and held on, both of them letting the emotion flow. Jax heard a sniff and pretended he didn't notice Zeyla crying.

Gunshots echoed across the house. Both the women stiffened and pulled out of the hug. Jax had his gun in his hand before they separated.

"I've got you covered." He started to turn toward the door.

Maizie touched his shoulder. "Love you, Jax." She leaned down and kissed his cheek.

He forgot all about the gunmen, and the guys fighting on their behalf, as his mind filled with thoughts of Kenna and Maizie and the family they were building together. "Love you, too, Maze."

She sniffed.

Kenna touched his cheek.

Someone stepped on a creaky board in the hall. Jax spun around in his crouch so fast he nearly fell over, but managed to catch himself and remain upright.

He got his gun up about the same second Preston came in, followed by Jax's father. Jax slumped to the floor, his back to the couch where Maizie and Kenna sat. Preston had a pistol by his side, and neither of them looked tense.

"Hey, guys." Jax blew out a long breath, and someone touched the back of his head, running a hand through his hair.

Preston came over and hugged Kenna.

Jax's dad crouched in front of him, a soft look on his face that Jax had never seen before. "You did good, buddy. You did real good."

Jax stared at his father, more tears burning in his eyes. He rubbed his nose and realized that was his gun hand. "I need to stop crying."

His dad shook his head. "Cry all you want."

Jax closed his eyes for a second, saying the biggest thank you of his life to the Lord, who had brought them all back together.

He heard Preston talking quietly to Kenna, filling her in on what had been happening.

He sat with the feeling for a minute, giving himself a

second to absorb the fact they were all back together. Alive and free.

No matter what happened in the months and years to come, they had this moment to remind them of what God could do. That He would bring them through it, walking beside them and guiding them as they kept going. Never quitting. Never backing down. Always fighting.

For their brand of justice.

Zeyla said, "You good, Maizie?"

"Thanks to you," she replied. "All of you."

Jax glanced over his shoulder. "Anytime."

She bit her lip.

"Don't worry about it. It's over. We're all safe." He could turn to her, on the floor where he was sitting by the couch, and they could hash this out. But Jax just didn't have the energy to do that.

"I'm still sorry I kept things from you," she whispered.

He nodded. "We'll figure it out."

Movement by the door caught his eye. When he turned, he saw Ramon at the door, lines of tension across his forehead. "We're clear."

Bruce appeared behind him, peering around his shoulder. Jax was pretty sure he saw Amara, too, out there in the dim light of the hall.

Ramon said, "You guys ready to roll?"

Jax nodded. "Thanks."

"As if you have to thank me."

"I will if I want to."

Maizie giggled behind him, leaning on his shoulder so she could stand. Ramon held her hand and helped up Zeyla at the same time.

Jax said, "Who is going to help me off the floor?"

His father smiled.

Zeyla put her arm around Maizie, and Ramon came over to Jax. His father and Preston shifted closer.

Kenna put her hand on his shoulder. "I've got this."

She leaned on him the same way Maizie had and stood before him. Hand held out. Pregnant with his baby, in need of a cheeseburger, hashbrowns, and a decaf cup of coffee.

Jax took her hand. What he didn't do was make her hold up his weight.

He lifted up, sat on the edge of the couch for a second, then stood. He discovered he was more unsteady than he'd thought, which meant his instincts were right that he'd needed help.

Preston got on one side of him, Jax's good arm around his shoulder. His father had Kenna put her arm through his, and they walked together, talking quietly. All of them headed for the door.

A man's heart plans his way, but the Lord directs his steps.

He was pretty sure he was paraphrasing some translation of it, but the Bible verse from days ago popped into his mind. That's what had happened, wasn't it?

First, he'd tried to use the FBI to solve his problem and find Kenna, even bringing Maizie along. Next, he walked away from them, and Kenna's team had helped him try to solve the case. He'd discovered far too many pieces he hadn't been expecting in that puzzle, and betrayal had stung. But in the end, it was the road that had brought him back to her—not even counting the fact his shoulder had been rebuilt in the process. Just as long as Kenna and the baby were safe.

Add to that the fact that all of them were here and walking out together?

They had come through it stronger.

Thank You, Lord.

Epilogue

FIVE WEEKS LATER
SOMEWHERE IN WYOMING

S un shined through the blinds, casting a yellow morning glow across the covers. Kenna Banbury-Jaxton slid to the side of the bed, trying not to disturb her husband. He lay face down, one arm hanging over the side of the bed. Scars on his shoulder, and more on the inside that no one would ever see.

She slid her feet into the slippers at the end of the bed and grabbed a zippered hoodie from Jax's side of the closet, one of the only things that closed over her pregnancy bump.

She ran a hand down the spot where their daughter resided, greeting the baby with a silent good morning.

The coffee pot had finished percolating, the beep likely what had awoken her.

She ignored the word *decaf* on the side of the bag, pressed into the corner with the sugar Jax used now, and poured herself a mug. Added a splash of milk. Petted the cat on her way past Jolene's perch on the recliner where Jax typically sat.

Kenna unlocked the RV door and left it open, closing only the screen.

Just yesterday they had the whole team on video chat, discussing what they were going to do next. Elizabeth and Craig Stairns were back in Colorado with Maizie in her Airstream. Ramon had just finished a job in Pittsburg, looking for a man they suspected had ties to *Dominatus*. In the middle of the meeting, Maizie had informed them of the breaking news.

The president and the FBI director had been having lunch in a DC hotel when they had both fallen deathly ill as a result of what the Secret Service believed to have been poison in their food. They had been dead before EMTs managed to arrive, and neither had responded to life-saving attempts by agents there for the president's protection.

Now the vice president had been sworn in.

Dominatus had taken out the top tier of the resistance in this country, and they likely had someone sympathetic in power now. Or at least a person willing to look away and ignore what was really going on.

Kenna tore her gaze from the mountains long enough to sit.

She offered some silent prayers for the coming day, determined to take each one as it came. Able to handle what was right in front of her. The rest she would leave in His hands, knowing He would take care of each of them.

Kenna sipped her coffee and watched the morning yawn itself awake.

A slight breeze ruffled wildflowers in the meadow in front of her. The only road was so far away that she couldn't make it out in the distance. Mountains all around them. So much space she didn't think she'd ever seen the world this open. Bursting with light, and growth. Warm to the touch.

Everything her life hadn't been.

Thank You.

The RV screen door snapped back on its hinges, and Jax came out, his hair sticking up in different directions. He wandered over and planted his hands on the arms of the plastic chair on either side of her. "Good morning."

She lifted her chin, and he kissed her. "Yes, it is good."

"Even though you started it without me."

She smiled. "You needed to sleep."

Neither of them had been immune to bad dreams, the fear creeping up at random moments and catching them off guard.

He slumped into the chair beside her and lifted her hand, kissing the back. Not letting go. "I'd rather be with you."

She lifted his hand to her lips. "Me, too."

Keep Reading For...

- Where to find more great Lisa Phillips books.

- How to sign up for Lisa's newsletter and get a FREE book.

- Where to find Lisa on social media.

About the Author

Find out more about Lisa Phillips at her website, where you'll discover more romantic suspense fan-favorite series and heart-pounding thriller novels.
https://authorlisaphillips.com/

If you loved this book, please consider sharing about it on social media. Or leave a review at your book retailer website, on Goodreads, or on Bookbub. Your review will help others find great books to entertain and encourage them!

Signup for Lisa's newsletter by scanning the QR code below to stay updated on sales, new releases, and recommendations for your TBR pile. New Subscribers even get a FREE book!

Find Lisa on Social Media!

facebook.com/authorlisaphillips

instagram.com/lisaphillipsbks

bookbub.com/authors/lisa-phillips

Also by Lisa Phillips

Find out more about Brand of Justice at my website:

https://authorlisaphillips.com/product-tag/brand-of-justice/

Book 1: Cold Dead Night

Book 2: Burn the Dawn

Book 3: Quick and Dead

Book 4: Over the Limit

Book 5: Skin and Bone

Book 6: Dust and Ashes

Book 7: Long Road Home

Book 8 : Dead to Rights

Book 9: Fear No Evil

Book 10: Out of Time

Book 11: Every Which Way

Book 12: One More Chance

Book 13: Storm and Tempest

Book 14: Now or Never (November 2025)

———

Other series by Lisa:

Last Chance Downrange

Chevalier Protection Specialists

Last Chance County

Northwest Counter-Terrorism Taskforce

Double Down

WITSEC Town (Sanctuary)

Numerous other titles including several with *Love Inspired Suspense*, find the complete list here (or scan the QR code):

https://authorlisaphillips.com/all-books/